Jon King is the bestselling au
Hidden Evidence and *Princess*
written with co-author John Bev
Books New York. As well as
journalist, screenwriter and music producer. He lives with
his wife in Somerset, England.

THE CUT-OUT

Also by Jon King

Cosmic Top Secret: The Unseen Agenda
The Ascension Conspiracy
Princess Diana: The Hidden Evidence
(with John Beveridge)
Princess Diana: The Evidence
(with John Beveridge)

THE CUT-OUT

JON KING

© Copyright Jon King 2013. All rights reserved. The author hereby asserts the moral right to be identified as the author of this work.

Cover artwork: Jon King.
Cover image: © Depositphotos.com/Viktor Gladkov.
Cover font: Bebas (thanks to Ryoichi Tsunekawa,
Bagel & Co).

For Casey
Without whom this book would be pointless

The identities of some of the characters in this book have been changed to preserve their anonymity. And my life. Several locations, and several events, and to some small extent the chronology of events, have also been changed.

Everything else is true.

CUT-OUT: A mechanism or person used to pass information from one agent to another; to create a compartment between members of a covert operation via which material or information can be passed. An intermediary. A go-between. A courier. *In more general terms a cut-out is a person or agency used as an unwitting pawn by intelligence services.*

1

Private Members Club, Whitehall—October, 1996

The day Rob Lacey walked into the Sincerity Club on an overcast day in October 1996 was the day that changed my life.

Lacey was a career MI5 officer who specialized in counter-terrorism and counter-proliferation. He was old-school. He'd entered the Service more on principle than ambition: more to help combat the threat posed by the IRA and other terrorist organizations than to run his own, private little empire.

The man he'd come to meet here at this exclusive members' club, on the other hand, was everything Lacey was not—a ruthless MI6 operative who for the past some years had been head of SIS Special Operations Europe, although his imminent posting to the British Embassy in Paris would officially log him as First Secretary Political, a common cover for undeclared MI6 agents in friendly territories. He was tall and fit with sharpened features and ice-cold eyes. His name was Richard Mason.

"Ah, Robert. Good of you to come." Dressed in dark city suit and Oxford brogues, Mason stood up from the table and offered Lacey his hand. "Cognac?"

"No thank you.".

"As you wish. Please, take a seat."

Lacey would in truth have welcomed a cognac. But he didn't like Mason. Declining the man's offer was a point made.

Peeling off his gloves Lacey seated himself and threw a cursory glance around the room.

The twenty or so other members present were mostly nestled on their own, he noted, behind magazines, or broadsheets, or books: or some other form of reading matter. Elsewhere small groups of establishment types chatted surreptitiously among themselves. He felt decidedly out of place in here. The plush leather armchairs, the dark-wood panels, the smoke-veiled alcoves like the one he and Mason occupied now—all added to the air of conspiracy hanging over the musty old place. It was like walking into a John Le Carré novel, he decided, halfway through. It put him on edge.

"So," he said, knitting his hands and eyeing the man opposite him. "I'm curious. It's not every day I'm summoned by MI6 special operations."

"We'd prefer if you thought of it as an invitation," Mason replied. "Off the record."

"In my reckoning everything you do is off the record. What is it you people say? *No paper trails, no ghosts*?"

"No recriminations, Robert. Only results. Nothing else is of any significance."

"Quite."

Downing the dregs of his cognac Mason set the empty glass on the table and beckoned to the waiter, who immediately left his duties behind the bar and made strides towards their table. "You're sure I can't offer you a cognac? Old times' sake?"

Lacey gave a single shake of his head: *No thank you.*

While the waiter served Mason his second *Cognac Grande Champagne Vintage 1885* Lacey pondered the *old times* to which his adversary had just referred.

It was a career-shaping secondment to MI6's special ops unit some twenty years earlier that had first seen him cross paths with Mason. At the time both were junior officers of their respective agencies, but Mason's ruthless ambition had been evident enough, even then, and Lacey had quickly grown to dislike the man. And the unit to which he was attached. Indeed, the same ungovernable air exuded by Mason, he'd soon realized, had been evident throughout the entire MI6 special ops unit, and he'd felt no disappointment at all when his secondment had finally ended and he'd been recalled to his post at MI5's domestic counter-terrorism branch, known in-house simply as 'T Branch'. The eighteen months he'd spent with MI6 had served his career well enough, he'd be the first to acknowledge that. But he'd been more than happy to put it behind him and move on.

Within six months of returning to MI5 Lacey was transferred to G Branch (MI5's international counter-terrorism and counter-proliferation division). It was a move he'd been pushing for and one that, as it turned out, kick-started his career for real. Through the course of the following decade and even to the present day he'd scored considerable success in the prevention of weapons-proliferation in countries like Libya, Syria and Yemen, as well as restricting the acquisition of weapons by 'hostile' groups like the PLO, Hamas, Hezbollah and others. And he'd won a number of recommendations and promotions for his efforts.

He'd also won enemies. In his decade and a half as a counter-terrorism 'target officer' he'd engaged virtually every core group within the Islamist *mujahideen* network, and on occasion had faced up some of its most notorious members. He still figured high on the Hezbollah 'wanted list'.

But despite that he'd given death more than a second glance, and on more than one occasion; despite that he'd shared the same acre as some of the world's most dangerous 'terrorists', he'd be the first to confess he'd known none more dangerous than the man seated opposite him now, Richard Mason—the man whose special ops mafia had not only fanned the flames of civil war in the former Yugoslavia: they'd also engineered more IRA bombings than Martin McGuinness, more terrorist attacks than Al Qaeda, and Lacey knew it. False flag operations, they called them: covert operations made to look like they'd been carried out by someone else—like the Provisional IRA, for example.

Or al Qaeda.

Oh yes, Lacey knew the dirty games on which Mason had built his career—the very reason he disliked the man with such intensity.

As the waiter made his way back to the bar, having just served Mason his second cognac, Lacey closed the door on *old times* and returned his attention to the present. Mostly, it was where he'd rather be.

"I'd appreciate it if we could get to the point," Lacey said, as Mason raised his glass to his nose and savoured the complex aroma of its contents. "I take it there is one?"

Swallowing a measure of the vintage cognac, Mason said: "You received the memo?"

Lacey nodded. "It arrived yesterday."

"Then you'll know our dilemma."

"Diana?"

"She's a nuisance, Robert."

"She's always been a nuisance. That's part of her appeal."

"To some, perhaps. But the nuisance has become more than a simple irritation. She's become a problem. That's a very different matter."

Lacey didn't much like where this conversation was heading. "You know, if we put half as much effort into outflanking the Libyans and the IRA as we do harassing the Prince of Wales' consort, this country would be somewhere to live."

"I dare say. But she's no longer the Prince of Wales' consort, that's the problem. In case it slipped your mind their divorce became final three months ago."

The dark shadow that fell in Mason's eyes as he emphasized those words confirmed what Lacey already knew: something very serious was brewing.

"And the point?" he said. "Why did you invite me here to discuss the Princess of Wales?"

Mason had just dipped his hand in his jacket pocket, and was now holding a regular-sized envelope, brown. He slid it across the table in Lacey's direction. "We need a courier," he declared. "Someone to circulate some information."

"A cut-out?"

"In a sense. Your name came up specifically."

"Well it shouldn't have." He picked up the envelope. "As naive as it may sound to someone of your unforgiving ambition,

Richard, my pride as an MI5 officer is in *protecting* innocent people, not in setting them up."

"Oh, we're not asking you to set anybody up, old boy. We're quite good at doing that, all by ourselves. You'll see why you're here when you've opened that."

Cognac in hand, Mason sat back and watched as Lacey started to open the envelope, reluctantly at first, almost nervously, as though by instinct he knew its contents might bite him. He wasn't wrong. In his hands now was a photograph of a man's face, a chiselled face with ragged brown hair and bookish eyes, around 40 years of age. It was a face Lacey knew well enough.

"As you can see," Mason said, draining the last of his cognac. "The person we have in mind—we believe he's an acquaintance of yours. We believe he's someone you know."

2

I'd known Rob Lacey for close on twenty years. We'd been introduced at one of the local bars in my home town of Sandhurst, and for whatever reason we'd got on pretty well from the outset. I considered him a friend—perhaps not a close friend, but I had his phone number, and he had mine. And in my world that meant we were friends.

On that first occasion, though, Lacey had been in town on business. I knew that. As did everybody else. But then the boundaries between business and pleasure in those days were perhaps less defined than they should have been, particularly when you consider the kind of business Lacey was in. It was the mid-1970s, the days when the West's post-war superpowers were busy divvying up the spoils they were still pillaging from their former African colonies: the days when the British government in particular was busy recruiting hired hands to do its dirty work in the former Portuguese colony of Angola. Some twenty years later, of course, Angola would become the focus for Princess Diana's massively publicized landmines campaign. But in 1976 it was making headlines for a different reason. Civil war was raging. Following the country's recent declaration of independence, a feat achieved only by means of another war, a devastating 'decolonisation war' which had ravaged Angola for the previous nineteen years, the country was again in conflict. One war had given way to another. The decolonisation war had given way to civil war. There were resources at stake. Oil, mostly. Vast reserves of the stuff. Diamonds, too. In order to safeguard these interests the British government needed forces on the ground. Not regular forces, of course; no way could regular British soldiers have been seen to fight alongside the opposition forces in another country's civil war. No. For this war the government needed mercenaries, soldiers for hire.

Which is the reason it sent Lacey to Sandhurst—

"I'm meeting Rob Lacey this morning," I said to Katie. "He said he could help me out with a story I'm researching. There's not much Lacey doesn't know about Angola."

I was in my office, at home, gathering up my papers, preparing to head up to London for my meeting with Lacey. Katie had just brought me in a cup of coffee.

"Thanks," I said, kissing Katie on the cheek and gulping down several mouthfuls of sweet black coffee before snapping my attaché case shut and throwing on my jacket. "I don't suppose you've seen my...?"

"It's in your case."

"My Dictaphone?" I reopened my attaché case. She was right. Of course she was right. There, glaring back up at me from the midst of an unruly stack of papers and sundries, my Dictaphone. What would I do without her?

"What time will you be home?" she said.

"Around tea time."

"It's your turn to cook."

"Then I'll try and get back sooner."

Another kiss, this one on the lips, and I swept up my case and headed for the door.

For London. To meet Lacey.

—By the end of the decolonisation war in 1975 Angola's vast resources were the envy of Western governments, including my government: the British government. Trouble was, these resources were now controlled by the country's new Marxist regime, the Soviet-backed MPLA. It was the MPLA who'd won power in the wake of the decolonisation war, and who'd won control of the country's oil fields and diamond mines in the process. This meant that, in order to continue siphoning off cheap Angolan oil, and to maintain its thriving trade in Angola's blood diamonds, the

British government, like its French, South African and American counterparts, was forced to do business with the MPLA—the political faction it had so rigorously opposed during the decolonisation war; the political faction it continued to oppose now, in the civil war.

But here's the twist. While Britain's oil and diamond merchants were cosying up to the MPLA, teams of British mercenaries were secretly fighting to overthrow the new regime and hand the reins of power to the opposition forces, UNITA—the political faction the West had funded and armed during the decolonisation war; the political faction it continued to fund and arm now, in the civil war.

Simply put, the situation was a mess—way too messy for the government to openly involve itself; way too lucrative for it to turn its back.

Enter MI6 and its 'black ops' mafia. Enter a young, naïve MI5 officer seconded to MI6 to coordinate special ops logistics on behalf of his faceless masters. Truth be told, Lacey was little more than a 'cut-out' himself in those days, the government's unofficial 'runner', its errand boy, its undercover liaison man tasked with brokering 'black asset' deals between Whitehall and the small group of private security firms on its payroll. One of these private security firms in particular had been set up specifically to supply mercenaries to fight the British government's dirty war in Angola. This firm was called Security Advisory Services, or SAS for short, and was run out of my home town of Sandhurst by former special forces maverick and self-styled colonel, John Banks, someone I knew well enough.

In fact I knew several of the mercenaries contracted to SAS, largely through my friendship with their younger brothers, with whom I'd grown up. Like Lacey, most of the mercenaries, including Banks, were half a generation older than I was, but a number of them had younger brothers who'd been friends of mine from an early age. We'd hung out together, attended the same schools, the same haunts; we'd played together as kids and partied together as teenagers. On any number of occasions I'd suffered the bragging rights of my friends' older brothers as they'd recounted their stories of African conquest—of how they'd brought down this or that soviet-backed dictatorship, of how they'd fought in this civil war or brought about that military coup. It was something they seemed to delight in talking big about, especially to us younger boys. And of course, us younger boys took it all on like most young boys would: wide-eyed and awe-struck.

And the flow of information didn't stop there. By my early twenties I was frequenting the same bars and hangouts as the mercenaries themselves, had actually come to know one or two of them quite well, and on occasion was even party to conversations one might expect would – and should – have been held in secret, behind closed doors.

But Sandhurst didn't work like that. Sandhurst was a small town with big ears and loose tongues. And consequently, few secrets, especially in those days, before modernity encroached and turned what was then a small, socially incestuous community into the sprawling suburban town it is today. Everyone knew everyone and everyone knew their business—even the kind of business dealt by SAS and Lacey. Perhaps this is why the meetings were held so casually, often over a beer and a game of pool—but always with the unspoken proviso that all present kept schtum about what they might have heard. And needless to say, on pain of some very nasty consequence, all present did precisely that: kept schtum.

Of course, I had no idea back then that these stories, the information they revealed, would provide so much background to my understanding of Princess Diana's landmines campaign and the can of deadly worms that campaign would threaten to spotlight. At the time the stories meant little to me except that they painted an exciting picture. But it was a picture full of surprises, as I would later discover.

It was in this place and this circumstance, then, that I first met Rob Lacey, the man who, over the course of some years, would not only provide me with nailed-on insights into the grubby, unscrupulous world of geopolitical espionage. But the man, too, who would play such a key role in my investigation into Princess Diana's death.

The man who would spill the beans.

3

Kensington Palace, Westminster—October 1995

The sound of the grandfather clock ticking time from the corner of the room seemed somehow portentous as Diana entered the study, closed the door behind her and sat herself down at her desk.

She was alone. It was where she always came when she wished to be alone, away from the madness, the constant turmoil and terrible anguish that seemed to have engulfed her life in recent years. It was where she came to gather her thoughts, and on occasion, like this occasion, to record them in writing.

Picking up her pen from off the desk top she gazed down at the blank page in front of her. *Could she do it?* The thoughts she wished to record seemed almost too upsetting for her to write down, almost too painful to relive, even in her mind. She'd known this even before she'd made the decision to come here, of course, even before the tears she was starting to cry had welled there in her eyes. But she'd made the decision, even so, and now her mind was made up. She would suffer quietly no longer. Her husband was cheating on her, she'd come to realize. His security team was spying on her and his cronies were surreptitiously bullying her and planning her demise. Should something untoward happen to her, as she so greatly feared it might, the letter she was about to write would at least reveal to the world who was to blame.

Who had planned her 'accident' and who had carried it out.

As she peered up at the grandfather clock standing so tall and unafraid there in the corner of the study, she knew the time had come. Despite her pain she would write the letter and release it to the safekeeping of her close friend and lawyer, Lord Victor Mischcon.

Dabbing her eyes with a handkerchief she adjusted the pen in her hand and started to write.

I am sitting here at my desk today in October, longing for someone to hug me and encourage me to keep strong and hold my head high…

A sound at the door, the creak of floor boards, the faint sound of footfall disappearing along the hallway.
Was someone spying on her?
Immediately Diana stopped writing and gave her full attention to the noise as she pushed herself up from her desk and tip-toed across the room to investigate.
Warily, so warily, she squeezed the handle of the oak-panelled door and turned it just sufficiently that she could pull the door ajar and peer out into the hallway.
Nothing. No one. Not even one of the staff going about their daily duties. She closed the door, and for several moments simply stood there, her back tight to the door, her hands grasping the handle behind her back as though too terrified to let it go.
Was someone playing games with her? she was thinking. *Was someone deliberately trying to unsettle her? Frighten her?*
She knew the answer, of course. She knew the answer to all of these questions. At length she let go the handle and made her way nervously back to her desk, and continued to write.

This particular phase in my life is the most dangerous – my husband is planning 'an accident' in my car, brake failure and serious head injury in order to make the path clear for him to marry…

She paused, considering whose name to write. *Camilla?* Or *Tiggy?* With which of his current mistresses was Charles most infatuated? Or perhaps more to the point: With which of his current mistresses was Charles expecting a child?

...To make the path clear for him to marry Tiggy, she eventually wrote. *Camilla is nothing but a decoy, so we are all being used by the man in every sense of the word.*

But still she was unsure...

She knew, of course, that Charles had been seeing Camilla all along, from the very beginning, from their very first introduction and throughout their extraordinarily public courtship. He'd even continued to see her throughout their marriage – their fake, ill-fated marriage – the fact of which Diana was only too aware. He simply couldn't bear to be without her was the truth of the matter, and Diana had always known this, even though she'd always tried not to believe it. Rather she'd tried to believe – so desperately tried to believe – that he would one day love her more than he loved Camilla: that he would love his wife and the mother of his children more than he loved his mistress. But now, of course, with the separation formalized and their divorce looming hideously, she knew it could never be. She knew now beyond all doubt that Camilla and Camilla alone could satisfy Charles' longing for love, the love he'd clearly craved from childhood, but never received—not from his mother, not from anyone during his formative years, except perhaps the string of older women in whom he'd found solace, both as a boy and, later, as an adolescent.

And there was the key, Diana knew. There was the reason for his obsession with Camilla, his infatuation with the older woman and divorcee who over the years had served him not only as lover, but as mother, too: mother, lover and wet nurse, all rolled in one.

His *whore*.

But now even Camilla was facing competition, from the boys' nanny, Tiggy Legge-Bourke, although Diana of course knew it wouldn't last. She knew that Tiggy, like so many before her, including herself, would never ultimately prise Charles away from his *paramour*, that she was simply another fleeting fancy who would fail to claim her prize the way so many had failed in the past. Charles would never love anyone but Camilla, and that was the end of the matter. The only difference on this occasion, if the hearsay was to be believed, was that Tiggy was already pregnant with Charles' child.

What a mess. What a horrid, horrid mess.

Letting her head fall desperately into her hands Diana again started to cry, the tears that had been welling there all morning finally breaching the banks of her eyes and spilling down her cheeks in small torrents. The grandfather clock counted a full two minutes before those tears finally ebbed and her crying ceased. Only then did she pick up her letter from the desk and, regretfully, fold it into an envelope marked *Lord Victor Mishcon*.

My Dear Victor, was the last thing she had written. *I entrust this letter to your safekeeping, so the world will know that if something does happen to me, it will be MI5 or MI6 who will have done it. Lovingly yours, Diana.*

4

At the time Lacey had his meeting with MI6 enforcer, Richard Mason, at Whitehall's Sincerity Club, I was working as senior editor of Britain's most popular independent *X-Files*-style magazine, *UFO Reality*. It was the mid-1990s and the *X-Files* was far and away the most popular show on British TV, setting a climate and a trend that had seen around a dozen or so similar magazines launched within an eighteen-month period. Of these, *UFO Reality* was the high street's most popular seller.

True to its name, the magazine for the most part covered UFO-related stories—anything from alien abductions (widely reported at the time), crop circles (widely reported at the time), UFO sightings (even more widely reported at the time), to well-known UFO incidents and alleged government cover-ups: Roswell, MJ-12, Area 51 and others. Plus many other aspects of a phenomenon that, quite simply, was more popular in the UK at this time than afternoon tea. Due largely to the success of the *X-Files*, and in particular Mulder's conviction that the truth about aliens was being covered up, what seemed to pique public interest most of all about this strange new phenomenon was the tantalizing notion that the British and American governments knew more about it than they were letting on.

And that's where I came in.

As well as editing the magazine and contributing various reports and articles, I also wrote a regular feature called *Jon King's X-File Document*, which became very popular with our readers—not least, I guess, because it helped introduce the nefarious activities of our governments to what until then had been a fairly drip-fed audience. Fair to say, in fact, that this was one of the first regular 'conspiracy' columns to hit the British high street. It was the days before the internet had reached orbit, don't forget, and the only access people had had to this information prior to the *X-Files* explosion was contained in a few difficult-to-acquire books, most of which were American. The timing couldn't have been better. So long as I could find at least a tenuous link to UFOs (and sometimes not even that much) the feature allowed me to explore areas of government 'conspiracy' and 'cover-up' scarcely before exposed to the public—illegally run advanced technology programmes, for example; top-secret biotech programmes.

And perhaps more to the point: the government's oil-and-diamond-driven crimes in countries like Angola.

Together with our more manifestly UFO-based features, these were topics that clearly caught the public imagination. At its peak, *UFO Reality's* circulation topped 60,000 (not bad for an independent magazine, even in those days). And the core contribution, edition-on-edition, was *Jon King's X-File Document*—the very reason, I would later learn, that *UFO Reality* would so suddenly and inexplicably disappear from the high street newsagents.

And I would end up the *munchkin* of Britain's Secret Intelligence Service.

5

Richard Mason's Office, MI6 Headquarters — March 1997

Mason sat alone in his darkened office, in a chrome-and-leather armchair facing the wall. In his hand a multi-purpose remote control. As his thumb selected a button on the remote and pressed it a false panel on the wall slid electronically back to reveal a bank of nine square plasma screens, each identical to the next. He then hit a second button on the remote and the screens came alive, all nine simultaneously.

All nine showed the same image.

It was an image of Diana. Or rather, a series of seemingly random images of Diana, one and then another, and then another, each one depicting the princess at a particular stage in her life. Mason was studying them intently, each one in turn, like a stalker obsessing on his prey — Diana as a child, diving into a swimming pool; a teenager, attending a garden party; the shy young children's nanny, recently introduced to the media as Charles' new love interest: *Lady Diana Spencer ... is this the girl he's going to marry?*

Mason hit another button on the remote. A new sequence of images started to play. Charles and Diana were now standing, arm in arm, before reporters at Buckingham Palace on the day they announced their engagement, cameras flashing, Diana appearing blushed and star-struck. Charles looked resigned.

"Can you find the words to sum up how you feel today?" the reporter put to the happy couple.

"It's difficult to say," was the best Charles could offer.

"In love?"

"Of course," Diana was quick to affirm.

Charles was more ambiguous. "Whatever in love means," he said.

Again Mason hit the remote and again the sequence of images changed—the wedding; Charles and Diana emerging on the steps of St Mary's Hospital following the birth of Prince William; Diana sitting alone at the Taj Mahal in India, the desperate, almost bereft expression on her face telling the story no words could. The sequence made little sense except to Mason, who's arctic stare never left the screens, even when the in-house phone buzzed beside him and demanded his attention. He took the call on speaker mode.

"We're settled on Paris, then?" the anonymous telephone voice said, before even Mason had spoke. When he did speak his eyes remained fastened to the screens.

"My posting at the embassy has been arranged," he confirmed.

"So I understand. But what I don't understand is … why Paris?"

"Because Paris is a deniable dreamland. A distinct lack of CCTV cameras, incompetent emergency procedures, an expendable agent inside the Ritz Hotel. It's the perfect location."

"When you say 'incompetent emergency procedures.'…?"

"The French emergency services are notoriously inept. If need be we'll make sure they live up to their name. The last thing we need are survivors."

"Ah."

Just then the image on the screens flicked to a newsreel shot of Diana in Angola, making her way bravely through a minefield, protected only by body-armour vest and a transparent head shield and visor. Mason's eyes flared. The sight of Diana spotlighting Angola, bringing the resource-rich country to the attention of a global audience, clearly rankled.

"You know the CIA favour Angola," the telephone voice was saying. "If she were to step on a misplaced landmine…?"

"The CIA can go to hell," Mason replied. "They're passengers on this one. They should remember that." He hit the remote and a new image came up on screen—a man of average height, if a little portly, emerging from the front entrance of the Ritz Hotel, Paris. A different control on the remote allowed Mason to zoom in on the face of Henri Paul. "On this occasion it's *our* man who's in the driving seat, if you understand what I'm saying. Everything's under control. He knows perfectly well which route to take."

The telephone voice cleared its throat. "Yes, well, we can't afford any mistakes with this, Richard. You know that. No paper trails, no ghosts."

"As if."

"Here's wishing you a successful posting, then. And remember, this conversation never took place."

With that, the line *clicked* dead.

Mason got back to his private movie show—just him, the princess, and the inebriated chauffeur: the man who would be 'patsy'.

6

It was a regular day at the office the day the phone call came...

Earlier that morning I'd said goodbye to Katie and the kids as normal.

"Don't shoot!" I said as I entered the breakfast area, hands in the air, confronted by the notorious King Boys. Fortunately Jack and Ben were only 9 and 7 years old respectively, and the guns they were pointing at me were of course make believe. Still, you could never be too cautious.

"We wouldn't shoot you, Daddy," young Jack reassured, beaming ear to ear, still pointing his imaginary gun in my direction.

"We'd have no one to pick us up from school," Ben pointed out.

They laughed.

Silly me. "I'm safe then?"

They both assured me I was indeed safe as they holstered their guns and got back to eating their cereal. I kissed them on the cheek and said goodbye.

"And you be a good girl for mummy," I turned and said to 4-year-old Rosie, and then I kissed her on the cheek, too. "Love you."

"What about me?" Katie said. She was busy helping Rosie butter her toast. "Are we still on for a date tonight? It's divorce papers if you say no."

"I've booked the table," I reminded her. "Babysitter's arranged."

I kissed her on the lips and grabbed my attaché case.

"Don't forget to pick the boys up from school," Katie said as I headed out the door.

"I'll be there."

Closing the door behind me, heading out to the car, I couldn't help thinking how very lucky I was. A beautiful wife, three gorgeous kids and I even had a job I quite liked doing. What more could I have wished for?

What I didn't know at the time, of course, was that the CIA was about to call me up. Everything was about to change.

I arrived at the office to find the team all there and ready for the tough week ahead. It was copy deadline week, when all the major stressing and fine-tuning had to be done prior to the magazine finally being designed up and sent off to the printers. For that reason I was happy to see a full quota of staff on parade, in particular JB (John Beveridge, my associate editor on the magazine, co-author of my book, *Princess Diana: The Evidence* and, perhaps more pertinently, my brother-in-arms during the gruelling investigation that neither of us yet knew lay in wait, just around the next bend). I knew when it came to the grind it would be JB who I could call on to put in the extra hours.

This week he'd been working on a story about Phil Schneider, the former US government structural engineer who claimed to have worked on the construction of top secret underground bases in America. He also claimed to have been involved in a gunfight with 'grey' aliens at the notorious Dulce underground base in New Mexico. Personally I never took these kind of stories too seriously, but I knew it would appeal to a large section of our readership. In particular news of Schneider's mysterious death the previous year was still the talk of the town in conspiracy circles, so I'd assigned JB the task of investigating.

"Any more on the Schneider story?" I put to him, sipping my hot coffee. It was mid-morning, and having just made my third caffeine hit of the day I was heading back through the editorial suite en route to my office. "Are they still pushing the suicide theory?"

JB shrugged. "The coroner's now saying he died of a stroke."

"What, by wrapping a rubber catheter hose around his own neck and strangling himself?" That was David, the magazine proprietor. He and his partner Claire ran the show.

"We don't know that for certain, David," Claire said from her adjacent desk.

"We do now," JB corrected, buffing up his John Lennon glasses with the hem of his *Nirvana* T-shirt. "His ex-wife says he was found with the hose wrapped three times around his neck. Evidently he'd been dead for days when his body was found. She believes he was murdered."

"Well, see if you can talk to her," I said. "We need to get something concrete before we run with it."

"I'm on it." He put his glasses back on.

"How about you, Mike?" I said, turning my attention to our features editor, the somewhat overanxious, though always industrious 40-year-old seated over by the window. "Still working on the Bill Cooper feature?"

Mike was probably the most experienced member of the team, so I often entrusted him with the more in-depth research projects. For this month's issue I was after a feature on well-known American conspiracy theorist and radio broadcaster, Milton William Cooper, probably best known for his groundbreaking book, *Behold A Pale Horse*, in which he claimed to have seen top-secret documents revealing US government collaboration with aliens. A prominent member of America's southern-belt militia movement, Cooper was convinced he'd become a government target for exposing classified information, and had famously stated on his radio show that he "would never be taken alive". He was right on that count. Some four years after Mike wrote his feature on him, in November 2001, Cooper was shot dead at his home in Eagar, Arizona, by US law enforcement officers. He'd been on the run for three years.

But this wasn't the only 'prophecy' for which Cooper had achieved notoriety. He'd accurately predicted another famous event, too, and some say this was the real reason he was taken out.

Four months prior to being shot, in June 2001, Cooper announced on his radio show that the United States was about to face a "major attack ... within weeks". He said the attack would actually be carried out by "those behind the New World Order", but that it would be blamed on a then unknown Saudi insurgent and CIA asset by the name of Osama Bin Laden. This was at a time, remember, when the world had never heard of Osama Bin Laden.

In any event, as we all now know, a little over two months after Cooper's prophetic broadcast, on September 11, 2001, the attack tragically happened. The Twin Towers in Lower Manhattan and a section of the Pentagon in Arlington, Virginia, were destroyed by hijacked aircraft, and almost 3000 people lost their lives. Overnight, Osama Bin Laden became a household name. And Milton William Cooper became a wanted man.

Of course, back in November 1996, when Mike was researching and preparing his feature, Cooper's forewarning of 911 was yet to hit the airwaves. But he was still a sufficiently well-known figure in the burgeoning world of conspiracy theory to warrant a feature in our magazine.

"Mike...?"

"Almost there," he said, a well-thumbed copy of Bill Cooper's book lying open on his desk. "I'm proofing it now. This guy really has something to say. I just wish he'd say it in a less belligerent fashion."

"He's certainly a bruiser."

"A war-monger, more like. Frankly I'd rather be working on the remote viewing story."

"Sorry, Mike," Jackie piped up. "That's *my* territory."

Mike mumbled something into his work; I turned to Jackie.

"How's it coming along, Jacks?" Jackie was our newest recruit, a student fresh from college, and I needed to be certain she was on target for the end of the week. "Any evidence the CIA are actually able to remotely view enemy targets?"

"I think they'd like us to think so," she said, the budding pragmatist. Then she quipped: "I've found plenty on Diana being remotely viewed by MI5, though, if that's any help."

Mike almost snarled. "Haven't they got anything better to do?"

"I know," Candi agreed, disapproving. "I think it's disgusting."

"Oh, I dunno," JB threw in. "I wouldn't mind remote-viewing Diana."

"You need a girlfriend, JB," I said, and with that, made a timely exit, the sound of jibes and laughter fading as I headed back to my office and closed the door behind me.

It was then, just as I sat myself back down at my desk and started to read through the article I'd been working on – *CIA Behind Arms-For-Oil Deals In Angola* – that the phone call came.

7

Thames House, Millbank, MI5 Headquarters — November 1996

Lacey exited the elevator into a corridor, accompanied by senior Whitehall spook Sir Philip Hemming. According to Lacey, it was Hemming who would later become the loudest voice of protest in the entire security sector *against* the planned assassination of Princess Diana.

"She's no longer HRH but she's still the mother of the future king," Sir Philip was saying as he and Lacey started off along the sterile, featureless corridor towards Room A6, where the meeting they were headed for was being held. "To make matters worse, Charles seems hell bent on marrying a divorcee. It's all so messy."

"What about the other one?"

"Which one?"

"Tiggy Legge-Bourke. I heard she was pregnant by Charles, that she'd had an abortion to cover it up."

"A vicious rumour." Sir Philip cleared his throat. "Anyway, I shouldn't worry about Tiggy. Charles may well have added her to his already populous harem but I doubt there's any danger of wedding bells. The public would never accept him marrying the royal nanny, not in place of Diana."

"But they'll accept Camilla?"

"At this precise moment in time, Robert, whether or not they accept Camilla is less a problem than his desire to marry her. *That's* the problem."

A short distance along the corridor they stopped outside a regular, dark-wood door marked 'A6'. Before opening it Sir Philip said something Lacey wasn't expecting.

"You know why you're here today, Robert? Request from the top, which evidently originated with MI6. I hope you're not keeping anything from us."

"Sir Philip?"

"A Security Service Deputy Director of Counter-Proliferation, such as you are, wouldn't ordinarily be expected to attend a meeting of this nature. Your presence here today is unusual, to say the least."

Lacey was a little taken aback by Sir Philip's almost accusatory tone. "I had a meeting," he heard himself say.

"With our cousins at MI6. Yes, we know. Head of MI6 Special Operations summoned you personally. Must have been important."

"I suppose it was, yes."

Lacey's mind was suddenly back at the Sincerity Club, the meeting he'd had with Mason scarcely a month earlier, when he'd learned about MI6's plans to use a cut-out in an operation he'd yet to learn the full details of. Since then his senses had been working overtime trying to figure out what the end game might be, not wanting to believe the most palpable scenario, but at the same time not wanting to ignore his best instincts. All he knew for certain at this point was that the operation was being run by Mason and his deniable ops team, a fact in itself sufficient to have put his mind on amber alert. The fact that he'd been called up by Sir Philip in person late last evening, and told he was to accompany him to a in-house crisis meeting, had upped the amber alert to red, even more so when Sir Philip had then informed him that the meeting was to decide the way forward following the Lord Chancellor's report on Diana's recent divorce from Prince Charles.

Again his mind raced back to his meeting with Mason at the Sincerity Club.

A way to resolve the problem must be found, Mason had said to him as he'd stood up to leave, citing this as the reason behind his decision to use a cut-out. *The situation has become unmanageable as a result of Diana's divorce from Prince Charles and the latter's desire to remarry while the former remains alive*. And that was the phrase that had lodged in Lacey's mind: *while the former remains alive*. It had left Lacey in no doubt that Diana herself was the 'problem'.

"You know they want her out of the way, don't you," Sir Philip said, interrupting Lacey's thoughts.

"They?"

"MI6. They want shot of her."

"Oh, they want shot of everyone they can't control," Lacey replied, endeavouring to shrug the remark off and yet at the same time conceal the growing sense of apprehension in him.

Sir Philip opened the door. "She's ruffled some very powerful feathers, Robert," he said, shadowing Lacey into the meeting room. "Some very powerful feathers indeed. If she thinks she can take on the establishment and win she's very much mistaken."

As Lacey and Sir Philip entered the meeting room they were greeted by a dozen or so faceless, suited officials, all but one seated at the impressive, oval-shaped table around which the meeting was about to be held.

The one yet to be seated, Lacey immediately saw, was Richard Mason.

8

"Mr King?"

"Speaking." I hit the button on my tape recorder and checked my wristwatch, a habit. It was 11.45 am. The tape recorder was wired to my telephone.

"I've just read your article on the US government's covert activities underground," the American voice informed me—a male voice, mature, intelligent, engaging. "Project Noah's Ark. Very interesting."

"Thank you."

"Sure."

"So how can I help you?" I was part with the conversation, part distracted by the article staring back at me from my computer screen: *CIA Behind Arms-For-Oil Deals In Angola*. It was still only part-way finished and the deadline was fast approaching. It was starting to bug me.

"The article," the voice went on, referring of course not to my CIA article, but to my *Project Noah's Ark* article, which I'd published in the previous month's issue. "It prompted me to call. I have some information."

"Go on."

"It would be best if you left your office," the voice said in a slightly more guarded tone. "We'll talk on another line. Go to a public call box and call this number."

"Now?"

"It'll be worth your while."

"Okay," I said, my mind no longer distracted by the article I was desperate to finish but instead now fully focused on the call. I jotted down the number. "Who should I ask for?" I said. "Can you ... hello?"

But the line was already dead; the caller, whoever he was, had hung up.

As the caller remarked, in last month's issue I'd written a piece on what was already being referred to in conspiracy circles as the American government's 'deep-underground programme'. Rumour had it that a series of highly covert and extremely controversial military-industrial projects were being carried out in the United States – or more precisely, several hundred feet *beneath* the United States – and I'd set myself the task of finding out what they were and why they so intrigued the conspiracy community. In the main, the activities said to be taking place down there were experimentations in advanced-technology and biotechnology, while the facilities themselves were said to be powered by illegally run nuclear reactors. Or at least some of them were. Of course, there were rumours, too, of alien-government collaboration in some of the programmes, which provided not only an intriguing dimension to the story – especially at this time when the *X-Files* was so popular – but also the perfect angle for our readership.

And in this regard there was an even more intriguing angle.

The buzz at the time was that many of these underground facilities had been built with an ulterior purpose in mind—that the city-sized facilities, linked by a high-speed underground rail network, had been built as a contingency in the event of some imminent global catastrophe. Hence the title of my article: *Project Noah's Ark*. When the apocalypse came, so the theory proposed, the elite would all dive underground while the masses would be left to the mercy of the 'flood'. An unlikely scenario, perhaps. But at a time when so many feared that *Area 51* really was a holding bay for captured aliens, that the recent Hollywood Blockbuster *Independence Day* was a precursor for the main event and that Fox Mulder really was the New Age Messiah come to save us all from alien takeover, it was a story worth the telling.

And in any event, it was this article that had prompted the mystery caller to contact me. Or so he'd said. And rightly or wrongly – wrongly, it would turn out – I took him at his word.

9

Avenue Marceau, Paris — April 1997

The number plate on the black Mercedes S280 parked up outside Café de Baron on this dark and moonless night read 680 LTV75. It was a number plate Clive du Bois knew well enough.

Having worked as a chauffeur for *Etoile Limousine* for the past two-and-a-half years he'd driven the vehicle on any number of occasions, and had come to memorize the number plate like he memorized everything else—faces, names, places. His mind was like a camera; it remembered everything, as it happened, frame by frame. The events of this night were no exception.

He'd met his clients at Le Bourget Airport earlier that evening and had delivered them without incident to a sumptuous address in the affluent Paris suburb of Passy. Then, realizing he'd made good time, that he still had the best part of an hour to kill before his next pick-up, and figuring a strong *café noir* might be just what was needed to help him remain alert, and awake, he'd made his way back across town from Passy, driving first down by the river, then heading up along Avenue d'Léna and Avenue Pierre 1er de Serbie before swinging left on Avenue Marceau and pulling up outside Café de Baron, where he was now. His photographic mind had registered every detail of his journey—or rather, every detail except one. He'd been followed. The headlights he'd noticed in his rear-view mirror on his way to the airport, and then again as he'd pulled away after dropping off his clients in Passy, had been tailing him, yet so discreetly that even *his* mind couldn't recall exactly when they'd appeared, or when they'd disappeared. And when they'd appeared again. From the moment he'd left the *Etoile Limousine* car lot at Place du Marché

Saint-Honoré, scarcely a stone's throw from Place Vendome and the Ritz Hotel in the centre of the city, and had driven all the way up to Le Bourget and back down to Passy, his pursuers had outmanoeuvred him. Now he was about to meet them, face on.

As he opened the driver-side door and started to climb out, his intention to cross the several yards of dimly lit pavement to Café de Baron and order his late-night *café noir*, the chauffeur was met by a gloved hand that seemed to appear from nowhere, from the shadows, simultaneously wrapping itself around his neck and yanking him from his seat so violently that he buckled instantly to his knees on the pavement. Less than a beat later a second gloved hand slammed down on his head and opened up a gash fully four inches long with the butt of the pistol it held, sending du Bois tumbling backwards across the pavement like a drunk. He tried to yell, but he couldn't. Instead he gave up this useless, stifled groan as the heel of a thick-soled boot thudded into his ribs and stole his breath. The last thing he remembered before losing consciousness was the number plate 680 LTV75 as it disappeared along Avenue Marceau and out of sight.

And then, darkness, as du Bois' photographic mind finally focused out.

10

"It's Jon King returning your call."

A raw November wind whipped through the call box in which I stood as I took out pen and notepad and thumbed my way through to an almost blank page—a page with space enough, at least, for me to scribble notes. I shivered. It was cold in here. The call box had been so convincingly demolished there was little of it left to keep the wind from penetrating my bones—windows smashed, door unhinged, so much so that a gap high enough for an ambitious limbo dancer to slither under now existed between the foot of the door and the concrete on which I stood. Kids with nothing better to do, I figured. To make matters worse, the line was bad, the stranger's voice faint and breaking up. I pressed a hand to my ear in an attempt to block out the drone of passing traffic. "Hello?" I said again. "It's Jon King."

"I hear you." The American voice was deep in tone, distinguishable from other stateside accents by its lazy, Southern drawl. "I hear you loud and clear."

I clicked open my ballpoint. "You say you have some information?"

"In relation to your article about the deep-underground programme in America, yes—Project Noah's Ark. Are you aware that there's a similar programme in the UK—?"

No, I wasn't.

"—I have the specifics. I can tell you all about it if you're interested."

"I'm interested."

A brief pause, a static crackle on the line, then: "The thing is, what's happening in America is happening over here, too. It's just that over there the focus is mostly on advanced-technology projects, while in the UK it's much more to do with biology, or more specifically, biotechnology—genetics, cloning, hybridization, all kinds of exotic bio-warfare experiments. It's all pretty much beyond your worst nightmares."

"And you can prove this?"

"I can help you build a case, put you in touch with those who are willing to speak out. I know people who work at these places. I can introduce you, help you get exclusives for your magazine. It would fit very well. For sure some of the biology involved in these programmes is pretty damn exotic, I can tell you that much, especially when it comes to the hybridization programmes."

"Exotic in what way, exactly?"

"Aliens, man. The hybridization of aliens and humans."

Here we go, I thought, this is where we enter the twilight zone, but I refrained from saying it out loud. Instead I said: "That's some claim."

"Yes, and I have the meat to back it up." He paused. "I also have some other information I think you'd be interested in," he said. "But if you want to take this any further we'll need to meet."

"Well, with respect, I'm a busy man. I would need to know…"

"As I've already told you," the voice calmly assured, "it'll be worth your while. But we would need to meet. This kind of information doesn't travel well over the telephone."

I paused for a brief moment. Was this guy crazy? Probably. What he was talking about was certainly crazy, there was no denying that. But then, in the eyes of Middle England I ran a crazy magazine. There was no denying that, either.

But there was something else, too, something I couldn't at this stage put my finger on. All I knew was it unnerved me somewhat, made me feel uncomfortable—something to do with the guy's tone, his understated, almost serene authority, it's twisted edge. This was not someone to be feared for his insanity, this voice in my head was trying to warn me, but his agenda. I made a mental note.

"Do you have anywhere particular in mind you'd like to meet?" I said.

"Avebury," came the reply. "Avebury Stone Circles in Wiltshire. You know the place?"

"I do, yes." In fact I knew it very well. Avebury and the surrounding area was a hotspot for UFO sightings and crop circles. It had featured in our magazine many times. "When?"

"This Saturday, midday, in the car park opposite the post office."

...*The car park opposite the post office.* I noted it down. "Okay," I said. "How will I recognize you?"

"You won't. I'll pick you out. Saturday. Midday. Avebury. Opposite the post office. Are we agreed?"

"I'll be there."

11

Thames House, Millbank, MI5 Headquarters—November 1996

"We all know why we're here, gentlemen." Addressing the dozen or so senior officials seated at the table there with him, Sir Philip Hemming opened the dossier he'd just pulled from his attaché case and officially convened the meeting. The dossier was designated *Top Secret – Delicate Source – UK Eyes A*. Its title read: *The Prince and Princess of Wales*.

Among the officials present were Lacey, of course; Deputy Director General MI5 Operations, Malcolm Garner; Chief of MI6, Sir Richard Dearlove; MI6 Head of Special Operations Europe, Richard Mason; Home Office Permanent Secretary Sir Martin Gray; a naval intelligence Commodore whom I would later be introduced to (he being, by some coincidence, a personal friend of Lacey's), and several other Whitehall spooks whose identity I never learned. By account, the Crown was also represented by a senior royal courtier and member of the secretive Way Ahead Group, Sir Gerald Cameron.

Sir Philip was in the chair. "We're here to discuss the recent divorce of the Prince and Princess of Wales," he informed those gathered. "In particular the constitutional implications engendered as a result of the prince's desire to remarry."

"Which are?" Sir Gerald Cameron wanted clarified.

"Very grave indeed," Sir Philip said.

"Surely he can't be allowed to remarry," one of the Whitehall officials put in.

"Try and stop him," said another. "You know what he's like when he wants something."

"We could whip up public opposition to the marriage," a third spook suggested. "Shouldn't be too difficult, given their fondness for Diana."

"And their dislike of Camilla."

"I'm afraid it might be too late for that." Sir Philip had just opened a second dossier on the table in front of him. This one was also designated *Top Secret – Delicate Source – UK Eyes A*, but was titled *The Office of the Lord Chancellor*.

"Why do you say that?" Sir Gerald Cameron was curious to know.

"Because the Lord Chancellor is already mooting disestablishment."

"What...?"

"The proposed marriage between the Prince of Wales and Camilla Parker-Bowles, in the event that Princess Diana is alive to witness it, would engender such a constitutional crisis that the only resolution would be to effect disestablishment." Sir Philip was reading from the dossier. "For reasons herein listed the marriage must be at all costs avoided for as long as the mother of the future king remains alive." He repeated the phrase, *"at all costs"* with some emphasis.

The room fell silent at this point, each to a man realizing the implications of such momentous reform. To disestablish the Church from the state would not only create a seismic chasm at the heart of the establishment: it would create a secular state in Britain for the first time in the nation's history. The power mongers in Whitehall would never sanction it.

"Do you understand what you're saying?" the Crown's representative, Sir Gerald Cameron, said.

Sir Philip was impassive. "The Lord Chancellor's words, not mine," he said. "But clearly he feels he has little choice. Prince Charles is fated to become Supreme Governor of the Church on his accession, and if he's permitted to remarry it would severely undermine the Church's position from a constitutional perspective. Camilla is a divorcee, is she not—?"

"Yes, but ..."

"—The prince's wife must one day assume the role of Queen Consort, by station if not by name. And to put things bluntly, gentlemen, Camilla cannot assume this role while Diana is still alive."

Again a deathly silence fell, and this time persisted for several moments. It was Sir Gerald Cameron who finally broke that silence.

"You do realize," he said, "that the last person to disestablish the Church was Henry the Eighth."

"Quite," Mason put in, making his first contribution to the meeting. In his eyes, demons. "And we all know what that means, gentlemen, don't we."

He left a deliberate pause as he eyed each man present, one and then the next, before concluding:

"One of the wives must go."

12

Avebury was even colder than the call box had been. But at least it was good, clean country air, and aesthetically more pleasing than the high street in which the call box had stood. I consoled myself with these thoughts as I threw on my jacket and wrapped up against the bleak November day.

I'd arrived at the Avebury car park about fifteen minutes earlier than our arranged meeting time. As usual it was more or less full, even at this time of year, but from what I could make out the American hadn't yet arrived. Having parked my car and gathered my attaché case I wandered over to the entrance and sat myself on a vacant wall, watching for the arrival of a single, middle-aged male, the mental picture I'd formulated on speaking to the mystery caller on the telephone. I didn't have to wait long for his arrival. Moreover, as he drove into the car park I noted that the mental picture I'd formulated was about right. In fact he looked how you might imagine a mildly successful, late middle-aged businessman to look, if a little weathered—around six feet, weighty, thinning to grey on top with a pallid, craggy jowl that added years. He drove a silver Vauxhall Carlton. His handshake was firm.

Following a brief introduction we wandered out through the car park's field exit – a wooden latch-gate that opened into a grazing meadow famed for its sheep and standing stones – and talked as we walked. Despite the time of year and the unfriendly weather there were a good many other people strolling around the field, though none seemed too interested in anybody else, preoccupied instead with being tourists. Hopefully we appeared the same.

At this first meeting – we would meet four times in all – the American told me he was a US special forces veteran who'd run numerous operations for the CIA, and that he'd chosen to pass information my way because he'd become disillusioned with the agency for whom he worked. Of course, if I'd had my wits honed – if I'd been more seasoned, more alert to the man's intentions, and more suspicious of his objectives – I might have realized there and then that he was pushing candy. That he was saying what I wanted to hear. That, for some as yet unveiled purpose, I was being groomed and reeled in. But I didn't. He'd read my articles on the American government's deep-underground programmes, he said, and this had prompted him to pass information my way regarding similar programmes being carried out by the British government, in particular – so far as I was concerned at the time, being editor of a conspiracy-based UFO rag – the privately funded advanced-technology programmes being carried out by the British-based aerospace industry, also underground; plus, of course, the alien-human hybridization programmes he'd mentioned to me on the telephone. He said he had information about these programmes that our readership would want to hear.

And once again, rightly or wrongly, I took him at his word.

Naïve? Yes, perhaps. But why should I have suspected any different? Why would a low-key conspiracy journalist ever suspect he was being set up in a high-profile intelligence operation? Especially when the initial information the American gave me was more to do with the UK government's dubious activities underground, at some of the country's most highly secret defence and research facilities, than anything remotely to do with deniable ops. Or indeed, political assassination. So far as I was concerned I was being gifted the ingredients for a seriously juicy story, one that our readers would relish. And that was it.

Truth be told, I thought I'd hit the jackpot.

The next time we met, again at Avebury, I was able to learn a little more about the American and in particular his covert military background. On this occasion conversation flowed freely between us, and for the first time I saw a side to the man I hadn't yet seen—a somewhat more disturbing side, it has to be said. Even so he seemed happy to talk about his past, including some of the more illicit 'black ops' he'd been involved in, and I for one wasn't about to discourage that.

But first he made reference to my magazine. "I noticed the Project Noah's Ark story you wrote was part of a regular feature in your magazine," the American said as we strolled anonymously among the standing stones and the few tourists intrepid enough to have braved this bleak winter's day. It was January, in every sense of the word. "Jon King's X-File Document. I guess that makes you a sort of real-life Fox Mulder."

"It keeps a roof over my head," I said, more than a little embarrassed by the association with the lead character in the *X-Files*. "Actually I'm more interested in what the CIA are up to in Angola than what happened at Roswell."

"You don't want to know if the US government has done a secret deal with aliens?"

"I'd like to know why they would have us believe that. I'm more interested in the agenda behind the story than the story itself."

"Well that's where I can help."

A short while later we rounded Avebury's reputedly haunted Red Lion pub, the mildewed odour of ale and cigarette smoke escaping its walls and thickening the otherwise fresh, if bitter, Wiltshire air. Either the ghosts were enjoying a lunchtime beverage, I mused, or the lack of tourists wandering among the stones suddenly made sense. They were all in the pub. It was coming up to 1 pm, after all, and the Great British 'liquid lunch' was under way, Avebury's customary complement of daytime visitors taking full advantage of the warmth and hospitality offered by the famous old watering hole. *At least someone has some sense around here*, I thought to myself as reluctantly I turned my back to the pub and partnered the American across the road as we headed for the cold and uninviting field where Avebury's second inner stone circle stood, the promise of warm hands and cold beer receding in our wake.

"You mentioned Angola," the American said as we started to slow-pace the field's raised perimeter—an earthwork bank and ditch enclosing the world's largest prehistoric stone circle. "That intrigues me. I have to ask myself why the editor of an *X-Files* magazine would wish to concern himself with what's going on in a troubled African republic?"

I shrugged. "Just my natural curiosity, I guess. I like to keep abreast of the seedier activities carried out by my government, especially when those activities are about exploiting another country's resources to the detriment of its indigenous population. It irks me. I think the way democracy has been hijacked by big business needs to be exposed wherever possible, so I try and write about it when I can—between UFO stories."

"Very conscientious of you."

"Not really. I'm just naïve enough to believe a better world's possible. And to speak up for it."

"There's no shame in that."

Strolling atop the earthwork bank bordering the southernmost edge of the field I suddenly spied another prehistoric wonder looming some way in the distance. Silbury Hill was Europe's largest human-made earth mound. It looked for all the world like a landed spacecraft.

"But why Angola particularly?" the American was keen to know, exhaling the smoke from a cigarette he'd just lit with a silver Zippo lighter. Its lid *clicked* as he flipped it shut. "The world's a big place."

"Good question." I thought about it briefly. "I guess my interest in Angola stems from the fact that I knew some of the British mercenaries who fought there in the seventies. I grew up in the town where they were based."

"In Sandhurst?"

"Yes, you know it?"

"I've never been. But I knew some of the British boys who fought in Angola."

He knew some of the Sandhurst boys? I logged the fact. "Small world."

"Smaller than you think."

Something about the way the American said that found its way home. It was as if he wanted me to think he knew more about me than I would have liked. No more than a nuance, but it made me feel itchy, uncomfortable.

"I was in Angola myself in the sixties," the American went on, unbidden. "And again in the seventies, between tours of Vietnam. Special Forces Operational Detachment Alpha—the Green Berets, effectively the CIA's own private army."

"I didn't think the CIA were in Angola in the sixties."

"The CIA are everywhere at all times." He gave a dry smile, and drew in a lungful of carcinogenic smoke. Then blew it out again. "Fact is we weren't supposed to be in Laos or Cambodia in the sixties, either. But we were there, making cross-border runs from western Nam on a regular basis. The Viet-Cong had bases set up in eastern Cambodia and Laos and we were the jerkies sent in by Nixon and his White House generals to ferret them out. The situation was not too dissimilar in Angola, except over there we were running back and forth across the border from Zaire. Same tactics, different outcome. Angola was a whole different ball game."

"So you were running arms to the Angolan rebels?"

"The FNLA, UNITA and the MPLA. In those days they were all on the same side, three conflicting rebel armies bound together by their struggle to drive out the Portuguese."

"A struggle to gain their independence."

"Correct. In which case you may ask what we were doing there at all. And the answer is it had nothing to do with supporting a bunch of overzealous warlords disguised as freedom fighters. Fact is we were there for the same reasons the British were there—oil and diamonds. Simple. On the face of it we were doing what the CIA always does, which is funding, training and equipping the opposition forces, as well as giving them tactical and logistical support. In other words we were fighting their god damn war for them. But at the same time we were pursuing an ulterior agenda, and that was more to do with power-brokering and money-laundering than freedom-fighting, I can tell you that much." He paused and stared coldly ahead at the near distance, as though reliving events in his mind. "You know," he said. "I still couldn't tell you which hell was the meanest—Nam or Angola. In their own way both were insufferable. But undoubtedly Angola was the most immoral."

The American slowed his pace to an eventual standstill, and I stopped beside him. He locked his gaze on mine.

"It's the same war," he wanted me to understand. "In the sixties they called it a war of independence. In the seventies and eighties they called it a civil war. But in truth it doesn't matter what you call it. It's the same war with the same players fighting for the same spoils—control of Angola's oil fields and diamond mines, even today."

"Today?"

"Oh, undoubtedly. Your country and mine are still waging an oil-and-diamond war in Angola. Don't ever doubt it. Others are involved, too—Russia, Cuba, South Africa, the French. Who do you think is keeping the new government in power? Coz they sure as hell ain't doing it all by themselves." He drew on his cigarette. "Angola's a dangerous place to be," he said, "something the Princess of Wales should be heedful of, incidentally. Have you seen her in the news recently, wrapping her arms around landmine victims and parading around in unexploded mine fields? She needs to tread carefully, no pun intended."

The American's claim that Angola's inner 'war' was still raging behind the scenes, even though it had officially ended three years previously, made me think. But his reference to Princess Diana slipped by me virtually unrecorded. I'd seen the recent images on TV, of course – Diana in visor and protective body-armour vest wandering dangerously in an unexploded mine field – all part of her campaign to bring the issue of landmines to the world's attention. And it was working; her landmines campaign was headline news. But right now I was more interested in my government's covert involvement in yet another illicit war than in what the world's most famous diva was up to. Even the American's insinuation that she should *tread carefully* washed over me.

"There's a lot going on behind the scenes in Angola and not much of it ever makes the front pages," he added, fixing me with that knife-edge stare of his. "But I guess that's the point, isn't it? Never believe the official line. Whatever they tell you is happening is never what's really happening. It's something else." He paused, it seemed for effect. "But I guess you know that anyway, right?"

"I generally try to read the small print."

He nodded. "As I figured. You and I are gonna get along just fine."

He snuffed out his cigarette underfoot.

13

Deserted Warehouse, Paris—April 1997

The black Mercedes S280 was now parked in a different place. But its number plate remained the same: 680 LTV75.

Both vehicle and plate were now parked at one end of a deserted warehouse on the outskirts of Paris, a mechanic in dark-blue overalls buried somewhere beneath the vehicle's bonnet, as though he might be fixing a worn hose or changing dead spark plugs. But he was doing neither of these things. Instead his hands were busy removing a miniature circuit board concealed beneath an internal cover, and replacing it with another, seemingly identical one. Difference was, wired into this circuit board was a micro-transceiver tuned to override the vehicle's steering and traction control.

Who needs a chauffeur when the vehicle can be driven by remote control?

As he finished fitting the new 'parasite' circuit board a second mechanic emerged from beneath the vehicle's front end.

"Right, the Blockbuster's in place," the second mechanic said, wiping grease from his hands with a grubby rag. "That'll take care of the brakes."

"And this'll take care of the steering," the first mechanic said, replacing the internal cover over the parasite circuit board and dropping the bonnet shut. Then: "You boys about done?" he turned and said to the two other men there with them. They'd just finished loading concrete blocks into a false floor built into the back of a white Fiat Uno parked up next to the Mercedes. "Time's moving on."

"Done," one of them said, closing the Uno's hatchback door. "You could hit this thing with a tank now and it would still hold the road, no problem."

"Good. Because this Mercedes coming at you at eighty miles an hour might just as well *be* a tank." The first mechanic had peeled off his overalls and was now immaculately dressed in charcoal suit and tie of the kind a chauffeur might wear. He opened the Mercedes' driver-side door and climbed in behind the wheel. "Now let's get this death trap back to its rightful owner."

He fired the engine.

Some forty minutes later the number plate 680 LTV75 pulled silently up at the side of the road, on Place du Marché Saint-Honoré, just along the way from the *Etoile Limousine* offices in the centre of the city. Dressed in charcoal suit and tie the vehicle's 'chauffeur' climbed casually from the driver's seat and transferred to a white Fiat Uno parked up some twenty or so yards back along the street. It was late, around 3.40 am as the Uno drove off with its extra passenger.

A little over six hours later, around 10 am, the Mercedes was spotted by one of the company's employees on their way to work. Evidently the vehicle had been 'abandoned'. Realizing it was the Mercedes that had been stolen at gunpoint some days previously the employee reported his find and following a routine mechanical examination and a forensic dust down the Mercedes was finally returned to its owners at *Etoile Limousine* a few days later. By the end of the week it was back in service, ferrying VIPs about town.

14

Saturday, August 23rd, 1997

Not all my meetings with the American took place at Avebury, but this one, like the first two, did. As it turned out it would be our last meeting that summer. So far as I knew at the time, of course, it would be our last meeting, period.

On my way to Avebury I had to stop off at the magazine offices to pick up my Dictaphone: one of the few essential tools of my trade. I always kept it in my attaché case, but on the one day I needed it most, of course, it wasn't there. I'd looked everywhere. I was late. I was starting to flap. *Where the hell had I left it? Why was I always mislaying my god damn Dictaphone?* As I rummaged desperately through the chaos littering my office desk in search of my precious recording device JB entered the building and appeared in the doorway behind me. Just what I didn't need. I was in a rush. I knew he'd grill me about the American.

"Jon." He looked surprised to see me. "I didn't think you'd be in today. It's Saturday."

"Tell me about it. I promised to take Katie and the kids out for the day and then I remembered I had this meeting and then I realized I didn't have my—*yes!*" My Dictaphone suddenly emerged from the clutter jamming up my desk drawer. I turned and held it aloft to show JB. "I was looking for this."

He nodded. "You meeting that American guy again? The one who reckons he's CIA?"

I knew it. "Ever the cynic," I said.

"Well it's unlikely, isn't it? Why would the CIA want to feed secrets to the editor of a UFO mag?"

"Thanks, JB."

"Well think about it."

"I have."

"And?"

"*And* … I'm really not sure what to make of him. He's interesting, there's no doubt about that. He's given me some good information, too, stuff I've been able to corroborate, so he's not all fob and fairy dust." I paused, trying to find the words. "I do have to admit, though … I feel like … almost like I'm being—"

"Led a merry dance?"

"—Groomed, JB. Groomed."

"For what?"

I shook my head. "That's the thing, I don't know. It's like he's drip-feeding me, like I'm forever waiting for him to deliver the punch line."

"Well be careful. When the punch line comes it might not be what you were expecting."

Ouch. JB had a way of cutting to the marrow, and more often than not he was right. Still turning his words over in my mind I set the Dictaphone back down on the desk and grabbed my jacket from the back of the chair JB was now occupying. I decided to change the subject. "What are you doing here anyway? Talk about me not working Saturdays."

He sighed. "I just thought I'd do a bit of research, that's all. Play catch-up."

"On Saturday?"

"Is that a problem?"

"No, of course not." I shrugged my jacket on. "You okay?" I said.

"I'm fine."

"You just seem…"

"I'm fine."

He wasn't fine. I could tell that. I hadn't known JB all that long at this point, a few years at most, but I knew him well enough to know he wore his feelings on the outside. If there was something bugging him a neon 'HELP!' sign started to flash just above his head, or it might just as well have done. He would also become cantankerous. He was one of the most deeply caring people I'd ever known—a people person, thoughtful and considerate, a man of the community who'd worked most of his life caring for the disadvantaged. In short, he was one of life's single malts. But he was unable to contain his feelings. If there was a problem you could smell it on his breath.

"You sure you're okay?" I said, one last time. "Only—"

"Jenna," he finally blurted. It was the name of his girlfriend. "We had a fight. We've split up."

"What again?"

"What do you mean *again*?"

JB and Jenna had parted company more times in the past few months than I could readily recount. But I knew I shouldn't have said it quite like that. It just came out. "I'm sorry, JB. It's just difficult to keep track. I didn't know you were back together after the last time you split up. I didn't know you were still together, period."

"Well we're not now."

"No. So what happened this time?"

"She just wants me to be a certain way and—"

"You're not prepared to compromise."

"—I'm not prepared to *change*."

"No, of course not." This wasn't going anywhere. "Look, if there's anything I can do…"

"Not really."

"Well maybe we can grab a pint when I get back."

"I'll be here."

I checked my wristwatch. "Jesus. I really must make a move."

"Better not keep the CIA waiting."

"Very funny." I picked up my attaché case and started towards the door.

JB called after me. "Jon?"

I turned. A smug grin had worked its way onto JB's face. He was reclining all the way back in my chair now, holding my Dictaphone in the air. "You'll probably need this mate."

"Right."

A couple of hours later I was seated next to the American at a table outside Avebury's famed wholefood restaurant, drinking coffee. My Dictaphone was placed discreetly in front of me, next to my coffee, recording the American's words as he spoke them. Though I didn't know it at the time, Lacey would later inform me that I wasn't the only one recording our conversation that day, that the entire transcript had been filed back at GCHQ, the British government's signals intelligence base: the eyes and ears of MI6. From there, he said, it had found its way into the hands of MI6 Special Operations Chief, Richard Mason, who in turn had shown it to Lacey at a meeting they'd had in a private members club in Whitehall. Whether an undercover agent had been secreted nearby, of course, covertly recording our conversation – or maybe that the American had had his own recorder tucked away inside his jacket – I would never know for certain. But of the fifty or so tourists seated there at the restaurant with us that day as I sipped my coffee and listened to the American's tale, and the hundred or so others milling about, I couldn't help but wonder which ones were the tourists, and which one the agent. To this day the memory of it makes me shudder.

"It's all smoke and mirrors, Jon," the American was saying between mouthfuls of filtered coffee, his tone perhaps darker than it had been at any of our previous meetings, more underground. "Psychological warfare. If we can make the Russians believe we have exotic technology it makes them more wary of our capabilities. Keeps them on the back foot."

"And they believe that?" I said, slightly incredulous. "They believe America has alien technology?"

The American shrugged. "They believe we put a man on the moon," he said, and forced a fake smile. Not a warm smile. More a challenging one. "See that's the thing, Jon. We can make anybody believe anything."

Again, something about the way the American said that found its way home. Not for the first time I felt decidedly uneasy. Not for the first time I tried not to show it.

Then, out of the blue: "You know why Kennedy was killed?" the American threw in as he flipped open his silver Zippo lighter and lit up a cigarette. "The real reason?"

Though slightly taken aback I managed to find a reply. "I always assumed it was because he threatened to pull out of Vietnam," I said. "That he vowed to end the Vietnam War sooner than the military-industrial complex would have liked."

"And there are those who would agree." He breathed out a lungful of cigarette smoke. "Others, though, would say it was because he threatened to disenfranchise the Fed and print government money. Still others that he pledged to smash the CIA into a thousand pieces. Then there are those who say he was killed because he was determined to put an end to the arms race. So which was it?" He didn't wait for me to reply. "Popularity," he said, and threw me an unforgiving look. "Fact is Kennedy could have achieved *all* of those things, such was the extent of his popularity. And that's the point, see Jon? When you hold public opinion in your hand like that – when your popularity is such that it enables you to influence the public mind and galvanize it against the status quo – that's when you become a threat. JFK. Martin Luther King. John Lennon. Think about what I'm saying."

I thought about it, but failed to make the connection. Of course, had I known then the real reason the American had sought me out I would perhaps have put two and two together and realized that the only other person in the world to hold public opinion in their hand in a comparable way to Kennedy – the only other person so popular they were able to win public opinion and turn it against the status quo; indeed, the only other person who was actually doing just that – was Princess Diana. But the thought never entered my mind. Why would it? At this stage Princess Diana didn't exist in my world. Despite that she was the biggest media attraction we'd ever known, her face on every front page, her every move a news headline, at this particular moment in time Princess Diana simply wasn't on my radar.

But that, of course, was about to change.

It was the fourth time we'd met, and the American had already indicated it would likely be the last. He'd told me pretty much all he'd set out to tell me, he said. Now it was up to me to use the information in whatever way I felt I could.

But he also said something else. He wanted to give me "one last pearl" of information that would substantiate his credential—he'd tell me something that was about to happen so that when it did happen I would know he was the real deal, at least in terms of his ability to access privileged information. It wouldn't necessarily prove that the information he'd given me was genuine or accurate, of course; I knew that. But it would, as he said, prove at least that he was party to information unavailable to your average Joe, and in this regard his credential would be rubber-stamped. Little did I expect, though, that the "pearl" he was about to impart would be so deadly.

We'd finished up our coffees and headed back towards the stones, chatting as we'd walked. It was August; the restaurant was crowded, Avebury was buzzing with visitors and the table we'd occupied had been set among other populated tables with more tourists arriving for refreshments by the minute. Too many ears in too close proximity for the American to drop his "pearl", he'd said, so we'd ambled back up to the stones where the tourists were more dispersed and, for the most part, on the move. Finding a relatively quiet corner we sat ourselves down on a fallen standing stone and I turned my Dictaphone on. If this was truly to be a "pearl of information" then I wanted to record it, verbatim.

"Remember I told you how certain people were taken out," the American said, avoiding my eyes, staring grimly ahead. "People whose message was a threat because of their popularity, and because of their ability to mobilize public opinion—Kennedy, Martin Luther King, John Lennon and others?"

"I do, yes."

He leaned over and switched my Dictaphone off at this point. "Well it's gonna happen again."

"What...?"

"Someone's gonna get hit, soon."

"Are you serious?"

"I'm telling you, Jon, there's a plot to eliminate one of the most prominent figures on the world stage. I don't know precisely where or when the hit will take place, but it'll happen within days from now. They've been planning it for months."

"Who? Who's been planning it?"

"The people I told you about. MI6, the CIA. Whoever. I can tell you, Jon, this one will be bigger than Kennedy. Even my own sources are extremely nervous about this one, so much so that provision for public reaction has already been considered, very carefully. They have good experience of how to deal with public reaction. It's being taken care of as we speak. The media is being primed, as we speak."

"Jesus."

Just then a small knot of tourists ambled by, some lost in conversation, others seemingly lost in thought. Momentarily the American fell silent. As the last of the tourists passed us by I wondered how people might react should the American's information prove correct; should someone of global renown – President Clinton? the Pope? – truly meet an untimely end *'within days from now'*, the result of political assassination. Indeed, I wondered how *I* might react. The prospect was chilling, terrifying and electrifying, both at once. So much so that I was glad when the American finally spoke again. It snapped me back to the present and away from the growing sense of trepidation that now seemed everywhere in me.

"I was told that this person has to go for a good many reasons," the American went on. "Not least because they've become 'carcinogenic to the system'. That's a quote, which basically means they've become a threat to the stability of corporate government, just like John Lennon and the others before him, the others I've told you about."

"How the hell do you know all this?"

"I can't tell you that."

"Well … who, then? Where…?"

"I can't tell you that, either." The American climbed to his feet and tugged his jacket across his chest, as though preparing to leave.

"No, wait!" Now *I* was on my feet, too, an instinctive response as panic started to run in me. The more the information sunk in the less sense it seemed to make to my hot-wired mind. "Is that it?"

"That's it."

"You just expect me to take your word that someone big is about to be assassinated? I mean, why are you telling me anyway?"

"So you can tell everybody else. Isn't that what a journalist does?"

"When there's a story, yes. But I need evidence—a time, a place, a name."

The American turned and fixed me in a way that he would do again, some years later, when I would finally learn the real reasons behind this unlikely charade and everything would suddenly make sense. Right now it made no sense at all.

"This is live intelligence, Jon. Read the papers. Watch the news networks. You'll know who it is soon enough." He paused at this point, as though to emphasize what he was about to say next. Then: "The media will tell you it was an accident. You'll know it wasn't."

That said, he held my gaze for a further long moment before turning and heading back towards the car park.

15

"Darren Adams, please."

The switchboard put me on hold.

As I waited for the call to go through I couldn't help thinking what a dumb idea this was. What was the point of calling Darren? Even before I did it, even before I fed my money in the pay phone and dialled the number I knew it was a dumb idea. Even before I jumped in my car and drove the six or seven miles from Avebury to Marlborough in search of an old-style phone box, every mile ruing the fact that I'd ignored Katie's advice and still hadn't bought myself one of those new technological marvels: a mobile phone. Even before that I knew this was a dumb idea. But I guess I was just desperate, mad to talk to someone about what had just happened, *what I'd just been told*. I had, after all, no more than an hour prior, been told that someone of global prominence was about to be eliminated and I needed to speak to an accommodating voice, even if it *was* a dumb idea: even if I had no real idea what to say or how to say it. Or indeed, what the accommodating voice might say in response. I just needed to talk.

So I drove to Marlborough, found a phone box and called Darren Adams, a *Sunday Mirror* journalist whom I'd know for several years, someone I'd bought the occasional drink for in exchange for hotwire leads, someone I'd fed the occasional UFO story to in return for the national coverage. Of all the people my scrambled head could think of Darren was the one person I figured might listen, might even be able to help in some as yet unfathomed way. The one person in any event that I hoped might lend a sympathetic ear. I was wrong, of course. But then I knew it was a dumb idea to begin with.

"Darren, it's Jon King."

"Jon, hi. How's it going? Seen any UFOs lately?" He laughed.

I didn't. "Listen, Darren. Something's come up. You might be able to use it."

"Go on."

"I've just met someone. He told me something."

"I'm with you."

"I don't know if I can say it over the phone."

"We can meet. Can you give me half an hour?"

"I'm not in London."

"Ah..."

"Look, Darren, I, ahh ... it was something really big, really important. I don't suppose you've heard anything?"

"I'll need a bit more information than that, I'm afraid, Jon. What did this person actually say?"

"Something ... you know, something ... CIA-ish."

"CIA-ish?"

"Well you know, something Kennedy-ish."

"You mean Dealy Plaza-ish?"

"Yeah. That's it. Something Dealy Plaza-ish."

"No, nothing like that's come our way lately, Jon. Sorry."

By now I was starting to realize how ridiculous I must have sounded. But I was too freaked out to do much about it.

"Are you sure this guy had a full set of wheel nuts?" Darren said.

"I've spoken to him before, several times," I said, as if this might prove the man's integrity. It didn't, of course. "He seems sound enough."

"Well if I were you I'd check him out before taking what he said too seriously—whatever he said."

"Of course..."

Just then, unexpectedly, my mind was momentarily distracted by something I'd just seen outside, through the call box window. A black Ford Granada with smoke-tinted windows had just slowed to a virtual standstill as it cruised past the call box, and had then picked up speed again and driven on along the street. *Had they done that deliberately? With intent to intimidate?* Given what I'd been told not more than an hour earlier by the American – that someone of global prominence was about to be assassinated – my mind was perhaps more prone than it might ordinarily have been to misinterpret, to imagine, to panic. I had to admit that. But there'd been no need for the Granada to have performed a manoeuvre like that—the traffic was free-flowing and there had been no obstacle in the road that would have caused the driver to slow down the way they did. Deliberately. Quite deliberately. I was sure of it. I couldn't see who the driver or passengers were through the darkly tinted windows, of course. But whoever they were, if their intention had been to freak me out they'd clearly succeeded. My heart was in my throat, pounding, as though trying to smash its way out.

"So, anyway," Darren was saying, obviously angling to wind down our conversation and get back to work. "How's your new book doing? What's it called again—Cosmic Top Secret, isn't it?"

I was still numbed by what I was sure had just happened. "Cosmic Top Secret," I echoed, absently. "It's doing okay, thanks. The review you did helped enormously. I really appreciate it."

"Hey, no problem. Any time. When your next book's ready to go you know where to come. Nothing like a rave review in a national to shift a few copies."

"Yeah, thanks." I was still frantically scanning the high street as I spoke, left then right, left again, back and forth and back again in search of the mysterious Granada. It was nowhere to be seen. My heart was still pounding.

"Anyway, Jon, listen. I'd better get back to it. It's pretty mad here. Saturday's always our mad day—the day before publication. Deadline in a few hours."

"Of course."

"I'll speak to you soon. And don't forget you owe me a pint."

"Next time I'm in town."

"I'll hold you to it."

With that Darren hung up.

I didn't put the phone down straight away. Instead I just stood there, for what could have been several minutes, the phone still tight to my ear as if I was still in conversation. Fear does strange things to a person, and I guess I was just too frightened to move, too frightened to leave the call box and make my way back to my car in case the mysterious black Ford Granada suddenly appeared again and I was jumped. It didn't, of course. It didn't appear again and I wasn't jumped. It was mid-Saturday afternoon in the centre of a busy Wiltshire market town, people everywhere. What was I thinking? If anyone wanted to jump me they would hardly choose this time and place to do it. After what seemed a small eternity I finally got a grip on my thoughts, hung up the phone and headed back to my car. I spent the entire journey home chasing ghosts in my rear-view mirror.

16

Sunday, August 31st, 1997

The week that followed my last meeting with the American was a strange one, to say the least, if not altogether surreal. I just didn't know what to think. On the one hand, I found it difficult to take what he'd said seriously enough for it to fully distract me. On the other, I just wasn't sure.

At random moments in the day I'd find myself faced with the ludicrous realization that I'd been forewarned of an imminent high-profile assassination. The next minute I'd have to remind myself that it was probably not true, that even though some of the information the American had given me in the past had stacked up, he was nonetheless a 'talker', someone known in the seedy world in which he claimed to operate as a 'flapper', meaning that he had a loose tongue. There was always the possibility as well, of course, that he was simply a stray bullet—or as Darren had put it, someone short of a full set of wheel nuts. Was that it? Had I been taken in by the inventions of a crazy person? I couldn't discount the possibility.

I knew in any event that he was someone whose claims I should treat with extreme caution. I had, after all, grown up listening to characters like him – the mercenaries who'd fought in Angola – most of whom had derived their daily gallon of ego juice from boasting about what they'd done or what they'd claimed to know. For all I knew this could have been just another ego massage: just another gallon of juice. So for the most part I just tried to push the whole thing to the back of my mind and get on with the rest of my life.

But it wasn't that easy.

The one thing that bugged me most of all was why he'd seen fit to tell *me*—why *me?* If what he'd said was true – if there really was a high-level plot to "eliminate one of the most prominent figures on the world stage", as he'd claimed – then why hadn't he told someone better placed to do something about it? Why hadn't he told someone like Darren Adams at the *Sunday Mirror,* for example, someone with an audience large enough to make a difference—someone the mainstream would listen to? Our magazine was doing pretty well, thank you very much, but compared to the nation's tabloids and broadsheets it was a minnow. Worse: it was a *fringe* minnow, read largely by UFO enthusiasts and conspiracy theorists. Why would he choose to inform the editor of such a goofy publication about something of such global importance?

I would later learn the answer to this question, of course: *I was being set up.* But at the time I just couldn't figure it at all.

So the week passed like that—kind of strangely. One minute I was sure the whole thing was a hair's breadth short of laughable. The next I was terrified. Or at least greatly concerned that what he'd said might pack some flesh: that someone of world renown might indeed have been earmarked by some powerful, faceless cabal to become the victim of a fatal *accident.*

"The media will tell you it was an accident," he'd looked me in the eye and pronounced. "You'll know it wasn't."

As each day passed the likelihood of this scenario coming real lessened in my mind by metre, it should be said. But I watched the news religiously, even so, waiting for the moment the Pope might fall from his pulpit, or President Clinton from his pedestal. Well who else could the American have been referring to? *This one will be bigger than Kennedy.* Who else but the President of the United States or the Head of the most powerful religious institution on the planet? Surely one or the other was about to be eliminated, I would think to myself. And then I'd rein myself in.

Don't be ridiculous. Get a grip. No one is about to be assassinated.

Then Sunday came—Sunday, 31st August, 1997: the day that changed not only my life, but for a brief moment in time, at least, most everybody else's life, too.

We'd planned a day out with the kids at a local aviation museum. On offer was a simulated helicopter ride and even a bombing raid over Dresden in a 1943-built Lancaster—or the 'Lanc' as it had been affectionately referred to during World War II. To minimize the loss of life, the bombing raid was also to be simulated.

Having showered and dressed I jogged down the stairs and entered the breakfast area to find Katie and the kids in buoyant mood. As was I. I'd put in long hours at the magazine in recent weeks and I was looking forward to a well-earned day off, in particular spending it with my family. But even though I felt pretty good I guess I must have looked pretty lousy, because the first thing Katie said as I entered the room was:

"You look like you need a coffee. I'll put the kettle on."

Maybe I'd been putting in even longer hours than I thought.

"So, today we get to fly in a helicopter," I said to the kids as I took my seat at the table with them. "How cool is that?"

"A real helicopter?" Jack wanted to know.

"Well no, not exactly. It's called a simulator. But it's just like real."

"Where are we going?" Ben put in.

"We're going to the aviation museum."

"What's an aviation museum?" Rosie said.

Both Ben and Jack rolled their eyes at this question. *Don't little sisters know anything?*

"It's a place where old aeroplanes are kept," I told her.

"And helicopters," she said.

"And helicopters, right."

"And fighter planes," Jack pointed out.

"Yeah," Ben agreed, and in perfect formation the two boys started dropping imaginary bombs from imaginary aircraft, complete with deafening sound effects. I hardly heard the telephone start to ring above the noise of exploding eight-thousand pounders.

"Is the museum far away?" Rosie was curious to know as I stood up to grab the phone.

"No, it's not far," I replied.

"Can I sit in the front?" Ben said.

"Well, I..."

"I'm sitting in the front," Jack came back. "I'm the oldest."

"That's not fair!" Ben complained.

"Yes it is!" said Jack.

I picked up the phone and put it to me ear. "Hello?"

"No it's not because I'll never be the oldest," Ben tried to explain. "That means I'll never be able to sit in the front."

Katie poured my coffee and brought it over to where I'd been sitting. "I'm older than all of you," she told the boys, settling what could otherwise have been a lengthy dispute. "I'm sitting in the front."

"Well done Ben!" Jack exclaimed. "Now look what you've done."

"I never said anything."

"Quiet everyone!" I suddenly demanded, drowning out even the loudest remonstrations from either Ben or Jack. The phone was pressed hard to my ear. "Quiet ... please..."

It was JB. He'd just told me the news. Princess Diana had been killed in a road traffic accident. I went so cold my blood turned to ice.

17

The next few days were a living nightmare. I just couldn't believe it had actually happened. *The media will tell you it was an accident. You'll know it wasn't.* The American's words kept resounding in my ears, in my head, repeating like some hideous, worst-case nightmare on relentless rewind. Not once had he mentioned the name 'Princess Diana', of course, I knew that. But everything else chimed.

"One of the most prominent figures on the world stage" will be assassinated *"within days from now"*, he'd said, barely a week prior. *"This one will be bigger than Kennedy."*

Who else could he have meant? At this point in time, whether Diana's death proved to be "bigger than Kennedy" remained to be seen. But undoubtedly she'd been "one of the most prominent figures on the world stage" – if not *the* most prominent – I couldn't doubt that. And the manner of her death he could scarcely have predicted with more precision.

"The media will tell you it was an accident. You'll know it wasn't."

Chance? Coincidence? Twist of fate?

Perhaps. But my churning innards wouldn't believe that. *Couldn't* believe that. Even before I'd put the phone down on JB I knew by instinct this was what the American had been referring to: that the *accident* he'd forewarned me about was the one that had just claimed Princess Diana's life; that the *assassination* he'd forewarned me about had actually come to pass. I'd just have to reconcile myself with the fact and, once the dust had settled, decide what I was going to do about it.

But first I had my family to think about.

I still hadn't told Katie what the American had said, that he'd forewarned me of Diana's *accident*. There'd seemed little point. I didn't want her worrying about something I felt sure would never happen. She knew about the meetings, of course. She knew about my meetings with the American just as she knew about my meetings with all the other 'cloak-and-dagger' characters who'd come forward over the years—informers, eyewitnesses, time-wasters, crazies. She just didn't know what the American had told me on that final occasion at Avebury.

This one will be bigger than Kennedy.

I would have to tell her soon, though, I realized that. But not before the mushroom cloud had settled in my head. Not before I'd processed what had happened and not until I'd figured out what to do next.

Should I go to the police? The media? Write a book?

I just didn't know. I couldn't think in straight lines. I was scared, and I didn't want Katie to have to deal with that. Not with any of it. So I kept a brave face and, for those first few days, said nothing, not a hint about what the American had said. I still didn't know where he'd got his information, for one thing—I didn't know who'd given him the information and I didn't know who else knew he'd been given it. *Worse*: I didn't know who knew he'd given it to *me*. How discreet had he been? Had he been followed to Avebury? Were the people who carried out the assassination aware that the American had spoken to me?

I just didn't know. My head was a mess. All I knew was, if I told Katie too soon she would realize immediately that we were in danger – or that we *might* be – and she would worry herself crazy about me and the kids. I just didn't want to inflict that on her, not yet.

Not ever.

So I stayed schtum, bottling up inside this deadly mix of confusion, disbelief and dread—not knowing what to do with it or where to take it. In the end I took it to JB, but at this early point in the game he was so reluctant to believe anything other than the official story that he didn't want to hear it.

"You don't know that he was talking about Diana," was his initial rebuff.

"Well who else could he have been talking about?" I said.

"It's just a coincidence, Jon. Nothing more than that."

"And that's what you think—honestly?"

"Why shouldn't I? A high speed chase, driver loses control. Two plus two equals a very nasty mess. It was an accident, Jon. Forget it."

I couldn't. "That's exactly what the American said they would say," I pointed out, hoping against hope that the real JB would stand up. "Is that coincidence, too? He said the media would say it was an accident."

"Well what else *would* they say? It was a car crash. In most people's minds that's an accident. If they wanted to kill her they would have shot her or something."

"Would they? If they'd done that we wouldn't be arguing over whether or not it was an assassination. We'd just be wondering who pulled the trigger."

"No one pulled the trigger, Jon. It was an accident. End of."

In those first few weeks following Diana's death this was JB's position on the matter. He was adamant. He wouldn't be budged.

Not knowing quite what else to do or who to talk to I called Darren Adams at the *Sunday Mirror* again, several times. But each time I called he was either 'not at his desk' or he was 'busy'. I called several other 'numbers'—people I knew who might know something, people I knew who *would* know something. But no joy. It seemed everyone had gone to ground and no one was talking. This one was just too hot. The only person I hadn't yet called was Rob Lacey.

Using an alias only he and I knew, Lacey had already tried to contact me at the office on the Tuesday after the crash, but I'd been out when he'd called and I'd decided to wait until I returned home from work that evening before calling him back. It was around seven in the evening when I finally wandered through into our living room and picked up the phone.

"Jon. Why the hell didn't you phone earlier?" Lacey demanded to know.

"Busy day. Sorry."

"I take it you've seen the news?"

The TV was on in the background as we spoke, images of shocked and grieving crowds gathered outside Kensington Palace amid an ever-expanding sea of flowers filling the screen. I'd never seen anything quite like it. "I've seen the news," I said.

"Then you won't be surprised to learn that all hell's broken loose up here. The security sector's on meltdown."

"Well maybe you shouldn't go around bumping off princesses."

"Careful what you say, Jon. I don't know who you've been mixing with but you're on file as a tap. Have been for some while."

"What? Well thanks for letting me know."

"I've only just found out."

"Jesus."

This was getting stranger – and more terrifying – by the minute. On file as a tap, Lacey had just said, meaning my phone was bugged—*meaning some sleazy agent holed up in a government listening post somewhere was probably eavesdropping my call right now.* Did they know who I was talking to? Wasn't Lacey being a little cavalier talking to me on the phone when he knew it was a tap?

Or was he too part of the plot?

What the hell was happening?

I glanced over at Katie, curled up snugly on the sofa with our black cat as she watched the images playing on the screen. I would do harm to anyone who dared lift a finger against her, I silently vowed. If I only I knew who they were.

"I spoke to someone," I said, my voice now a paranoid whisper. "About a week ago."

"A week ago...?"

"He told me something."

"Well whatever he said you can rest assured our people heard it, too."

"So what am I supposed to do? Go to the police?" Even before I said it I knew it was a stupid thing to say. But it did provoke an interesting response from Lacey.

"Do that and you'll find yourself in more trouble than you're already in."

"What's that supposed to mean?"

"We need to talk. Thursday—"

Thursday? But today's only Tuesday. That's two more days. What might happen in the meantime? To Katie? The kids…?

"—Usual place. Protocols apply."

"But…"

Too late. The phone clicked dead. As I replaced the receiver Katie looked up from watching the TV, her eyes heavy with concern, even though she didn't know who I'd just spoken to or what the content of our conversation had been. Still she knew all was not well.

"Be careful, Jon," was all she said. She looked so vulnerable.

Without words I crossed the room and cuddled in beside her on the sofa.

18

Lignières, France—September 1997

Jean-Paul led a secret life.

On the face of it he was a man at the pinnacle of his career—an annual income in excess of £500,000, a sought-after chateau in the Loire Valley, a luxury apartment in Paris. He owned two BMW saloons, a white Fiat Uno and a sparkling red classic BMW 650 motorbike. He dined at the best restaurants and smoked the finest Havana cigars, and was respected among his peers as France's leading photojournalist.

Simply put, Jean-Paul was a successful man.

He was also well-connected, unusually so for a man of his social standing, it has to be said. Brushing shoulders with prime ministers and other high-ranking politicians, as well as Europe's most powerful corporate czars, was all in a day's work for Jean-Paul. Influential friends. Powerful contacts. Exclusive access— access to people and places out of reach to most other press photographers. And it was this more than anything that had set the rumour mill turning. While some maintained his success was down to good fortune, that Jean-Paul had been blessed with a rare intuition that enabled him to 'be there' – right place, right time – to capture that elusive photograph for which every press agency, every magazine and newspaper editor would offer top dollar, others suspected a more sinister explanation. There were even those who suspected Jean-Paul had made a pact with the devil.

Or rather, if the rumours were to be believed, with MI6.

And the rumours were certainly persuasive.

The life of a paparazzo could be tough, after all, anyone who'd ever run with the pack in pursuit of that elusive photograph would tell you the same. Ambition and ruthlessness drove that pack, no doubt about it, each to a man jealous for the photograph that would make tomorrow's front page, inside cover, page three, four: *any page*. The pressure was immense, the success rate subzero, with many aspiring paparazzo falling by the wayside within the first six months. To make it past twelve required real self will. Either that, or a helping hand. And by all accounts Jean-Paul had received the latter. For years he'd struggled to be the first man there, to receive that vital tip-off that would leap-frog him instantly to the front of the pack, but with little or no success. And then one day, seemingly at random, everything changed. Suddenly Jean-Paul was *Paparazzo Uno*, no longer struggling to sell his photographs but able now to negotiate substantial rewards for his work as the very same agencies that had once shunned him now began to seek him out. Clients, too. Overnight Jean-Paul's name rose to the top of the pile. His income quadrupled. His beat-up old Fiat Uno became a shiny new BMW. The struggling press photographer he'd always been became a glittering, frontline paparazzo. And the reason, they say, was that Jean-Paul had been recruited.

It was a simple enough assignment that had first introduced him to the life of a part-time intelligence asset. All he'd been asked to do was glean what information he could from a certain left-wing politician he'd been hired to photograph and to pass the information back to his handler. Simple for a man of Jean-Paul's social reach. And well paid. From that moment on success was assured. In exchange for information gleaned from his high-ranking friends, Jean-Paul's intelligence handlers would in future provide him with all the tip-offs he needed – where to be for that sought-after photograph, and when – as well as 'arrange' exclusive access whenever exclusive access was required. This made Jean-Paul untouchable as a paparazzo, always one step ahead of his peers, and because of this, the most successful among them. The now famous image of Prince Charles kissing royal nanny, Tiggy Legge-Bourke, while on a skiing holiday at Klosters, had been taken by Jean-Paul, and had scooped him a reputed £100,000. The tip-off that Charles and Tiggy would be sharing an intimate moment, of course, the precise time and location, had come not from good fortune, nor even from that honed intuition some maintained he possessed. Rather it came from his MI6 handler—the same MI6 handler who would later 'arrange' exclusive access to Princess Diana aboard the Al Fayed yacht, *The Jonikal*, just a few days before her death. The same MI6 handler who would, in exchange for up-to-the-minute information on the princess's movements, arrange for Jean-Paul to be in Paris on the night of the crash, and remain undetected. Little wonder, then, that Jean-Paul had become a successful man.

Problem was, he wanted more—more fame, more wealth: more *success*. And the photographs he was developing now, this minute, in the darkroom at his chateau in central France, would be the currency he would use to get it.

Just then, there was a knock at the door.

"James?" It was Jean-Paul's wife, Elisabeth, calling him from the hallway. A self-professed anglophile – a lover of all things English: the people, the culture, even the weather – Jean-Paul had long since adopted the quintessentially English name of 'James'. It was the name he preferred everyone to call him by—even his wife. "Dinner will be ready in ten minutes."

"Be there in five."

James Andanson started to peel the last of the photographs he was developing from the tray containing the photographic liquid. The image on this last photograph was perhaps the most telling of all the photographs he'd developed that day. Indeed, it was the most telling photograph he'd ever taken, period.

As he removed the print from the liquid and hung it up to dry he studied the image it displayed with some satisfaction. It had been taken inside the Alma Tunnel on the night of Diana's fatal crash, and showed the immediate aftermath—a crumpled black Mercedes S280, the tail lights of a white Fiat Uno escaping the scene, a high-powered motorbike parked up alongside the crumpled Mercedes. A second Mercedes was also parked in the tunnel, next to the motorbike, a man in city suit and Oxford brogues standing imperiously beside its open rear door. The man was looking grimly into camera, as though this was a photograph he didn't want taken. It was of course the face of MI6 Head of Special Operations Europe, Richard Mason—Andanson's personal handler.

Smiling smugly to himself, James Andanson switched off the light and headed downstairs for dinner, leaving the scowling face of Richard Mason hung audaciously out to dry.

The black diplomatic limo with smoked-out windows carved a path through the dense Parisian traffic as it cruised past Élysées Palace and swung right on Rue du Faubourg Saint Honorè. It was headed for l'Ambassade de Grande Bretagne, where Mason's new office was located. Though he'd been here at the British Embassy in Paris barely two weeks, the Foreign & Commonwealth Office log would later declare he'd been on station for eighteen months. Later still, the log would be expunged.

In the back seat of the limo Mason was thumbing through a file he'd received earlier that day. It read: *Jean-Paul 'James' Andanson. Formerly Jean-Paul Gonin. French celebrity paparazzo. Anglophile. MI6 contact—4 years.*

Mason turned the page to reveal a mug shot of Andanson smoking a Havana cigar. "We'll need to wait until the French inquiry clears his name," he said into the car phone as he studied the image in detail, like he was searching for clues. "If anything happens to him while he's under investigation it'll look too suspicious."

"What makes you think the inquiry will want to question him?" The voice on the end of the line was English. Cultured.

"His name will come up," Mason assured. "Until then we'll watch and wait."

"As you say, Richard. But if the photographs are leaked in the meantime…"

"They won't be."

"They'd better not be. The operation isn't over yet. Far from it."

The limo turned right and disappeared into the embassy compound, the little piece of Britain in the heart of the French capital. Mason closed the file and snap-shut the folder containing it.

"This operation may never be over," he said with some irony. "I'll be in touch."

He terminated the call.

19

The journey to my agreed meeting place with Lacey had been fraught. Not to mention circuitous.

"You're on file as a tap," Lacey had said the last time I'd spoken to him, and I felt sure that whoever was listening in on my phone calls would be monitoring my movements, as well.

Especially my meeting with Lacey.

So instead of taking a direct route to our rendezvous point I'd made several deliberate detours across London via bus and tube train in an attempt to throw my pursuers, imagined or otherwise, off scent. At one point I'd even stopped off at the British Museum, deliberately wandering through the less populated areas to see who, if anyone, might be treading my coat tails. So far as I could tell, no one was. But just to make certain I took one last bus ride to Oxford Circus—bus rides were perfect for exposing a tail, Lacey had always said, for noting who boarded the bus when you did; whether they made a mobile call or texted during the journey; whether they alighted at the same stop as you. But again, so far as I could tell, no one did. So next I caught the tube to Lancaster Gate. From there the Pump House in Hyde Park, where I was scheduled to meet Lacey, was just across the road.

Paranoid? I don't think so. I was still shaken up by what the American had told me, even more so now that it had actually come to pass. Had he been acting alone? I didn't know. Did his masters know about our meeting? I didn't know. Did they know he'd told me about what I now believed was Diana's assassination?

Was my life in danger?

What I did know was that my mind was still fractured, its thoughts running riot in my head, crashing around in there like a pinball out of control. Diana had only been dead a few days, after all, and I still hadn't had time to process things—still hadn't had time to get a marshalled grip on my senses and think in straight lines. So when Lacey had said to me on the phone that 'protocols apply' – his way of telling me to use an SDR, a 'surveillance detection route', when travelling to the meeting – I'd simply followed his instruction, best I could. He knew I hadn't been properly trained in surveillance detection but he knew I'd been around those who had, and that I was capable of at least a rudimentary attempt at what in truth requires highly skilled training. I followed instruction regardless. Hence the detours, the bus rides, the visit to the British Museum. Not that I stood a realistic chance of exposing my highly trained pursuers, I knew that. But at least they would know by my erratic movements that I was deploying an SDR, and that would tell them that I knew I was under surveillance: that I knew they were following me.

If nothing else, Lacey had always said, it kept the buggers on their toes.

Momentarily lost in these thoughts I gazed out from the Pump House in Hyde Park, where I now stood, taking in views of the Italian Gardens and the expanse of Hyde Park beyond as I waited for Lacey to show. It was a glorious September morning. Sunlight was arcing across the garden's five pools and casting miniature rainbows in the spray thrown up by the pools' sculpted fountains. People were coming and going in every direction, some with purpose, others perhaps not so. Still others appeared distracted by the garden's anaesthetizing stimulus, and were wandering quite aimlessly, it seemed, back and forth, one fountain to the next. The scene was a meditation.

And then suddenly the meditation was interrupted.

Seated alone on a bench beside one of the fountains I spied a casually dressed man in dark blue denims and linen blazer. He'd just ended a call on his mobile phone and was now unfolding a newspaper, preparing to read it. Unremarkable in appearance— perhaps thirty-five, average build, short dark hair greased to one side and clean shaven. But for some reason he'd caught my attention, tugged my mind from its more contemplative thoughts and screamed at me to notice him. *Who was he?* I suddenly found myself asking, furtively studying the man now with my peripheral sight. *Who had he been speaking to on his mobile phone? Had he followed me here? Had he just reported my location to other members of his surveillance team?*

It was the sound of Lacey's voice that plucked me from these fretful thoughts.

"Charming view," he said, standing suddenly beside me, the two of us now staring out across the gardens, the expanse of Hyde park beyond. "Shall we walk?"

A few minutes later we were strolling together through the park, the Pump House and Surveillance Man some distance behind us, Serpentine Bridge and the lake some way ahead. Even though it was a weekday morning the park was nonetheless busy with its customary quota of tourists, joggers, skaters, people hotfooting it from A to B. Others simply chilling on the grass. I wondered which ones – if any – might be Surveillance Man's covert accomplices.

"So how are you keeping?" Lacey enquired. It had been a year or more since I'd last seen him, since I'd made the trip to London to pick his brains for my article on Angola. It seemed like a lifetime ago. "I don't get to see so much of you these days, not since you moved out of London. How's Katie?"

"She's good, thanks." Katie and I had moved a few years earlier in a bid to escape the city rat race, something we'd happily achieved, or so we'd thought. Now, it seemed, our *quiet life in the country* was in danger of becoming a living nightmare. "We're really happy where we are, or at least we were until this happened. It's hard to know how this might affect our lives."

"Have you told Katie about your American friend?"

"Not yet. I wanted to speak to you first, talk things through, make sure I wasn't losing the plot."

"Yes, well, speaking of plots, I suggest we cut to the gristle. There's a lot to talk about." Self-contained and quietly spoken, Lacey was a man of few words. But when he did make utterance it was generally to the point. "Let's start with your man, the American—who is he?"

I shrugged. "I can't say for certain. He claims he's CIA."

"Well if he is he'll know about UDS."

"UDS?"

"United Defence Systems, one of America's largest defence contractors. Committed substantial funds to a certain general election campaign recently. Even more to a certain cabinet minister's personal portfolio."

"And MI5 knew about it?"

"Of course. But if we prosecuted every politician guilty of accepting inducements there'd be no one left to run the country." He cleared his throat. "In any case, UDS were only a small part of a much larger investigation the industrial ops boys were running. If they'd hit on any one single beneficiary it would have compromised the entire operation. Sacrifice the worm to catch the bird, as they say."

"Meanwhile the worm grows fat on tax-free bungs."

"That's usually the way of it, I'm afraid, yes."

We headed up past the war memorial towards Serpentine Bridge. As we did so a green 4x4 pulled over to the side of the road a small distance ahead of us, its driver talking on a mobile phone. I couldn't help wondering who the driver was, and who he might be talking to. My paranoia was running amok.

"What does this have to do with Diana, anyway?" I said, eyeing the green 4x4 with some distrust.

"Landmines," Lacey came back. "UDS-built landmines, to be precise. Diana caught wind that some of Britain's high and mighty were involved in trade-offs with UDS—trade-offs that implicated the government. She was compiling a dossier, threatening to name names."

"Anyone we know?"

"Oh, yes. We know some of them very well indeed. They're household names. That was the problem."

"Wow. So what happened to the dossier?"

Lacey slid me a sideways glance. "It had an accident," he said.

"Ah."

A few paces further on we came on a small lay-by where a vending kiosk sold drinks and snacks—hot dogs, burgers, sandwiches, ice cream. As we approached the kiosks we were forced to negotiate a route through a flock of hungry pigeons that had swarmed there at our feet, pecking at the scraps. Somehow, I knew how they felt.

"And that wasn't the only problem," Lacey said. "Are you aware of Diana's recent visit to the White House?"

"It was on the news," I said. "By all accounts she turned the president's head."

"She did more than that, Jon. She damned near turned US defence policy on its head." He emphasized the point. "She managed to convince the President of the United States to sign a treaty banning landmines, worldwide. UDS were not happy. They were on the verge of closing some very lucrative deals with the British government for one thing—one reason they took such a keen interest in the outcome of our general election." He added: "The CIA were none too pleased, either."

"Because of a few landmines?"

"A few landmines! Is that what you think? I should be careful where you tread, my friend." Lacey indicated that I was inches from walking into a generous pile of pigeon shit.

I skipped around it. And the pigeons responsible.

"There are millions of landmines in Angola alone, Jon. You know that as well as I do. There are three-hundred-million deployed worldwide and a further three-hundred-million stockpiled and ready for use. That's not counting the billion-plus antipersonnel submunitions stashed away in America's hidden arms caches." Lacey stopped, mid-stride, turned and caught my eye. "When Diana convinced Clinton to sign that treaty the entire military-industrial complex sat up and took note. You can be sure of that."

"And so what—the CIA murdered her?"

"I'm not saying that."

"So what are you saying?"

"I'm sure you can work it out."

"Work it out?" I was starting to get frustrated. "Look, Lacey," I said. "Less than two weeks ago I was told someone big was about to get hit. A week later Diana dies in a highly suspicious car crash. Now you're telling me all this. I just need to know the truth. What are you saying—black and white?"

"If only life were that simple," Lacey said, and dug around in his pocket for loose change. "Excuse me one moment, would you?" He turned and headed for the vending kiosk.

A beat later my new mobile phone rang, the one Katie had finally persuaded me to buy. I checked the number. It was JB.

"Just making sure you're still alive," he said. "How's London?"

"All good so far, thanks. At least I think so."

"Meaning...?"

I was still preoccupied with the green 4x4 that, by now, had driven by us a couple of times and was circling back around for another pass. Probably just a park ranger going about his daily business, my rational mind tried to tell me. But at this precise moment in time it wasn't my rational mind I was listening to. "Ever had the feeling you're being watched?" I heard myself say.

"Sorry, Jon. I didn't quite catch that. The line broke up..."

"I doesn't matter," I said. "How are things back at the office?"

"In good hands, though I say so myself." A small pause, then: "Your literary agent Rick Devlin called, by the way. Simon & Schuster want the book."

"What book?"

"*Our* book?"

"Oh, so now someone's showing interest you want part of it?"

"Very funny."

I was kidding. Even though JB was still less than convinced that Diana's death was anything other than a tragic accident, he'd nonetheless agreed to help me investigate the incident and research material for the book I proposed to write. That I planned to use the book as a platform to petition for a public inquiry appealed to his sense of justice, and that, it seemed, overrode his personal opinion on the matter. I was very glad it did. I needed all the help I could get. And the help and support I would receive from JB over the coming years would prove invaluable.

"Listen, Jon, it gets even better," JB was saying, undaunted by my jaundiced sense of humour. "Evidently two more of London's top publishers want the book, as well. Not sure who they are yet, Rick didn't say. But he reckons there could be a bidding war for it."

"Well, let them bid away. The more they're prepared to pay for it the more they're likely to get behind it when it's published. It'll means more sales, and the more copies we're able to shift the bigger the platform we'll have to launch our petition for a public inquiry." I glanced up and noticed Lacey was making his way back over to me from the kiosk, a paper cone of monkey nuts in his hands—food for the pigeons. "Listen, JB. We'll talk about it later. I've gotta go. Thanks for checking in."

"No problem-oh."

A few moments later I was strolling with Lacey again, beside Serpentine Lake. Lacey was scattering nuts among the pigeons as we walked.

"What I fail to understand is why the CIA would become involved in the death of a British princess," I'd just said to him.

"Think about it, Jon. Why would the CIA become involved in anything?"

I remembered what the American had said about the reasons for the CIA being in Angola in the sixties, and the seventies, and the eighties.

Oil and diamonds.

"They say for every landmine deployed in Angola more than a thousand barrels of oil go missing," Lacey went on, "siphoned off in illicit arms deals. Then one day a meddling princess arrives on the scene and threatens to expose the entire operation. And not only that. She gets Clinton onside, as well."

We stopped outside Dell Café, on the shore of Serpentine Lake. Maybe fifty yards behind us the green 4x4 drew to a halt, too. "The landmines treaty is due to be signed in Oslo in two weeks time. But at some point between now and then Clinton will announce he's changed his mind and decided not to sign the treaty after all."

"What? But there'll be an outcry."

"Not now there won't. Diana's death will act as the perfect distraction. In a couple of weeks everyone will have forgotten that landmines even exist. As for Clinton, I have it on impeccable authority he's about to run headlong into a very public sex scandal."

"Even though he's agreed not to sign the treaty?"

"Call it insurance—a reminder that he should never have agreed to sign it in the first place. *And* a warning not to cross the line again. From what I've been told he'll do well to survive impeachment. Coffee?"

I nodded. "I think I need one."

•

"What I've told you so far is top-secret. What I'm about to tell you is nothing short of treasonous. Listen very carefully, Jon. I will only ever say this once."

Only very occasionally in the twenty or so years that I'd known him had I seen the face Lacey was wearing now—lips tight, brow knitted, eyes stark and doing the talking. It was his sincerity face, his *I really mean this* face. He only ever wore it when the heat was on, when he was about to say something that perhaps he shouldn't. Or at least something that he felt should be treated with particular confidentiality. It was apparent that he was about to say something of this magnitude now.

We were sat outside Hyde Park's Dell Café, drinking our coffee, watching the geese and the ducks and the pedal boats on

Serpentine Lake. It was around midday and the café was populated by people taking an early lunch—chatting, eating, drinking: enjoying the views and the unusually clement weather. Three tables away a woman in her late twenties, hair swept fiercely back in a pony tail, glanced up from the magazine she was reading and seemed to peer over askance at Lacey. A fleeting glance, no more. I don't think he noticed. I found myself wondering whether the ear phones she was wearing were attached to a walkman or a two-way radio device. My paranoia again.

Leaning slightly forward in his seat, his tone discreet, Lacey proceeded to tell me about the meeting he'd attended the previous year with senior Whitehall security advisor, Sir Phillip Hemming. As well as a representative from the royal household, he said, the meeting had been attended by some of Whitehall's most influential voices, including the heads of MI5 and MI6, and of course MI6 Head of Special Operations Europe, Richard Mason—a man, evidently, Lacey had known for some years. It was almost certainly Mason, Lacey said, who had overseen the operation in Paris.

"It's not his real name, of course" he'd wanted me to understand. "Mason. It's an all-purpose code name he uses. He's a high-ranking Freemason and I think the notion of using 'Mason' in this context indulges his deviant mind."

"Do you know his real name?"

"He doesn't have one."

Lacey went on to recount the general substance of the meeting, which, he said, had been ordered from the "very highest level". He said a "constitutional crisis" had arisen as a result of Prince Charles' desire to marry Camilla Parker Bowles "while Diana was still alive" – he emphasized that – and that MI6 had called for a "swift and decisive action" in order to avert the crisis.

"It was decided that there was only one course of action available to us," he said. "And it was of necessity extreme."

He went on: "The situation at the time was far more critical than you may think. For one thing the Church was in danger of being disestablished, and if that had happened the establishment as we know it would have come crashing down like a biblical tower. It really was that serious. Ultimately it was decided that one of the wives had to go," he said, surprisingly matter-of-fact.

"You mean Diana or Camilla?"

"One or the other, yes. Of course, MI6 had wanted the head of Diana for some while anyway, and this was the opportunity they'd been waiting for. We, on the other hand, argued that if anyone should go it ought to be Camilla. This way the crisis facing the establishment would be averted, public reaction would be minimized and Diana would be terrified into toeing the line. To us it was the perfect solution, given the options available."

Lacey paused at this point, his brow creased, as though somewhere in there he was reliving a very unpleasant scenario. And ultimately, I guess, he was. Realizing his fingers were drumming a nervous rhythm on the table top he clasped his hands together in a tight, white knot in an effort to keep them still.

"Up to this point, of course, it was all rhetoric, all in the planning stage, as they say. It had been agreed in principle that Diana or Camilla had to be taken out, true, but I still don't think at this stage anyone would seriously have sanctioned such an action. It was more a mutually agreed contingency plan, shall we say."

"So what happened?"

"Two things, one after the other. Firstly, the success of Diana's landmines campaign brought the CIA into the equation. That changed the complexion of things irrevocably."

"And secondly...?"

He grimaced. "Secondly, Dodi Fayed appeared on the scene," he said, and sighed, as though with resignation. "That really was the last straw. We knew then that if we didn't act immediately, MI6 and the CIA would."

"You mean if MI5 didn't get rid of Camilla—"

"—Then MI6 would get rid of Diana, yes. And they would have the full support of the CIA – surveillance, logistics, intelligence – everything you need to assassinate a princess."

"Jesus. So … what happened? I mean, Camilla's still alive…"

The look in Lacey's eye told me: *yes, but she shouldn't be*.

He asked me to cast my mind back a couple of months, to a night in June 1997, just a few weeks before Diana's fatal car crash in Paris. On that night, he reminded me, Camilla Parker Bowles had been involved in a car crash, too. The only difference was Camilla had survived.

"Camilla's car crash…" I heard myself say. I remembered the accident, all right. I just hadn't put two and two together, hadn't for one moment considered it might have been an assassination attempt, by MI5 or anybody else. "…I remember, of course. It was all over the papers. But I never thought…"

"Why would you?" Lacey said. "It was just an accident. Accidents happen all the time and people think little of them, which is why they're a favourite with deniable ops teams."

"My God…"

The newspapers had described how Camilla Parker Bowles had survived the crash despite her Ford Mondeo ploughing headlong into an oncoming Volvo Estate. She'd been on her way to Highgrove to meet Prince Charles, the papers had reported, when inexplicably she'd lost control and veered across the road into the path of the oncoming Volvo.

"She thought it was an attempt on her life," I said, recalling the newspaper story. "She said she thought someone was trying to assassinate her."

"Yes, and now you know why. But it all went stupidly wrong."

"Jesus…"

"Ironic, isn't it. Camilla's survival signalled Diana's demise. There was no way back after that. We'd had our shot and we missed."

Three tables away the woman with the swept-back hair and pony tail stood up to leave. Had she been listening in on our conversation? I shuddered at the thought. Even though a warm September sun was gently beating my back I gave a genuine shiver as I watched the woman fold her magazine into her bag and head off back towards Serpentine Bridge.

Lacey downed the dregs of his coffee and checked his wristwatch. "My goodness, is that the time? I must go," he said. He pushed himself up from the table and buttoned his jacket. "Time waits for no one, not even a spy."

"Why are you telling me all this, Lacey?" I suddenly found myself saying. We were friends, I knew that, and it wasn't the first time we'd discussed sensitive information. But never anything quite like this. I needed to know his intention was straight. "I mean, if they find out you've spoken to me..."

"I'll be in very serious trouble. Yes, I know." He picked up his attaché case.

"So why, then?" I pressed. "Why lay your career on the line for—"

"She was pregnant," he said, and left a pause long enough that the impact would bite. It did. In fact it stunned me to silence. "There were four lives lost in that accident, Jon, one of which was unborn. Not that this in itself was enough to prick my conscience if I'm honest. But it jarred, nonetheless."

He let another small silence hang between us before turning and heading off.

20

Brigade Criminelle Headquarters, Paris, February 1998

"I am confused, Monsieur Andanson."

Capitaine Laurent was leafing through a statement laid out on the table in front of him. He was chewing on the end of a pencil, turning the pages of the statement with his thumb and occasionally glancing up at James Andanson as he spoke. Andanson was seated opposite him, smoking the last of a fat Havana cigar; the sparsely furnished interview room was thick with spools of aromatic smoke. Beside the Capitaine, Lieutenant Gigou took notes.

"Pardon, Capitaine?" Andanson said, the slightest hint of derision in his voice. "You are confused?"

"Yes, Monsieur Andanson. Confused. First you say you were in Saint Tropez. Then you say you were at home. Which is it? Where were you on the night the princess died?"

Andanson drew on his cigar and blew out a thick plume of smoke. "I was at home with my wife," he said. "You can ask her. She will tell you the same."

"We have asked her, Monsieur Andanson. She says she was in Paris."

"Not at the time of the accident."

"Were you not in Paris as well, to photograph the princess?"

"No. My wife arrived home at nine o'clock. I was already at home. We spent the evening together—at home."

"Strange. That is not the recollection of your son."

Capitaine Laurent fingered the pile of papers in front of him until he found the statement given by Andanson's son, James Jnr. Referring to the statement, he said:

"Your son says you were not at home that night—"

"He is mistaken."

"—He says..." reading from the statement "... *I do not know where my father was. But one thing is certain, he was not at home.*" He looked back across at Andanson. "Why do you think he would say that, Monsieur Andanson?"

Andanson shrugged as he tapped ash from the end of his cigar. "Like I said, Capitaine, he is mistaken."

"He says here that he was at home all day, but that you were not. He says he went out in the evening, and that when he returned home sometime after midnight, you were still not home."

"What can I say? He is young. His mind is everywhere. That is all there is to it." He edged forward in his seat. "Look, Capitaine," he said. "On the night you are referring to I was in bed by midnight. I had a photographic assignment in Corsica the next morning and I had to be up early. I left my home at around four am and drove to the airport. You know this is true because you have the motorway toll receipt right there to prove it." He motioned at the pile of papers on the desk in front of Capitaine Laurent.

Fingering those papers the Capitaine retrieved a regular-sized chit and turned it face up on the desk. "This receipt proves only that you purchased the toll ticket at five-forty-eight in the morning. On your BMW motorbike you could easily have been in Paris at the time of the crash and back in time to purchase the ticket. This receipt proves nothing."

Andanson sat back in his seat.

For a long moment Capitaine Laurent studied the man opposite him. He did not believe his story, of course. He'd been a police officer for too long, almost thirty years, a detective for twenty-two of those years. He recognized the signs. He knew the signals given up by people like Andanson—the understated arrogance, the slight dilation of the pupils, the look that said *I know you know I am guilty, but you will never prove it.* Andanson was giving him that look now, and it made the Capitaine more determined than ever to find a way past the photographer's defences.

Again he fingered the pile of papers on the table in front of him, and this time pulled out a photograph of a white Fiat Uno. He flipped it around and slid it across the table so that Andanson could view it.

"We have evidence that a white Fiat Uno, like this one, was involved in the crash," he said.

"And?"

"You own a white Fiat Uno, Monsieur Andanson."

Andanson grinned. "Not anymore," he said. "I sold it."

"Oh?"

"It was old. I drive a BMW now, and so does my wife. I haven't used the Uno for more than a year."

"And yet only now you decide to sell it? After more than a year?"

"It is not against the law to sell a car you no longer use, Capitaine."

"That depends, Monsieur Andanson—on what the car had been used for."

Andanson glared, but made no further reply. Instead he pushed himself upright in his seat and bit his teeth. He was becoming agitated. The Capitaine was taking this line of questioning too far and he didn't like it. Of course he'd been in Paris to photograph the princess; where else would he have been? Photographing celebrities was his job. The world's most famous couple in Paris and he at home with his wife? Preposterous. Of course he'd been there—he'd been there at le Bourget Airport to photograph their arrival that afternoon and he'd been there outside the Ritz Hotel to photograph their departure that same evening. He'd also been there in the Alma Tunnel, barely a heartbeat after the crash, to photograph their demise. Not that he was about to confess any of this to the Capitaine, of course. How could he? There was too much at stake—his own life, for one thing. If he so much as breathed a word about his presence in the tunnel that night his cover would be blown, the entire operation would be compromised and he'd be in danger of meeting a similar fate to the princess. He valued his life too much for that. Had he known the operation had been intended to kill her, of course – had he known from the outset that the couple were to be murdered – he would not so readily have agreed to his part in it, certainly not for the amount he'd been paid. He was an informant, after all, not an assassin. He was a go-between, no more: someone who obtained information and passed it back to his handler—for money. Always for money. The sum he'd been paid for keeping his MI6 handler informed of the couple's movements during that final day in Paris – indeed, throughout the entire summer – was handsome enough. Or at least it *would* have been, in any other circumstance. But this operation had been destined to culminate in murder from the outset, he now realized, and if he'd known that he would have negotiated a higher fee – *demanded* a higher fee – before agreeing to do what he did. As it was he'd received the same as he would in any run-of-the-mill, kiss-and-tell operation, a fact that rankled, especially now that he'd been pulled in on suspicion of murder for his trouble.

Simply put, James Andanson had been suckered. They owed him. He would get his own back.

As the Capitaine continued to leaf through his notes, one by one, Andanson sat back and chewed on his half-smoked cigar, and thought of better days to come. Though unhappy he'd been duped into playing such a central role in an operation he'd had no foreknowledge of, he was nonetheless content to reap the rewards that operation was now about to bequeath him. That he'd been there, on the ground, in the tunnel, the only paparazzo in France to have photographed the entire event, from the Ritz Hotel to the Alma Tunnel, and had managed to escape the scene with the photographs intact, meant his life was about to change. Copies of the photographs – the copies he'd made for himself before handing the negatives over to his MI6 handler – were now locked safely away. And they would remain locked safely away until the moment was right for him to publish them in the book he'd been planning for the past six months. He'd already spoken to his good friend, Frédéric Dard, one of the world's most successful authors and France's most famous crime writer. Dard had readily agreed to write the book's narrative; indeed, like Andanson, Dard was simply waiting for the dust to settle before embarking on perhaps the most exciting project of his already stellar career. A publisher had already been agreed, as had a seven-figure advance. It would be the biggest-selling, most explosive book ever published, and would afford James Andanson the kind of reward his intelligence bosses had, in effect, cheated him out of.

Oh yes, he was thinking as he peered smugly across at the imbecile seated opposite him, MI6 would regret the day they made a fool of James Andanson.

He made a show of checking his wristwatch. Then: "I am a busy man, Capitaine," he said. "Unless there is anything else…?"

The Capitaine continued leafing through his notes for a moment or two longer, making a point of letting Andanson know who was in charge. Finally he produced a photograph of Princess Diana aboard the Al Fayed yacht, the *Jonikal*. It was a photograph Andanson himself had taken.

"You like to photograph the princess?" he said.

"I am a photographer, Capitaine. It is my job to photograph celebrities."

"But you particularly like to photograph the princess," the Capitaine said. "Last summer, in the weeks before she died, you followed her to, let me see …" flicking through his notes "… to Saint Tropez, to Monaco, to Sardinia…"

"I went where she went."

"She went to Paris," the Capitaine reminded him.

"Yes, but I did not."

"Every paparazzo in France followed her to Paris, but you did not? You expect me to believe this, Monsieur Andanson?"

"I expect you to prove otherwise, or let me go."

Just then, the in-house telephone interrupted proceedings. Capitaine Laurent lifted the receiver.

"Allo? Yes, but … but … surely not…?"

James Andanson watched as opposite him the Capitaine visibly sunk into himself, his expression turning increasingly incredulous as the conversation progressed. When he finally replaced the receiver Capitaine Laurent was shaking, Andanson could see, his cheeks flushed, his eyes flared. Beside him Lieutenant Gigou seemed bemused.

Then, through clenched teeth: "It would appear you have powerful friends, Monsieur Andanson," the Capitaine finally announced. "You are free to go."

Andanson stubbed out his cigar. Said nothing. Got up and left the room.

21

It was a little over two weeks since my meeting with Lacey, almost three weeks since Diana's death. I was driving home from yet another meeting, another source with something to say about how Diana had died, about who had killed her, and why. I was tired. It was early evening and already turning to dusk as I followed the beam of my car's headlights along the stretch of country road that would, on any regular night, have led me home without event. But this night, it seemed, was different.

"The government has said it was a miracle no one was killed by the car bomb that exploded in Northern Ireland yesterday…"

As the evening news came on the car radio I happened to glance in my rear-view mirror and noticed the headlights of a vehicle some way behind me, perhaps two-hundred yards back down the road. Could have been more. At first I thought little of it, but found myself checking the mirror anyway: checking to make sure the headlights remained a safe distance behind me. Which they did, for a mile or so. But then they started to close, rapidly, a fact I noted but again tried not to make too much of. With everything that had happened these past few weeks my senses were heightened, I reminded myself, and I was perhaps prone to make more of a situation than I normally would. I told myself there was a simple explanation: the driver had decided to speed up because he'd suddenly realized he was late, for dinner, for a date, for some other appointment. Or maybe it was a boy racer who got his kicks burning rubber after dark, when there was less traffic on the road and less chance of getting caught. We'd just entered a stretch of dual carriageway, after all, and within the next half-minute or so I fully expected the vehicle's tail lights to disappear off into the distance ahead of me as the driver closed me down and overtook me. Nothing untoward about that. I checked my speed – sixty miles an hour – then again narrowed my gaze into the rear-view mirror. The headlights were still there, much closer now. But strangely they were no longer gaining on me. And neither were they moving out into the fast lane to overtake me. Rather, having closed me down at some speed they had now, for some reason, settled in behind me and were just sitting there, on my tail, as though observing me. And they were a little too close for comfort.

It was something the newsreader said that momentarily snatched my attention away from the rear-view mirror and gave it back to the radio—something to do with landmines.

"Foreign news now and a treaty banning the use of landmines has been agreed by all the Western world's leaders, with the exception of one..."

Still flicking anxious glances at the rear-view mirror – at the headlights still tailing me – I felt for the volume switch and turned the radio up.

"...In a shock statement earlier today President Clinton revealed that America would not now be signing the treaty. The statement comes despite a recent pledge from the White House to support Princess Diana's landmines campaign. Critics say the president has bowed to pressure from the Pentagon and America's military-industrial complex."

For a brief moment my mind was back in Hyde Park, my meeting with Lacey, scarcely two weeks earlier.

"The landmines treaty is due to be signed in Oslo in two weeks time," he'd told me. "But sometime between now and then Clinton will announce he's changed his mind and decided not to sign after all."

I flicked another glance in the rear-view mirror – *headlights still there, even closer now—who the hell was that?* – then sent my attention back to the radio, which was now playing a recording of a statement President Clinton had made at a press conference earlier that day.

"Last month I instructed a US team to join negotiations then under way in Oslo to ban all antipersonnel landmines," Clinton announced. "Our negotiators worked tirelessly to reach an agreement we could sign. Unfortunately I cannot in good conscience add America's name to that treaty."

I cannot in good conscience add America's name to that treaty. The phrase bounced around inside my head like some garbled public address announcement. *I cannot in good conscience add America's name to that treaty.*

The newsreader concluded the piece.

"The shock announcement comes less than three weeks after the death of Princess Diana, and just one day before the treaty is due to be signed. The world can only wonder if the president's decision would have been the same were Princess Diana still alive."

Had I the presence of mind I perhaps would have pulled over at this point and allowed myself to more fully digest the news. *I cannot in good conscience...* But by now there was a maniac breathing down my neck—*literally*. The headlights that up until this point had been content to sit on my tail and track me were now on full beam, and so close behind me they were virtually whiting out the inside of my car, glaring off my rear-view mirror in every direction and making it extremely difficult for me to see. Who the hell was this madman? Boy racer? Government agent? As I squeezed my eyes almost shut against the dazzle of the blinding lights my mounting panic came down on the side of *government agent*. Surely it had to be. Well why would a boy racer – or anyone else, for that matter – have wanted to chase me down and run me off the road? For no apparent reason? I had no answers. Which was why I decided the maniac in the vehicle behind was more likely a government spook than a teenager in search of thrills.

I knew I had to do something. Terrified though I was, I knew I couldn't just sit there and allow this creature to bully me into making a fatal driving error. Already my mind was conjuring images of the Alma Tunnel, Henri Paul, the car chase that had resulted in Diana's assassination. Maybe this was my time, I was thinking. Maybe this guy was out to run me off the road and herd me into the nearest concrete pillar, or telegraph pole, or lamppost.

Maybe he'd been sent to silence me, or at least terrify me into dropping my investigation, scare me off so that what I'd been told would never come to light. I didn't know. And right now I hadn't the presence of mind to think it through. All I knew was I had to do something to get this maniac off my back.

By instinct I found myself feeling for the gear lever, sinking the clutch, dropping down a gear and hammering my foot to the floor in an attempt to put distance between us. It worked. Initially. But in no time the maniac was on me again, nose to bumper now, so close I could feel the thunder of his engine rumbling through the floor of my own car, almost smell the rubber he was burning on the road behind me. The smell was acrid, and terrifying.

And now there was a second factor to consider: a roundabout was looming in my front windscreen, no more than a hundred yards ahead, I estimated, and hurtling towards me at a full seventy miles an hour, seventy-five: eighty. *Jesus*. My mind was a compound fracture. Half of me was trying to judge the speed, the distance, trying to hold it together. The other half was praying there would be no other cars on the roundabout when I got there.

I drove it blind. No other way to do it. Hitting the brakes as late as I possibly could I screeched around the roundabout and almost lost control, my steering wheel spinning wildly left then right before finally straightening up as – *thank God!* – I managed to negotiate the exit and scream off along the road ahead, unscathed. Behind me, the maniac did the same.

Who the hell is this guy?

Then, suddenly, with the roundabout disappearing into the distance behind us, the maniac backed off. Suddenly he dimmed his headlights and trimmed his speed, although not completely, sufficiently though that now he was tailing me once again from perhaps twenty yards back, still too close for comfort but at least making no attempt to run me off the road, just the occasional reminder that he was still there as his headlights flashed to full beam, then back to normal again. For the next half-mile or so he simply sat there, on my tail, menacing, a steady twenty or so yards behind me. Even when I varied my speed – sped up, slowed down, deliberately – he kept the same distance between us, like he was fixed to my tail on a tow bar. Whoever it was driving that vehicle, I realized, he was no ordinary driver—a fact that gave me no comfort whatever.

And then another disquieting fact: up ahead, perhaps 300 yards into the ever darkening distance, I could see traffic lights. And they were red. Again I checked the rear-view mirror. Headlights still there, still twenty yards back, precisely. By now I was shaking, sweating. My heart was beating so hard it bruised, and I was finding more and more difficulty in keeping my thoughts level, my head composed. My mind was a battle field, debating now whether I should stop or just drive on through those fast-approaching traffic lights. I didn't want to cause an accident, of course. But I didn't want to stop, either: didn't want to leave myself vulnerable to the actions of the lunatic behind me. Whether it was the speed-check camera hovering above the lights threatening to film me, or whether it was the thought of causing serious injury to some or other innocent driver if I were to jump the lights and plough head-on into their vehicle, I'm really not sure. Perhaps it was neither of these things. But as I approached the lights I found myself slowing to a stop and pulling up beneath the red light, despite the threat posed by the maniac attached to my rear. And then I just sat there, staring straight ahead, almost too scared to look in my rear-view mirror. It must have been a full ten seconds before I finally plucked up the courage to check behind me, but when I did I was hit with a genuine surprise: the maniac and his headlights had disappeared.

Where the hell had they gone?

I was shivered. I just couldn't figure it. Now he was playing mind games with me. *Was he?* For the life of me I just couldn't figure where the maniac could be, where he could have turned off the road without me noticing. It was quite simply impossible—*wasn't it?* He'd followed me across the roundabout, I was certain of that. I remembered seeing him in my mirror, fighting his under-steer and sliding broadside around the roundabout, just like I did, before straightening up and locking on to me again as I powered along the exit road in a futile attempt to get away. He was there, behind me, no doubt about it. He was there as we'd approached the traffic lights. No doubt about that, either. I was certain we hadn't driven past a junction or a turning since then, not even a dirt track where he could have turned off the carriageway without me noticing. True, I'd been so preoccupied with trying to stay alive I guess I could have missed his departure. Then again, surely not. Surely I would have seen him turn off, or at least noticed that the headlights were no longer there, tailing me from a menacing twenty yards back. It just didn't make sense.

I took a breath. Okay. No matter. He was gone now, and that was the end of it. I closed my eyes, breathed deeply, was about to tell myself what a paranoid fool I'd been to think there'd been anything sinister in the fact that I'd been followed by an over-enthusiastic boy racer, that I was just jumpy because of what I found myself involved in, that MI5 had better things to do with their time than harass inconsequential conspiracy theorists like me … when the headlights suddenly reappeared. Seemingly without warning they were on me again, no more than fifty yards back and closing fast. *Where the hell did they come from?* As I sat there waiting for the traffic lights to change from red to green, watching the headlights approaching at breakneck speed in my rear-view mirror, I remember thinking this was it, that I was bound to die – here and now – or at the very least sustain serious injuries as a result of this maniac slamming into my rear bumper at eighty miles an hour. I thought about wrenching off my seat belt and leaping from the car, but I was frozen to my seat, rooted there, unable to move, think, anything, certain the vehicle bearing down on me was about to plough full throttle into the back of my car … when suddenly I heard the deathly screech of brakes as the maniac skidded to a velocity-defying halt and came to rest no more than a whispered threat from my rear bumper.

Then, silence…

…For a beat … two…

Then: *flash!* The headlights were again on full beam, again filling my rear-view mirror, blinding, bewildering. Throwing a desperate glance back across my shoulder I could just make out the silhouette of the maniac as he spun his steering wheel and simultaneously threw his car into reverse, spinning a full one-eighty degrees, tyres squealing and blistering on tarmac before screeching off back down the road and out of sight. It felt like I was watching some Hollywood action sequence, eyes and mouth wide, unable to believe what I was seeing, unable to move or respond. *Did he just do that? Who the hell was he?* I just sat there for what seemed a small eternity, numbed to the marrow, not knowing quite what to do, or think. By the time I'd stopped trembling sufficiently that I could at least think about continuing my journey home the traffic lights must have changed from red to green and back again several times. The next time they changed, I promised myself as finally I felt the blood starting to thaw in my veins, I would slot the car in gear and attempt the journey home.

Which, a few moments later, is precisely what I did…

…When I arrived home some twenty minutes later I was still shaking. Katie was in the kitchen preparing dinner. We both worked and were used to eating late, sometimes not until eight-thirty or nine—symptom of the times, I guess, but at least we made it a rule that, whenever possible, we ate together. The other rule on evenings when we were both late home was 'first home does the cooking'. This night was no exception.

Slowing my thoughts, pulling myself in, best I could, I dumped my jacket and attaché case in the hallway and made my way through to the kitchen.

"Hi babe." Thankfully my voice sounded pretty normal, even though I probably looked a little shaken up. I poured myself a glass of red wine.

"You okay?" she said.

"I'm fine."

"Only you look a bit—"

"No, really, I'm just tired." I kissed her on the cheek. "How was your day?"

"Busy," she said. "I haven't been in long. We had to do a last-minute stock take."

"Oh? Why was that?"

"I think mum might have to close the shop."

"What? Why…?"

Katie turned the potatoes up to boil, then took the wine glass from my hand and started to drink from it. "May I?"

"You already did."

"I'm worried about her, Jon."

"Your mum…?"

"Dad left her in so much debt. It's difficult to see a way forward. She doesn't really have a choice but to close the business and call in the receivers."

"Jeez. Poor mum."

"Poor *us*. I'll have to get another job."

"Of course." The reality suddenly hit me. Katie's dad had walked out on her mum some months earlier, and it turned out the business they'd run together – an art and colour shop, selling prints, postcards, original works of art, plus other colour-themed *objets d'art* – was not as healthy as we'd all been led to believe. Katie's mum had been left to pick up the pieces. And the debts.

But as Katie had just reminded me, it wasn't only her mum who would suffer as a result: Katie losing her job would have its impact on us, too. It was bad news all round.

I curled my arm around Katie's shoulder. "Don't worry, babe," I said, as convincingly as I could. "I'm sure we'll be okay."

"I hope so." She handed me back what was left of my wine.

"So," I said. "How long before…?"

"Ten minutes," Katie said. "Just waiting for the potatoes."

"I meant…"

Katie knew what I meant: *How long do we have before your mum shuts up shop and you're out of work?* But the look on her face told me she didn't want to talk about it. Not right now. "I'll call you when it's ready."

"I'll be in the office."

I kissed Katie one more time and made my way through to my office. I deliberately didn't say anything about my journey, about the maniac who'd followed me and tried to run me off the road. Katie had enough on her plate as it was; I didn't want to worry her more than was necessary. Besides, my mind was already busy attempting to fathom another mystery, one that had been bugging me ever since the maniac had left me mind-numbed and trembling at the traffic lights perhaps half an hour earlier. How did they know I was going to London today? No one had followed me from the house this morning, I'd made amply sure of that. How did they know where I was going, and when?

How did the maniac and whoever he worked for know I would be travelling back from London tonight?

There was only one possible answer.

"You're on file as a tap," Lacey had told me, which was MI5 speak for 'your phone's bugged'. They must have been listening when I'd arranged the meeting – the time and place – last night, on the phone. It was the only explanation.

I have no idea – had no idea then, have no idea to this day – what made me think I would solve this mystery by dismantling my office phone in search of a microchip-sized bug. I knew as well as anyone that, if my phone *was* bugged, then it would have been achieved remotely, by wire tap, not by installing a physical bug inside my phone. Taking my phone apart to look for this non-existent 'bug' nonetheless seemed the expedient thing to do. I guess given my state of mind it was almost understandable.

Katie, on the other hand, didn't think so. "What are you doing?" She'd just entered my office without me realizing, and had caught me red-handed, stupidly trying to fit the pieces of my handset back together. She looked at her wits' end. "What's wrong with the phone?"

"Oh … nothing," I said, feeling like a schoolboy caught smoking a cigarette. "It was … it was making a strange noise. I think it's okay now."

She gave me that look. "Jon, are you okay?"

"I'm fine."
"It's this Diana thing, isn't it?"
"What do you mean...?"
"Don't you think you're taking it too far?"
"Too far...?"
"Too seriously."
"No."

"You're making me nervous, Jon." She started to well up. "Seeing you acting in this way. It makes me nervous."

"I'm sorry, babe ... I..."

"Why are you so interested in Diana all of a sudden anyway?"

"I'm not. I'm interested in who murdered her."

"But you don't know that she was murdered..."

"I do, Katie. I *do* know. That's the point."

All this time I'd been holding bits of telephone in my hand. I let them down on my desk top and went to Katie.

"I'm so sorry, babe. I'm really sorry." I wrapped my arms around her, held her close for several heartbeats. Then stood back, gently brushed her hair from off her face and looked her in the eye. "Katie, please. I need your support right now. I know Diana was murdered. I feel like I'm the only one outside of MI6 who does."

Katie didn't reply. Instead she cuddled into me again, and this time started to cry. Not desperately, but in that way we all do when it just gets too much, when there's just nothing left to say. There was nothing left to say tonight. So I just held her.

It was the first time Diana's death had truly impacted on our home life, on our relationship. But needless to say, regrettably, it wouldn't be the last.

22

JB was at the bar getting drinks.

Distracted by a discarded copy of the *Daily Mail* lying face up on a table by the window I made my way over and sat myself down, started to read it.

Chauffeur Henri Paul Drunk the headline bellowed.

The accompanying article boasted a photograph of Diana's death-crash driver enjoying a night out at some or other Parisian bar, drink in hand, as though toasting the camera. It was as predictable as English rain, an irony that was not lost on me. "The media are being primed as we speak," the American had said. He was right. I folded it up and threw it back down on the table.

"Not even subtle about it," I said.

"What's that?" JB had just returned from the bar, a pint in either hand—his lager, my Guinness.

I tipped my head at the paper. "Results of the blood tests. They reckon Henri Paul was three times over the limit."

"And…?"

"What do mean, *and?*"

"Well in layman's terms that means he was pissed, Jon. Very drunk indeed." JB planted my Guinness on the table in front of me. "Like I said, it was an accident. Cheers."

He picked up the discarded newspaper and started to read it.

I picked up my Guinness and started to drink it.

The thing with JB, I'd learned in the few years I'd known him, was that he took time to change, time to adjust his somewhat entrenched perspective and consider an alternate point of view. For all that he lived life at a hundred miles an hour, out the box, he did so with his seat belt on, I'd realized, especially when it came to serious issues—which was no doubt why he still refused point-blank to entertain the possibility that Diana had been murdered. Or even that she might have been. He just wasn't ready for it, I told myself, not yet, even less that she might have been the victim of some dark establishment conspiracy. Like so many people at the time, though he shared the mood of the nation, even felt the instinctive unease – suspicion even – experienced by vast swathes of the population, still he didn't want to believe that the establishment might have sanctioned such an operation—that his tax dollars might have paid for it. The existence of UFOs, aliens at Area 51, even that aliens may have conspired with the US government to take over the world—all of these notions, crazy as they may have seemed, were nonetheless harmless: *safe*. When the day was done and the kids were tucked up snugly in bed they posed no real threat, not to the daily routine, not to the status quo. Ultimately they were nontoxic. That a powerful cabal within the heart of the British establishment might have orchestrated the assassination of the Princess of Wales, on the other hand, was a notion with a nuclear trigger. Not so much explosive as apocalyptic. Which was why JB, along with half the nation, was reluctant to entertain it.

I swallowed a third mouthful of Guinness and turned back to face him. "Do you really believe he was drunk?" I said.

JB's nose was still buried in the *Daily Mail*. "Why shouldn't I? They've done the tests. Look," … pointing at the article … "it says it here in black and white. The tests say he was drunk."

"The tests will say whatever they want them to say."

"They? Who's they?"

"Whoever's responsible for the cover-up."

"What cover-up?"

"The one that says Henri Paul was raving drunk. You've seen the footage taken by the Ritz security cameras, the footage of Henri Paul walking around the hotel less than an hour before the crash, up and down the stairs, talking to guests, bending down to tie his shoe lace and standing up straight again—acting perfectly sober."

"You can hardly conclude anything from that."

"Are you serious? If Henri Paul had had half as much alcohol in him as they say he did, he would've been staggering all over the place. There's no way he could even have walked out of the hotel, let alone driven that car."

"So what are you saying?"

"I'm saying maybe he wasn't drunk."

Again JB jabbed a finger at the article he was reading. "These are the results of the blood tests, Jon. The *official* results."

"I know that. But…"

"But what?"

"Well, maybe they switched the blood samples."

"What…?"

"Maybe the blood they tested didn't belong to Henri Paul. Maybe whoever murdered Diana switched the samples."

"Oh, come on, Jon." He threw the paper down on the table. "Headlights following you home, bugs on your telephone, blood samples being switched. You're starting to sound like you just escaped."

"I'm beginning to feel like it."

Just then, our magazine proprietor David and his partner Claire wandered into the bar, looking like they wished *they* could escape, but were unable. They made their way over to our table.

"What's wrong?" JB said, seeing the desperation on their faces.

David was the one to break the news, and he didn't pull any punches. "It's the magazine," he said. "It's gone under. We've been nobbled. As from today I'm afraid you're both out of a job. I'm so sorry."

So was I. In fact I was steamrollered, not just for the fact that I was now out of work, but also that such a sudden and final closure seemed to me frighteningly suspicious. At its peak, including subscription and overseas mail-order sales, the magazine had been selling around 60,000 copies per edition, with sales increasing month on month. Now, suddenly, it was gone. Suddenly it was no more. Suddenly, suspiciously concurrent with my decision to investigate Diana's death and write an accompanying book about what I'd been told, it had been banished from the shelves, the most successful *X-File* magazine on the market, just like that. David informed us that our wholesaler in America had pulled the plug and our distributor here in the UK had closed our account. Advertisers had discontinued their accounts, too. No explanation, he said. No reason given. We were finished, and that was that.

I was struck dumb, on the spot, there and then, just kept staring and staring at the sheer, cold frustration and utter despair written on David and Claire's faces. What had they done to deserve this? What would they do? How would they survive? I had no words, but my mind was an industry. Had someone behind the scenes orchestrated this? I was already thinking. Were we the victims of sabotage? If so, *why?* Why would they – whoever *they* were – why would they have gone to such extraordinary lengths to close down what to all intents and purposes was an innocuous UFO magazine? To warn me off? Was that it? Was *I* the reason David and Claire had suffered this devastating loss? Did they really deem me such a threat that they would do this? I mean, what I'd been told by the American was explosive, true—or would be, if ever I could prove it. But, of course, the chance of that was less than zero, a fact they must surely have known. So why such extreme action? I couldn't fathom it. But as I stood there, speechless – legs trembling, jaw loose – clasping the dregs of my Guinness as though clinging fast to the dregs of some other, more familiar reality, neither could I deny my gut-felt suspicions that, as David had just announced, we'd been 'nobbled'. Like Diana's death, it seemed, the unexpected closure of our magazine was no accident, a thought that ran me cold.

I felt scared. I felt isolated. I felt numb.

And things didn't improve from there, either. Over the next few weeks, in fact, they became decidedly worse, to the point that even JB started to believe sinister forces might have been behind events, especially when a few days later we heard more bad news from Rick Devlin, my literary agent. The three big publishers who until now had been bidding against each other for the right to publish our book about Diana's death – Simon & Schuster, Jonathan Cape and Hodder – had all pulled out, he informed us, all three of them, within days of one another. One minute wined and dined, the next, dumped. Again, no explanation. In the space of just a few short weeks we'd been hung out to dry—no job, no income: no prospect of either. And now no publisher for our book, to boot.

With Katie also losing her job due to the closure of her mum's shop things had overnight become pretty desperate, to say the least. Even so we soldiered on. We had too. It was our only option.

23

"You were in the SAS, Dave. You must know how it was done."

"Those boys weren't SAS, not serving SAS, anyway. The SAS wouldn't get involved in something like that. Too risky."

"Who then?"

"A private firm, probably made up of old boys—former SAS and other special forces, other elite divisions, plus a few chancers."

"So a private firm like the one you worked for as a mercenary?"

"Something like that, yeah. But don't ask me to name the firm, coz I won't."

I was in a working men's club near my home town of Sandhurst. I'd travelled back there to talk to Dave Cornish, a former SAS sergeant and member of John Banks' infamous Angola mercenaries back in the 1970s—the ones hired by Rob Lacey on behalf of MI6. I was looking for insights into how – if Diana's 'accident' had indeed been orchestrated – how in reality it could have been achieved. I knew from my association with some of the mercenaries that operations of the kind I believed had been used in Paris were more common than people might readily believe. But I needed to know more about how they worked, whether such an operation could feasibly have been used to assassinate such a high-profile personage as Princess Diana. And if it could, who would likely have carried it out. Having known Dave from my teenage years I knew he was the man to talk to, so I'd arranged to meet him for a game of snooker and a liquid lunch—and the chance to pick his brains. My first impression on seeing him again after all these years was that he really hadn't changed that much at all. Despite that he was now approaching fifty he was still lean and fit, still the equal of most men fifteen years his junior, although his closely cropped hair was these days seasoned with a dusting of salt-n-pepper grey.

Even so, you'd still be unwise to piss him off.

"It's not till you go private that you learn what really goes on," he was saying as he placed the wooden triangle over the cluster of reds and lined them up, ready to go. "I've run Semtex for the IRA, arms for the MPLA—we were supposed to be at war with both of them. I've even run drugs for the CIA, raw opium, but that's another story. Who's first?"

"After you."

Dave broke off, then stood up straight to analyze the result. "As for Diana," he said, "that's a different level completely. I've been involved in things you'd never believe, taken out more political targets than there are balls on this table—" I counted them. There were twenty-two. "—But Diana? No, never anything as big as that."

I guzzled a mouthful of Guinness and lined up my shot. "But it could be done? I mean, assassinate someone in that way, by car crash. It could be done?"

"Oh, for sure. Absolutely. Unlucky."

I missed, so I stood back from the table and chalked my cue. "You know the car was stolen prior to the accident," I said.

"Yeah, well that's how it's done, isn't it. Borrow the car for a couple of days, fix it, send it back good as new. No one would ever know."

"When you say 'fix it'…?"

"The brakes. Maybe the steering, too, depending on what you want it to do. I presume there were other vehicles involved apart from the tail car…?"

"There were, yeah. There were reports of a second Mercedes, a motorbike and a white Fiat Uno, as well as an as yet unidentified car, a dark-coloured car about the same size as the Uno."

"But it was the Uno that collided with the Mercedes, right?"

"Right."

"Then the Uno was the scraper. The second Mercedes was the tail car and the Uno was the scraper. The Uno would've been weighed down low to the ground, maybe with cement bags or concrete blocks. That way it holds the road when it collides with the bigger vehicle."

A white Uno colliding with a black Mercedes.

I took my next shot, and sure enough the white collided with the black. Problem was I was aiming for the pink.

"Witnesses say they saw a bright light in the tunnel," I said. "They say they saw a bright flash just moments before the crash."

"A strobe gun, probably. My guess is they would've used it in combination with the Brakes."

"The Brakes?"

"The Boston Brakes, to give it its full name. It's the name of a technique used by the ground teams. They favour it for its deniability, and its reliability."

"I don't suppose you've—"

His laughter cut me off. "Plenty of times," he said. "Oman, Gambia, Afghanistan. Many a warlord or tribal chief ended up slamming into a concrete wall at ninety miles an hour. And then there was Northern Ireland—"

"Northern Ireland?"

"—We used the Brakes so many times over there we got it down to a fine art."

"Jesus. So how does it work?"

"Pretty simple, really. A small explosive device called a Blockbuster is attached to the brakes, and a parasite is fitted somewhere under the bonnet, maybe integrated with the EMS."

"The EMS?"

"The electronic management system, basically the vehicle's on-board computer, assuming it's got one. The parasite is a tiny transceiver, not much bigger than a microchip, and tuned to receive a signal from a remote control activated from … well, from anywhere close-by. Maybe from inside the tail car, but more likely the scraper."

"The Uno...?"

"Right. There'd be two boys in the Uno, the pilot and the engineer. When the engineer triggers the remote the Blockbuster kills the brakes and the parasite takes over the steering. The driver's got no chance, especially if he's on the receiving end of the strobe gun as well. I'll tell you, Jon, it's a cinch. They would've stood no chance. The minute they got in that car they would've been snookered—just like you."

"Eh…?" I'd been so engrossed in Dave's explanation of the Boston Brakes as a deniable assassination technique I'd taken my eye off the game. Bad move. As he'd been talking he'd potted three reds and then managed to tuck the white up behind the green. I was indeed snookered.

"O' course, once the car's been fitted up they have to make sure that's the one they're gonna use."

"The limousine company have confirmed it was the only car available that night," I said, the hairs on the back of my neck starting to stand up and prick me as I realized what I was saying. "They couldn't have used another car if they'd wanted to."

"Well there you go, then. People think, how did they know they'd be in Paris on that particular night? How did they know they would use that particular car? But intelligence like that is easily acquired. Nothing's left to chance. They're like bloody magicians, that lot."

Thankfully I was something of a magician myself, I realized, as – more by chance than ability – I managed to escape the snooker at the first time of asking.

"Jammy git."

Standing up from the table I stole a moment to study the man there with me—former SAS, former mercenary, and God only knows what else. He'd seen it all and done it all, no doubt about that. He'd been there at the dirty end of the game more times than he would care to remember and he knew what he was talking about. But a 'Boston Brakes' car accident to assassinate a princess? It seemed like a plot even Hollywood might struggle to construct.

"How sure are you about all this, Dave?" I said.

Dave just shrugged, fired home the last of the reds and started to clear the colours. "One hundred per cent, mate. From the minute the decoy car left the Ritz to the moment the tail car closed in, it was obvious what was going down. Any of the lads'll tell you that." He chalked his cue and lined up his next shot. "But you don't have to take my word for it," he said as he sunk the pink and then sent the final black crashing into the corner pocket. "Ask around. Anyone who knows what they're talking about'll tell you the same."

24

"Professor Mackay? Jon King. And this is my colleague, John Beveridge. It's good of you to see us."

"Oh, you're welcome. Please come in."

JB and I had come to Birmingham University to interview Britain's foremost expert on road traffic accidents, Professor Murray Mackay. On behalf of the government, Professor Mackay had visited the crash tunnel in the days following the incident and had reconstructed the crash using state-of-the-art computer technology. We were hoping to gain some insights into how the crash had actually happened, from the professional's point of view—how fast the Mercedes was *really* travelling on impact, what *really* caused it to lose control, exactly what role the mysterious Fiat Uno had played in the crash.

And whether or not, in Professor Mackay's opinion, the crash could have been orchestrated.

We were also hoping for a sneak preview of the professor's computer-generated 3-D simulation of the crash in the hope that it might just reveal something – *anything* – to challenge the drink-drive version of events. We weren't to be disappointed.

Professor Mackay ushered us into the cramped and cluttered room that served as his office. Paint flaked from the ceiling and walls. Bits and pieces of engines – pistons, cylinders, flywheels: a crankshaft – lay scattered on the bench top that ran the length of one wall, along with an *ad hoc* array of engineering tools—drill and pin chucks, calipers, squares, a pocket-size vice, a micrometer, as well as other, less familiar gizmos.

Above the bench top, concealing at least some of the wall's flaking paint, were posters of badly crashed cars and mangled engine parts. A framed photograph of the professor in his younger years hung there, too, together with a diploma proudly displaying his credential and status. Opposite the bench top stood the professor's desk, itself host to a chaotic array of office paraphernalia, while beneath the desk a wastepaper bin overflowed with screwed up bits of paper. In sum the place was, frankly, a tip. But it was a tip clearly beloved by the man who occupied it.

"You'll have to excuse the mess," the professor said, as he cleared a path through the debris and directed us to our seats—a pair of time-worn wooden chairs parked at one end of his desk. "Officially it's my office, but it sort of doubles as my play room, as you may have guessed. Please, take a seat."

I sat myself down and dug around in my attaché case for my Dictaphone. "Do you mind, Professor?" I said, as I pulled out the pocket-sized tape recorder and set it on the desk in front of him. "It means we can record an accurate record of what you say."

"Of course. That's perfectly okay. In fact I'd rather you did." Then he added: "Can I order you a coffee, or…?"

"I'm fine," JB replied.

"Me too," I said, and switched the Dictaphone on.

A few minutes later we were locked in conversation.

"There certainly was a lack of tyre marks for a crash of this nature," Professor Mackay was saying. "Although I must emphasize, that doesn't necessarily imply anything suspicious."

"But it does imply some pretty skilful driving on the part of the Uno driver," I said.

"I would agree there was some rather abnormal driving just prior to the crash, yes."

"Abnormal?"

"Well the Uno did cross lanes as the Mercedes approached it from behind, causing the Mercedes to impact its rear wing. There doesn't seem to be any meaningful explanation for that. Or indeed, for the lack of tyre marks found at the scene."

"So even if there were no skid marks as such, you would still expect there to have been at least some degree of tyre marks on the road in a crash of this nature?"

"Well yes, of course, made either by the Uno as it tried to avoid a second collision with the Mercedes immediately after it crashed, or by the Mercedes as it slammed its brakes on to avoid crashing into the concrete pillar."

"But there weren't any—no skid marks, no tyre marks."

"Correct."

"Doesn't that imply the Mercedes brakes might have failed?" JB put in.

The professor thought about this for a moment. Then: "I suppose it's possible," he conceded. "We haven't concluded all our tests yet."

"But if Henri Paul slammed his brakes on, as you might expect any driver to do in that situation, surely he would have left skid marks on the road?"

"You would have thought so, yes."

"Or at least tyre marks," I pressed. "At least some evidence that Henri Paul tried to apply his brakes and avoid the crash."

The professor cleared his throat, in a way that said we were perhaps pushing him a little too hard. "As I say, there was some rather abnormal driving just prior to the crash. But beyond that I really can't say."

"Of course." I decided to change tack. Consulting the notes I'd made prior to our meeting, referring to one of the many inaccurate headlines blazoned on the nation's tabloids in the days and weeks following the crash, I said: "The media reported that Henri Paul was driving at a hundred-and-twenty miles an hour when he crashed."

Professor Mackay was shaking his head. "That's nonsense," he said. "Our research clearly shows the Mercedes was travelling at around sixty miles an hour on impact."

"But the media stated the speedometer was stuck on a hundred-and-twenty miles an hour following the crash."

"I'm afraid that's inaccurate, too. Mercedes design their speedometers to revert to zero in any high-velocity impact. And that's precisely what happened in this case."

"So why do you think the media would print false facts like that?" JB wanted to know.

But Professor Mackay wasn't prepared to speculate. "That's a question you'll have to put to them, I'm afraid. I can only tell you the facts as we know them."

"But you *can* confirm the Fiat Uno was definitely involved in the crash?"

"Oh, yes, most certainly. I can show you if you'd like?" the professor said, already pushing himself up from his seat. "If you'd care to follow me, gentlemen...?"

We did. Having quickly gathered up our bits we were ushered out of the office and along a short corridor that led through a set of double swing doors into Professor Mackay's laboratory. Less dishevelled than his office, I quietly noted. Peeling off left on entry the professor then led us through a second door and into a small computing room furnished with a bank of perhaps half a dozen consoles and monitors. The professor's assistant – a nerdy looking fellow in his late thirties with acne, glasses and a thatch of wire-wool hair, and wearing a grey lab coat – was seated at one of the consoles, hunched over a keyboard. He looked up from his work as we entered.

"These gentlemen would like to see the Alma Tunnel simulation, if you wouldn't mind, Martin," Professor Mackay said to the man. "They're researching the crash for a book they're writing."

"Certainly," Martin said, and immediately interrupted what he was doing to open up the computer's animation program. He tapped letters and digits on the keyboard as he spoke. "If you're writing a book you'll need to get your facts right. And for that you couldn't have come to a better place. This program has produced the most accurate reconstruction model in the world, bar none."

A few more letters and digits typed in by Martin and we were viewing, as he'd rightly pointed out, the world's most accurate computer reconstruction of the crash that killed Diana. It was a highly revealing, if slightly disturbing, experience.

"Okay, look. Here's the Fiat Uno, and here's the Mercedes," Professor Mackay commented as the 3-D simulation played out the crash sequence on the computer screen. It showed two vehicles travelling on a dual-lane highway, approaching an underpass—Diana's Mercedes travelling at speed in the outside lane, and a white Fiat Uno travelling a good deal slower in the inside lane. As the vehicles approached the entrance to the underpass – the Alma Tunnel – the Fiat Uno clearly pulled out, causing the Mercedes to collide with the smaller vehicle and lose control as a result. A third vehicle – a high-powered motorbike – then entered the fray. Professor Mackay's commentary continued: "And here's where the Mercedes collides with the smaller car, the Uno—*there!* And then a motorbike suddenly appears, pulls alongside and overtakes and ... well, you can see for yourself what happens next. The driver of the Mercedes, Henri Paul, struggles to retain control as he drives on into the tunnel. *There*—you see? The Mercedes swerves violently left, then right, then left again and into a concrete pillar on the central reservation. The result, I'm afraid, was fatal."

"Left, then right, then left again…"

"Yes, you can see how the Mercedes responds after colliding with the Fiat Uno. It swerves violently left, then right, then left again into the concrete pillar."

"What about the motorbike?" JB put in. "Where did that come from? Who was riding it?"

"I'm afraid we don't know."

"Well, did it influence the crash?"

"Again, I'm afraid we can't say at this stage." Professor Mackay turned to his assistant. "Could you run it again please, Martin?"

Martin ran the sequence a second time.

"What we do know is that the Fiat Uno influenced the crash. *There*—do you see? The Mercedes clips the back of the Fiat Uno and Henri Paul loses control, swerving first left, then right, then left again and into the concrete pillar."

"Left, right and left again. Yes, I see."

"Of course, there's nothing in that sequence of manoeuvres that would necessarily suggest foul play."

"Can you be certain of that?" I put to the professor.

The strained look on Professor Mackay's face told me that perhaps he hadn't seriously considered the possibility. And what's more, considering it now seemed to make him a tad uncomfortable. I logged the fact. Then, with no response forthcoming from the professor, I moved the conversation on.

"What about the Fiat Uno?" I said. "Don't you think it's strange that its driver didn't appear to brake, or at least perform some kind of correction manoeuvre to avoid colliding with the crashed Mercedes? You say there were no tyre marks on the road?"

"That's correct, yes."

"So the Mercedes hit the back of the Fiat Uno, causing Henri Paul to lose control, and two seconds later the Mercedes crashed into the concrete pillar—right in front of the Uno?"

"Correct."

"But there were no tyre marks on the road to suggest the Uno driver either braked or was forced to make any other kind of correction manoeuvre?"

"Well, as I think I've already said, there was certainly some abnormal driving that occurred, but..."

"Who do you think was driving the Fiat Uno?" I said. I knew the answer before it came.

"I'm afraid I can't speculate on that—"

"Of course..."

"—But I'd be very interested to read your findings. When did you say your book would be published?"

The question stopped me dead. Since we'd been mysteriously dumped by the three publishers who, in the immediate wake of Diana's death, had fought tooth and nail over the right to publish our book, we'd struggled to gain interest from any other. It was as if word had been put round the industry that no one was to publish our book, and as a result, every UK publisher of any standing had closed the door in our face. True, I was no Stephen King, but I was nonetheless a published author with Hodder & Stoughton and my readership was sufficiently established, as they say in the trade, that a book deal would ordinarily have been guaranteed—especially for a book with such obvious commercial potential as the one JB and I were now writing. If not Hodder then any number of other major publishers would, on any regular day, have stepped in and snapped it up. But not this one. Not this book. Not on this day. Professor Mackay's question drove the fact home. And it stung.

"I'll be sure and let you know as soon as it's available," was the best answer I could muster.

"Well I'll expect a signed copy."

"No problem."

25

St Tropez, France—April 1998

James Andanson lit up a Havana cigar, sucked in a satisfying lungful of its aromatic smoke, then lounged back in his seat and admired the million-dollar scenery.

He'd seen it all before, of course, on many occasions. But on this occasion the air smelled just that little bit sweeter, the sun shone brighter, the yachts, their owners and the gold they displayed seemed to gratify his senses just that little bit more licentiously. He knew St Tropez like an old friend, but this day it felt more like a new lover.

"Beautiful," he said to the man seated across from him. The two men occupied a seafront table outside La Souchet Café. "We are lucky men."

"We are?"

"Yes, of course. In the space of just two short years you have masterminded and carried out the most audacious MI6 operation in the history of the organization. And I, Monsieur Mason, have become a very wealthy man."

"Yes, well, let us hope your luck holds long enough for you to enjoy your newfound wealth, James. From what I hear it might just be about to unravel."

"What do you mean?" Andanson's buoyant mood was suddenly undone by Mason's cloaked threat. He'd worked for his MI6 handler long enough to know when a warning had been issued, cloaked or not. This was one such moment. St Tropez suddenly seemed a tad less appealing.

Dressed in casual cream suit and silk cravat, Mason swilled the ice around in his Cognac and Club Soda and gave Andanson his coolest stare. "I hear the police are interested in your car," he said.

Andanson's reply was dismissive. "They asked a few questions, that is all. I told them I sold it."

"And the photographs?"

"What photographs?"

"Do you intend to sell them, too?"

Suddenly Andanson realized what this meeting was really about, and the fear this realization spawned in him tried its damndest to close his throat. "I ... *ahem* ... I gave you the photographs," he managed to say.

"You did?"

"Yes, of course. You know I did. The only photographs I have now are of the couple on holiday, in Monaco, Sardinia, and here in St Tropez."

"You were in Paris, James—"

"Yes, but..."

"—In the tunnel. We wouldn't want those kind of photographs falling into the wrong hands."

Feverishly Andanson stubbed out his unfinished cigar and leaned forward across the table. His voice became an urgent whisper. "Do I look crazy? Do you think I would keep photographs of MI6 agents on the ground, outside the Ritz, inside the tunnel?"

"Why not? Tabloid editors would give their rectal virginity for photographs like that. Worth a lot money."

"But I already have a lot of money, Monsieur Mason. Thanks to you I have a very good life."

"Yes."

As though deliberating Andanson's fate Mason sat back in his seat and swilled his Cognac and Club Soda in its glass one more time. Then downed the liquid in one.

"Long life, James," he said, replacing the empty glass on the table between them. "Long life."

26

I was flustered. I'd promised to pick the kids up from school and I was late. It was raining outside like it never meant to stop, and I was dashing back and forth from closet to cloak cupboard looking for my rainproof. I couldn't find it—anywhere. Reminding myself that, for the most part, I'd be in the car anyway, I decided to leave it and started fumbling around for my car keys. *Where the hell had I left my car keys?* In my jacket pocket. *But which one? Which jacket had I worn last?* Not that I owned a rich man's wardrobe bulging with surplus outfits, but ... *shit!* Now my phone was ringing. The last thing I needed right now was a phone call from the office. From *anyone*. I decided to ignore it; the kids would be waiting – *in the rain!* – and I needed to get myself down to the school, pronto. No time for phone calls.

It kept ringing. Damn it! Still searching for my keys I pulled the phone from my pocket and checked the number: *Unknown*. Who could it be? No time to think about it. Right now I needed to find the keys and get the kids. *Where the hell did I...?* There! Glancing up I finally saw my car keys out the corner of my eye, on the mantelpiece, in clear view, gleaming at me like cheap diamonds: staring me full in the face! *Why hadn't I seen them?* I made a bee line for the mantelpiece, snatched up my keys and headed for the door. All the while my phone was still ringing; all the while the number calling me was still *unknown*. Should I answer it? No! I'd be crazy to answer the phone right now, especially as I didn't know who was calling. Opening the front door I stepped out into the rain and hit the *answer* button anyway.

"Hello?"

"You're late," the voice said. It was a male voice, English, with a seductively cultured accent.

I froze. "Who is this?" I heard myself say.

"Your alarm call," the voice said. "You'd best be on your way. Your children are waiting for you. They've been let out early. They're looking for you."

"What...? How do you know...?"

"I can see them from where I'm sitting. They're standing around in the rain, getting very wet. Little Rosie, Ben, Jack. You'd better hurry or they might think you're not coming. You *are* still coming, aren't you? I mean, if you can't make it I could give them a lift ... if you'd like."

"No!" I was instantly shaking: *raging*—part anger, part terror. "Who the hell are you?" I demanded to know as I slammed the door behind me and sprinted over to my car. "You hear me?" Turning the ignition. "You'd better back off, pal!" Screeching off down the road. "I'll be there in two minutes, less than that. *Back off!*"

"It's you who needs to back off, Jon. Back off and you'll never hear from us again, never be followed home again, never have your livelihood pulled from under you, ever again..."

By now I could see the school ahead, maybe fifty or more kids wandering out of the gates, looking for their parents. I could also see a car I was certain I'd seen before, a black Ford Granada with smoke-tinted windows parked up opposite the school. It was the same car I'd seen in Marlborough on the day I'd met the American, I was sure of it.

"Back off and your family will be safe."

I hit the *end* button and cut the caller off, then discarded my phone on the passenger seat. Whoever he was, whatever his threats, I didn't need to hear anymore from him. I was there now anyway, pulling up behind the row of parked cars stretching back from the school entrance, jumping out and running over to the gates in search of my children, oblivious to the rain, the umbrellas, the parents escorting their kids out of the school gates and scurrying them off across the road into the warm, dry safety of their vehicles. I was oblivious to the black Ford Granada pulling off from across the street and coasting down the road away from the school, as well—too intent on finding my kids to even notice the son of a bitch, to give him even the merest glance. It wasn't until I discovered all three of them hanging out in the school cloakroom, keeping themselves dry, out of the rain; wasn't until I'd gathered them all up and escorted them back to the warm, dry safety of my own car that I noticed the Granada had gone. I didn't care. In that moment I didn't care. All I cared about was that the kids – Rosie, Ben, Jack – were all safely belted into their seats, chatting about their day, oblivious to the threat with smoke-tinted windows that only moments before had loomed outside the school gates like an ominous death cloud. I took a deep breath and sighed, inwardly. I was the most relieved dad in the world in that moment. As I signalled to pull off and head back home I even shed a solitary tear, discreetly wiping it away before the kids saw their daddy crying.

And then I made a vow: this would be the last time ever I would be late picking the kids up from school.

•

The next few months were tough. Both Katie and I had lost our regular employment. I managed to sell a few articles, get a few other scraps of freelance work to help keep us going, but it was a real struggle. Katie, meanwhile, worked desperately hard on a new venture with her mum—a new shop that, initially, struggled even to pay for itself, never mind pay Katie and her mum anything resembling a regular salary. If it hadn't been for JB I think I would have given up at this point; I think I would, at least, have forgotten about the book and the investigation and got myself another job. A *regular* job. A *paying* job. But thanks to JB I didn't need to. For the several barren months following the collapse of our magazine he not only odd-jobbed in his second profession as a care worker to keep himself afloat. Every spare minute he had he also worked tirelessly to help me find outlets for my articles, as well as a publisher for the book, and at the same time arranged meetings with potential investors in a new magazine we were endeavouring to get off the ground. It was a heroic effort on his part, one that in the end paid dividends.

"Got it!" JB was suddenly standing there, in my home, in my office doorway, the smile on his face so broad it touched both his ears.

Startled, I looked up from the article I was writing on my computer and swung round to face him. "Jesus, you made me jump. Got what?"

"A deal."

"A deal?"

"A book deal. A company in New York want to publish the book. They're not offering much of an advance but it's enough to get us to Paris."

"Really?"

"And that's not all. I think I might have found an investor for the new magazine as well. I think we might be back in our proper jobs in a few weeks."

"You're kidding me."

"Deadly serious."

"My God…"

I could scarcely believe what I was hearing. JB had well and truly come through, a fact reflected in the size of the smile still separating his ears, a smile mirrored on my own face now. True, it was a smile that would later disappear as we learned that the publishers he'd found would, in many ways, prove more hindrance than help, and would leave us ultimately to question them as much as we questioned everybody else. But for now JB's news was manna from heaven.

"You say the advance is enough to get us to Paris?" I said.

"If we go by train."

"I'll pack my bags."

27

Paris — Friday, July 31ˢᵗ, 1998

Richard Tomlinson was a wanted man.
He'd just served five months of a twelve-month jail sentence for breaking the Official Secrets Act and now here he was in Paris, in breach of his parole conditions and hell-bent on giving evidence to the French Inquiry implicating MI6 in the death of Princess Diana. No wonder he was number one on MI6's 'wanted' list. True, others had given evidence claiming MI6 had murdered Diana, but their information hadn't originated from inside the organization. Tomlinson's had. He was himself a former MI6 officer, after all, and until his dismissal three years ago he was party to highly privileged information, some of which – the more juicy bits – he was about to make available to the Inquiry's presiding magistrate, Judge Hervé Stephan. Indeed, he'd already prepared his affidavit, which revealed not only that MI6 had undeclared agents stationed in Paris on the night of Diana's death, an unprecedented number of them, in fact; but also that Diana's chauffeur, Henri Paul, and well-known French paparazzo, James Andanson, were both high-level MI6 assets. He'd seen the files containing this information, he said; the files were colour-coded and numbered and he would reveal the full extent of what they contained when he testified before the Inquiry in just a few days time.

He would also reveal their colour-codes and numbers.

And that's not all. He would reveal too that, when serving as a deep-cover agent in Serbia in 1992, he'd been made party to an MI6 plot to assassinate then Serbian president, Slobodan Milosevic, by road traffic accident. According to Tomlinson, the plans he'd seen had outlined the proposed operation in some detail, and had involved firing a powerful strobe light in the eyes of Milosevic's chauffeur as he drove his president through a tunnel, causing him to lose control of the limousine so that it crashed into the tunnel's concrete wall—identical in many respects to the operation that had killed Diana.

And still there was more. The question of who, ultimately, was behind the operation was already the subject of fierce speculation, on the street and in the press. Tomlinson threatened to add to that speculation by revealing the names of senior MI6 officers who, he said, enjoyed a 'special relationship' with senior members of the Royal Household. The implication was that certain 'requests' made by the Royal Household were routinely filtered through to MI6 Special Operations and carried out as 'deniable ops'.

And there was the problem.

In short, the reason Tomlinson was a wanted man was not just that he'd pissed off MI6, nor just that he threatened to spill their secrets. More that those secrets led directly back, via the Royal Household, to the man currently in charge of MI6 Special Operations. And the man currently in charge of MI6 Special Operations, of course, was Richard Mason.

If you mess with the Devil, as they say, expect Him to call you up...

...Mason picked up the phone. "Put me through to DST," he said, urgently, eager to speak to his counterpart at the Directorate de Surveillance Territoire, the French equivalent of MI5. The call went through in a matter of seconds.

"Monsieur Mason?"

"Tomlinson's arrived at Charles de Gaulle airport. He'll be at his hotel within the hour. I take it you'll be there to greet him?"

"Of course."

"Good. I'll be over later."

Mason put the phone down and started to thumb through the document lying open on his desk. It was a photocopy of Tomlinson's affidavit that had found its way into Mason's office at the British Embassy in Paris by way of the DST. The thick folder lying next to the affidavit contained Tomlinson's MI6 file—a 6 x 4 photograph and detailed history of the man Mason knew as a traitor. For a brief moment he studied Tomlinson's photograph, the puffed-up, self-assured expression the man always seemed to wear—his charm, his *savoir-faire*, his bright, athletic good looks. Mason loathed him, with interest. Discarding the photograph he gave his attention back to Tomlinson's affidavit as he leaned across his desk and picked up a different phone to the one he'd just used to call DST. It was a direct line to London.

"Have you seen what Tomlinson intends to say at the Inquiry?" an unusually fractious sounding Mason enquired, again thumbing his way through the traitor's affidavit.

"We have a copy."

"And...?"

The stuffy, dispassionate voice on the other end of the line seemed unperturbed. "Oh, I shouldn't concern yourself overly, Richard. No one will believe him, not ultimately, except perhaps the usual gaggle of liberals and conspiracy theorists. Which I would say is rather the point anyway."

"Let's hope so."

"Speaking of conspiracy theorists, how is your cut-out shaping up? Still fighting the good fight?"

"Rather more fervently than we'd anticipated, as a matter of fact. He's found a publisher for his book. In America."

"But that's what you wanted, isn't it?"

"Yes, of course. But it's just ... I think we should keep an eye on him. I'm meeting with DST a little later. I'll have them maintain a covert surveillance."

"DST?"

"He's on his way to Paris."

"King...?"

"He's travelling here with his accomplice, John Beveridge."

"Rather a coincidence, isn't it? Messrs King and Beveridge in Paris at the same time as Tomlinson?"

"I rather prefer to think of it as forward planning."

"Ah." There was a slight pause on the other end of the line, the sound of muffled voices, as though plans were being discussed. Then: "Sir Robert requests you keep us abreast of developments. King and Beveridge are of little importance at this stage, but keep a shadow on them anyway, just in case. And make it one of our own. DST are not to be trusted."

"Affirmative."

"As for Tomlinson, let him know we disapprove of his decision to inform the Inquiry. But let him do it anyway."

"Right."

"Then throw him the hell out."

28

"You know what's bugging me, JB?"

"What's that?"

"The world's most famous couple are killed in a car crash in the centre of Paris, one of the world's busiest cities. At least three other vehicles are involved in the crash and yet they all just vanish, without trace. Can you imagine that happening in the middle of London?—"

"Well, I...."

"—She was the mother of the future King of England, for Christ's sake. I mean, didn't anybody get a number plate? What about the CCTV, or the speed cameras? Don't they have cameras in France?"

"I guess that's what we need to find out."

We were in the back seat of a cab, on the outskirts of Paris. It was a muggy, overcast morning as we picked our way slowly through some of the city's less desirable suburbs on our way downtown to meet a contact Lacey had said might be worth talking to. We'd arrived here the night before, and had booked a room at a modestly priced pension on Boulevard Saint-Germain, just across the river from Place de la Concorde and the affluent side of town. Although we'd fully intended to travel here by rail, on the relatively new *Eurostar* Channel Tunnel train, in the end JB had managed to find a last-minute deal on flights so we'd flown to Paris after all. And now here we were, somewhat out of our comfort zone and entirely out of our depth, on our way to meet a mysterious character called Thierry who, according to Lacey, was the man to plug the gaps. Or at least some of them.

As we turned off the main drag into what turned out to be a seemingly endless warren of backstreets and alleyways I couldn't help but wonder who might know we were here, and that we were on our way to meet a prime contact introduced to us by a serving MI5 officer: Lacey. I shivered. Strange how being in a foreign city, away from home, can make you feel vulnerable. Exposed. Paranoid.

Right now I was feeling all three.

According to Lacey, Thierry was a middle-aged down-and-out who'd resorted to the bottle when his career as a Whitehall civil servant had ended prematurely. Despite his name, it seemed, Thierry was English, having worked most of his life for some or other government department before 'retiring' to Paris (although, as Lacey had made a point of explaining, Thierry's 'retirement' had been more the decision of the department he'd worked for than his own). In any event, Lacey had assured us that Thierry remained well-connected. If there was anything – or anyone – worth knowing that hadn't yet surfaced in the media, anything at all, Thierry was the man to talk to. And so here we were, on our way to talk to him.

As the cab pulled up in the grimy, run-down back street we now found ourselves in I immediately realized why we'd received such strange looks from the cab driver when we'd told him our destination. He still wore the same bemused look on his face now as he peered back at us across his shoulder and motioned across the street towards what looked like a derelict rail yard. On closer inspection we could see that the yard was populated by around thirty raggedly dressed and unwashed denizens, most of them male, most sleeping under fetid blankets and cardboard: all of them homeless. I presumed Thierry was among them.

"Voila," the driver said, fidgeting nervously in his seat as though anxious to get the hell away from here.

I reached through from the back of the cab and gave him his money. "Merci bien."

"Bon chance!" he said—*Good luck!* He obviously believed we would need it.

Somewhat hesitantly we climbed out of the cab and watched the driver disappear back into the warren of backstreets and alleyways before making our way across the street towards

Cardboard City. I felt at once conspicuous and edgy as we picked our way mindfully through the debris—the filth, the trash, the makeshift cardboard beds, one of which was empty, we soon discovered, its occupant already up and rummaging for cigarette butts.

I called to him. "Pardon, Monsieur? Hello? Bonjour?"

The guy looked over at me like I'd just arrived from another planet, then mumbled something under his breath and carried on rummaging for nicotine.

I tried again. "Bonjour Monsieur. Thierry est ici? Uh? Thierry?"

Still no response.

Had he understood me? I wondered. I didn't know, but I figured I knew a way to find out. "Monsieur?" I said again, taking a cigarette pack out of my pocket and offering it to him. "Thierry? Est-il ici?"

The way the fellow's eyes suddenly lit up at the sight of the cigarettes told me that, if he hadn't understood me before, he understood me now, clearly enough. Wiping the palms of his hands on his grubby coat he crossed the few yards between us without uttering so much as a grunt and took the cigarettes from my hand. Having opened them up he checked inside the pack, presumably to make sure it wasn't empty. Then, satisfied with his prize, he pointed to a heap of rag and cardboard perhaps twenty yards away.

"Thierry," he said, and no more.

I looked over at the makeshift bed, laid out beside the remains of a small fire above which thin strands of smoke still hung.

"Merci," I said, but I don't think he heard me. Or if he did, he took no notice. He'd already turned his back on us, and was busy scraping a match on the remains of a ripped up matchbox in an attempt to light the cigarette he'd just pulled from the pack. We left him to it.

And made our over towards the inanimate heap of rags and cardboard the guy had pointed out. Sure enough, as we drew closer, the shape of a male face – craggy, unshaven, florid with too much alcohol – became visible beneath the rags. It appeared far older than its fifty-two years.

"Thierry? Hello?"

Thierry didn't reply, so I nudged his boot with my foot. Still no response.

I tried again. "Thierry? Lacey said you might be able to help. He said you were English, so I know you can understand me."

"He also said you like whisky," JB added, and from his jacket pocket produced the brand new bottle of *Teacher's* we'd purchased in the duty-free store on the way over from England. We'd actually purchased two, but we didn't want Thierry to know that, not yet.

A beat later Thierry's weathered features emerged from beneath the rags. "Lacey sent you?" he said, finally, in the plumiest Queen's English.

"Yes. He said we'd find you here."

"And you are?"

"My name's Jon King. And this is my colleague, John Beveridge. We're investigating the death of Princess Diana. Lacey said you'd be able to answer some questions."

"Did he?" Thierry pushed himself up into a sitting position and rubbed his eyes, then stoked the remains of last night's fire with a length of charred wood. "You're treading on hot coals, gentlemen. If Lacey sent you here, others will know you came. I take it that's for me?" he said, flashing a hopeful glance at the whisky bottle in JB's hand.

"In exchange for information, yes."

"Then let's talk. I have nothing better to do, after all."

JB handed him the whisky, and immediately he unscrewed the bottle and started drinking from it, guzzling its contents as though the whisky was neat water. It was shocking to witness. I couldn't help but wonder how such a quintessentially English civil servant had ended up living here, in Cardboard City, Paris. Though part of me felt sorry for him, the greater part of me remained for some reason slightly suspicious of the man. While I had no evident reason to doubt his story – that he was a former government official who'd been 'retired' and had since fallen on hard times – even so it seemed an unlikely tale, it has to be said, one I couldn't help but treat with some scepticism. For all I knew his life here as a hobo could have been a cover; he could still have been working for the government, an MI6 deep-cover agent tasked with overseeing the clean-up operation still very much under way here in Paris in the aftermath of Diana's death. My paranoia surfacing again, I knew that. But apart from those closest to me I just didn't know who was who anymore—who I could trust, and who I should be wary of. So I'd chosen to be wary of everyone.

Thierry made a face that said the whisky had burned on its way down.

"We're interested to find out more about the driver of the Fiat Uno," I said. "The one involved in the crash."

"What about him?"

"They say he was a paparazzo, that he owned a Fiat Uno identical to the one that hit the Mercedes. Lacey said you'd know him."

"Everyone knows him."

"Everyone?"

"He's well known in town. But it wasn't his car in the tunnel."

"How can you be so sure?"

"Would you use your own car in an operation of that kind?"

"No," I conceded. "But we'd still like to talk to him. Do you know his name?"

"Perhaps." Thierry took another mouthful of whisky, and swallowed. Then wiped his mouth with the back of his hand.

I cast a glance at JB.

"We were also hoping to talk to this man," JB said, and pulled out a photograph of someone who claimed to have been in the tunnel at the time of the crash. He handed the photograph to Thierry.

A beat, then: "Francois Levistre," Thierry said.

"You know him?"

"Of course. He says he saw a light in the tunnel. A flash. No big deal."

"No big deal?" I said.

"Not really."

"We were told it could have been a strobe gun," JB put in.

"I suppose it could have been, yes. But in Levistre you're looking for the wrong man. He won't tell you anything. Not anymore."

"What makes you say that?" I said. "Has he been threatened?"

"My God, no. They've long since substituted their bully-boy tactics for a far more effective practice. They don't *threaten* these days, they *lampoon*, make you look stupid. No one takes the word of a clown. Discredit the messenger, discredit the message. It's their new motto."

"And this is what they've done to Levistre—discredited him?"

"If they haven't yet, they will. Mark my words." He handed the photograph back to JB.

"Who are they, Thierry?" I said. "Who are *they*?"

Thierry shrugged. "Who fixed the Mercedes?" he said. "Who switched the blood sample? Who killed the princess and ruined the wedding plans? Answer those questions and you'll know soon enough who they are." He took another mouthful of whisky before adding: "But be careful. They have the advantage. They already know who you are."

They already know who you are…

He was right about that, of course. And I guess in broad terms I knew who *they* were, too. But right now I needed specifics: I needed a name. As I stooped down on my haunches and watched Thierry slug away at what little remained of his liquid breakfast I felt sure he had more to tell: that he knew the name, the one we'd come to discover.

Figuring the promise of a second bottle of whisky might just loosen his tongue even further I gestured to JB, who sunk his hand inside his jacket pocket, ready.

Then: "I need a name, Thierry," I said. "The name of the paparazzo."

"What makes you think I know his name?"

"You said you knew him. You said everyone knows him."

"Figure of speech."

"Was he working for MI6?"

"We've all done that from time to time. It's easy money."

"What about the network, then? What's the word on the street?"

"The street doesn't talk to strangers."

"Not even strangers with whisky?" JB cut in, and pulled out the second bottle from inside his jacket.

"We need a name, Thierry," I said. "Who's the street talking about?"

29

James Andanson was by now a very worried man.

His recent conversation with his MI6 handler, Mason, had reminded him what a dangerous game he was playing. Keeping copies of the photographs he'd taken in the Alma Tunnel immediately after the crash – prior to the arrival of the emergency services, when the assassins were still there, on the ground, yet to make their getaway – suddenly felt like the most foolish thing he'd ever done. He was in a panic. He knew he needed to remove the photographs from his office safe and stash them somewhere else before Mason's bloodhounds found them and then came after him. They knew where to find him, of course; he'd been working for the prestigious SIPA press agency in Paris for almost a year now and his office there was open territory, easily accessible to someone like Mason and his highly trained goons. Had he not feared that Mason might have set a trap he would have removed them immediately after his meeting with the MI6 man in St Tropez. As it was he'd decided to wait, play it cool so as not to arouse suspicions by rushing back to his office in Paris straight from St Tropez. His next scheduled trip to Paris would be the least conspicuous time to do what had to be done, he'd decided. And now that time had arrived. Now here he was, on this thickly humid Parisian afternoon, making his way to the SIPA press agency to collect the telltale prints before someone else did.

Turning right off Place de la Porte de Saint-Cloud, Andanson's cab drew up outside the SIPA building on Boulevard Murat in Boulogne-Billancourt, and the paparazzo climbed out.

"Quinze minutes," he said to the cab driver, instructing him to wait fifteen minutes. The driver nodded, pulled out a pack of cigarettes, tipped one in his mouth and lit up. Carrying an empty duffle bag Andanson turned and headed into the building.

"Bonjour, Monsieur," the receptionist said as an anxious looking Andanson entered the main reception area and made his way hurriedly through to the elevator. He did not speak, not to the receptionist, not to anyone. His mind was so focused on the task facing him he scarcely even noticed the sound of the woman's voice, much less the surprised expression on her face as he strode obliviously past her. Clearly put out by the paparazzo's poor manners she made a face that showed her displeasure, then turned her head and continued to paint her nails.

Less than two minutes later Andanson stepped from the elevator and made his way hurriedly along the short corridor to his office. Once inside he closed the door and locked it, then headed straight for the safe where his photographic archive – or a good deal of it, at least – was stored safely away. Many of his prints were of high value, after all, and storing them in his office safe, away from prying eyes and gloved hands, had become routine priority. Even more so now that his name – James Andanson – was synonymous with success. Dialling in the safe's combination he opened it up and took out the neat bundles of prints and rolls of photographic negative it contained, then sat himself at his desk and started flicking through the material, sifting the innocent from the incriminating.

At one point he paused as he pulled out what appeared on the face of it to be a regular photographic album, though the title scrawled on its inside cover gave it away as something far more prized than that. *Rapport sur le Voyage de Lady Di* the title read— '*Report on the Voyage of Lady Di*'. It was a photographic record of Andanson's pursuit of Diana and Dodi the previous summer, during the days and weeks leading up to their deaths. As he thumbed through its pages now he was reminded of just how revealing its contents were; some of the world's most familiar photographs of Diana and Dodi were contained in the album, many of which had already made the front pages of Britain's tabloids. Others were still yet to do so. Each had notes scrawled beneath them, like captions in a scrapbook.

But there were other photographs in the album, too, less familiar photographs, more dangerous. These were the images Andanson had come to remove—photographs of MI6 agents on the ground in Paris on the night of Diana's death, agents known to Andanson, their faces dotted among the swarm of paparazzi outside the Ritz Hotel, in the afternoon and in the evening; and then again around midnight as they waited for the couple to depart on their fateful journey. There were even photographs of Mason himself, at the rear of the Ritz Hotel, outside Dodi's apartment, in the Alma Tunnel immediately after the crash. Again, beneath each of the images were scrawled notes, giving the album the appearance of a scrapbook.

Carefully sifting out the incriminating prints Andanson stuffed them in his duffle bag and placed the remainder of the material back in the safe, locked it.

He then left the room, smugly content in his belief that he'd outpaced MI6 and could now stash the material safely away until the French Inquiry was done and he could publish his planned book without fear of reprisals.

But of course, he was wrong. As he exited the building and climbed back in his cab on Boulevard Murat in Boulogne-Billancourt, two miles away in Mason's office at the British Embassy on Rue du Faubourg Saint-Honoré, the phone rang.

MI6 chief Richard Mason picked it up.

"He's just left, sir," the voice reported, referring to Andanson's departure from the SIPA press agency offices.

"Did he take the entire archive?" Mason wanted to know.

"We don't know that, sir, not yet. We'll need to take a look around his office ourselves."

"Negative. The climate is still too sticky. I'll organize a black bag, have someone do it for us."

"Sir."

"Stay on his tail, though. We need to know where he deposits the backup. Once we have it in our possession we can tell Wilkinson Montpellier's go."

"Should we close the contract on site, sir?"

"Affirmative. But wait for the green light. I'll arrange things through the embassy."

That said, Mason put the phone down and closed the photograph album laying open on his desk in front of him. Its cover was titled *Rapport sur le Voyage de lady Di'* —'Report on the Voyage of Lady Di'. Beneath the title the name of the album's author: *James Andanson*. He slid the album back in his desk drawer and locked it.

Twenty-four minutes later Richard Mason arrived at 7 rue Nélaton, headquarters of the DST.

Half an hour after arriving at his hotel from Charles de Gaulle Airport, Richard Tomlinson was seated at the dark, apple-wood table in the corner of his room, checking notes on his laptop, when suddenly the door burst open. Two plain-clothes agents accompanied by three gendarmes were on him before he could even spit.

"Aghhh! What the...?"

The searing *crack!* of a pistol butt brought down on the back of his head and the *crunch* of someone's boot slamming into his ribs was the only introduction he received. He couldn't remember hitting the floor but as he forced open his eyes he found himself at the foot of the apple-wood table, rolled up in a foetal ball, clutching his screaming ribs. They hurt so bad he could scarcely breathe.

"Who are you?" he tried to say to the men ransacking his room. "What do you want? Where's your ID?"

The plain-clothes agent seemingly in charge of the raid turned to the gendarme whose boot had just cracked Tomlinson's ribs. "Show him our ID," he said, and the same boot thudded into Tomlinson's kidneys, like a sledgehammer.

The high-pitched squeal Tomlinson effused sounded more like a pig being slaughtered than anything human. The horrific sound lasted less than a beat. Then Tomlinson passed out.

"Bring the computer," the senior agent instructed. "Clothes, attaché case, even his fucking toothbrush. If there's a reason to prevent this son of a bitch giving evidence at the inquiry, I want it found."

"What did you get?" Mason asked.

"Everything," the DST agent replied.

"Let's hope so."

The two men were in a minimally furnished office at DST HQ in Paris, Mason poring over papers and studying a list of names on a computer screen set on the table in front of him. The DST agent was standing by the open window, smoking.

"Langman," Mason muttered, almost to himself, as he scrolled down the list of names on the computer screen. His tone carried a hint of discomfort. "Nicholas Langman ... Richard Spearman..."

"They are names on the Diplomatic Service List," the DST agent reminded him. "They are a matter of public record. The fact Tomlinson knows them is no cause for alarm."

Mason didn't agree. The look on his face said so.

"What is wrong?" the DST agent probed. "All is as it should be, is it not?"

Again Mason made no reply, but his expression told its own story.

"Are you telling me some of these names are covers?" the DST agent said, reading Mason's expression, realizing what the MI6 man was refusing to say. His own expression was now one of mild panic. "Are you saying there were undeclared MI6 officers in Paris on the night the princess died?"

"Well if there were it appears the secret is safe," Mason said, his eyes emotionless and glued to the computer screen, the list of names it displayed. "Fortunately no operational code names are included in Tomlinson's list. All is good."

The agent wanted to say: "Operational code names? You mean like *Mason*? Are you included on the Diplomatic Service List as well, under your *real* name?" But he knew better than to ask further questions. Instead he gazed back out the window and sucked anxiously on his cigarette, leaving Mason to complete his trawl of Tomlinson's computer...

...In a different section of the building Richard Tomlinson sat upright on the cell's single wooden bench, naked from the waist up but for the heavy adhesive strapping that kept his ribs from caving in. Even so, they throbbed. His head pounded. He was hungry and thirsty and wanted nothing more than to throw in the towel and walk away from this nightmare in which he found himself, self-inflicted though it was. But he knew he wouldn't. Despite the discomfort he knew he would see this nightmare through and do what he'd come to Paris to do. He had his reasons for wanting to give evidence, after all, and they outdid any amount of pain the authorities could deal him. They couldn't keep him here for very much longer anyway, he knew that. They would find nothing on his computer to warrant his extended detention, and so would be forced to release him without charge, sooner rather than later. In two days from now he would stand before the judge at the French Inquiry, and he would reveal everything he knew—even Mason's name. Then he would get the hell out of France before MI6 terminated him.

30

JB and I were sitting at a table outside a café somewhere in downtown Paris. In fact JB had slipped inside to use the bathroom, so I was sitting on my own, talking on my mobile phone to Jackie, the girl who'd joined our magazine straight from college and had since proved her weight in gold. She'd called me up with an update from England.

"Richard Tomlinson's in the news over here," she was saying. "He claims one of the paparazzi worked for MI6. Evidently he intends to name him at the inquiry."

"So I heard. We think the paparazzo in question was a guy called Andanson. James Andanson."

"Anderson…?"

"No, no, *Andanson*. Jackie…?" A strange crackle on the line kept threatening to interrupt us; our friends back at GCHQ, no doubt. "Hello? Jackie, did you get that…?"

"Ander…? Anderson?" Jackie said through the crackle and pop of MI5's best eavesdropping endeavours. At which point the noise suddenly abated; the line cleared. "James Anderson?"

"No, not Anderson—*Andanson*. A-N-D-A-N-S-O-N. *An-dan-son*. We don't think it was his Fiat Uno in the tunnel but it seems he was definitely in Paris on the night of the crash, involved in the operation in some way or other. We need to see what we can find out about him."

"I'm on it."

Just then, the waitress arrived at my table with pencil and note pad in hand.

"Ah, deux grand cafés noirs, s'il vous plaît," I said in my best schoolboy French. Then: "Jacks, are you still there?"

"Still here."

The waitress scribbled on her pad and headed back inside.

"We also need to find out what's happening with a character named Francois Levistre."

"I can tell you that now," Jackie said. "He was splashed all over the tabloids yesterday. They crucified him."

"Levistre?"

"Francois Levistre, yes. The media seemed more interested in the fact that he has a criminal record than in what he had to say about the crash, even though he's only ever been convicted for petty offences."

"What does his criminal record have to do with what he saw in the tunnel?"

"You tell me. And that's not the end of it, either. They also made a point of highlighting the differences – the *alleged* differences, I might add – between his version of events and his wife's, saying they contradicted each other."

"Therefore their accounts are unreliable."

"Correct. The article concluded that Levistre demonstrated 'a complete lack of credibility', and therefore his account should be ignored. Basically they implied he made it all up to gain notoriety."

"Jesus." I recalled to mind what Thierry had said earlier, that these days intelligence agencies were less likely to threaten witnesses, more likely to lampoon them, make them look stupid, discredit them in the eyes of the public so that their stories lost credibility, too. I was gobsmacked. "It seems Thierry was right, after all," I heard myself say.

"Thierry?" Jackie questioned.

"Oh, someone we spoke to earlier. He said they would make Levistre out to be a clown. Looks like he was right."

Just then, the waitress returned with two large black coffees. She placed them on the table with the bill.

"Merci bon."

"Monsieur."

I sugared my coffee and stirred it. "How are things coming along with the new magazine, by the way, Jacks?" I said, sipping my coffee, changing the subject. "Any developments?"

"Yes, as a matter of fact," Jackie reported. "Mark met with the new distributor yesterday. We should have a nice new office for you when you get back."

"Excellent, can't wait to get back to it … Jackie? Hello…? Jacks…?"

The signal again, and this time it was terminal. Just before we were finally cut off, though, I thought I heard Jackie say: *"Don't forget Richard Tomlinson is due to testify in court today."* But I couldn't be certain. For one thing the line was so bad. And for another, my attention had just been stolen by a wholly unexpected sight; indeed, it was a sight that would stay with me for the rest of my life. Because just then, as Jackie tried to remind me that the former MI6 officer was due in court later that day, I saw him, Richard Tomlinson, drive past me in a cab. And what's more he saw me, too. I hadn't yet met the man in person, of course, but I'd seen his face often enough – in the papers, on the news – enough that I could recognize him in a crowd. Sounds crazy, I know. Improbable, even. But if it wasn't him then it was a spit, his absolute double, and that double was staring right back at me now from the back of a passing cab. It was a strangely out-of-time moment, one that caused the hairs on the back of my neck to stand up and take a look, as though to confirm the sighting. And they did. It was the reappearance of JB from inside the café that finally teased me back to reality.

"You all right, Jon? You look like you've seen a ghost," he said, seating himself opposite and tipping his head at the *grand café noir* peering back up at him from the table. "I take it this one's mine?"

I didn't reply. Instead, as JB claimed his coffee and started to drink it I found myself glued to Richard Tomlinson's cab, watching it disappear along the street and into the near distance, unable to remove my eyes until it had been swallowed entirely by the city traffic. It was an image I would never forget. Not ever. Not even in my sleep.

31

Richard Tomlinson stood in the dock facing Hervé Stephan and Marie-Christine Devidal, the inquiry's presiding magistrates. Other court officials were also present, but it was Stephan who was in charge of proceedings. And it was Stephan who was about to address Tomlinson.

Around forty years of age with hawkish nose and sterile eyes, Stephan had of course been handpicked for the job. The eyes of the world were on France at this historic moment, and the inquiry's outcome, the French authorities had soon enough realized, should be swift and unremarkable. If not inevitable. Stephan's reputation as an investigating magistrate had been noted in this regard. He'd already studied Tomlinson's affidavit, of course, had already noted the wild and dangerous claims it contained, and on this basis had decided that his cross-examination of the former MI6 man would be brutal. No agonies spared.

Glancing up he peered briefly across at the man looking back at him from the dock, then perched his reading glasses on the bridge of his nose as he looked back down and read purposefully from his notes. "D/813317," he said. "Does this number mean anything to you, Monsieur Tomlinson?"

Tomlinson shifted his weight to one side to ease the stabbing pain he still felt from his fractured ribs, but did so in such a manner that no one would readily notice. If what he had to say was to cut through the court's stark, hostile atmosphere, he realized, he would need to be as strong in his character as he was clear in his testimony. Unflinching, he looked straight ahead at Judge Stephan when he made his reply.

"It was the code I was designated when I worked for MI6," he said.

"By MI6 you mean the British Secret Intelligence Service?"
"Yes."

"And why did you leave the Secret Intelligence Service, Monsieur Tomlinson?"

"I was dismissed."

Judge Stephan made a laboured point of noting the fact. Then: "I see you spent some time in Serbia," he said, referring to his notes. "And also Moscow?"

"I was assigned deep-cover operational duties in those countries, yes. It was in Serbia that I learned of the MI6 plot to assassinate President Milosevic, by road traffic accident."

"It's also where you witnessed a particularly unpleasant incident. Is that correct?"

"I witnessed a civilian lose their life, if that's what you're referring to. They were blown up in front of me."

"So I understand." Judge Stephan looked up from his notes and peered enquiringly at Tomlinson, as though to assess his response. "The experience affected you deeply, would you say?"

"Of course..."

"And the subsequent loss of your girlfriend to cancer ... these experiences, they affected you deeply. Yes?—"

"Well, I..."

"—You suffered severe psychological trauma as a result—"

"Look, what are you trying to...?"

"—So much so your superiors deemed you no longer fit to be an MI6 officer."

"That's not true! I was dismissed because I spoke out about accountability and protocol, about how too many MI6 officers do as they damn well please!"

Tomlinson's mouth immediately tightened over his clenched teeth. *Damn!* First blood to Stephan, he knew. Inwardly he chastised himself. He should have seen it coming, should have seen where Stephan was heading, that the magistrate was contriving to discredit him to make what he had to say less believable. He breathed, took a moment to regain his composure.

Then: "Monsieur Stephan," he said. "I came here because I have valuable information that may well help prevent a miscarriage of justice. I came here to inform you that the crash in which the Princess of Wales died was no ordinary accident. It bore all the hallmarks of an MI6 operation."

"That doesn't mean MI6 were involved."

"But it does mean they might have been."

"*Might have been* is not sufficient grounds for prosecution, Monsieur Tomlinson. If we truly wish to prevent a miscarriage of justice we must adhere to the facts." Judge Stephan left a lengthy pause, as though to allow his comments to percolate, then turned briefly to confer with the magistrate at his side. Marie-Christine Devidal was a fraught-looking woman in her early forties, tight and officious, her hair so heavily lacquered it scarcely moved as she turned her head to confer with her fellow magistrate. Stephan mouthed his concerns; the two of them nodded their agreement. When finally Stephan turned back to face Tomlinson he initiated a new line of questioning. "Do you resent being sacked by MI6?" he said with a breath of cynicism in his voice. "Is that really why you're here today, to get back at your former employers?"

Tomlinson was visibly incensed. "That's preposterous!" he retorted.

"Is it?" Stephan removed his reading glasses, as though to emphasize his point. "You tell me MI6 formulated a plot to assassinate a foreign leader in a car crash. You expect me to take this as evidence that MI6 assassinated Princess Diana. Do you have anything of any real substance to say?"

"What I've told you already, as stated in my affidavit, is easily sufficient for you to initiate proceedings against the British Secret Intelligence Service. But for the avoidance of doubt, let me reiterate. There were at least two undeclared MI6 officers based at the British Embassy on the night of the crash. I have both their names. One of them was a very senior officer."

"That doesn't mean he was here as part of an MI6 plot."

"Well he wasn't here for the summer sales," Tomlinson fired back. "He was an illegal, Monsieur Stephan. We do not post illegals to friendly countries without very good reason. Why else would he have been here?"

"It is not for us to speculate—"

"Are you aware that MI6 officers are immune from prosecution for crimes committed on foreign soil?"

"Monsieur Tomlinson—"

"Would you care to know why illegals were posted to Paris at the time in question? Would you care to know their names...?"

"Monsieur Tomlinson, please!" Judge Stephan's clenched fist thumped the top of the bench. "This is not the place to speculate on the business of foreign diplomats. Now if you have finished..."

"I have not." Again Tomlinson shifted his weight in an attempt to ease the discomfort of his throbbing ribs. "I have information regarding Henri Paul. He was an MI6 agent. He had worked for MI6 for at least five years."

"And you can substantiate this claim?"

"I have seen his personal file. It was shown to me when I was working undercover in the former Soviet Union."

"And Henri Paul's name appears in this file?"

"No. Assets are designated by code-number, not by name."

"Then how can you be sure this particular code-number you say you saw belonged to Henri Paul?"

"If you'll let me explain—"

"I repeat—did Henri Paul's name appear in this file?"

"No, for the reason I gave you. But—"

"Evidence, Monsieur Tomlinson. I need evidence. At this time there is no evidence that Henri Paul was a secret agent."

"That's because it's being withheld by MI6. If you subpoena the file you will find all the evidence you need."

"But you say Henri Paul's name does not appear in the file."

"The code-number will be associated with a name via the asset's handler. I can tell you the name of Henri Paul's handler—"

"Is there anything else, Monsieur Tomlinson?" Stephan said, dismissively, waving away Tomlinson's offer of a name.

Tomlinson bristled. "Yes. I can also tell you that one of the paparazzi who followed Princess Diana was a member of UKN."

"UKN?"

"It's a small corps of part-time MI6 agents who provide surveillance and photographic expertise. I can confirm that one of these agents is a French paparazzo who was here in Paris on the night in question. Examination of UKN records would reveal his identity."

"And then what, Monsieur Tomlinson?"

"And then you can question him."

"On what grounds? Providing information to a foreign intelligence service isn't necessarily a crime."

"It is when the intelligence service in question is responsible for murder."

"Monsieur Tomlinson!"

"If you would just order MI6 to produce the records for the court you could at least question the man and eliminate him from your enquiries."

Visibly infuriated now, Stephan's eyes turned to fire. *"We'll decide who is to be eliminated, Monsieur Tomlinson,"* he said, and the fire in his eyes all but ignited.

There was another fire burning in a carved out acre of secluded woodland just north of Montpellier in southern France, this one more deadly. It was 9:45 pm.

Almost twelve hours earlier James Andanson had set out from his home in Lignières for a meeting in Paris with the Deputy Editor of *Paris Match* magazine, Christophe Lafaille. Andanson was a close friend of Lafaille, and an even closer friend of Lafaille's boss, Tony Comiti, who once made a documentary about Andanson working the patch in St Torpez during the 'paparazzi season'. But it wasn't a film Andanson wanted Comiti to make on this occasion. On this occasion a very different deal was in the offing. *Paris Match* was arguably France's most successful magazine, and James Andanson had targeted its million-selling circulation as the ideal vehicle in which to serialize his forthcoming book based on the contents of his diary: *Rapport sur le Voyage de Lady Di — Report on the Voyage of Lady Di*. Which is why he'd set out for Paris that morning, for his meeting with Christophe Lafaille, scheduled for 1.45 pm. And for a further meeting at the SIPA press agency offices with Sophie Deniau, scheduled for 4 pm.

But he never made it to either of those planned meetings. He never got to within 100 miles of Paris that day. He'd only travelled as far as the A71 intersection at Bourges, in fact, when the phone call came — the phone call that persuaded him to head south on the A71 towards Clermont-Ferrand and Montpellier instead of north towards Orleans and Paris. It was the phone call that not only *changed* his life, but effectively *ended* it.

"Head south, James," the caller had instructed. "Meet me at the Hotel Campanile in Millau, in the car park. Meet me there at four o'clock."

"But I have a meeting in Paris at four o'clock," Andanson protested.

"Cancel it. This is extremely urgent, James, we have a job for you. I'll see you at four o'clock."

Andanson discarded his mobile on the passenger seat of his black BMW 320d Compact and turned right on the A71, south. He'd thought about ignoring the caller, of course, had thought about defying his instruction and heading on up to Paris anyway. But he knew better than to cross Richard Mason. At the first opportunity he pulled over and called Christophe Lafaille to cancel his appointment – tried to contact Sophie as well but couldn't get through – then continued his journey south towards Millau and the Hotel Campanile.

At around 3.30 pm that afternoon Andanson arrived in the panoramic town of Millau. Six minutes later he pulled into a petrol station situated opposite the town's Hotel Campanile and filled his tank. He also refilled the spare petrol container he carried in the boot of his car, having emptied its contents a few days previously when he'd run low on fuel en route to an unexpected photographic assignment. The years of constant travelling had taught him to be prepared. Having paid for the fuel and returned the refilled container to its place in the boot he climbed back in his car and drove across the road to the Hotel Campanile car park where, he'd been led to believe, Mason would be waiting for him.

But waiting for him instead was an unwelcome surprise.

"Mr Mason couldn't make it," the man said. He'd watched as Andanson had pulled into the car park and, Glock 17 unholstered, had made his way over to the paparazzo's BMW and climbed in beside him. "He asked me to meet you instead."

Andanson didn't bother to ask the man's name. The semiautomatic pistol levelled at him now told him everything he needed to know. He'd been set up. This man had been sent to kill him.

"Drive," the man said. "I'll direct you."

Andanson fired the engine.

Sometime later Andanson found himself driving along an isolated dirt track, across farmland towards a fenced-off, wooded area up ahead. It was early evening, around 8 pm and it was beginning to get dark. His headlights were on full beam.

"Turn off your lights," the man beside him instructed, and indicated left with the pistol he still brandished. "Take this track here."

Andanson doused his lights and turned off left along an even more primitive dirt track. He knew this area pretty well, but daylight was disappearing fast and it was becoming more and more difficult for him to see ahead. To some large extent he was trusting to luck, but luck was something that was about to desert him.

"In there." The man with the gun pointed to a clearing in the woods just ahead of them. "Drive into that clearing, turn off the engine and give me the keys."

Andanson followed instruction. "So what now?" the paparazzo said. "You are going to kill me?"

"No," the man said. "You are going to kill yourself."

Back in the courtroom Judge Stephan started gathering up the papers on the bench in front of him. "Conspiracy to murder is a very serious allegation, Monsieur Tomlinson," he said. "It must be supported by hard evidence. I have heard nothing to persuade me your claims are anything but wild speculation."

"But you will order the release of the files?" Tomlinson wanted to know.

"What files?"

"The files I've told you about. They will identify the embassy staff, as well as the Ritz informant and the paparazzi agent."

"The court will examine everything it deems pertinent to the inquiry. Now, if that is everything." He tapped the edge of his papers on the bench top and turned to confer with his assistant magistrate, Marie-Christine Devidal.

Tomlinson could scarcely believe what was happening. "But you must at least order the release of the files," he said, his voice raised, more in desperation than annoyance.

But: "That will be all," Judge Stephan said and the two magistrates stood up to leave. "You will be contacted in due course."

For what seemed like several minutes after Stephan and Devidal had departed the courtroom Richard Tomlinson simply stood there, aghast, motionless, the questions in his eyes almost audible.

At length he turned and headed for the door. He'd been gagged.

32

While Richard Tomlinson was being discounted by the French Inquiry, JB and I had decided to visit one or two key locations, if for no other reason than to familiarize ourselves with what until now had been little more than points on a map. From the downtown café where we'd had our morning coffee – the café where I was sure I'd seen Richard Tomlinson, or his double, drive past me in a cab; and where I'd spoken to Jackie on the phone – we'd made our way back to the more affluent 1st arrondissement of Paris and Place Vendome, where among other palatial constructions the Ritz Hotel was situated. Place Vendome was the most uptown and fashionable square in Paris, the centre of chic, the place to hang your hat, for those who could afford to. It was also where Diana and Dodi had taken their last supper and from where they'd begun their last journey amidst the melee of turmoil and confusion that had marked that fateful day. Indeed, as we made our way, on foot, across the square, past the imposing Vendome Column towards the entrance to the Ritz Hotel, I found myself picturing the commotion that must have ensued here, almost a year earlier—the day the princess was killed.

Diana arriving here with Dodi in the late afternoon sunshine, alighting from the limousine and having to fight her way through the scrum of paparazzi already gathered here, outside the hotel's front entrance—largely the same scrum that had pounced on her at Le Bourget Airport some two hours earlier, when she'd arrived in Paris from Sardinia.

Then being whisked away to Dodi's apartment on Rue Arsène Houssaye, just off the Champs-Élysées, some two-and-a-half hours later, only to find the same salivating media scrum already there and waiting, like hyenas stalking a kill.

Then being forced to return here for dinner later that evening, to the Ritz, it being simply too dangerous for them to dine at their favoured restaurant, Chez Benoit, scarcely a diamond's glint from Dodi's luxury apartment. On this occasion, too, the couple would have to fight their way through the ever-madding media scrum, past the avalanche of cameras and flash bulbs and into the relative calm of the Ritz Hotel's exclusive Imperial Suite.

But there was yet one more journey to be made: *the getaway*.

As I stood there now, lost in this bizarrely evocative moment, strangely mesmerised by the hotel's lavishly baroque façade, I pictured Diana at twenty past midnight having to sneak out via the hotel's rear entrance in order to evade the pack of wolves still baying for her blood, here, at the front. She must have been terrified. Indeed, as the images of her ill-fated escape played hauntingly on my mental screen I seemed in some small, insignificant measure to relive that terror—as though the ghost of that terrible night had momentarily resurrected itself and shared its forbidding secrets for all to see. Inwardly, I shivered.

"You look like you've seen that ghost again, Jon," I heard JB say.

"Just thinking," I said, and folded my arms around myself as though to ward off the chill I was feeling, even though it was twenty-plus degrees in the shade. "I was wondering what it must have been like, you know, having all that attention constantly heaped on you. She couldn't even leave the hotel without the security guards having to deploy decoy cars."

"Why do you think they did that?" JB said, unexpectedly, taking me by surprise.

I shrugged. "To try and fool the paparazzi into chasing the wrong vehicle, I guess."

"Yeah, that would be my guess, too."

"So…?"

"Well, it's just … I can't help wondering…"

"What…?"

"Well if that's really what they were trying to do, why didn't they just keep driving? I mean, they could've kept going in that direction…" he said, indicating north along Rue de la Paix. He then spun round and indicated south across the square in the direction of Rue de Castiglione. "…Or in that direction. Why didn't they just keep driving away from the square, at least for a mile or so, before coming back here? If they really wanted to lure the paparazzi off the scent why didn't they take them on a wild goose chase across town? It doesn't make sense."

"What are you getting at, JB?"

"Well, think about it. All they actually did was drive the so-called decoy cars once around the square and straight back here. They didn't fool anybody. In fact all they succeeded in doing was create even more hysteria, to the point that the paparazzi became even crazier than they already were. It just seems odd."

This was the most fired up I'd seen JB since we'd started investigating the case. JB the doubter, the sceptic. "Do you think they might have done it deliberately, then?"

He made a face. "I dunno about that. It's just … well it's not what I would've done, that's all."

"No, me neither," I agreed. "Not unless…"

"Unless what?"

"Unless I was deliberately trying to whip up emotions so they got out of hand."

"And why would you want to do that?"

Again I pictured the out-of-control media scrum that was gathered here, outside the hotel's front entrance, Diana having to sneak out the back in an attempt to get away unseen. Again the image was terrifying. "Because when things get out of hand," I heard myself say, "that's when accidents happen."

JB offered no further response, but I could see he'd taken on board what I'd just said. I wondered if maybe, just maybe, the doubter in him was starting to ask new questions.

A few moments later: "Come on, let's check out the embassy. It's about half a mile up the road, this way," I said as we turned and strolled off in the direction of l'Ambassade de Grande

Bretagne, the British Embassy. Ten minutes later we were standing on Rue du Faubourg Saint-Honoré, opposite the embassy—a commanding bourgeoisie town house renovated and modernized for twentieth-century use. Evidently the British government had purchased it in 1947.

"Well, here it is," I said, eyeing the building opposite with both eyes—one on its impressive architecture, the other on the secrets it housed. If the operation that led to Diana's death had been run out of this place, I thought, it would likely remain secret forever. Or at least for a very long time. "Base of operations."

"What, the embassy?" JB said.

"Where else? Where better to locate your operational control room than right here in the heart of things?"

"I s'pose, but…"

"The Ritz is only half a mile back that way, remember, the Alma Tunnel a mile away in that direction, the headquarters of French Intelligence a mile beyond that. All comfortably within touching distance. MI6 would have had a team based here anyway, under diplomatic cover. It was the perfect location."

"Except for one thing," JB said, considering my hypothesis with some cynicism. "It was bank holiday. The embassy was closed that day."

"Exactly," I came back.

"Eh…?"

"Think about it. If you were running an operation as clandestine as this one, you'd hardly want the place to be crawling with extraneous staff, would you, much less open to the public." I caught his eye, purposely. "Like I said, it was the perfect location."

"You know, you could have a point there," JB agreed after a moment's thought. "You actually could have a point."

Place de l'Alma was busier than I'd imagined. More tourists. More traffic. But only one camera to capture all the action—one traffic-monitoring camera looking back along Cours Albert 1er and Cours la Reine towards Place de la Concorde, Place Vendome and the Ritz Hotel. Cours Albert 1er was the riverside highway along which Diana's Mercedes had been chased by at least three still-unidentified vehicles on the night of the crash. If any camera should have captured the chase – in particular the moment the Fiat Uno dipped out in front of her Mercedes and forced Henri Paul into a violent and, as is turned out, deadly correction manoeuvre – it was this one towering above us now, mounted near the top of the lamppost overlooking the entrance to the Alma Tunnel. The official word, of course, was that no cameras had captured the event—not any part of the journey from the Ritz Hotel had been captured by CCTV or traffic camera: not the departure, not the chase, not the crash. Standing here now with JB, on the Place de l'Alma overpass, having just walked from the embassy, past Place de la Concorde and along Cours la Reine, following the same route Diana had taken on the night she died, it seemed all the more evident why no images or footage of the journey existed. There were, quite simply, no cameras. Or at least very few.

"Notice anything, JB?" I said. We were standing by the lamppost, beneath Place de l'Alma's solitary traffic-monitoring camera, gazing back along the route we'd just walked. The camera was filming every vehicle that entered the tunnel. "Anything different?"

"Everyone's driving on the wrong side of the road, for a start."

"What else?"

JB shrugged. He didn't know.

"Cameras," I said. "Traffic cameras. This is the only one. There are ten or so private security cameras I counted back along the route, two attached to a couple of the embassies and the Chamber of Commerce over there and several others on some of the buildings on Cours la Reine. But this is the only traffic camera."

Suddenly latching on to where I was going JB scanned the horizon and his eyes locked onto the solitary security camera attached to the front of the Chamber of Commerce on Cours Albert 1er. It seemed to be working fine.

"They say all the security cameras were facing the wrong way on the night of the crash."

"All of them?"

"That's the official word."

"Well what about this one?" JB wanted to know, craning his neck and gazing up at the traffic-monitoring camera whirring above our heads.

"According to French Traffic Control it wasn't working at the time of the crash."

"Convenient."

"Evidently everyone at Traffic Control goes home to bed at eleven o'clock, and when they do they turn the cameras off. It was gone midnight when the crash happened."

"So all the cameras, what few there are in Paris, were either facing the wrong way or they were out of action when the crash happened?"

"Correct."

"There's scarcely any cameras, anyway."

"Correct."

JB let this information sink in. At length he said: "I guess that makes Paris the ideal place to assassinate a princess, then—without being seen."

"Or filmed."

"Or filmed, indeed. All part of the plan from the outset."

"The plan?" Was I still talking to JB, the doubter? The hardened sceptic? "You're beginning to sound like a conspiracy theorist, JB."

"Well if I am," he said, "it's because I'm beginning to sense a conspiracy. Come on, or we'll miss our flight home."

33

"I'm there now," Mason said into his mobile phone, as the cab he was travelling in drew up in the SIPA press agency car park. It was around 3.30 am, and dark. "We'll have the remainder of the archive soon enough."

As the cab driver killed engine and lights Mason ended the call he'd just made and immediately dialled a different number. At the opposite end of the car park the headlights of a Renault Master van flashed on and off, once. Mason cut the call and climbed out.

"Wait here," he said to the driver. It was no ordinary driver, of course. It was no ordinary cab. "If anything goes wrong, kill them."

Unbuttoning his jacket Mason's 'driver' unholstered his Glock 17 semiautomatic pistol and cocked it, *click-click*.

Closing the door noiselessly behind him Mason felt for his own semiautomatic as he stepped cautiously into the shadows, all six senses alive and alert. Though mounted security lights illuminated the SIPA building's main entrance, he saw, the car park remained largely in shadow, and for a beat Mason had to allow even his sharply trained eyes to grow accustomed to the dim light. He scanned the scene. There, perhaps twenty yards ahead of him, he could just make out the form of a tall, rangy man dressed all in black and wearing a black ski mask rolled up so that his face was partially visible. He was standing by the Renault Master van, and even at this distance Mason could now see it was the man he'd come here to meet. He let his grip on the semiautomatic relax, just a little, but left the safety lock off as he softpadded his way around the perimeter of the car park to where the man stood.

Then: "I trust there were no problems?" Mason said.

"Nothing we couldn't handle," the man replied, but in a way that told Mason things perhaps hadn't gone as smoothly as they might have.

"What do you mean?"

The man shrugged his shoulders. "One of the security guards tried to play the hero. He tried to take the gun off me. There was a struggle and it went off."

"And…?"

"He's okay. He took the bullet in the leg, or the foot, I'm not sure. He's still alive anyway, tied up with the others in the lobby."

"Great."

The news that a firearm had been used in the raid momentarily angered Mason, but only momentarily. The armed gang he'd hired to break into the SIPA offices – and more precisely, into James Andanson's office – were of course professional criminals. But they were far from professional agents. The shooting of the security guard would make it look all the more authentic, he quickly realized: make it look like the break-in had been carried out by a gang of amateur thieves and, if anything, negate any suggestion that the intelligence services might have been involved. The gang's incompetence would work in his favour, then.

"Let's get our business done," he said. "I take it you managed to find what we were looking for?"

"It's in the van with the other stuff."

"The other stuff?"

"A few desktop computers, half a dozen laptops, a couple of scanners, one or two other bits and pieces—whatever we could find that we knew we could sell on. You did say so long as we got the hard drive and the photographs we could take whatever else we wanted and keep it for ourselves."

"Well let's hope you find a favourable price," Mason said. "Shall we?"

Turning, the man opened up the back of the van and craned inside. While he did so, Mason kept his hand tucked discreetly in his pocket and firmly clasped around the butt of his semiautomatic pistol. One false move and the man was dead.

"One hard drive, one folder," the man said, as he re-emerged from the back of the van with the goods Mason was about to pay him for. "The photographs are in the folder."

"They'd better be." Mason handed the man a brown envelope. "If you get caught…"

"I know the rules, Monsieur," the man said. "If we get caught it was all our own idea. They would never believe me anyway, even if I told them the truth."

"Correct. Now you'd best be gone; the police are on their way."

The man nodded. He understood. He stepped around the side of the van, climbed in the driver-side door and fired the engine. Then drove off into the night.

Mason hit the call button on his mobile phone. A beat, then: "Tell Sir Robert all is well. The archive will go the same way as the man himself: it will be incinerated."

A few moments later, hard drive and folder containing Andanson's entire photographic archive safely in his possession, Mason's climbed back in the 'cab' and closed the door.

"Jon, it's Jackie," my voicemail told me. Evidently she'd phoned when JB and I had been out and about and I'd only just retrieved her message. We were at this moment making our way back to the UK, or more precisely, we were stuck in a somewhat disorderly queue at Paris's Charles de Gaulle airport. In any event we were on our way home, and despite being nudged ever closer towards the customs security gate, shuffling along with my bag between my ankles, mobile phone pressed hard to my ear with my shoulder as I fumbled in my pockets for my passport and boarding pass, I was eager to listen to what Jackie had to say. I'd recently asked her to find out what she could about James Andanson, and I guessed the message she'd left contained her report.

I was right. "It looks like you were right about James Andanson being in Paris on the night of the crash," her message began. "Friends of his say he took telltale photographs in the tunnel immediately after the crash, and that he was planning to publish them in a book. But it seems someone had other ideas. His death was announced today…"

No way…

I almost dropped the phone. *James Andanson dead? How? Had he been murdered?* I asked myself. *Who else were they prepared to bump off to keep the truth from showing its teeth?* A shiver cut through me as I sent an instinctive glance left and right, then behind me, as though to make sure I wasn't being watched. My paranoid instincts surfacing again.

"He's dead," I mouthed to JB. I could scarcely speak.

"Who's dead?" JB wanted to know.

I motioned for him to keep his voice down. "James Andanson," I soft-toned. "It's Jackie on the phone. James Andanson's dead."

"What? Well … how…?"

I shook my head. I didn't know. I continued listening to Jackie's message.

"The authorities are saying it was suicide," she went on. "What they're not saying is that, according to an initial report by AFP, Andanson was found four-hundred miles from where he was supposed to be with a bullet hole in his left temple. He was found in his car, in a clearing in secluded woodland just north of Montpellier. The car was completely burnt out. Andanson was unrecognizable." She paused, and then added: "The AFP report has been withdrawn, by the way. They're now going with the suicide story."

"Jesus." The terrors were growing in me with every word Jackie spoke. Again I scanned around me, just in case.

"There's more," Jackie continued. "AFP are also reporting that Andanson's office at the SIPA press agency was broken into by an armed gang last night. His entire photographic archive was stolen, including presumably his portfolio of Diana, possibly even his photos of those who killed her. Whoever was behind this certainly did a thorough job."

"My God…"

"Anyway, Jon, that's all for now. Have a good flight home. I'll see you when you get back. Bye."

I hit the *End Call* button and turned to JB. "It was suicide," I heard myself say. "James Andanson committed suicide. Evidently he shot himself in the head, then threw his gun away, locked himself in his car, disposed of his keys, then set fire to himself."

"He was murdered, then," JB said.

I didn't respond. And JB didn't speak again. In fact I don't think either of us spoke again until we landed in England. We were just too numb.

34

2 Years Later, Odyssey Magazine Offices—November, 2001

The sound of the phone ringing in my office. An electronic *click-click* on the line as I picked up the receiver and pressed it to my ear. Then a short silence, followed by the faintest of crackles as the call was rerouted through GCHQ's echelon screening system and redirected via satellite back to me. All this in the space of a heartbeat.

Was it worth it? All that taxpayers' money to fund the surveillance of a 'whacko' conspiracy theorist—someone who, after all, they'd conspired to set up in the first place?

No, I didn't think so, either. But then, I wasn't the one trying to cover up the murder of a princess.

Though being back in England had made us feel a little less vulnerable, being constantly reminded that our phones were tapped was still a cause for concern. They weren't even clever about it. It had reached the point now that every time I made a call or answered the phone the electronic crackles and pops on the line were louder even than the person I was talking to. At least that's the way it seemed. Whether or not this was a deliberate ploy, of course, a form of psychological warfare designed to keep us freaked, I couldn't say for certain. But if it was, it worked. If not, then to judge by the radio-ham crackles and pops that accompanied our every call, MI5 was in serious need of some new technology.

On a positive note, we'd arrived back from our second trip to France to find that our new magazine *Odyssey* – a more straight-line investigative journal, no UFOs, no aliens – had received the green light from the new distributor we'd managed to find and was now doing well enough. Our new offices were comfortable enough, too. My office in particular – where I sat now, at my desk, answering the phone call that had just interrupted a feature I'd been working on for the past few hours – was clean and airy, and even boasted a reasonable view. All in all, it was good to be back in work—good to be earning an honest dollar again and able at least to some manageable extent to pay the bills, even though at times it seemed like I was having to share my new office with the gangsters at MI5: *click-click*.

I slapped the receiver against the heel of my hand and put it back to my ear.

"Hello?" I said, a little aggressively. "Who is this?"

A small run of several more *clicks*, then: "Jon, it's me," Katie said. "Is everything okay?"

"Oh, Katie, hi…"

"Only, you sound angry at something."

"No, no, everything's fine," I lied, narked more than intimidated at the thought of some upstart tea boy at GCHQ listening in on my private calls. "I'm just not so keen on the company we seem to be attracting these days, that's all."

"You mean the clicks on the line, don't you. Jon, I find this all really frightening. Who are they? What do they want?"

"I don't know what they want, babe. It'll be all right, though. I promise."

I could hear the alarm in Katie's voice, and it cut me to the bone. She'd been really suffering with the stress of it all lately— the financial struggles we still faced, the phone taps, the insanely long hours I'd been working in an effort to keep it all together. And the mood-swings that had plagued me as a result.

But I guess the worst thing Katie was having to deal with was my seeming obsession with finding the truth about Diana. Without me realizing, it had grown to overwhelming proportions, even to the point that I was putting the investigation, my *obsession*, before everything – my work, the kids, my wife – and Katie was the one who was having to pick up the pieces. Which wasn't fair. Katie had supported me from the very beginning, had stood by me while others had laughed, and scorned. She deserved better. And so did the kids. Trouble was, at this precise moment in time I was just too immersed to realize it.

"It'll be all right, I promise." I heard myself saying it again, as if saying it twice would somehow make it more defensible. But if anything it just made it sound more hollow. I changed the subject. "What are you doing with yourself on your day off, anyway?"

"Well at the moment I'm watching the news. Al Fayed's lawyer has just been on. The French court of appeal upheld his claim but still ruled against a second inquiry."

"Can they do that…?"

"They just did. Judge Stephan was found guilty of serious wrongdoing for failing to prosecute the paparazzi, but the verdict still stands. It was a drink-drive accident."

"Henri Paul was the lone gunman."

"Fraid so."

"Jesus. They're not even subtle about it."

A short pause, then: "Anyway," Katie said, and in a way that told me she was coming to the real point of her phone call. I braced myself. "The good news is mum can babysit for us tonight."

"Tonight…?"

"Is that a problem?"

"Well, I…"

"You did promise…"

"I know, but…" *Damn!* Katie was right. I did promise. *See if your mum can babysit*, I'd said. *We'll book a table, drink some wine, spend some quality time—together*. It had completely slipped my mind.

"Jon…?"

"I know, babe, I know. I'm sorry," I said, tripping hopelessly over my own excuses. "It's just …there's so much to do here and … I'm just so busy…"

"You're always busy. You spend more time with Diana than you do with me."

"That's ridiculous."

"Is it? I'm serious, Jon. We can't go on like this."

"Well … can we arrange for tomorrow?"

"Mum can't do tomorrow."

"The weekend, then? Saturday evening, I promise. I'll make a note—"

"I'll tell you what, Jon, make a note of this. I'll be staying at mum's tonight. I'll see you when I see you."

"What…? Katie, no, *wait*…" But it was too late. She'd already hung up.

As if to underline the fact that I'd just been dumped, MI5 hung up, too. The familiar *clicking* sound that accompanied the conclusion of all my office phone calls – my home and mobile phone calls, too – punctuated the end of the call. I slammed the phone down in its cradle, frustrated.

At which point JB came bounding through the door.

"You need to pay more attention to your love life, mate," he said, and dumped a pile of ripped-open envelopes on my desk. "Readers' letters."

"That was them again," I said, deliberately ignoring his sideways remark. "On the line. It was them."

JB raised an eyebrow and shrugged. "I can report it," he said, tongue-in-cheek. "See if we can get a trace."

"Trace MI5? Ha-ha."

"Well have you got any better ideas?"

"Yes, as a matter of fact." I stood up and threw on my jacket. "I'll go and talk to them face to face," I said. "At least that way we cut out the middle man."

That said, I stormed out the office and headed for Hyde Park.

"I did tell you your number was on file," Lacey said, as if this would make everything all right. "You can't say I didn't warn you."

"No. But surprisingly that doesn't make me feel any better. Do you realize what it's like being watched by faceless spooks all the time? Being followed everywhere, having your every conversation monitored and recorded? Not being able to talk about it to anyone because they'll think you're a paranoid idiot? I mean, for Chris' sake. It's gone beyond a joke, Lacey. It's no longer funny."

"Well you know what they say, Jon. If you want the wheel to stop spinning, stop peddling."

"That's not what I wanted to hear."

We were standing on Serpentine Bridge, Hyde Park's impressive artificial lake stretching out before us, Kensington Gardens hiving at our back. I cast a glance across my shoulder, and in the near distance, through the trees, I could just make out the majesty of Kensington Palace, where Diana had spent her life as a wife and mother, as a divorcee: as a princess. A palace on the outside, she'd once told friends, a prison on the inside: the place, ultimately, where her coffin had spent the night before her funeral at Westminster Abbey, more than four years ago now. I could hardly believe it. Four years of lies, spies and cover-ups, and an ever-growing obsession to uncover the truth behind her death. *My obsession.*

And throughout that time Katie had borne the burden of it all.

I sucked in a deep, heavy breath and held it for several heartbeats. When I released it again my shoulders sagged. "It's really started to affect my personal life," I said, calmer now, more resigned. "The kids hardly recognize me these days. My wife hardly sees me anymore, and when she does I'm usually too involved or ... or too tired ... well, you know. It's just, if I'd known at the start of all this what I know now I would never have—"

"Don't be so sure about that," Lacey cut in. "It's in your nature, Jon. No doubt that's why you were selected. They would have profiled you well in advance." He turned and caught my eye. "The American, as you call him, he knew when he fed you the information that you'd act on it. That's why he told *you* and not someone else."

"When he *fed* me the information? When I was *selected*? What are you saying?"

"More than I should."

"Are you saying I was set up? But … why? Why would they want to tell me their secrets in advance? It doesn't make sense."

"It's not supposed to, not yet."

"Lacey you're starting to creep me out. I can't take much more of this, and neither can my family."

"You should have thought of that before you decided to write a book about it. It's too late now, Jon. You're in too deep." He added: "But you do have one thing in your favour."

"And what's that?"

"They need you—alive. That's why they keep such a close eye on you. It's when the surveillance stops you'll need to start worrying." He threw a brief glance at a man standing on the road below us, on the water's edge. He was in his thirties, dressed in bomber jacket and jeans and seemed intermittently to touch his hand to his ear, like he was listening to music on a walkman. Lacey knew different. "If it's any consolation, I can assure you you're causing them more of a headache than they're causing you," he said, tipping his head towards the man, discreetly, so as to point him out to me without him realizing. "Ask him."

I threw a discreet glance down at the man below. The realization that I was looking at an MI5 surveillance spook, that once again they'd known in advance of my meeting with Lacey and had turned up to monitor it, made me feel sick. How did they always know? "Did you tell them about our meeting?" I put to Lacey.

"Of course not," he said with a touch of irony. "You did."

Stupid question. Of course I did. I'd arranged the meeting on the phone a couple of days previously, and they'd obviously been listening in. Again I felt sick. "I just wish I'd never met the American," I said. "I wish none of this had ever happened."

"Yes, well, foreknowledge doesn't always come with twenty-twenty vision, does it. You of all people should know that." Again he turned and caught my eye, as though to emphasize what he was about to say next. "Listen, Jon, if you take my advice you'll hang in there. You may not get the public inquiry you're pushing for, but you may yet force an investigation, and that would likely result in a judicial inquest. A jury, Jon. It would mean the coroner would be forced to appoint a jury. It's your best hope."

"You really thinks that's possible?"

"It won't be easy. But yes, it's possible. That's the other reason they're still showing such a keen interest in you."

I thought about this for a moment, and even though I felt like a fly in a spider's web, unable to move, or even breathe, without the spider knowing about it, I had to confess the possibility of forcing the government to order an investigation did make it seem somehow worthwhile.

The only downer was still that my marriage was on the line because of it.

Again I sucked in a deep breath, and refocused my mind on the primary reason I'd arranged to meet Lacey again after all this time. Until now the possibility that Diana might have been pregnant when she died had been off-menu; we'd so far found no real evidence and had thus paid the possibility little heed. Recently, however, we'd got word that the pregnancy theory might just hold some liquid.

"When we first spoke about this you said Diana was pregnant," I said to Lacey, and noticed the guy down below us touch his hand to his ear again.

Lacey noticed him, too. "Did I?" he said.

"I received a message from someone, a student doctor. He said his lecturer knew Diana's nutritional guru. He said they both knew she was pregnant."

"If you're fishing for motive, Jon, you're casting the wrong line. Whether or not she was pregnant is neither here nor there.

Fact is, she didn't need to be pregnant. The possibility that she could have fallen pregnant at any time was motive enough."

"You mean because she would've fallen pregnant with a Muslim child?"

"Something like that."

"Who gave the order to embalm her?"

"I can't tell you that."

"But you do know she was embalmed illegally, and that the embalming process made it impossible for pathologists to ascertain whether she was pregnant?"

Lacey didn't answer.

"Who was it, Lacey? Who gave the order?"

"I've told you, I can't tell you that."

"Can't? Or won't?"

Lacey's expression soured at this point, his eyes seeming to narrow, his mouth tightening as it always did when he felt he'd said more than perhaps he should have. He glanced down at the guy in the bomber jacket and jeans, who threw a sideways glance back up at Lacey before turning and wandering on along the road. At length Lacey turned back my way and fixed on me.

"Listen, Jon," he said. "A lot has happened in these past four years. There are some very powerful people involved in this. Be careful. They know who you are and they know what you know."

"I thought you just said they need me—*alive*."

"I can help you this one last time," he told me, ignoring what I'd just said. "I can give you a lead. But beyond that, I'm afraid there's little more I can do."

35

Richard Mason's Office, MI6 Headquarters, London

It wasn't only me and JB who were back in the country. Mason was back, too, ensconced once more in his seat of power at MI6's Vauxhall Bridge headquarters. Much of his day-to-day work, though, still involved him covering the tracks he'd left behind in Paris four years earlier—cleaning up the mess he'd made there: making sure it stayed there.

Which is why the agent there with him now, standing at one end of the sprawling smoke-glass table claiming centre-stage in Mason's minimalist, space-age office, was briefing him on the latest known whereabouts and activities of one Richard Tomlinson. The agent's name was Wilkinson.

"I fear he's too close in and too well-known for us to close the contract on him, sir," Wilkinson said. "I think a deal is our best option."

"Another deal?" Mason wasn't convinced by that. "Tomlinson's not a man we can trust," he pointed out, no trace of emotion in his voice at all. "He's leaked information before. We paid him a large sum of money and set him up in a job many others would have died for in return for his silence, and he bleated."

"Yes, sir."

"Most of what he says is deniable, of course. But that's not the point. He's already presented himself to one inquiry. If, God forbid, a British investigation is launched, what's to say he won't repeat the exercise? What's to say he won't try and expose us again, if only to get his own back?"

"For that precise reason, sir, I think a deal is the way forward." Wilkinson laid the folder he was carrying on the table in front of him and snapped it open so that he could read from the notes he'd prepared. "If I may, sir?"

"Go on."

As Wilkinson proceeded to deliver his report, Mason turned and gazed dispassionately out the window at London and its time-dirtied river some 200 feet below, his hands clasped firmly behind his back. His body language betrayed his displeasure. If it was up to him, and him alone, he would order the contract closed on Tomlinson with immediate effect. A simple accident would suffice, somewhere discreet. That way they could deal with the traitor permanently, once and for good. But he knew there were times when even he had to listen to reason. And this was one of them.

"The deal you refer to, sir," Wilkinson began, "was when Tomlinson was living in Spain in nineteen-ninety-six, a year after he left the service. As you rightly point out, we secured him a fifteen-thousand pound loan and a lucrative marketing position with the Stewart Formula One racing team. In return, Tomlinson pledged not to reveal in-house protocols or operational secrets, but as you also pointed out, he reneged on that pledge. He bleated. The recent publication of his book, *The Big Breach*, contained several instances of confidentiality violation, although in truth it didn't actually reveal anything an avid reader of spy novels wouldn't already have known."

"Quite. But that's hardly the point." Mason unclasped his hands and pocketed them, but continued to gaze out on London. "Anyway, it's not his book I'm worried about, Wilkinson. It's what he knows about the Paris operation that remains our primary cause for concern."

"Yes, sir. I'm just coming to that."

Wilkinson turned the page.

Following his humiliation at the hands of Judge Hervé Stephan in Paris, Wilkinson reported, Tomlinson fled to Switzerland. But his stay was cut short by the Swiss authorities who, wishing to avoid a diplomatic *contretemps* with Britain and MI6, promptly threw him out. Tomlinson then caught the first plane home to New Zealand and spent several months there, in the place of his birth, and several more in Australia, before finally returning to Europe. There he spent brief spells in Germany and Italy before eventually moving to the French Riviera, where he was currently working as a yacht broker with a company called BCR Yachts. Between times he'd been refused entry into the United States (where he'd been detained by US customs officials on arrival and, at Mason's intervention, had been interrogated by the CIA) and on his release had slipped quietly – and briefly – into Russia for the publication of his book.

He'd then headed back to France.

Amid all this international border-hopping Tomlinson had taken great pains to sidestep the attentions of his former employers at MI6. The last thing he'd wanted was Mason coming at him like a wounded rhino, especially as more recently Tomlinson had been framed for releasing the so-called *Alpha List*—an ostensibly damaging list of alleged MI6 officers arranged in alphabetic order. The list had found its way onto the internet by way of US news magazine, *Executive Intelligence Review*, and although Tomlinson had in fact had nothing to do with its release, the singular fact that MI6 I/Ops had mooted his name in connection with the leak had given Mason sufficient grounds to hunt him down and have him extradited back to Britain to face the music. Mason's music.

Which was why Tomlinson was currently lying low.

"As we know, sir," Wilkinson concluded, "the Alpha List was a hot cake. But although Tomlinson wasn't responsible for its release, it's still something we can use as leverage in any deal we may decide to offer him."

"Where exactly is he now?" Mason wanted to know.

"Cote d'Azur, sir, just outside Cannes. We have a team on him."

For a brief moment Mason pondered Wilkinson's assertion that a new deal should be offered to Tomlinson to keep him quiet about Diana and the 'Paris Affair'. At length he said: "So what exactly do you propose we offer him?"

"Immunity, sir." There was no easy way of saying it, Wilkinson had known that. So he'd just come right up front with it. The backlash he was about to receive was expected, and instant.

"Immunity?" Mason growled, simultaneously snapping his gaze back from London and jerking it round to eyeball the man who'd just uttered the unutterable. "Are you seeking a swift demotion, Wilkinson, or planning an early retirement? Because either can be arranged."

"No, sir. But in the event that a British investigation *is* launched, as you say, and a judicial inquest results, we have to prevent Tomlinson saying more than he already has. We need somehow to make him dilute even that much. Given that elimination is off the menu, a deal seems the only reasonable option."

"But immunity?" Again Mason swung his gaze out the window at London. "That means he could walk the streets of this city again without being arrested or prosecuted."

"Yes, sir."

"We would be a laughing stock, Wilkinson."

"More than that, sir. There are other considerations."

This time as Mason retrieved his gaze and gave it back to Wilkinson it narrowed to the width of a sharpened razor. "Other considerations?" he said.

"I'm afraid so, sir. We would need to unfreeze his assets and issue an apology for his mistreatment."

"An apology...?"

"Yes, sir. Of course, this is only in the event that a jury is used at the inquest. In any other event we can just leave him to rot in France."

For at least half a minute Mason said nothing, but pocketed his hands again and paced. It was more than four years since the Paris operation, he was thinking to himself, and by now everything should have been done and dusted. The French Inquiry should have expunged all possible doubts and closed the book on the matter, period. And so it would have done had it not been for Tomlinson bleating about MI6 involvement in Diana's death and that man King being suckered into the game by some Tom Fool plan conjured up by the CIA. Bloody Americans should have kept their noses out of it. Their part was purely logistics and support, and that should have been the sum of it. Of course, there were other conspiracy theorists out there claiming assassination, but the difference here was that King was part of the web. He was one of the team; he'd been set up, duped and used as a pawn in a stupid, elaborate and unnecessary subplot, and now there was every chance the subplot was about to backfire. Not that King had uncovered any smoking-gun evidence, of course; no, that wasn't the worry. Mason was far too skilled and experienced to have allowed that to happen. But the fact King had been used from the outset to propagate the 'assassination theory' did give his account added substance. It gave him, and what he had to say, more weight, more leverage with the public—even more so now that Tomlinson's public bleating had tended to endorse King's argument and make it sound more convincing. He pursed his lips. Yes, Tomlinson had to be silenced, one way or the other, he realized. But despite Wilkinson's reasoning, offering the traitor a deal would happen only as a last resort, and never so long as he remained in charge.

Meantime he would have a quiet word with the CIA about further dissuading the conspiracy theorist, King.

"That will be all," Mason suddenly said to Wilkinson as he paused by the window and again turned his gaze on London "I'll deal with things from here on in."

"Sir." Wilkinson sensed, rightly, that he'd failed in convincing his boss that a deal should be offered to Tomlinson, and he knew there was no point restating his case. Not now. Of course, the time would come when such a deal would indeed be struck—when Tomlinson would indeed be granted immunity from prosecution and have his assets unfrozen by MI6 on condition he discontinued in speaking about the 'Paris Affair', and all other MI6 operations. Much to Mason's chagrin, MI6 would also offer Tomlinson a public apology.

But as Wilkinson realized, that time was not yet.

Gathering up his notes from off the table Wilkinson turned and left the room.

A few moments later Mason picked up the phone. "CIA, London" he said. "Paris liaison. I need to arrange a meeting."

36

The message reached us via email, anonymously.

It read: *I am a final year medical student. My tutor is a friend of Diana's nutritional guru, one of Harley Street's elite practitioners. If you want proof that Diana was pregnant when she died, you should speak to him.*

End of message.

I read it again: *If you want proof that Diana was pregnant when she died, you should speak to him.*

The medical student in question had posted a comment on one of several online forums we were running on the death of Diana. The forums were all part of our effort to force a public inquiry—to gather signatures for our online petition, which we intended to deliver to Downing Street, or Scotland Yard, or both, if a British investigation failed to materialize. The student had also stated in his post that he had some information that he didn't wish to post on a public forum, so I sent him my email address and the above message formed the main thrust of his reply. It piqued my interest, not only because it seemed to suggest Diana might have been pregnant at the time of her death. But because it also contained evidence of a cover-up, as follows:

The name of the Harley Street practitioner is Roderick Lane. My tutor said that just prior to Diana's Mediterranean holiday with Dodi Fayed she visited Mr Lane for nutritional advice. She feared she was pregnant. Shortly after her visit Mr Lane's clinic was broken into and his computer was stolen. Diana's personal records were stored on the computer. It seems someone didn't want the world to know about the baby.

I telephoned Roderick Lane. No joy. He flatly denied that his office had been broken into and refused to talk about Princess Diana. In the meantime JB spoke to the contact Lacey had given me at our last meeting in Hyde Park—well-known investigative journalist and independent television producer, David Campbell, evidently a personal friend of Roderick Lane. During the conversation Campbell inadvertently let slip that, *yes*, he'd been made aware of the break-in but, *no*, he didn't believe "it had anything to do with Princess Diana's visit". *Bingo!* Despite Lane's denials it seemed the break-in probably had occurred, after all. We were on to something, then. We went to see Roderick Lane.

It turned out Mr Lane's clinic wasn't actually on Harley Street, but New Cavendish Street, which intersected Harley Street from Tottenham Court Road. Like most other Harley Street clinics, surgeries and medical facilities it was housed in one of the area's typically Georgian-styled mansions, with their customary rectangular sash windows and parapets that gave the illusion of a flat roof. Owned by the superrich De Walden dynasty, one of the UK's wealthiest families, the Harley Street Estate, together with the surrounding Marylebone Village, was worth billions. Indeed, the average person's entire annual salary would scarcely have covered the booking fee for most of these exclusive health parlours, much less pay for the treatments they offered. But mercifully that wasn't why we were here. We were here to question one of this elite community's more high-profile members about one of its more high-profile clients, Princess Diana.

Had she been pregnant when she died? Had she confided in Roderick Lane? Would he tell us if she had?

These were the thoughts foremost in my mind as, by some twist of irony, we passed by the Royal College of Midwives on our left as we made our way along Mansfield Street on approach to New Cavendish Street and Roderick Lane's clinic. The oak-panelled front door that confronted us on our arrival was impressive and imposing, and for a beat and two more we simply stood there, staring at the door, its solid façade, its engraved bronze plaque, wondering if we'd made the right decision to come here at all, much less to turn up unannounced and expect to be seen. I turned to JB and gave him that look that said *Ready?* He nodded, affirmative.

I pushed the door open and we stepped inside, and were greeted by a traditionally furnished reception area supervised by a traditionally humpy receptionist.

"Good morning. Can I help you?" The receptionist didn't look at me as she spoke, but squinted slightly off to one side, as though addressing an imaginary parrot on my shoulder. Everything about her seemed fake, even her pimped-up accent.

"We'd like to see Roderick Lane," I said.

"I see. One moment…" She ran her finger down the long list of names in the appointment book. "…Your name?"

"It's King. Jon King. I'm afraid we don't have an appointment."

"Oh, I see. Are you clients?"

"No, not exactly. But we've spoken to Mr Lane on the phone."

"You'll have to make an appointment, I'm afraid."

"Well, couldn't we just…? I mean … we've come a long way, you see, and … we only want a minute or two of his time. If you could just let him know we're here…?"

Just then, as luck would have it, a door opened midway along the corridor that led off from reception and a man in office shirt and tie stepped out, reading notes. For a man closing on forty he looked in good shape.

"Mr Lane…?" As he neared reception I made a point of stepping in front of him and offering my hand to ensure he couldn't sidestep me. I didn't know if this *was* Roderick Lane, of course, but I was running on instinct at this point. As it turned out, my instincts were right. "My name's Jon King. You might remember we spoke on the phone…?"

The man didn't answer, not right away. But he did stop in his tracks and look me up and down, like he was viewing an unwanted curiosity. *Who is this man? What does he want?* "On the phone?" he said, finally. "Mr King…?"

"Yes. And this is my colleague, John Beveridge. If you recall, we're investigating the death of Princess Diana. We understand she was one of your clients."

"Well, I…"

"We were told she came to see you just prior to her Mediterranean holiday with Dodi Fayed."

"Well, as I'm sure I would have told you on the phone, if she did I'm afraid it's none of your business."

"Our source said she came to see you because she thought she might have been pregnant—"

"Who told you this?"

"—And she wanted nutritional advice."

"Sophie?" He turned to the receptionist.

"I'm sorry, Mr Lane," Sophie said, flustered. "I did try…"

He turned back to me. "Mr King, you can't just barge in like this."

"Did Diana tell you she was pregnant?" I demanded to know.

"What the princess may or may not have said is confidential."

"So she *did* visit you, then?"

"As I just said, that is confidential information. Now if you don't mind I'll have to ask you to leave." Again he turned to the receptionist. "Sophie, would you show these gentlemen out, please."

"No, wait! Please, Mr Lane…"

He'd already turned his back on me and was now headed off along the corridor, back the way he'd come. I swung a glance at JB, who shrugged, as if to say *I guess that's it, then; I guess we'd better leave*. But something inside me snapped in that moment. Perhaps it was all the dead ends we'd encountered over the past four years, or the strain of being watched and followed and duped and manipulated. Could even have been my personal life catching up with me, as Katie and I were still struggling to keep it all together under the stress. Who knows? Maybe I'd just clambered out the wrong side of bed that morning. But whatever it was, it caused something in me to snap, and I found myself chasing Roderick Lane along the corridor, glued to the man's heels like a hound on a hare.

"Jon!" JB yelled, but I was already on my way.

"Could you at least confirm that your office was broken into following the princess's visit?" I shouted at Roderick Lane's back. "Mr Lane...?"

He just kept walking.

"Your computer was stolen, wasn't it—"

No response.

"—The one containing the record of Diana's visit?"

Still no response.

"They feared she could have been pregnant and they wanted to destroy the evidence before the press got hold of it, didn't they?"

Finally we reached the door to Roderick Lane's office, where he stopped, suddenly, and swung round to face me. His eyes were narrow and searching, as though trying to figure me out. *How do you know all this? Who told you? Where did you get this information?*

"Please, Mr Lane. Whatever the princess told you, whatever she confided in you, it could be crucial in helping to establish the truth about her death. The *truth*, Mr Lane."

It was at this point that the inquisitive look in Roderick Lane's eyes darkened to one of veiled terror. He was too frightened to confront that truth. "The princess died in an accident, Mr King," he said. "A simple, tragic accident. Now if you'll excuse me I have other clients to attend to."

That said, Roderick Lane turned and shuffled into his office, closing the door behind him.

"Well handled, Jon," JB said with pointed sarcasm as we made our way back along New Cavendish Street towards Harley Street Car Park, where we'd left the car. The way he was striding out told me he wasn't in the best of moods. "What the hell got into you?"

"I'm sick of being palmed off, JB. He was hiding something."

"You don't know that."

"Well he must have known about the break-in, about his computer being stolen. He must have suspected something."

"Why?"

"Because just prior to the break-in Diana had been to see him. That's why we're here, remember? His computer was stolen, the one containing Diana's personal file—the one containing the answer to whether or not she was pregnant. He must have known."

"Maybe he just didn't want to talk about it."

"What…?"

"He probably thinks it's a coincidence—"

"Some coincidence…"

"—And that we're just a couple of conspiracy nuts jumping to crazy conclusions."

"Are you serious?" I halted, sharply, grabbed JB's arm and swung him round to face me. "Is that what *you* think, too?"

"I sometimes wonder." He snatched his arm free from my grasp. "There are ways of doing things, Jon. Jumping on him like that is not one of them. It got us nowhere."

"Well how would you have gone about it?"

"Not like that."

I wanted to say: *Well what the hell else was I supposed to do? The guy wasn't talking. Nobody's talking. There's a massive cover-up in place and everyone's too scared to say anything.* But I didn't say any of those things. Instead I simply stood there, searching JB's eyes for some measure of empathy, understanding, support: but there was none—just this cold, hard stare that told me he believed he was right.

And of course he was. I'd overreacted. I'd let things get the better of me and I'd lost control. And as JB had just said, it had got us nowhere.

"Okay, you're right," I said, finally, not wanting to admit it but having nowhere else to take it. I let go a frustrated breath. "I should have done it differently."

"I know." A lingering look from JB, just long enough that I was left in no doubt – he was right, I was wrong – and then he turned and started across the road ahead of me, towards Chandos Street and Harley Street Car Park. "Come on," he said. "We can stop by Canary Wharf on the way back, call in on Darren Adams and see him about the book serialization."

Call in on Darren Adams and see him about the book serialization.

I started after JB. At least this day would give up something worthwhile, I told myself as I followed him across the road and back towards the car park. At least Darren would want to talk to us—wouldn't he?

•

Half an hour or so later we pulled into the underground car park on Canary Wharf, home to much of the nation's tabloid press, including the *Sunday Mirror* offices where we were hoping to catch Darren Adams. Darren, of course, was a news reporter with the *Sunday Mirror*, someone I'd known now for six or seven years, someone with whom I'd exchanged leads, tips, stories, and who'd been my main 'Fleet Street' contact ever since my days as editor of *UFO Reality*. As JB had reminded me as we'd made our way back to the car from Roderick Lane's clinic around half an hour earlier, our book was finally on its way from America. It was due to arrive here next week (two years late, I might add, but that was another story), and the *Sunday Mirror* had agreed to serialize it. Which for us was a coup. Even though, somehow, we'd managed to secure a deal with an independent UK distributor, there was still no publisher here willing even to look at the book, much less license it for publication in the UK. Which meant we had no corporate publicity machine to tell everyone it had arrived. So when Darren managed to persuade his editor that our story would sell his newspaper we were made up, to say the least. Not that his editor had needed much persuading, by all accounts. Quite the opposite: *the hottest story since Squidgygate*, he'd coined it. He'd even instructed Darren to run a feature on us to run alongside the serialization, so keen was he for the story. Indeed, we'd spent the best part of the last twelve months trying to keep him at bay as we'd waited and waited for the book to finally arrive—constant phone calls, lunches, meetings, at which he'd tried desperately to convince us to let them run with the story *now*. We'd said no, and no again. Not until the book arrived. We wanted the story to make waves, we'd told him, and we felt that running the feature prior to the book's arrival would lessen its impact. Thankfully he'd listened to reason.

But now the book was finally here there would be no further prevaricating. The feature would appear in this Sunday's paper. The serialization would begin the week after that.

Next Sunday, Darren had said when I'd spoken to him a couple of days ago. *Barring World War Three breaking out and snatching all the headlines, the feature will be next Sunday's lead story, front page.* He'd added: *You'd better tell your distributor to be well prepared, coz you're gonna sell a lot of books.*

Needless to say we were elated, more than a little apprehensive, as well. We knew, of course, that coverage on a national scale like this would publicize not only the book, but also our call for a public inquiry into Diana's death. As we approached the *Sunday Mirror* offices, standing tall and gleaming there among the other sky-scraping office blocks on Canary Wharf, I couldn't help but feel the tingle of anticipation running through my veins.

On reaching the giant-sized glass-panel doors at the foot of the Trinity Mirror skyscraper I hit the button on the intercom and waited for a reply.

Then: "Sunday Mirror," the female voice came back, almost immediately. "Can I help?"

"I'd like to speak to Darren Adams," I said. "News desk. It's Jon King"

"One moment."

In the short space of time it took the receptionist to put me through, a strange sense of foreboding came over me, like a dark cloud descending on an otherwise sunny day. It felt heavy, almost sinister. Why was I suddenly feeling like this?

"Jon," the male voice said on the intercom. "It's Darren. How can I help?" His tone was unusually short, unwelcoming, unlike the Darren Adams I'd come to know: unlike the Darren Adams I'd spoken to only two days before.

"I just thought I'd drop by and offer to buy you that pint," I said, throwing a slightly puzzled glance at JB – *what's wrong with Darren?* – while at the same time endeavouring to keep the conversation upbeat. "I'm with JB. We were in town and we thought it might be a good idea to touch base prior to the story coming out next Sunday. A good excuse for a drink if nothing else."

"I see. Actually I'm quite busy at the moment, Jon— deadlines, you know how it is."

"Too busy for a quick pint?"

"I'm afraid so, yes."

"Oh, right, well … no problem…"

"Maybe next time."

"Next time, yeah, sure..." An awkward silence fell, one that only added to the growing sense of unease I was undoubtedly feeling. At length: "Well … listen, the book will be here in a couple of days," I said, endeavouring to smooth out the silence. "Maybe I'll drop by and bring you a copy then?"

No reply.

"Darren …?"

"I'm still here."

"Well, what's the problem? I take it the deal's still on? I take it you still want the exclusive?"

"That might prove difficult, I'm afraid, Jon."

"What? But you've been chasing us for the past twelve months. I thought it was a done deal?"

"It was, but … look, I'm sorry, Jon. Orders from above."

"Above? What's that supposed to mean?"

"Exactly what it says." Another short silence before Darren could bring himself to explain. And even when he did, he did so stutteringly. "Listen, Jon, I … I'm not supposed to tell you this…"

"What? Tell me what…?"

"I'm afraid you've been D-Noticed."

"D-Noticed…?" I was stunned. Being a magazine editor myself I'd had some experience of the D-Notice, or what had recently been rechristened the DA-Notice, though most journalists still referred to it by its former name. Simply put, and despite its official designation as an 'advisory notice', a DA-Notice was an official government warning issued to media editors and producers, preventing them from publishing or broadcasting material the government didn't want published or broadcast. Evidently our book fell into that category. "But that's ridiculous," I said. "How can the government issue a DA-Notice when the book hasn't even arrived yet?"

"I'm sorry, Jon, but that's the way it is."

"But … on what grounds?"

"I think you know that, Jon. DA-Notice Five, United Kingdom Intelligence and Security Services—"

"And *Special Services*, whatever the hell they are," I heard myself say.

"—And Special Services, exactly. It prevents us publishing information that the government fears might compromise covert operations and those involved in them. Need I say more?"

"But surely that's an admission that the crash was a covert operation. By D-Noticing our book they're admitting involvement in Diana's death."

"What they're doing, Jon, is preventing us from running the feature and serializing the book."

"Yes, but…"

"I'm afraid that's the bottom line, Jon. That's just the way it is. Now, look … I'd really better go. We'll catch up soon."

With that the intercom died. And almost, so did I.

I virtually crawled home that night, not because I was drunk, although God knows the idea of consuming a little too much alcohol seemed very appealing as I trudged up the garden path, turned the key to the front door and stepped inside. Katie would be in bed, I was pretty sure of that, so I closed the door and slipped through to the kitchen as noiselessly as I could. I didn't even turn the lights on. Knowing the reception I would receive for being home late, *again*, I didn't want to wake Katie up. Just couldn't face another confrontation. Not now. Not after what had transpired in the past few hours. I was simply too exhausted. I felt winded, battle-scarred, and no less pissed off that yet again JB and I had been turned over by the *powers-that-be*—powers bigger and stronger than both of us. It felt like we'd been turned over and shaken until the entire contents of our pockets had emptied on the ground, and there seemed precious little we could do about it.

And that was the worst thing: knowing there was no means of recourse, no way of punching the bully back except by remaining resolute. By keeping on. By not giving in. Which for the past four years, of course, was precisely what we'd done. Tonight, though, I felt like nothing more in the world than turning my back and walking away: *giving in*.

Instead I sat myself down at my computer and sipped the coffee I'd just made. It burned my tongue.

Despite the fact that Roderick Lane – like pretty much everyone else we'd spoken to – had refused to cooperate; and despite, too, the *Sunday Mirror's* sudden and unexpected U-turn, we still had a book to promote and a lecture tour to organize, and I'd promised our PR, Mark, that I would have a press release ready for him the following day. Since raising the finance to fund the new magazine, Mark had become a pivotal part of our team, not only as magazine proprietor, but also as our campaign manager—running the promotional campaign JB and I had planned for the book's arrival in the UK, a campaign that had already seen us interviewed on all the major radio and TV shows in the country, and which would soon involve us travelling the length and breadth of Britain, giving talks and signing books. I was tired, dog tired. It was closing on midnight. But I'd promised Mark I'd have the press release ready and I didn't want to let him down. Taking another sip at my hot coffee I opened up a Word document and started to type.

I'd barely written the first paragraph when the light splashed on and virtually blinded me.

"You're back then," Katie said, suddenly standing there by my office door, looking anything but pleased to see me. She'd just switched the main light on.

Startled, I spun round on my chair and almost knocked what was left of my coffee crashing to the floor. "Katie," I said, squinting through the bright light suddenly abusing my eyes. "You made me jump."

"What are you doing?"

"Oh, I … I'm just polishing up the press release for the book."

"At midnight?"

"Mark's waiting for it."

"*I'm* waiting for *you*. I've been waiting for you for the past four hours. What happened this time?"

I had no answer.

"You missed Rosie's bed time—*again*."

"I know, I…"

"You missed mine, too."

"I'm sorry, babe. It's just … the conference is coming up, the book tour … we need to be up to speed."

Katie didn't respond, not verbally. But the look in her eye told me she was more disappointed with my excuse than angry with it. Which made me feel worse.

"Look, Katie, please … it's important…"

"To who, Jon? Important to who?"

"To me, to us. To everyone, including Rosie."

"Rosie?"

"Yes, Rosie."

Katie considered this for a moment. But only for a moment. Her eyes were by now raw with tears. "My guess is she'd rather have you kiss her goodnight," she said, then turned and left me alone, shutting the door firmly behind her.

"Katie…"

I should have gone after her, should have followed her out of my office and told her I was sorry, that I loved her, that she was more important to me than this stupid Diana thing: than *anything*.

But I didn't. Instead I turned my attention back to my computer and took up where I'd left off writing the damned press release. That's how obsessed I'd become.

37

Vietnam had been hell. The heat, the paranoia, the madness; the fever and the dysentery and the ever-present stench of 'jungle rot'—the open sores and tropical ulcers that lacerated your feet after six days and nights out on patrol, without a break. Sometimes longer.

The constant fear of being captured. And tortured. Of dying a slow, excruciating death in the dungeons of the Hanoi Hilton, the famed North Vietnamese torture facility where so many of his buddies had met an untimely end.

The leaches. The mosquitoes. The fear of stepping on a mine.

Or on a snake's tail. Most of the snakes in Vietnam were as lethal as any Viet Cong sniper, after all, as deadly as any enemy ambush or booby trap. As his unit commander had once wisecracked, the ones that didn't bite simply crushed you to death. And he'd never quite known which – venom or asphyxiation – he would have plumbed for, given the choice.

Lighting a cigarette he exited the American Embassy and made his way mindfully through London's mid-morning drizzle towards Grosvenor Gate and Park Lane. The drizzle was cool on his skin, a far cry from the sweat and the swamp rash that had stung his face in Nam's My Lai Jungle, he mused. And then again in Ha Long Bay. Quite why these memories of his days – weeks, months, years – in Vietnam had resurfaced in him on this dull, winter's day he had no idea. But as he paused at Grosvenor Gate to hail a passing cab they played on his mind like an old-school newsreel, no denying that. Stubbing out his cigarette underfoot he climbed in the back of the cab, and his memories climbed in with him.

His first tour of Vietnam had been as a regular special forces soldier with America's Green Berets. In all he'd spent more than two years with this elite fighting force—training South Vietnamese troops to kill their communist neighbours, rescuing downed American helicopter pilots from behind enemy lines, carrying out guerrilla incursions deep in enemy territory. He'd been decorated no less than five times during this period. He'd also witnessed more horrors than any one person should.

But it was what had occurred during his fourth, possibly his fifth, tour of war-ravaged Vietnam – he'd been there so many times, and witnessed so many horrors, he could scarcely remember which – that had shaped his life so indelibly. It was during this tour that he'd been selected out and transferred to the highly secret MACV-SOG (Military Assistance Command, Vietnam-Studies and Observation Group). This was the elite CIA-US Army Special Forces unit the American government had crafted specifically to carry out its covert missions in Laos and Cambodia—places the American military was not supposed to be. It had proved his introduction to the darker side of unconventional warfare, to covert and deniable operations—and ultimately to the agency for whom he would work for the rest of his days: the CIA.

Throwing a glance out the cab window as they drove along Victoria Embankment he caught sight of a river cruiser ferrying Japanese tourists from Blackfriars Pier to the Tower of London. The image was strangely evocative, and for an instant there Old Father Thames became the Mekong River, flowing red with Cambodian blood. It was a memory he would never erase.

"Not far now, guv," the cabbie turned and said across his shoulder. "Just up past the Tower and on through Limehouse. East India you wanted, wasn't it?"

"A place called Trinity Buoy Wharf at East India Docks, yes."

"I know it. Be there in no time."

"Oh, there's no rush," the American said. "The person I'm meeting is of no consequence. He can wait."

Not knowing quite how to respond to this remark the cabbie gave a slightly bemused look in his rear-view mirror, then sent his eyes back to the road ahead. He didn't speak again.

In the back of the cab, the American flipped open his silver Zippo lighter and lit up another cigarette.

For over half his life, in one capacity or another, he'd been a CIA runner. Still was, of course, although these days he was more messenger than mercenary, more ambassador than assassin. With age comes temperance, someone once said, temperance and insight. And this had surely been the case with the American. The agency he'd been so proud to serve, he'd come to realize, had long since been hijacked by the gangsters who ran the oil companies, the banks, the pharmaceuticals: *big business*. His loyalty to the cause, to the government it served – to *democracy* – had seemed suddenly to make less sense, to the point that a measure of cynicism now shaped his opinions, disenchantment even, where before he'd known only duty. Oh, he still worked for *The Company*, of course, still skivvied for the CIA; well what else was he supposed to do, now, at his age, closing on sixty-five? But at least these days he was less a soldier in the CIA's unseen wars than a mover in the games they played, and the fact that he was warmed him. Compared to the things he'd seen and done in Vietnam, and in other places since – in the Congo, Rwanda, Angola – his assignments now were, for the most part, measured. He could live with that.

They were easier, too, and his current mission was no exception. A British princess had been taken out and he'd been assigned to set-up a little-known conspiracy journalist in the ensuing cover-up, simple. Or at least it should have been. To judge by the call he'd received earlier that day from one of his cousins over at MI6, however, it seemed said journalist had become more of a nuisance than they'd anticipated he ever would. Still, it was nothing he couldn't take care of. The biggest problem in the equation wasn't the journalist, it was the MI6 faggot who'd sanctioned his plan to set the journalist up in the first place, one

Richard Mason, a man with whom the American had crossed swords one too many times in the past.

He was about cross swords with him again, now—the very reason he was on his way to meet him.

38

JB and I were on our way to meet Steve O'Brien, a graphic artist and computer program developer. Steve was a friend of ours who'd offered to design a 3-D animation of Diana's crash based on Professor Murray McKay's computer-generated model, the one he'd shown JB and I when we'd interviewed him at his office at Birmingham University some years before. We wanted to compare the sequence of events that had led to the crash to those of another, similar crash that we'd recently been made aware of. By chance, a friend of JB's had just read a book written by world famous explorer, Sir Ranulph Fiennes. A former SAS officer himself, Fiennes had penned a novel called *The Feather Men* in which he'd recounted the assassinations of four SAS officers, including that of Major Michael Marman—who, Fiennes revealed, had been killed in a staged car crash. Like former SAS Sergeant Dave Cornish, whom I'd known since my teenage years and whom I'd interviewed over a game of snooker some years previously, Fiennes too had referred to the crash as the 'Boston Brakes'. The correlation had sounded my in-built alarm.

"We believe the car crash that killed Princess Diana could have been a Boston Brakes operation," I'd put to Sir Ranulph on the telephone, having obtained his number from Darren Adams at the *Sunday Mirror*. Though Darren was unable to serialize our book, he was nonetheless more than capable of coming up with the odd famous person's contact number, for which I was eternally grateful. "Would you agree?"

"I can't honestly say I've ever thought about it," Sir Ranulph said.

I didn't believe him. "In your book, The Feather Men, you explain in some detail how a professional hit squad was hired to carry out high-profile assassinations."

"Yes, it happens all the time."

"You specifically cite the Boston Brakes as a known method of assassination, whereby the target vehicle is taken over by remote control and crashed at high speed."

"Correct."

"And you say that this method was used to assassinate one of the SAS officers featured in your book."

"Major Michael Marman, yes. But you must remember the book is a novel, Mr King, not an historical document."

"But you're on record as stating that the story is true, that it's based on actual events. And all the characters in the book are real people, like Major Marman—"

"Yes, he was a real person…"

"—And Sir Peter Horsley, whose BMW was also involved in the crash. All this is on police record; it's historical fact."

"All the police records show is that Sir Peter was involved in a very bad accident."

"An accident that killed Major Marman."

"Yes."

I pressed the point. "Sir Peter didn't think it was an accident," I said. "He believed his car was taken over by remote control and made to crash into Major Marman's car—exactly as you describe in your book."

"I'm afraid I can't speak for Sir Peter."

"No. But thankfully he's already spoken for himself."

A decade or so before his death Sir Peter had published his autobiography, *Sounds From Another Room*, in which he described in chilling detail what had happened to him on Tuesday, November 11th, 1986, while driving from his home in Wiltshire to a business meeting in Plymouth, Devon. He was driving his BMW along the west-bound carriageway of the A303, he said, not far from the megalithic monument of Stonehenge, when suddenly he became aware of a grey Volvo in his rear-view mirror, closing on him "at high speed". A few moments later the Volvo took up position "immediately behind" him.

"With alarming suddenness," Sir Peter wrote, "my BMW spun sharply to the left, and then, with tyres now screeching, equally sharply to the right and then back again."

I remembered pausing at this point, and reading the sentence over and again. It seemed to trigger a memory in me, something Professor Mackay had said when we'd watched his 3-D animation of Diana's crash some three years previously. "There," the professor had said, pointing at the computer screen as Diana's Mercedes collided with the white Fiat Uno on entry to the Alma Tunnel. "The Mercedes swerves violently left, then right, then left again and into a concrete pillar on the central reservation." And again: "What we do know is that the Fiat Uno influenced the crash. *There*—do you see? The Mercedes clips the back of the Fiat Uno and Henri Paul loses control, swerving first left, then right, then left again and into the concrete pillar."

I read the line from Sir Peter's autobiography one more time.

"With alarming suddenness, my BMW spun sharply to the left, and then, with tyres now screeching, equally sharply to the right and then back again."

Had I stumbled on something here, I wondered? I thought I had. But little did I realize at this point that what I'd stumbled on was more than a simple coincidence of events. It was the signature of the Boston Brakes: the proverbial smoking gun.

Sir Peter continued: "I saw the grey Volvo accelerating past me at high speed. My car had now developed a mind of its own as it swung broadside and skidded down the road. With a lurch it hit the central reservation … and crossed over into the opposite carriageway. I just had time to see a small car approaching from the opposite direction. I hit it sideways on with tremendous force. In a split second the driver's horror-stricken face was visible and I clearly heard his hoarse scream above the tearing metal of the two cars momentarily locked together; then came silence as the small car disappeared, catapulted off the road by the sheer force of the impact."

For the record, Sir Peter suffered horrific injuries in the crash, but survived. Major Marman was killed outright.

"Like I said," Sir Ranulph wanted me to accept, "it's just a story."

"With respect, it's more than just a story. Major Marman was a real person. Sir Peter Horsley was a real person. Police records show that the crash actually happened and that Major Marman was killed. The only question is whether or not he was murdered, as you clearly state in your book."

Indeed, according to Sir Ranulph, Major Marman had been the target of a professional hit squad known as *The Clinic*, whose speciality was carrying out assassinations that were made to look like accidents. The night prior to the crash, Fiennes explained, members of *The Clinic* had broken into Sir Peter's garage and secretly fitted a radio-controlled 'parasite' to his BMW, which had allowed the assassins to take out his brakes, take over his steering remotely and steer his BMW into Marman's oncoming Citroen 2CV. An intriguing plot, if it were fiction. But it wasn't. As Sir Ranulph had previously asserted, and as police records clearly showed, it was a real story involving real characters, real people. Air Vice Marshall Sir Peter Horsley was certainly a real person. He was a Second World War hero, formerly Deputy Commander-in-Chief of Britain's Atomic Strike Force and Equerry to both the Queen and Prince Philip. He was very real indeed. As was Major Michael Marman.

"I'm just asking you to confirm that Major Marman was, as you state in your book, the victim of a Boston Brakes operation in which Sir Peter Horsley was used as a proxy."

"And if I do, you'll take it that Princess Diana's car crash was similarly a Boston Brakes operation. Is that it?"

"Well the two incidents do share striking correlations."

I recalled to mind my conversation with former SAS Sergeant Dave Cornish, who'd explained to me that, in the case of

Diana's crash, the person holding the remote would have been in the white Fiat Uno.

"There'd be two boys in the Uno," Dave had said. "The pilot and the engineer. When the engineer triggers the remote the Blockbuster kills the brakes and the parasite (transceiver) takes over the steering. The driver's got no chance."

The same must have been true with the Marman crash, I was beginning to figure, in that the Clinic member responsible for working the remote – the 'engineer' – would have been in the grey Volvo that had closed on Sir Peter's BMW and overtaken it just as the BMW had spun out of control.

"That's pure conjecture," Sir Ranulph said. "As is the theory that Princess Diana was murdered."

"So you're not prepared to acknowledge the correlations between the two incidents?"

"Princess Diana died in an accident."

"That's what they said about Major Marman."

"And I really don't have the time to continue this conversation. Goodbye."

And that was the end of it. He hung up. I never got the chance to speak to him again.

"Steve, hi, thanks for doing this." JB and I followed Steve O'Brien along the short, rickety first-floor corridor and into his partially darkened office, where we seated ourselves in front of the giant-sized computer monitor commanding the centre of his desk. He closed the blinds so the office fell darker still. "We really appreciate it."

"No worries, guys. Anything to help the cause. Here you go."

A few codes and digits typed into the keyboard and a click of the mouse for effect and Steve's 3-D animation opened up on screen. I was immediately impressed. I'd asked him to reconstruct not only Diana's crash, but also the crash that had claimed the life of Major Marman as described in Sir Ranulph Fiennes' book. It was this animation that appeared on screen first. He'd done an excellent job.

"That's superb, Steve," I said, instantly captivated by the detail he'd managed to incorporate, even down to the make of the cars involved.

On screen now was a black BMW saloon travelling west in the slow lane of a dual carriageway. Suddenly a grey Volvo closes on the BMW from behind and takes up position on its rear bumper. The Volvo then pulls out to overtake and the BMW starts to lose control.

Excitedly I turned to JB and nudged his arm. "Here we go, JB. Watch this."

"I'm watching."

Lurching first to the right, then to the left, then to the right again the BMW suddenly skidded broadside across the central reservation and slammed into an oncoming Citroen 2CV, travelling in the opposite direction.

JB looked a little perplexed. "I don't see a tunnel," he said. "And that doesn't look like Paris."

"That's because it's England, nineteen-eighty-six," I told him. "The A303 in Wiltshire, in fact. Play it again please, Steve."

"Coming up."

Another click of the mouse and the animation started running a second time.

"The guy driving the 2CV, here," I said, pointing at the screen. "That's Major Marman, the target. And this is Sir Peter Horsley's BMW. Watch how the BMW reacts just as it's overtaken by this vehicle here, the grey Vovlo—*there!* It lurches one way, then the other way, then back again before slamming into the target vehicle. D'you see that?"

"First one way, then the other way, then back again," JB said. "Yeah, I see that."

"Now watch this."

At the controls, Steve typed in a different set of codes and digits and clicked the mouse again. The result? A different animation on screen.

"This one's a reconstruction of Diana's crash," I said to JB. "It's based on Professor Mackay's original."

"I remember it, yeah."

"Watch as the motorbike overtakes—*there!* Diana's Mercedes lurches one way, then the other way, then back again before slamming into the concrete pillar."

"Jesus."

"D'you see that?"

"One way, the other way and back again. The manoeuvres are identical."

"That's because both crashes were caused by the same method, JB. I'm convinced of it." I stood up and started to pull on my jacket. "Dave Cornish called it the 'Brakes', basically a microchip transceiver that controls the steering and a Blockbuster that…"

"…Blows out the brakes," JB said, completing my sentence.

"Right."

"But didn't Tomlinson say a flash gun was used?"

"An anti-personnel strobe gun, yeah. But Dave Cornish seemed sure it would have been used in conjunction with the Brakes."

"The *Boston Brakes*."

"Correct."

"But where does the Fiat Uno fit into all this? If whoever was riding the motorbike that overtook the Mercedes as it entered the tunnel was responsible for triggering the … what did you call it, the parasite?"

"The parasite, yeah. The microchip transceiver."

"So if the motorbike's pillion rider triggered the parasite, what part did the Uno play?"

"Well according to Dave Cornish there would have been two operatives in the Uno, the driver and the engineer. It would have been the engineer who worked the remote control once the parasite had been triggered."

I caught the look on JB's face. It said he was having trouble.

"A bit too James Bond?" I said.

"Well it does seem a bit far-fetched. I mean, who would ever believe it?"

"Exactly, JB. That's why it's known as a deniable op." I checked my wristwatch. "Come on," I said. "We're late."

39

Trinity Buoy Wharf looked very different to how the American remembered it. He'd last been here in the 1980s, when it had still been in transition from industrial ghost town to artistic playground, a status it had most certainly now achieved, he mused, as he waited by the gault brick lighthouse and took in the scene about him—the new pier with its recycled pontoon and floating office space; the trendy cafe and diner; the colourful patchwork of rehearsal rooms, studios and workshops recently built from recycled shipping containers. The ironies of life, he thought to himself, knowing as he did that those very same containers, back in the 80s, had been used to fulfil a different purpose altogether. But then, back in the 80s, so had Trinity Buoy Wharf.

A derelict wasteland in appearance back then, the wharf had been part of a multi-location live drop utilized by MI6 and mujahideen runners trafficking opium to the UK from Afghanistan. Millions in hard sterling had been funnelled, via Swiss bank accounts controlled by MI6, back to Afghanistan to help fund and arm the country's network of Islamist warlords against the Soviet occupation. MI6 was not alone in this endeavour, of course; the CIA was hard at it, too. Indeed, between them, MI6 and the CIA helped smuggle untold quantities of opium out of Afghanistan in those days, not only trafficking the stuff to Europe and the West to help raise money for the Afghan resistance, but also into Russia in a deliberate attempt to weaken Soviet morale by feeding the country's already acute heroin problem. Psychological warfare at the dirty end. For his part in this backstairs arms-for-drugs operation, the American had worked alongside his cousins at MI6, both in Helmand and in London, in his capacity as CIA special forces liaison. At the time, of course, the world remained oblivious to the West's involvement in drug-smuggling and the funding of Islamist armies. Not even the American himself knew the full extent of what he'd been involved in. But then, he'd never asked. He'd been paid well enough for his contribution and his interest had ended there. The only problem he'd encountered was the asshole under whose command he'd been forced to operate—a newly promoted MI6 Special Operations Commander called Richard Mason.

Stubbing out a half-smoked cigarette underfoot the American glanced up and saw that very same asshole approaching him now in the back of a diplomatic limo. As the limo slowed and pulled alongside him its tinted rear window slid down to reveal the asshole's face.

"Get in," Mason said to him. "It's unlocked."

The American opened the door and climbed in. "Long time," he said. "Your manner hasn't changed."

"Neither has your smoker's breath," Mason rejoined, then turned and gave instruction to the limo's driver via the in-car radio. "Drive," he said. "It doesn't matter where. Foreign diplomat status applies."

As the limo pulled away its doors locked automatically and the bulletproof window through which Mason had greeted his *foreign diplomat* guest wound back up, all by itself. In that moment the limo became as attack-proof as any Chieftain tank.

"It wasn't my fault," Mason was saying a few minutes later as they cruised along East Smithfield on approach to Tower Bridge. "Not that I need to justify myself to you. But there was no viable option."

"You could have pulled them out."

"If I'd done that we'd have lost the target."

"That's bullshit, and you know it. We had the cell completely noosed. If we'd waited for backup to arrive we would have accomplished the mission without any losses on our side. Home and dry."

"Naïve speculation. Typical CIA. If we'd waited as you suggest the entire operation could have been compromised."

"That's a matter of opinion—*your* opinion. The boys on the front line were totally exposed."

"It happens."

"Oh really?" The American flicked a glance at the man seated opposite him. The closest Mason had ever come to the front line was playing prop forward for Gordonstoun Boys rugby team, and he knew it. "And what would you know about the front line, anyway?"

"That's hardly the point," Mason said. "In any case, it's in the past. What's done is done. The operation was a success. And that, ultimately, is all the matters." He slid his gaze out the window.

The American bit his teeth. He didn't agree with the way the operation had been run and he didn't like the idea that two young operatives had lost their lives, unnecessarily in his opinion—the result of Mason's personal ambition. He knew well enough that Mason had given the order to go in purely for the badge he'd won as a result—gaining promotion to his current rank of MI6 Chief of Special Operations, Europe. But now wasn't the time to argue the point, he told himself for the umpteenth time. It wasn't his concern. He'd taken the money for his part in the operation and that was where he'd laid his hat. Any case, there were more pressing issues to be dealt with, he reminded himself—the very reason he was here.

Swallowing his disquiet – for now – he said, simply: "So why did you request this meeting?"

Mason visibly tightened. "The cut-out," he said. "*Your* cut-out."

"Jon King?"

"He's making a noise."

"That's what he's supposed to do."

Mason pursed his lips, in a manner that said he was unhappy with this reply.

The American noted it. "So what would you have me do?"

"You tell me," Mason said. "You're the one who fed him a line. This was your idea."

"To give the public something to hang their grief on, yes. And so far it's worked."

"I would say that depends on how you measure success."

"Like everyone else—by results." He paused, as though to punctuate what he'd just said. Then: "Look," he went on. "The tide is against us, as we predicted it would be. We had to make provision for public reaction—"

"Bah…"

"—Have you read the opinion polls? Have you any idea how people are feeling out there? They're angry. They need to feel vindicated."

"Vindicated?" Mason huffed. "You Americans pay too much attention to public mood. The public will eat what we feed them."

"Maybe so. But if we keep feeding them TV dinners we need to be prepared for when they throw up."

Again Mason huffed. "And that's another thing. You're too fond of platitudes. If this results in a public inquiry…"

"It won't."

"It had better not, because that could make things very difficult for a lot of people."

"You mean you could get found out and lose your job."

"I mean we need to maintain a closed operation—at all costs. An inquiry forced through by public opinion could prove extremely embarrassing, for your government and mine."

"Well like I said, it won't come to that."

"And like I said, it had better not."

For the next few moments a jagged silence settled between them, the American throwing a fractious glance out the darkly tinted window as they cruised past the Bank of England and the Royal Exchange and on towards Mansion House in the heart of London's financial district: Mason stared coldly ahead. But only briefly. By the time they'd reached St Paul's Cathedral the MI6 man had opened a compartment by his side and pulled out an A4 portfolio. He handed it to the American.

"This is the other reason you're here," he said. "The prodigal prince."

Opening the portfolio the American retrieved a photograph of a man in his late thirties, small in stature and wearing overstated glasses. He was also wearing a tartan sash and kilt. "The prodigal prince?" he said.

"Michael Roger Lafosse, aka Prince Michael James Alexander Stewart, seventh Count of Albany. The tartan he's wearing belongs to the Scottish clan of the Stuarts, the lot who occupied the Throne in the seventeenth century. Lafosse thinks he's a descendant of Bonnie Prince Charlie and therefore a legitimate claimant to the Scottish Throne, which of course no longer exists. He's Belgian. Moved to Scotland in nineteen-seventy-six to pursue his claim."

"Hence the prodigal prince." The American was reading through the notes in the portfolio. "It does say here he has a birth certificate proving his lineage."

"Not anymore, he doesn't. I arranged a black bag team to gain entry to his apartment and pick up anything that might legitimize his claim. We've had his passport for a while now so he can't go anywhere, and we've also rewritten his birth certificate so he's no longer who he wants everyone to believe he is. He is now officially a fraud. To help your cause I've arranged the necessary introductions with someone who'll convince your cut-out King that the prince is genuine."

"And is he?"

Mason's eyes hardened at this question. "He is who we say he is," was his flat response.

"But you're confident King will take the bait?"

"I don't see why not. He's waltzed into every trap we've set for him so far. No reason to suspect he won't waltz headlong into this one." He paused, then added: "That is if he doesn't incite a national revolution first."

"King? Oh, come on. He's a two-bit conspiracy theorist. No one will take him *or* his book seriously. We've blocked all reviews and serializations in the mainstream press and we've also blocked the book being licensed by any of the major publishers over here. He's walled in."

"Well all I can say is, for someone who's *walled in*, as you put it, he seems to be making a very good fist of things. Despite your efforts he's managed to get himself on every radio and TV station in the country and I'm reliably informed he's planning a national book-signing and lecture tour. What's more, the public are right behind him."

"They're meant to be. That's the whole point. Give him enough ammunition and eventually he'll shoot himself." He held up the portfolio in front of him. "All the more so now that we have a new ace card."

Mason remained unmoved. "Just make sure this doesn't go any further," he said, a noticeable chill in his tone now. "Nip it now, or I'll hold you personally accountable." Again Mason turned and spoke into the in-car radio. "Pull over," he told the driver. "Our guest is getting out."

At Mason's command the limo pulled over and came to a halt at the side of the road. Mason continued to stare straight ahead as the American tucked the Stuart Portfolio in his attaché case, then opened the door and started to climb out.

"You know what?" the CIA man turned and said to Mason as he stepped from the limo and out onto the pavement. "You're an abject son of a bitch."

Mason didn't reply, didn't even bother to look as the American closed the door behind him and walked on along the street. Instead he leaned to one side and again spoke into the in-car radio.

"Drive," was all he said.

And as if by the power of the word alone the limo pulled off and drove on.

40

Okay, this was where it started to get weird. Really weird. For all that we'd faced up phantoms in our attempts to uncover the truth; for all that we'd been surveilled, monitored and manipulated like puppets on some insidious, invisible string: indeed, for all that we'd become slave to what appeared to be, to all intents and purposes, some pernicious, calculated mind game controlled by fear and paranoia – and our lives had been turned inside out in the process – for all that and more, things were about to get even weirder.

Had we realized what was happening at the time, of course; had we known the agenda behind our extraordinary meeting with the man we would know only as 'the Doctor', we would almost certainly have turned our backs and walked away. Or at least dealt with the situation differently. But we didn't. And ultimately, I was glad we didn't. But I didn't know that at the time.

Confused? So were we. All I would ask is that you stay with us. The following twist, as bizarre and unlikely as it might at first seem, will unravel edifyingly in the end. At which point the sting will become evident, and the lengths to which the intelligence services were prepared to go to silence John and I will become all the more evident, too.

We were on the London Eye, looking down on Big Ben and the Houses of Parliament. Only three of us occupied the capsule—myself, JB and the man we'd come here to meet: a man who'd been introduced to us simply – and rather curiously – as the Doctor. Dressed in fine mohair overcoat, white silk scarf and wearing a neatly trimmed, steel-grey beard, the Doctor was everything you might expect of a multi-generational Scottish aristocrat—honed features, straight back, cultured English accent cut with a fine Scots lilt. Not that we'd heard much of that lilt. Aside from the customary pleasantries on greeting our guest at the foot of the Eye some ten minutes earlier, in fact, scarcely a word had passed between us, and we were beginning to wonder if the Doctor had forgotten his lines. Or maybe even that he'd changed his mind and wished now that he hadn't arranged to meet us. Turned out we were wrong, on both counts.

For our part, we'd been told the Doctor had worked for a Foreign Office department responsible for certain historical and genealogical documents, some of which dated back centuries— possibly even as far back as 200 AD. We didn't know documents went back that far (or if they did, what possible relevance they might have had regarding our investigation), but we'd been assured that the information the Doctor had for us might be significant, and may even be useful in terms of identifying a motive for Diana's death. As if there weren't enough motives already. Needless to say, neither JB nor I bore the faintest inkling quite where all this might lead, if anywhere at all. But having spent an arm and a leg booking a private capsule on the giant Ferris wheel overlooking the River Thames – the *London Eye* – we were hoping for at least a half-decent return on our investment. And in a strange kind of way, we received that and more.

"Westminster," the Doctor finally announced, gazing thoughtfully out the capsule window, across the river at Parliament. "It's where it all began. The English inveigled James the Sixth of Scots into becoming James the First of England, and Westminster finally gained control of Britain. It was the greatest conspiracy ever perpetrated on the British people." He threw a reconciled glance our way. "Too late to do anything about it now, of course."

"Of course." Not knowing quite what else to say I turned to JB, who pulled a face and shrugged.

The Doctor turned and peered back out the window. "Oh, there were one or two half-hearted attempts to regain the Throne in the early days," he went on, unbidden. "One or two aborted efforts to win back the crown from Westminster. But of course they came to nothing. Power was already in the hands of the bankers, you see. It was what you might refer to as a *financial coup d'état*. Secretly Parliament had signed away the nation's fiscal powers to the Anglo-Dutch oligarchy that had taken over the City, and in the process the Stuart monarchy was sold down the river. That was the beginning of the end."

Without removing his gaze from Parliament, the Doctor stood up straight and stretched his back, then rolled his tongue around the inside of his mouth, as though musing. I took the opportunity to study the man.

For all that he seemed a little quirky, I considered, he was nonetheless engaging, and strangely enigmatic. Standing a full six feet, perhaps even more, he had the feel of a man half his age, and I couldn't help noting how much he reminded me of Sean Connery. Of course, none of this explained why he'd wanted to talk to us, and that was what bothered me. He was, after all, a government man; had been all his life, or so the person who instigated our meeting had claimed, and I was yet to figure why a man in his position would have wanted to engage with a couple of conspiracy freaks—which, I presumed, was how someone of his social station would have thought of us. The letter I'd received, which had been delivered to our magazine offices and marked *Personal and Confidential*, had said simply that someone of some note had expressed an interest in talking to us about Diana and went on briefly to give details of this person's status and credential. By now I'd grown accustomed to receiving anonymous letters, phone calls, and sometimes the odd email, with offers of information, so I'd thought little of it. If we wished to accept the offer and meet the Doctor in person, the letter said, we would have to do so on his terms.

I put it to JB. He agreed we should meet him.

And so now here we were, wondering what it was the 'Doctor' had to say that was so unutterable we'd had to meet him here, in secret, in our own private capsule on the London Eye, in order for him to reveal it. Hopefully it wasn't just to give us a lesson in alternative history, which was all we'd received so far.

"We were told you might be able to shed some light on the death of Princess Diana," I finally ventured, attempting to steer the conversation in our direction. "We were told you were a special remit Foreign Office historian and—"

"You were told that?" The surprise on the Doctor's face as he swung back round to engage us was stark, but it quickly dissolved to a look of resignation. "Oh, I suppose it scarcely matters now," he said. "Quite a mouthful, though, isn't it—special remit Foreign Office historian?"

"What exactly does it mean?"

"It means I was paid a lot of money to maintain the status quo. To ensure the version of history you were taught at school remains the *only* version of history, no matter how extreme the measures taken to keep it that way."

"And there was I thinking we live in a democracy," JB threw in.

"Democracy, my arse!" the Doctor shot back. "You live in a conspiracy, gentlemen, one that was born with the overthrow of the Stuart Monarchy and the founding of the Bank of England. Well that's what they wanted, you see. The bankers, the oligarchy—that's what they wanted. That's why they plotted the demise of King James and at the same time funded the arrival of the Dutch usurper, William of Orange. The Stuart kings had always opposed the establishment of a central banking system for fear that the country would be taken over by the money men. Charles the First, and then Charles the Second, and then James the Second—all of them. Each in their time refused to sanction a central bank, refused to give in to the bankers and hand them control of Britain. So in the end the Stuarts were dispensed with and replaced with a more, shall we say, compliant monarchy. It's been that way ever since." He pursed his lips, and again rolled his tongue around the inside of his mouth, as though remembering the moment Parliament had become a corporate puppet. It was evident the thought displeased him. "Aye," he said, somewhat bleakly. "History will tell you the Stuarts were raving Catholics hell-bent on re-establishing Catholicism as the national religion, and that's why they were ousted. But nothing could be further from the truth. They were ousted because they stood up to the bankers." He threw us a sideways glance. "That, and for the legacy they carried in their blood."

Having made his point the Doctor cast his gaze back out the window at Parliament.

"Look, I'm sure there's a lot of truth in what you're saying," I said, still trying to work the man out. "But we're not sure what all this has to do with Diana?"

"Like I said, gentlemen, we live in a conspiracy. Those who conspire at the highest level decide for us all. The rest of us do as we're told—or pay the price." He turned and caught my eye. "You do hear what I'm saying?"

"You're saying Diana paid the price for not doing as she was told?"

"She upset the wrong people, Mr King. She stepped out of line. In the process she became the biggest threat to the monarchy since Bonnie Prince Charlie. I know, because my job was to counter that threat."

"The threat posed by Princess Diana?"

"In part, aye. She carried the blood, you see. The genes. It was all there in the documents I looked after, the documents I was employed to conceal." As though to consider how much he should say, and how much he should keep to himself, the Doctor again fell momentarily silent. But only momentarily. "My *special remit*, as you put it, was to modify the content of certain historical and genealogical documents in the government's possession, and to ensure the continued concealment of others that would prove very damaging to the Royal Establishment if ever they were to be released—if their content were to be made public. Needless to say that won't ever happen."

"So what do these documents contain that's so damning?"

"Secrets," the Doctor said, matter of fact. "Plots. Conspiracies. More specifically, information about a certain bloodline."

"A bloodline…?"

"Yes, gentlemen, a bloodline. Or more precisely, *the* bloodline, the one that rules the Western world, which is why everyone wants to possess it." A shadow darkened his eyes as he added: "Centuries ago it was a *legitimate* bloodline, of course, a *royal* bloodline of some credential, passed down from generation to generation in rightful succession. Some even referred to it as *messianic*. Certainly it dates back centuries, as far as records go and beyond. It was this bloodline from which the Stuart kings themselves descended—the very reason they were so manipulated and persecuted."

"Forgive me, Doctor," I said. "But when you say ... a *messianic* bloodline ... are you able to elaborate?"

"Is it not self-explanatory?"

I didn't know. Was it? Maybe I just didn't want to draw the obvious conclusion. I moved the conversation along. "You say that certain people still strive to possess this bloodline?"

"Using everything in their power to do so, yes."

"But how do you go about *possessing* a bloodline?"

"Oh, that's simple. Marry into it, produce children, get rid of the mother."

Marry into it, produce children, get rid of the mother.

Peering out the capsule window the Doctor bore his full glare down on the Foreign Office, and beyond, on St James Park and Buckingham Palace, standing tall and impregnable in the near distance. "It's called viticulture," he said. "Political and masonic viticulture—the grafting of bloodlines from one vine to another, one family to the next. Of course, this only creates a bastardized strain of the original bloodline, but it's enough to fulfil the ambitions of those who possess it."

"And who does possess it?"

"Let's just say it's in the hands of an extremely powerful mafia of families and their heirs." He was still glaring out the window at Buckingham Palace as he added: "Interlopers they may be, but their control of the bloodline is supreme. And because it is, they occupy the seats of Western power today."

Again I glanced across at JB. Again he shrugged. We really were quite bemused by what we were hearing—unsure whether the Doctor bore genuine secrets, or if he was simply unhinged. At this point I was running with the latter.

"You mentioned Bonnie Prince Charlie," I said, inviting the Doctor to say more.

"Aye. The last of the Stuart pretenders, the last legitimate heir to the bloodline who carried any real threat. At least that's the official story. You have me to thank for that." He gave a wry smile. "If you were to read the documents, on the other hand, you would learn the real story—that in fact the Bonnie Prince had a son by a secret marriage, Edward James Stuart. In effect Edward was the first legitimate heir of the male line to be written out of history in order to protect the ambitions of the money men. But he wasn't the last." He sent JB and I a knowing look. "It's all there in the documents," he said, "in the genealogical records they contain. The entire legitimate line of descent from the Bonnie Prince—all the way to the present."

"The present?" My mind quickly computed the ramifications of this statement. "But ... that means—"

"Aye. It means the Stuart bloodline, as it became latterly known, is alive and well, as is its senior male heir in the line of the Bonnie Prince."

"The bloodline's senior male heir is alive today? Who? Where is he...?"

The Doctor balked slightly at this question. "All in good time," he said. And then he said: "The point is that the bloodline has survived intact, and there are some very powerful people ready to support a Stuart revival – even a restoration – especially if it were headed up by someone with influence." He paused. What he said next almost sucked the breath from my lungs. "You are aware that Diana was a Stuart by blood, that she too was a descendant of the Bonnie Prince and the original bloodline—?"

Diana was a descendant of Bonnie Prince Charlie...?

"—She was a bigger threat than either of you realize, gentlemen. In years gone by she would have ended her days in there." He motioned out the window behind us, at the Tower of London, looming there over the time-tortured river like a bad memory.

I turned to JB, who seemed equally as anaesthetized as me. *Where the hell was this conversation going?*

I turned back to the Doctor. "Look," I said, still trying to piece together what seemed to me now a very complex, very implausible jigsaw. "Are you seriously suggesting the Foreign Office was aware of some kind of plot to overthrow the monarchy by modern-day Jacobites?"

"Hijack would be a more accurate term."

"And that Diana was somehow involved in this plot?"

"I'd thank you not to put words in my mouth."

"But that's what you inferred."

"People can be manipulated, Mr King. She carried the blood. She also had the support of the nation, and that made her very dangerous."

"Dangerous enough to have her killed?"

"I didn't say that. But yes, perhaps."

"You honestly believe Diana could have been killed because of her Stuart blood?" JB wanted clarified.

The Doctor gave half a shrug. "There were other factors," he said. "The Fayed boy, for one."

"Dodi Fayed?"

"Aye."

"Because he was a Muslim?" I said.

"Precisely that."

"But this is the twentieth century," JB argued. "Don't tell me you're pulling the race card now."

"*Blood*, gentlemen. Not race: *blood*." He paused, just long enough for his words to embed. "You can take it back as far as you like, to the Crusades and the battle for Jerusalem. Even before that. A long way before that, to the Judaic kings of ancient Israel and beyond." Again he fixed us, this time with unforgiving emphasis. "Our God is Jehova," he said. "Theirs is Allah. And never the twain shall meet."

Realizing JB and I were more than a little uncomfortable with this analogy, he added: "You must understand what I say in a *political* context, gentlemen. Whatever else she may have done to upset the Castle, she should never have got together with the Fayed boy. It was political suicide."

We were reaching the end of our trip around the Eye, descending slowly to the point where we'd first stepped aboard. The Doctor turned and fixed us one last time.

"It's all a matter of blood, gentlemen," he said. "Stuart blood versus Windsor blood. Western blood versus Arab blood. Judaeo-Christian blood versus Muslim blood. *The clash of civilizations*. Politically speaking, you belong to one or the other. When she got together with the Fayed boy she crossed the invisible line."

Our capsule was nearing the ground, and the Doctor was preparing to exit.

"Before you leave," I said, keen to get at least some understanding of who this man really was, his motives. "Why did you ask to meet us and tell us all this?"

The Doctor thought about this for a moment. Then: "My family are Jacobites, Mr King. We go back a long way, to Robert the Bruce and beyond, even to the first High Stewards of Scotland. We are descended from the original, legitimate strain of the bloodline which has since been hijacked and stolen from us. My work at the Foreign Office, well ... you might say this is my way of helping to set the record straight—a sort of penance for betraying the family tradition all those years." He reached into his top pocket, pulled out a small business card and handed it to me. "Call this number," he said. "Give my name. Tell them you want to speak to Michael."

"Michael...?"

"You asked me who was the rightful heir to the bloodline today. Call this number."

I took the card and slipped it in my pocket without reading it.

"One last thing," the Doctor turned and said, tucking his silk scarf in the lapels of his mohair overcoat. "I'd appreciate it if you didn't follow me. I've arranged for you to enjoy a second time around—all paid for." The attendant opened the door and ushered the Doctor from the capsule. "Good day, gentlemen. It's been a pleasure. Enjoy the views."

That said, the Doctor stepped from the capsule and disappeared along the gantry. We would never see him again.

41

The next few months were purgatory, pure frustration, as we waited and waited for our book to arrive from America. It was now more than eighteen months late and still no sign of it, and we were seriously beginning to wonder at our publisher's motives for failing to meet the agreed deadline. Or the *extended* deadline. The *super-extended* deadline. *Any* deadline.

It'll be with you in May. No, sorry, September. It'll definitely be with you in January. No, April. May. June…

Even our UK distributors were growing ever more sceptical, and no less displeased, at the lengthy delays, and the indefensible excuses our publisher was using to explain them.

We've had problems with the layout. The fonts are incompatible. Our system's crashed and we've lost the entire manuscript—would you send it again?

Meantime, any number of books about the death of Diana were being churned out in the UK, each one a government mouthpiece: each one, we felt sure, lessening the impact our own book might otherwise have made had it been here on time.

Could this be the reason for the delays? we wondered. To undermine the book's impact? Were the same intelligence agencies responsible for tapping our phones and surveilling our lives responsible for delaying the publication of our book, too?

Was our publisher part of the plot?

Had we been inclined, of course, we might have taken these thoughts more seriously than we did—might have believed a more sinister reason was lurking behind our book's late arrival. As it was we just grew more and more frustrated by the day, the week, the month. But we did put the time to good use.

Our meeting with the Doctor on the London Eye some weeks behind us, I suddenly remembered the business card he'd given me on his departure. To be honest, until now I'd paid it scant attention. Although the all-singing, all-dancing hardback edition of our book hadn't yet arrived in the UK, we *had* been sent a box of *galleys* (low-quality soft-back copies for promotional use), and we'd been so busy sending them out to media outlets, requesting interviews, scheduling book signings and organizing our upcoming speaking tour that, although I hadn't totally forgotten about the card, I had consigned it to the back of my mind, mostly due to its seeming irrelevance in relation to our investigation. I was of course aware that the Doctor could have been a nut job with a fairy tale to spin; at times during our meeting he'd certainly sounded like one. I was equally aware that he could have been a government agent, a plant sent to feed us disinformation and put us off scent. But as the weeks rolled by, each one promising the arrival of our book, I found myself thinking more and more about what the Doctor had said. And the more I thought about it, I had to admit, the more intriguing it had started to sound.

As the London cab I was travelling in with JB turned into Portland Place and pulled up outside BBC Broadcasting House, I found myself feeling in my top pocket for the business card the Doctor had given us. It was still there. In that moment I reached a decision. It was a decision that would turn our investigation on its head, well and truly.

"The Doctor," I said to JB as we made our way from the cab and headed for the entrance to Broadcasting House. It was early evening and the West End was just coming to life.

"What about him?"

"I think we should follow up the lead he gave us. I think we should phone this number." I held up the business card I'd just pulled from my top pocket.

"I'd been wondering when you might get round to that." JB gave a wry smile, then led the way through the big swing-doors into the foyer of the famous old building. Once inside, he took the card from my hand and slid it in his pocket. "I'll phone the number when we get home tomorrow," he said. "See who answers the phone. Right now we've got an interview to deal with."

We headed for the elevator.

Several minutes later we were seated in the stuffy, regimented waiting area outside Studio 4, preparing ourselves for the latest in a long line of media interviews we were currently undertaking as a result of the galleys we'd sent out. Tonight's interview was one of the biggest so far; it was being simultaneously broadcast the length and breadth of the country via the BBC's network of regional radio stations, so we were being extra-meticulous in our preparation – scanning the latest news, tooth-combing our notes, second-guessing the questions our host might ask – although it should be said that we were fairly in the zone anyway from the string of media appearances we'd already made.

"The French Inquiry found that Diana's death was the result of a drink-drive accident," the host had put to us on BBC's *Breakfast Time* TV show a few days earlier. "Why aren't you satisfied with this finding?"

"Because in our opinion it's flawed," I'd said. "The results of the blood tests carried out on Henri Paul are completely incompatible with each other. Initial tests gave widely differing results to tests carried out four days later. They are wholly unreliable. And yet these are the samples on which the drink-drive verdict is based."

"The French pathologist doesn't even know how many samples were taken," JB had added. "All we know is they were taken from the wrong part of Henri Paul's body, wrongly labelled and stored in the wrong place. What's more there's no supporting evidence to show they even belonged to Henri Paul. They were never DNA-tested."

"That doesn't mean it wasn't Henri Paul's blood," the host had made a point of saying.

"Perhaps, but the fact that the samples were found to contain enough carbon monoxide to poleaxe a mountain gorilla must say something," I'd fired back. "They also contained an alcohol level *three times* the drink-drive limit, and yet Ritz CCTV footage shows that Henri Paul was able to bend down and tie his shoe laces, chat coherently to guests, walk unaided from the hotel and drive a Mercedes S280 limousine in the presence of trained bodyguards. And this is only one of many anomalies that have never been explained. For the record, forensic pathologists at Glasgow University say the blood samples could not possibly have belonged to Henri Paul."

"So who did they belong to, then?"

"That's what we need to find out. That's why we're calling for a public inquiry."

We were ushered inside Studio 4.

As well as being prepared for whatever our host might ask, we'd also learned to prepare ourselves for any on-air surprises—something we'd learned to do ever since our appearance on *The James Whale Show* some weeks earlier.

James Whale was perhaps Britain's best-known talk-show host, and we'd been invited to guest on his show the minute he'd received our media pack. It was a popular show, with a big audience, so naturally we'd accepted, but we hadn't expected to be censored barely five minutes before going on air. There was a *live DA-Notice action* on our book, we were told, which meant there were vast swathes of the book we weren't allowed to talk about on air. It turned out this was the same 'live DA-Notice action' that Darren Adams of the *Sunday Times* had told us about some months previously: the same DA-Notice the newspaper itself had received, and in consequence, had shelved plans to serialize our book. It really was a strange situation we found ourselves in. As the past few weeks had demonstrated all too clearly, it seemed we could do as many ten-to-twenty-minute interviews as we could eat—interviews that skimmed the surface and dealt with the less controversial, more generic questions:

Wasn't it the paparazzi who made her crash? Wasn't Henri Paul drunk? Why would anyone want to kill Diana anyway?

But the longer, more in-depth interviews were being censored.

Our 2-hour, in-depth interview with James Whale on London's *Talk Radio* was a case in point. It was Whale himself who'd informed us of the situation, explaining that the radio station had received the Notice that same day and that, even though it had been issued as a 'guideline' rather than an 'order', if the station ignored it they could lose their licence. As if to prove what he was saying, Whale opened the copy of the galley we'd sent him prior to the interview and held it up for us to see, flicking through the pages a dozen at a time. We were horrified. Page after page had been scored through with red marker pen, highlighting those sections of the book we were not allowed to talk about on air. More than seventy-five-percent of the book had been expunged, and as a result, we'd spent two hours talking about why we believed the French Inquiry was flawed and whether or not the emergency services had done a good enough job. The real meat of what we had to say never saw the light of day.

As we seated ourselves and slipped the headphones over our ears inside BBC Studio 4, then, we were kind of relieved to find this particular broadcast was a question-and-answer phone-in format. As well as being less censored than an in-depth interview, it would also give us an insight into the public mood, something we were ever keen to monitor.

"Okay, let's go to the phone lines," our host said after a brief introduction and a few cursory questions. "Ahmed from Birmingham, what would you like to say?"

"I'd just like to say well done to the two authors. They're saying what we all think anyway."

"I agree," said Linda, the next caller. "I had a gut feeling the minute I heard on the news that Diana was dead. I just knew it wasn't an accident."

"Yes but you can't just go on a gut instinct, Linda," the host argued. "You need evidence."

"What's the point? It'll only be covered up."

"Oh, right." The host pulled a face that said he thought the caller was batty. "Let's go to our next caller, then. Robert in Edinburgh, do you buy into these conspiracy theories?"

"Aye," Robert affirmed. "JFK was shot by a lone gunman and the Roswell UFO crash was a weather balloon."

This time the host's face distorted in confusion. "Sorry, Robert, not sure what you're saying there…?"

"I'm saying she was murdered."

"Oh, right. Okay, you made your point." He cut Robert off. Hit a different button. Then: "Anne from London, you're on the radio. What would you like to say to the authors?"

"I'd just like to say that I feel for William and Harry. It must be awful for them, all this talk of murder."

"So you think the authors should back off?"

"I do, yes."

"But what if they happen to be right? What if the French Inquiry was wrong and Diana *was* murdered?"

"I still think they should let her rest in peace, for the sake of the boys."

"What do you say to that?" we were asked.

"Why don't you ask the next caller," JB said.

"All right, I will." He hit another button. "Nick from Cardiff, did you hear that?"

"I did yes, and I think the last caller was talking rubbish. How can Diana rest in peace if she was murdered? As for upsetting the boys, if my mother had died like that I'd want to know the truth."

"You don't think the French Inquiry delivered the truth?"

"No. I don't think a British Inquiry would, either. But like the rest of the country I support the authors' efforts to try and force one through."

And so the theme continued. It seemed in general the public were onside. Our push for a public inquiry was gaining support, and momentum. All was looking good. Until we left the building.

42

"A car has been called for you, Mr King," the doorman said as we stepped from the elevator and made our way across the foyer towards the exit. "It's waiting outside."

"Thank you," I said, not thinking anything of it.

We'd made our own way to Broadcasting House earlier purely because we were in town on business and it had seemed easier for us to jump in a cab than arrange a pickup point and hang around for a BBC limo to come and collect us. But it was now 9.45 pm. We had a train to catch, and a free ride back to the train station seemed a very agreeable idea. It was customary for the bigger media outlets to provide transport anyway—one of the perks of being in demand. What we didn't know at this point, though, as we exited the building and made our way over to the waiting limo, was that this perk was about to turn sinister.

"Mr King? Mr Beveridge?" Dressed in full chauffeur's livery and sporting a clipped, ginger-grey beard, the driver emerged from the front of the vehicle and opened the rear door.

"Waterloo station, please," I said, as I climbed in the back with JB. The chauffeur closed the door behind us.

A few minutes later we were heading east on New Oxford Street, the lights of the West End dancing burlesque-like in the distance behind us. Even though it was closing on 10 pm, it seemed, London was still wide awake, though it became progressively sleepier the further south and east we travelled. Indeed, by the time we'd reached the far end of High Holborn, past the junction with Chancery Lane, and had turned right on Holborn Circus into New Fetter Lane down towards the river, London's light show had all but ebbed completely. The only illumination now was the glare of oncoming car headlamps and the light spilling out from still-open offices and convenience stores. That, and the radiance from a three-quarter full moon doing its best to dodge the clouds.

As we reached the end of New Fetter Lane and turned left on Fleet Street towards Ludgate Hill, the moon finally disappeared for good.

That's when it first struck me. That's when my gut suddenly fisted as my mind all at once awoke to the route the chauffeur was taking. Fleet Street? Ludgate Hill? Surely we'd come the wrong way, hadn't we? If we turned right up ahead on New Bridge Street it would take us down to the river, true. But that route would take us down to Blackfriars Bridge when we should have been aiming for Waterloo Bridge, a mile back up-river. Of course, for all I knew it could have been a route the chauffeur took on a regular basis, perhaps to avoid the traffic on Aldwych and the Strand. Perhaps he would take an unexpected turning off Fleet Street and cut back along Victoria Embankment, perhaps even take a route I was unfamiliar with. Perhaps. But for some reason this sharp stabbing pain in my gut was telling me that wasn't about to happen, even more so when we turned left on Queen Victoria Street and Upper Thames Street and starting heading down towards the docks.

I threw an uneasy glance at JB, then at the chauffeur, his deadpan profile reflected in the glass partition separating us from the front of the car. Then back at JB.

"Where's he taking us?" I said.

"Down to the docks, by the looks of things." JB was peering anxiously ahead out the front windscreen. "Why the hell is he taking us down there?"

"Only one way to find out," I said, and rapped on the glass partition in an attempt to get the chauffeur's attention. "Hello? I think you've taken a wrong turning. I think we're going the wrong way…" No response "…Hey! Where are you taking us…?"

But the chauffeur didn't respond. Didn't even flinch. He just kept driving, as though he couldn't hear me: as though the increasingly distressed madman pounding away on the glass partition in the back of his vehicle didn't exist.

"Hey! You're going the wrong way! Waterloo's in the opposite direction—back there!" I jabbed a thumb at the mile or so of murky River Thames disappearing behind us. *"You need to turn round!"*

But it was useless. The guy obviously had no mind to turn round and take us back to Waterloo: no mind to let us in on where he was taking us, either. Seriously panicked now, I scanned the glass partition for a handle or a latch so I could slide it open and make my protests better heard. But there was no handle, I immediately realized, no latch. It must have been operated electronically from the front dashboard, like the doors. Realizing there was no way out I turned to JB, saw that he was as panicked as I was. Following which, not knowing quite what else to do, I collapsed back in my seat and let my heart beat me. Which it did, like a sledgehammer.

"We're turning off," JB suddenly said, the alarm in him constricting his voice to a tight whisper. "He's indicating now."

And sure enough, less than fifty yards further along the road the chauffeur slowed and turned right into a small, narrow impasse that led down to a quayside overhanging the river. It was dark, very dark, the only source of illumination being the vehicle's full-beam headlamps reflecting off the buildings to left and right. And then that was gone, too, as we pulled over and the chauffeur cut the engine and dimmed the lights. Suddenly all was quiet, deadly so, the only sound to be heard the electronic *click* of the door locks being freed as the chauffeur hit the release button on the dashboard in the front. And then silence again, eerie, foreboding.

What the hell was going on? Why had he brought us here? Were we about to be beaten up? Worse?

The answers to my questions were only moments away, I suddenly realized, because just then the chauffeur turned and motioned that we should get out.

"What, here?" I said. "But…"

"Let's not argue with him," JB said. "At least he's letting us go. Come on."

Reluctantly we did as the chauffeur said. As we opened the doors and started to climb out I fully expected something very unpleasant to happen, someone to jump us, or mug us, maybe start roughing us up. But nothing like that happened. Instead, as we closed the doors behind us the chauffeur simply fired up the engine again and started to reverse back along the narrow street, switching the headlamps back on full beam as he did so. They were blinding, forcing us to crease up our eyes and shield them with our raised hands … a beat, two … and then the lights disappeared, casting us back into pitch darkness. By the time our eyes had overcome the glare and accustomed themselves to the surrounding gloom the chauffeur and his vehicle were out of sight. We were alone.

For what seemed a small eternity JB and I just stood there, not knowing what on earth was going on, or why we'd been driven to a dark, neglected alley in southeast London and unceremoniously dumped by the river. Not that we could see where we were; by now the night's cloud cover had obscured the moon entirely and the pervading darkness prevented us from making out detail. But we knew we were by the river. We could smell it. We could hear it, too, lapping up against the quayside wall barely five yards from where we stood. And shivered. If we'd had our wits about us, of course, we would have taken to our heels the minute we were released from the car: slammed the doors behind us and followed the river back up towards Waterloo Bridge as fast as our legs – and our lungs – could manage. But we didn't. For some reason we just stood there, rooted by shock, and fear, and utter confusion: wondering what to do next and where to go: thinking about getting the hell out of there but for reasons we couldn't explain unable to actually do it. By the time we came to our senses and finally decided to try and find our way back to Waterloo a full half-minute had passed. Maybe more. By which time it was too late. Because by this time we were no longer alone.

"Princess Diana," this voice suddenly said from somewhere in the shadows. "She was murdered. I can tell you why, and who did it."

There was scarcely a person in the country who didn't have an opinion on Diana's death—on why she might have been killed and who might have done it. Even those who said they believed she'd died in an accident secretly held opinions on the possible motives for her murder, and MI6 man Richard Mason knew this.

Mason also knew that public opinion on the matter, both pro and con, had to remain divided, not only between the 'accident theorists' and the 'conspiracy theorists'. But more importantly, between the different schools of conspiracy theorists themselves. That way the truth, whatever it was, would become fogged, confused, and of course diluted, sufficiently so that it could never stand up as evidence—not *hard evidence*. And that's what he was after. This was the game's objective. This was why he'd called in the I/Ops team (I/Ops – Information Operations) MI6's in-house 'black propaganda' unit, who'd been planting stories in the mainstream press and influencing the public mood for decades. As his MI6 training had long since taught him, far better to obfuscate the truth with smoke and mirrors than try to conceal it with lies. Deny, debunk, discredit. Allow the truth – or at least a version of it – to be filtered out to the masses, and then ridicule it to the extent that it no longer appeared credible. On its own, that Diana might have been the victim of political assassination seemed worthy of consideration, he was well aware of that. Her involvement with landmines, or with Dodi Fayed, or that she'd pissed off the establishment to the point of no return, all served to bolster this probability in the eyes of the grieving public. He knew that, too. Mixed with a little disinformation, however, stories planted in the press and on the internet by I/Ops – *Henri Paul was drunk; he was driving way too fast; the paparazzi forced him to crash*: and then the vividly fantastic: *Diana had been abducted by aliens; she'd been murdered by the lizards who rule the world; she was still alive, having faked her own death and was living happily with Dodi (and Elvis) on an idyllic island somewhere, away from the media glare* – mixed with these confabulations even the most credible arguments lost their muscle, making the case for murder almost impossible to believe. Indeed, the effort to steer public opinion away from 'assassination' and towards 'accident' was actually now beginning to work. Due largely to I/Ops' strategically managed media campaign, people were gradually coming round to the idea that a drunken chauffeur and a pack of rabid paparazzi could have been, all by themselves, responsible for Diana's death.

But despite this, the problem of motive remained. And this was causing Mason something of a headache.

While the majority seemed ready to accept, even though reluctantly, that the princess could have died in a drink-drive accident, still they seemed unable to sidestep the undeniably glaring motives that continued to suggest foul play. They had, after all, seen for themselves how Diana had waged a very public war on the establishment, how she'd made enemies of some of Whitehall's most powerful czars—not to mention her relentless, media-fuelled campaign against the Royal Family and, indeed, her unprecedented public attack on the Queen. They'd seen, too, how her hugely publicized landmines campaign had threatened to expose the grimy underbelly of Britain's illicit arms trade, and how her romantic involvement with Dodi Fayed had brought the Church to the brink of collapse. She was a rebel, a nuisance, a problem, an enemy of the state in all but name. Multiple motives for her murder existed, plausible motives, viable motives, a fact the public were well enough aware of. No matter how many times the media told them the chauffeur was drunk, no matter how willing they were to accept that 'drink-drive accidents happen every day', the fact that credible motives existed for her murder seemed sufficient to keep the public baying for answers. And this was Mason's problem. This was the source of his headache. This was the stumbling block in his otherwise textbook operation.

And this is why he'd turned the screws on the prince.

"The prince?" I said, still not knowing who I was talking to, although a vague outline of the person to whom the voice belonged was beginning to emerge, several feet in front of me, as my eyes grew gradually more accustomed to the darkness. The person's features, though, remained concealed. "What prince?"

"The Doctor gave you a number."

"He did, yes."

"You didn't call."

"How … how do you know that?"

"Because it was *my* number."

"Ah." I was thinking on my feet now, not knowing whether to stay and chat or make a dash for it while I still could. My mind was whirring, computing possible escape routes as my mouth, thankfully, kept the conversation turning. "But that still doesn't answer my question," I said, scanning the shadows for gaps in the dark. "What prince?"

"If you'd called me you'd know the answer to that."

"Yes, but I didn't call."

"No."

"So what prince are you referring to?"

The voice paused for a moment, as though for thought. Then: "Prince Michael of Albany," it announced. "The legitimate heir to the Throne."

"The Throne? You mean … the Throne of England?"

"Of Scotland."

"But Scotland doesn't have a Throne. It doesn't have a monarchy, not anymore."

"No, but that's all part of the conspiracy, isn't it. That's what you're supposed to think. Remember what the Doctor told you?"

"Yes, but…"

"We think you should meet the prince and decide for yourselves. If nothing else it will open your eyes to who was really behind Diana's death, and why."

Jesus.

I flicked a sideways glance at JB, who responded with a slight shrug of his shoulders and the tiniest shake of his head, as though to express his disbelief, both at the situation we found ourselves in and the conversation we found ourselves having. He too, it seemed, was wondering whether to stay and listen to what this voice from the shadows had to say, or simply make a run for it. In the event neither of us seemed able to decide, either way. So by default, we stayed.

But I continued to scour the darkness for escape routes, just the same.

We were still down by the river, in an unlit, derelict alleyway, not far from the docks, where we'd been dumped by our fake BBC chauffeur just minutes earlier. It was difficult to see much at all, but from silhouette and sound I *was* able to form a vague picture of our immediate surroundings, and the prognosis for escape wasn't good. Scanning briefly left and right I could just make out what appeared to be a palisade steel fence blocking off the end of the alleyway, separating alleyway from quayside and the sound of the river beyond. Escape route number one: blocked. The only other route out of here that I could see was a tidy two-hundred yards or more back up the alleyway towards the main drag, the way we'd been driven in, but the voice – its owner, and possibly its accomplices, too – stood between us and that particular exit route. We were trapped. And worse still, we now found ourselves in dialogue with a disembodied voice that professed to know who killed Diana, and why.

Was this real? Was it really happening? Had we really just been abducted outside BBC Broadcasting House and taken against our will to a derelict alleyway in London's dockland?

We had, there was no avoiding the fact. And it felt like some kind of mad dream, one of those dreams where your heart pumps faster than your mind's able to think. What was most disturbing of all about this particular mad dream, though, was that the owner of this voice – a man's voice, cultured, if a little plummy – clearly knew who we were and what we were up to. He knew, at any rate, that we'd recently spoken to the Doctor, the former Foreign Office historian whom we'd interviewed on the London Eye several weeks earlier; he knew the Doctor had given us a telephone number to call and that we hadn't yet made that call. He obviously knew, too, that we'd been scheduled to give an interview at the BBC earlier that evening because he'd sent his chauffeur to pick us up.

How did he know these things? Who the hell were these people?

One thing was clear: the owner of the voice and the Doctor, my rationale was telling me, must have been accomplices. Or at least acquaintances, perhaps members of the same covert cabal, some or other masonic cabal maybe, or even a more official organization, like MI5 or MI6. The Doctor had said he'd spent most of his life working for the Foreign Office, after all, MI6's official face. Maybe he'd never really left. Maybe he was still working for them, or for some other Whitehall department—who knows? As for our captor, it was patently clear that whoever he was he must have been someone with genuine muscle—someone, at least, with the means to have organized our abduction from outside the BBC building and then have us transported to this dark and deserted alleyway on the edge of London's dockland. That fact alone unnerved me. And to judge by the look on JB's face, it unnerved him, too.

"Look," JB finally said, bravely, the anxiety in his tone almost palpable. "If you expect us to stand here and hold a friendly conversation you'd better think again. You just abducted us. Whoever you are you can't go around abducting people and expect them not to object."

"Yes, I'm sorry about that," the voice calmly replied. "It was the only way to ensure we met in private."

"That's ridiculous," I said.

"Ridiculous but true. You're being followed. This was the only way of ensuring that your pursuers wouldn't be able to listen in on our conversation. What I have to say is for your ears only."

"Well whatever you have to say, please make it brief. We have a train to catch at Waterloo, and if we miss it we'll be stranded in London for the night with nowhere to stay."

"There's no need to worry about that," the voice assured. "If you miss your train I'll arrange your passage home. But first I want to tell you something that might provide the key to your enquiries into Diana's death. I know why she was murdered, you see."

"So you said."

"I also know who did it. But before I tell you anything I need to be convinced that you're serious in your commitment to uncovering the truth."

"I'd have thought the fact that we've been constantly monitored by MI5 and MI6 for the past God-knows-how-long would confirm that much."

"All that tells me is that you're of interest to the intelligence services. Nothing more. The fact is you didn't call the number the Doctor gave you. You met with him almost a month ago and you still haven't called the number. That tells me you're less than efficient in your endeavour, even if you do profess to being serious."

"We'd planned to make the call tomorrow," JB said, picking the business card I'd given him earlier that evening from his jacket pocket and holding it up in front of him, toying with it nervously as he spoke. "I have the card with the number on it here—look."

"So why haven't you called before now?"

"Because we wanted to give it our full attention," I said plainly, growing less nervous as the conversation progressed, and even a little narked that now we were having to justify ourselves. "If you've been monitoring us like everybody else seems to have been doing you'll have noticed we've been somewhat busy with media commitments these past few weeks. We simply haven't had the time. From what the Doctor said it seemed it would involve us having to follow up new lines of enquiry, and we wanted to wait until we had a few days to ourselves so that we could do the job properly." I paused, then added: "And anyway, you needn't have gone to all this bother just to tell us who you think killed Diana. We know who killed her."

"What you know is that MI6, or a renegade element within MI6, was responsible for orchestrating the operation. What you don't know is who was personally behind it and why it was ordered in the first place."

"We have a good idea," JB came back. "We have our own sources. We know more than you may think, as our book will show when it arrives."

"Ah, yes, your book," the voice said with some irony. "I was coming to that." A brief hiatus followed, during which JB and I exchanged anxious glances, our eyes searching each other's resolve, then flitting back in the direction of the voice in search of its still-concealed owner. The darkness was too thick for us to make out the man's features, but had I been able to glimpse his face my guess was he would have been chewing his lips in thought right now, mulling over what he was about to divulge next—which, as it turned out, fairly shook us to our bones. "You know you've been snared, don't you," he unexpectedly said after the short silence. "You know you've been trawled and netted by the shop front network—"

The shop front network...?

"—You were turned down by every British publisher worth its weight. As a result you were forced to set your sights further afield, on American publishers in particular. Eventually you were turned down by virtually all of them as well, until finally you were forced to sign your work over to … well, to the only publisher willing to take you on."

"What of it?" I wasn't at all surprised that he knew all this; in recent weeks we'd spoken openly on both TV and radio about our difficulties in finding a UK publisher, and about how we'd been forced to go to America in order to get our book published. It was no secret. What did strike me, though, was how meticulously this man must have been listening to our story. "What are you getting at?"

"Intelligence agencies have their own network of what they call *shop fronts*, companies either owned by them or otherwise utilized by them for their own purposes. Have you ever stopped to consider why this particular publisher took you on when all the others turned you down?"

"No, I've never really thought about it."

"Well think about it now."

I did, but only for a beat. "Are you saying our publisher is a shop front?"

"What I'm saying is that certain publishing houses are set up specifically to publish books that major publishers have been warned *not* to publish. MI6 have their shop front publishers; the CIA have theirs. Both agencies know that to ban a book like yours outright would only create more publicity, and therefore more demand for the book. So instead they make sure the book is published not by any of the major publishers – because that would give the book credibility – but by one of their shop front publishers, which are invariably smaller, independent outfits whose list includes any number of, shall we say, fringe titles."

"You mean conspiracy books."

"If you prefer. Either way, by association anything revealed by authors such as yourselves, anything that otherwise might be deemed serious enough to be officially investigated, is immediately discredited, and tarred with the same wacko conspiracy brush as all the other conspiracy theories out there — many of which, in particular the more ludicrous ones, have been concocted by the intelligence services anyway. It's a game at which they've become particularly proficient."

I found myself resisting what the voice was telling us, scarcely able to believe – not wanting to believe – what I was hearing. In all truth I found it difficult to accept that our publisher was anything but a regular New York publisher, but with everything else that had happened over these past few years I knew I couldn't just dismiss the notion out of hand. "Are you sure about this?" I said, still trying to reconcile myself with the idea that we might have been duped.

"How long is the book overdue?"

"Almost two years now."

"Long enough to lessen its impact when it finally does arrive."

"I guess."

"Have any British publishers shown an interest in licensing the book over here?"

"Yes, John Blake Publishing. We had a meeting with John Blake personally and he was very keen to licence the rights."

"So what happened?"

"Our American publisher kept quibbling over the terms, unnecessarily in our view. We told him we were happy with the offer but in the end negotiations broke down completely because of our publisher's intransigence."

"I see. And what about your British distributors? Do they enjoy a good working relationship with your publisher?"

"I'm afraid not, no. They've already said they won't be distributing the paperback edition when it comes out because the publisher has messed them about too much already. In their own words our publisher has been 'thoroughly unprofessional' and a 'nightmare to work with'."

"Am I sensing a pattern here? Would you say your publisher is doing all possible to make your book successful? Or perhaps the opposite?"

I didn't answer that question, not right away. Perhaps I was afraid of hearing my own answer. "But if what you're inferring is true," I said, finally, "that would mean we've been manipulated all along, from the outset?"

"I'd say we have to consider that a possibility, wouldn't you? The *powers-that-be* would never have allowed your book to be published by one of the mainstream publishers. On the other hand, of course, they knew they couldn't openly ban it, either. Publication by a shop front was the obvious solution."

The obvious solution.

Beside me, I heard JB fold…

…A few moments later: "Look, you said you could tell us who killed Diana," I said, gathering myself, forcing what I'd just been told to the back of my mind and attempting to move things along. Time was progressing. I was tired. There'd been no sign of the moon in these past ten minutes and London seemed to be getting darker and colder by the minute. The sooner we could get to the meat of the matter and wrap this conversation up the sooner I would be tucked up in my warm, comfortable bed next to Katie. The thought was all-consuming. "You said you could tell us who was personally behind the operation that killed Diana and why it was ordered."

The voice didn't reply, not straight away. Instead it sounded as though it was sucking its teeth while it considered how best to respond. It was several moments before it finally said: "I can tell you the name of the man in charge of the operation."

"I can tell *you* that."

"Oh...?"

"Mason," I said, recalling to mind what Lacey had told me the last time I'd seen him in Hyde Park. "Richard Mason. Head of MI6 Special Operations, Europe. Mason's not his real name, but a code name he likes to use because he's a high-ranking Freemason. Evidently he gets off on the idea."

The voice seemed genuinely surprised. "Very good," it said. "Very good indeed."

"Yes, well, like JB said, we've done our homework. What we really need to know now is Mason's real name."

"Ah. I'm afraid that's where we all come unstuck. Like all true legends he doesn't appear to have one."

That's exactly what Lacey said, I thought to myself, but didn't say it. "So what's the big secret then?" I said instead. "Why did Mason order the operation?"

"Oh, it wasn't Mason who ordered it. He might have been the project manager, but the architect was someone else entirely, although of course it wasn't just one person."

"A group?"

"A very secretive and powerful group, yes, a consortium of, shall we say, socially elevated people—people with a vested interest in maintaining the status quo. People with a vested interest in keeping the blood pure."

"Now you're beginning to sound like the Doctor. Cryptic was *his* middle name, too."

"How about if I told you it was the oligarchy that underpins the House of Windsor and its impenetrable power-circle. Would that be straightforward enough for you?"

"Not really, no. You can't just infer that it was the royal family and expect us to accept it as though you've just revealed the world's biggest secret. Everyone and their dog has pointed their finger at the royals. You have to have evidence. You can't just say it was Prince Charles because he wanted to marry Camilla, or that it was Prince Philip because he didn't want the future king to have Muslim stepbrothers or stepsisters."

"Now you're getting warm…"

"Perhaps. Perhaps not. But the point is you have to back up your claim with evidence."

"If we could do that I wouldn't be standing here now, talking to you. It's not that simple. The people who did this are extremely powerful. And dangerous. They will go to any lengths to protect their legacy."

"Their legacy?"

"The bloodline. No doubt the Doctor would have mentioned it when he spoke to you?"

"He did, yes."

"To retain control of the bloodline they would even murder a princess. Why? Because to control the bloodline is to control GOD."

"GOD…?"

"Yes, GOD—Gold, Oil and Diamonds, the bloodline of global power. It's not just about the royal blood, Mr King. That's easily manipulated, and has been for centuries, as I'm sure the Doctor would have informed you. No, it's not just about that. When all is said and done it's about money, and power, and that means control of the world's resources—GOD. That's the Holy Grail of political power, though to separate it entirely from the bloodline is not possible."

I was trying to keep with the thread. "You're talking in riddles again. Who exactly *are* these people? Does anybody actually know?"

"I've just told you who they are. They occupy the seat of power because the legitimate heir to that seat has been usurped. I'm afraid I can tell you no more than that."

"But you've told us nothing."

"If you want to know more you must ask the prince yourself. He's expecting you for lunch at the Balmoral Hotel in Edinburgh, at one o'clock the day after tomorrow. Now you'd better be on your way or you'll miss your train. My chauffeur will be here in a moment to take you to the station."

"That's it?" I said, my tiredness – my frustration – nearing boiling point. "You abducted us and brought us here against our will to tell us this? That the prince – whoever he is – requests our presence?

"One o'clock, the day after tomorrow, the Balmoral Hotel. Goodnight gentlemen."

As the voice turned and retreated into the darkness the headlamps of the limousine that had brought us here swung into the top end of the alleyway and shone directly on us, blinding us and preventing us from witnessing the stranger's departure. I wanted to turn and run after him, question him further, yell at him, throttle him. But I knew it was pointless. We still didn't know who or how many others might have been loitering in the shadows. All we knew was, whoever they were, these people were organized and potentially dangerous. Frankly, at this point all I wanted to do was go home.

"Déjà vu," I said sarcastically to the chauffeur as JB and I climbed in the back of the limousine for the second time that evening. "Straight to Waterloo Station this time, please."

I closed the door.

Easing myself back in the seat and snapping my seat belt on I realized that *déjà vu* perhaps wasn't the most appropriate phrase to have used. After all, I hadn't seen this night coming at all.

241

43

It wasn't the first time he'd broken into this apartment. On explicit orders from his MI5 field boss he'd been here before, had picked this very lock, had let himself in and installed two covert listening devices similar to the ones he was about to install now. On that occasion he'd also been instructed to locate and photograph specified personal effects—passport, bank statements, credit cards, pin numbers: and most important of all, an original copy of the occupant's birth certificate. Due to the occupant's naivety, and the agent's proficiency, he'd managed to collect a full shopping bag. Bank and credit card transactions had since been meticulously monitored back at GCHQ, and on occasion, blocked; while the occupant's passport had been confiscated and revoked. The birth certificate, meanwhile, had been falsified and reclassified as counterfeit, but unlike the passport, had been allowed to 'float' until such times as it might be needed to prove 'false identity'—to show the world that its owner was not who he claimed to be. That time had now arrived. And because it had, surveillance on the subject had been stepped up. Which was why the agent had returned to carry out another 'black bag' operation. The covert listening devices he'd installed on his previous visit had, for some inexplicable reason, stopped transmitting, GCHQ had reported, and he'd been sent back to replace them. As he ascended the refurbished Georgian complex's outer staircase and made his way along the elevated landing for the second time that year he was again reminded of the subject's identity. It forced a dry smile on his lips. It wasn't unusual for MI5 to bug the homes of known 'resident aliens', of course, in particular those deemed a threat to the security of the United Kingdom. What was unusual, though, was the status of this alien in particular. This alien wore the title: *HRH*.

"Safe to go," the voice in his earpiece told him as he approached the apartment's front door "The subject has just arrived at the Balmoral Hotel, on schedule. He'll be there for some time."

"Noted." A furtive glance left then right to ensure there was no one else about, and the agent set to work.

Dipping his hand into a built-in tool pouch concealed in the inside pocket of his sweat jacket he pulled out a flattened-steel lock-pick and inserted it into the door's pin-and-tumbler Yale lock. Deftly, he started to feel for each of the lock's key pins, easing each one in turn from its mooring and releasing the springs and tumbler pins that would free up the lock's inner cylinder. Then, using the lock-pick as a surrogate key he turned that cylinder, opened the door and let himself in, being sure to close the door securely behind him.

Once inside he made his way through the reception hallway and into the open-plan lounge and dining area, where he set his eyes on the bookcase lining the far wall. Bypassing the rosewood dinner table and chairs, negotiating a careful path around the low-slung sofa dividing lounge from dining area, he made his way over to the bookcase, where he reached up and ran his fingers behind the small pile of magazines stacked precariously on the top shelf. There he felt for the air-conditioning vent-cover on the wall behind the magazines, and using the small screwdriver he carried in his tool pouch, unscrewed it. This was where he'd installed device 'A' on his first visit, but having removed the cover and felt inside the cavity his fingers told him it was empty. Device 'A' was no longer there. It had been removed.

Making a mental note he replaced the cover, then turned and retraced his steps back around the sofa and headed for the frosted glass-panelled door over by the breakfast bar. The door had been left slightly ajar, he could see; it opened into a cramped, windowless office space scarcely big enough to house the desk, chair and – more pertinently – the computer he knew he would find in there. It was inside the computer casing that he'd installed device 'B' on his last visit, in a cavity between the motherboard and the CPU, and he'd done so in such a way that, to the untrained eye, it looked every inch one of the computer's core components. Changing the screwdriver head – *click-click* – he stepped into the office and removed the computer's outer casing, and was not the least surprised to discover that device 'B' had been removed, too. Mystery explained, he thought to himself. The subject must have had the apartment swept for bugs. This time he would have to be more discreet.

Having replaced the computer's outer casing he quickly disconnected the machine from the wall socket, removed the plug and replaced it with one he carried in his tool pouch. It was no ordinary plug, of course; it contained a built-in microphone and micro-transmitter, voice-activated, and worked on a closed-cell digital network similar to GSM, though infinitely more secure, and sophisticated. Indeed, the spies back at GCHQ listening to the conversations it transmitted would hear them no clearer if they were here in the apartment in person. Even so, he would fit a second device as backup before he left, in a specially adapted light bulb he also carried in his tool pouch. He would fit that in the lounge.

"Shopping list completed," the agent said into his concealed mouthpiece as he exited the apartment around fifteen minutes later. "He's all yours."

He then started back along the elevated landing and disappeared down the staircase—anonymously, like a ghost.

"Subject One already in the building," a different agent said into her mobile phone. She was standing beside the Duke of Wellington statue, outside the National Archives of Scotland Building in Edinburgh, dressed in jeans and camel tweed jacket, milling discreetly with other pedestrians and sightseers. The Balmoral Hotel was in her sights, on the opposite side of the street. "I have subjects Two and Three approaching now."

"Remain positioned. Call in when they leave."

"Affirmative."

As we approached the Balmoral Hotel my eye was for some reason taken by the commanding figure of the Duke of Wellington on the opposite side of the street. The old duke, cast in time-blackened bronze, was mounted magnificently on his rearing steed outside the National Archives of Scotland Building, and was the focus of a small group of interested parties—an Asian couple taking notes, and photos; a young man making a sketch on a pad; and several others, perhaps tourists, standing around, admiring the old soldier, him and his horse.

There was one other there, too, a woman dressed in jeans and camel tweed jacket standing slightly apart from the small crowd. I'd noticed her glance over at JB and I as we'd approached the hotel entrance. And now, flicking a sideways glance, I could see that she was talking on a mobile phone. It bothered me. I couldn't help wondering who she was, who she was talking to, why she was there. My paranoia again? Possibly. But given that we seemed to have entered a new phase of our investigation of late – our meeting with the Doctor on the London Eye, our 'kidnapping' outside BBC Broadcasting House and our subsequent *tête-à-tête* with a faceless voice down by the river in London's dockland; and now our 'pre-arranged' meeting with a self-styled prince – I figured it more likely than not that our movements were being monitored.

One eye still on the woman in the camel tweed jacket – still there, still talking on her mobile phone – I followed JB into the Balmoral Hotel.

"Good day, gentlemen." We were greeted at the door by a rather camp concierge who ushered us through the foyer and into the hotel restaurant. He motioned towards the window table. "Your party is waiting."

As we made our way over to the table I couldn't help feeling this whole charade was a setup, or at best a distraction. I couldn't help wondering what we were doing here in this chic, five-star restaurant with its walnut floors, dark-wood furniture and its 1930s-style Art Deco surrounds. Not that I was averse to luxury, nor indeed the stylized décor. But I *was* averse to this grumbling sense of feeling out of place, not so much in the restaurant as in myself, wary of the recent deviation our investigation seemed to have taken and wondering where it might lead us next. The seemingly random surfacing of such dubious characters as the Doctor and the 'kidnapper' in the past few weeks, appearing out of nowhere, like pop-up dummies at a shooting gallery, had unsettled me. JB, too. Who were they? Why, at this late stage in our investigation, had they emerged from their secret place and offered us cryptic insights into Princess Diana's death? It just didn't seem real.

"Ah, Jon and John I presume," the diminutive figure seated at the table said as he stood up to greet us and offered his hand. He was not what I was expecting. Elegantly dressed in dark-blue suit and nutmeg brogues – groomed hair, stylish spectacles in transparent frames, a winning smile – he seemed every bit the princely brand he claimed to be. Except, that is, for his stature. If he was five feet standing upright, that's all he was.

I shook his outstretched hand. "I'm the Jon without the H," I said. "Jon King. And this is my colleague, John Beveridge."

"Yes, I believe we spoke on the phone."

"That's right," JB said. "It's a pleasure to meet you … your … *highness*…?"

He chuckled, boyishly. "Good Lord, no. Please, call me Michael. It's my name."

"But I thought…?"

"I am Prince Michael James Alexander Stewart, heir to the Honours of Scotland, although I doubt I will ever in truth accede to those Honours. And even if I do, my name will always be Michael to my friends. Formalities are for functions and funerals. Please, take a seat."

And that, surprisingly, was pretty much how it was: loose and informal, despite the five-star surroundings in which we found ourselves and the elevated social class of the man there with us (despite also, that I still couldn't help feeling we were the unwitting stars in some elaborate reality show—any minute I expected the show's host to appear and exclaim: *You've been framed!* And then we'd all wake up and go home.)

But that didn't happen. There was no show and there was no host. Just this slightly surreal situation in which JB and I found ourselves, lunching with a guy who was either the rightful-though-deposed King of Scotland, or he was a nutter. And although the latter option seemed perhaps the most apposite, right now I just couldn't be sure—a fact that only served to make things seem even more bizarre, even more surreal. Inwardly I counted to ten. Then, tightening the belt of my mind I sat myself down at the table and opened my attaché case in search of my ever faithful Dictaphone, and reminded myself that it wasn't us who'd gone in search of Michael; rather, that it was the Doctor, and then our mysterious kidnapper, who'd compelled us in his direction. Why these two obscure characters had been so adamant we meet this charismatic little man remained to be seen. Hopefully all would now be revealed.

Over lunch we spoke extensively about Michael's alleged Stuart heritage, about how, as the Doctor had affirmed, he was descended from Bonnie Prince Charlie, and about how he'd been born in exile, in Belgium, and had returned to his ancestral home of Scotland in 1976 to pursue his claim as Scotland's rightful king.

"I'm the first one since eighteen-eighty-seven to raise the issue of the Stewart claim," he told us, making a point also of explaining that, since the heady days of the Stuart reign in the seventeenth and early eighteenth centuries – James I, Charles I, Charles II, James II, Mary II, Anne: plus of course, Prince Charles Edward Louis John Casimir Sylvester Severino Maria Stuart, popularly known as Bonnie Prince Charlie – the family name had reverted to its original spelling of 'Stewart', derived as it was from the High Stewards of Scotland in the 12th century. It was Prince Michael, we were enthusiastically informed, who was the current Head of the Royal House of Stewart.

"I felt it was my duty as *de jure* constitutional monarch to return to my ancestral homeland and endeavour to restore Scotland's freedoms."

"And they actually allowed you to do that?" I said between mouthfuls of to-die-for Shetland salmon. "They don't mind you being here, doing what you're doing?"

"Well, it's not quite as simple as that," Michael said in his 'born-in-exile' accent: native Belgian with a manifest Scots lilt. "I have been in Scotland now for twenty-five years and not a week goes by without some or other contact from, shall we say, Her Majesty's errand boys. If they're not harassing me in person then they're doing it behind my back. Only last month I had my apartment swept for listening devices by a private counter-surveillance firm. Not for the first time, I might add. It cost me a small fortune." He dabbed at the corner of his mouth with his napkin. "Anyway, this time they found two devices concealed in my home. Last time it was only one. But the point is they're always breaking into my home and planting their surveillance equipment. I can only assume they enjoy my conversation."

He laughed at his own quip, that boyish chuckle again.

Then: "They even came knocking on my door when I was in, as brazen as you like" he said, shaking his head, as though even he found that one difficult to believe. "*Just checking up on me*, they say. *Harassing me*, I say, reminding me they are always there, watching me, keeping tabs on me." He grinned. "I of course invited them in and made them a cup of tea! Well, why not? It was eight o'clock in the morning and I was making one anyway, and I wanted them to know I wasn't afraid of them and that I had nothing to hide. On that occasion they asked to see some of my personal family papers, and I told them I didn't keep them at home, that they were in a vault in the bank. Do you know what they said?"

"No…"

"They said I was lying, and they pointed to a drawer in my sideboard, the top drawer, where I keep what I call my *Albany File*, which contains some of my family papers, my birth certificate, various letters from MPs, from the Home Office and the Prime Minister and so forth. A lot of my important papers. They said the papers we want to see are in that drawer."

"And were they?"

"No, thankfully. As luck would have it I had moved them about a week or so before. But the point is, how did they know that I kept my important papers in that particular drawer? There is only one answer: they had seen them. They had broken into my home and searched through my personal belongings when I wasn't there."

For the first time since our arrival the ingenuous spark in Michael's eye dulled to a sober, almost cynical hue.

"So you see, gentlemen, although they have allowed me to remain here, it has been at a cost. I've had my passport revoked for one thing, even though I am a naturalized British citizen. All I have now is this." He produced a 1995 British visitor's passport from his inside pocket and handed it across the table to me. Sure enough it bore the title *HRH Prince Michael James Alexander Stewart of Albany*. "It's out of date now, of course, which means I am unable to travel. You might also find this of interest."

Dipping his hand in his inside pocket once more he pulled out a letter addressed to *HRH Prince Michael of Albany*. The letter was from British Home Secretary, Jack Straw.

"I spoke to him," JB said, suddenly animated, peering excitedly across me at the letter in my hand. "Or at least I tried to. They said he was unavailable for comment."

"Why did you want to speak to Jack Straw?" Michael asked.

JB suddenly looked a little sheepish. "I was checking up on you, to be perfectly honest," he confessed. "Doing a bit of homework."

It was a confession Michael found particularly amusing. "Ha! And what did you find out?"

"I found out that the British Government doesn't like talking about you."

And JB was right, as we'd discovered only twenty-four hours earlier.

Given that we'd arrived home late following our enforced *tête-à-tête* down by the river, and given also that our lunch with Prince Michael had been prearranged for just two days after that, there'd been scarce time for us to do very much homework, much less compile a casebook on the mutinous prince. We had, nonetheless, made the most of what little time we'd had.

From a couple of rather obscure articles we'd managed to dig up, one in a Scottish magazine and the other tucked away in the pages of a *Guardian* supplement, we'd learned about Michael's citizenship problems and also that Jack Straw had indeed written to 'HRH Prince Michael of Albany' outlining the government's reasons for revoking his passport (even so, to hold that letter in my hand now made it seem all the more real). We'd learned, too, that the government had branded Michael a fraud, and even a 'terrorist', and had gone to some lengths to 'prove' his birth certificate counterfeit by circulating a copy that contained one or two significant alterations. Either the man was what the government said he was, we concluded, or he was the victim of an orchestrated smear campaign. And if the latter, why? We could only assume that, for one reason or another, Michael posed a pretty substantial threat.

For the record, we also discovered that in 1807 Parliament had declared the Stewarts 'extinct in exile', which basically meant that the British Government was no longer obliged to recognize the Stewart line or claim. And that included Michael. Yet Jack Straw, one of the articles affirmed, had addressed Michael as 'His Royal Highness' in the letter he'd written to him. Why would he have done that? we wondered. Why would Jack Straw have addressed Michael as 'His Royal Highness' if the government considered him a fraud and a terrorist? It didn't make sense.

So we decided to ask him. Or at least his spokesperson. Just the day before we travelled to Edinburgh, JB called the Home Office and questioned them on why – if Parliament had declared Michael's family 'extinct in exile', and no longer recognized the Royal House of Stewart; and indeed, if they considered the man a fraud and a terrorist – why Jack Straw had written to Michael and addressed him as 'HRH Prince Michael of Albany'?

"We remain unconcerned with this person unless he makes a direct and formal challenge for the British Throne," the Home Office spokesperson said in the absence of Jack Straw.

"Fine, but that wasn't my question," JB replied. "The Home Secretary wrote to Prince Michael and addressed him as 'His Royal Highness'. Can you confirm that this means the government now recognizes Prince Michael's status and that it will support him in his efforts to restore the Scottish monarchy?"

"We have no further comment."

"Do you see him as a threat?"

"No comment."

"A terrorist?"

No reply.

"Well can you tell us why you refuse to grant him a British passport?" JB demanded to know. "Prince Michael is a naturalized British citizen and yet, it would seem quite arbitrarily, you decided to revoke his passport. Can you explain to me why you did this?"

"That would be a matter for the Home Secretary to decide."

"Can I put the question to him, then?"

"I'm afraid Mr Straw is unavailable."

"Well can't you give me an answer on his behalf?"

"I just did. We have no further comment."

"But I'm a taxpaying British citizen. I have a right to an answer."

"I'm afraid I'm unable to comment further."

Realizing he was getting nowhere fast, JB terminated his call to the Home Office and phoned the Prime Minister's residence instead. Ten Downing Street was equally evasive.

"I'd like to know why you refuse to grant Prince Michael of Albany a British passport?" JB said to Number Ten.

"Who?"

"His Royal Highness Prince Michael James Alexander Stewart of Albany."

"I'm afraid that would be a matter for the Home Office."

"I've just spoken to the Home Office and they say they're not prepared to comment on the matter. The Home Secretary recognizes Prince Michael's royal status and also that he's a naturalized British citizen, but he refuses to issue him with a passport. I'd like to know why."

"One moment, please." There was a brief pause, a faint rustling sound on the end of the line, as though the secretary was gathering paper and pen. Finally: "Would you care to tell me who this Prince Michael is, exactly?"

"He is the current senior heir to the Royal House of Stewart."

"The Royal House of Stewart? But the House of Stewart is extinct, in exile, I believe."

"That's not what Prince Michael says."

"Well it's what the British Government says."

"Does the British Government acknowledge the existence of Prince Michael?"

"Well I suppose if the Home Office has been in communication with him the answer must be yes."

"But he can't have a passport?"

"I'm afraid you'll have to ask the Home Secretary that."

"He won't speak to me."

A further pause, this one a little tense. Then: "Look," the civil servant finally said, clearly exasperated. "Are you saying this person, this … this Prince Michael … are you saying he's laying claim to the British Throne?"

"No. The Scottish Throne."

"But the Scottish Monarchy is extinct."

"No it isn't. Prince Michael is the senior hereditary descendant of King James the Second Stuart of Great Britain and he is very much alive and well. Jack Straw recently wrote to him and addressed him as 'His Royal Highness'…"

"Yes, so you said. But there is no Scottish Monarchy, not anymore. There is no Scottish Monarchy and there is no House of Stewart."

"So where does that leave Prince Michael?"

This time the silence was acid. "We remain unconcerned with this person unless he makes a direct and formal challenge for the British Throne."

Or words to that effect. JB gave up.

•

Some moments later we'd finished our lunch and the waiter had just cleared the table and disappeared back to the kitchen with our used plates and crockery stacked cockily on his shirtsleeve. I brought the conversation round to the primary reason we were here.

"We were told you might be able to shed some light on Princess Diana's death," I put to Michael.

"Go on."

"We think she was murdered and we're investigating possible motives."

"Then investigate her blood, her lineage."

I glanced over at JB, then back at Prince Michael. "That's what the Doctor said."

"The Doctor?"

"He was one of the two sources we spoke to who suggested we speak to you. The other one was—"

"Yes, I know who the other one was. He told me what happened and I can only apologize."

"So who is he?"

"Let us just say he's a particularly fervent supporter of the Stewart claim to the Throne. He is not alone." Before we could question him further, Michael added: "You mentioned the Doctor?"

I nodded. "He said he'd worked for a government department that dealt with what he referred to as the counter-monarchy problem."

"I know of this department," Michael said. "I've been on the wrong end of its bully-boy tactics too many times. But I'm afraid I have no idea who this Doctor is, not unless you have a name..?"

I gave a single shake of my head.

"Well if he truly worked where he said he worked then he would have been very aware of the Stewart claim, not only through me, but also through Diana. That's probably why he sent you to me."

"The Stewart claim through Diana? Can you elaborate?"

"Diana was very much of the Stewart heritage; she carried the Stewart gene, the blood. It's all to do with the blood. There are those who want the bloodline restored to what they see as its rightful place. I am certain they would have had Diana in their sights as someone who could have helped them achieve their aim."

"Really? It sounds like you're implying Diana could have been persuaded to make a claim for the Throne if she'd lived—"

"Well…"

"—It's something the Doctor also alluded to, or at least that she was in a position to head up some kind of counter-monarchy setup within the Royal Household."

"Oh, I think she was already doing that. But to make a claim for the Throne? No, I don't think so. I don't think that's what your man was alluding to."

"What then?"

"More likely that some or other group was planning such a move and they saw Diana as their perfect figurehead—not only because of her Stewart blood, but also her popularity. She had the British public eating out of her hand. Couple that with her royal heritage and you start to see why the Doctor and his department might have considered her a threat."

I was gobsmacked by this statement. "Some or other group?" I said. "But what kind of group would contemplate making a claim for the Throne? In this day and age the very idea seems absurd, and completely unrealistic."

"Perhaps."

"So who? What group would dare conspire to challenge for the Throne?"

"One that supports the bloodline, is the simple answer. Or perhaps I should say one that supports the restoration of the bloodline to the thrones of Europe, and that includes England. Of course, I don't mean that they would attempt some sort of military coup or anything of that nature. The days of William of Orange marching on London with his army and ousting the incumbent monarch are long gone. And thank goodness for that!" He laughed out loud again. Then: "I'm talking more of hijacking the system, infiltrating the Royal Household and manipulating events from the inside, in much the same way as the bloodline was overthrown in the first place. In much the same way as the Carolingians usurped the Merovingians, and later the Hanover-Windsors usurped the Stuarts—more by political manoeuvring than military might. And for this Diana was the perfect candidate. You must remember that Diana was more royal than many people think, in many respects even more so than Prince Charles. Her lineage can be traced directly back to King James I of Great Britain and beyond, to the great Merovingian kings, Clovis and Dagobert. And that means she was of messianic stock; at least those who support the restoration believe this to be the case."

Messianic stock?

My head was beginning to reel—part with bewilderment, part with disbelief. The Doctor had made some pretty wild claims himself, claims similar to those being made here, now, by Michael. He too had referred to the bloodline as *messianic*; he'd said that it dated back centuries – *as far as records go and beyond* – and that it *ruled the Western world* today. He'd also said that the Stuart kings had descended from this bloodline and that this was why they'd been persecuted and ridiculed by history. Of course, the *messianic* hypothesis was not a new one; that the bloodline in question stretched back via the Merovingian kings of Dark Ages Europe to the ancient kings of Judah and even that it included the historical Jesus was an idea that had permeated popular culture in recent times. It was a sentiment echoed in the works of Donovan Joyce and Barbara Thiering, I knew; others too, not least Michael Baigent, Richard Leigh and Henry Lincoln, international bestselling authors of *The Holy Blood And The Holy Grail*. But even so, these were all hypothetical works based on the authors' own research and their interpretations of what that research had exhumed. They were tantalizing but unproven theories. What JB and I were encountering here, on the other hand, was real—real and extraordinary. It involved real characters with extraordinary claims. I was scarcely able to wrap my head around it all.

"There's an inference in what you say that brings to mind the Knights Templar and the Priory of Sion," I felt I had to put to Michael. And it was true. The bloodline that Michael – and the Doctor – had referred to was what others had coined *the bloodline of Jesus and Mary Magdalene*, which, they said, had passed down to the present day via the Merovingian kings of Dark Ages Europe and later the Stuart kings of 17th-century Britain. It was the Priory of Sion and its military arm, the Knights Templar, so the story claimed, that had been formed at some point towards the end of the 11th century to protect the secret of that bloodline and its *messianic* heirs. According to Pierre Plantard, the French draughtsman who in 1956 revealed the Priory's existence, the bloodline was still extant today, something both the Doctor and now Michael seemed to have affirmed in their own way. But I was aware of the story; I'd read about it, I'd followed it, and I knew that more recently Plantard's claim about the Priory of Sion had been shot to pieces by journalists and scholars alike. "I thought all that had been exposed as a hoax," I said.

Surprisingly, Michael was in agreement. "Yes, and a good thing, too," he said with some meaning. "I never did believe the Priory of Sion was anything other than a clever deception on Plantard's part. But that doesn't mean the bloodline is a hoax as well. Not at all. The bloodline is very real, and has been the focus of a constant power game that has lasted centuries. Certainly the neo-Templar groups who support the bloodline today do so because they believe in its authenticity and its right to one day be restored to power. The problem is these groups include some rather radical factions who would give anything to wrest the British Throne back from its current incumbents, the Windsors. I would suggest it was one of these factions who saw Diana as the potential figurehead for their ambitions." He again leaned across the table, napkin in hand and pinched tight to the corner of his mouth, in a manner that told us he was about to say something he'd rather no one else heard. "Through various channels they have even approached me," he wanted us to know, his voice scarcely more than a breath. "But my only interest is in restoring the Scottish Throne. Nothing more."

He sat back and deposited his napkin on his empty plate.

"Would you like to see the dessert menu?" the waiter said, suddenly there at our table. The slightly tanned young man with striking green eyes and perfect teeth seemed to have appeared from nowhere, taking all three of us by surprise. I wondered if he'd heard any of what Prince Michael had just said.

"Just a coffee for me, please," I said. "Black."

"Yes, I'll have a coffee as well," Prince Michael said. "But with milk."

JB echoed him. "I'll have mine with milk, too."

"Three coffees, one black," the waiter confirmed, then turned and disappeared towards the kitchen.

I peered back across the table at Prince Michael, who had momentarily removed his spectacles and was busy buffing them up with a spare napkin. My mind was still whirring with thoughts of the bloodline and some cloak-and-dagger attempt by a secret cabal of neo-Templars to restore it to the British Throne, using Diana to do it. Or Michael. *Through various channels they have even approached me*, he'd just said. Was this man for real? Was he even who he said he was? I churned this question over in my mind for what seemed a small eternity, back and forth, and then again, but never quite finding the answer. So I rephrased it: Would this man – *anyone* – have given twenty-five years of his life, struggling against the odds, with no realistic chance of ever achieving his goal, if he *wasn't* who he said he was? Why? What would have been his motive? It seemed the bleakest prospect. He'd left everything, after all, I reminded myself – his family, his friends, his job – left it all in his native Belgium and had arrived penniless in Edinburgh in 1976 with the sole intention of pursuing his claim to a throne that no longer, in reality, existed: a throne and a monarchy that had been extinct for several hundred years. The actions of a madman? A self-deluded soul? Or a person of unrivalled conviction? I didn't know. All I knew was, whatever anyone else thought of him, whatever anyone else believed about him – indeed, whatever the truth about the bloodline and the neo-Templars and Diana's Stewart heritage – one thing was evident: Prince Michael James Alexander Stewart of Albany believed lock, stock and several smoking barrels that he was the senior male heir to the Royal House of Stewart. And as such, that he was the rightful heir to the defunct Throne of Scotland.

Who was I to argue the point?

"One last thing," I said. JB had gone to the bathroom and I was seated at the table alone with Prince Michael. I sensed a vulnerability in him, one I felt sure might feel challenged by the question I was about to put to him. I felt I had to put it anyway. "If you are who you say you are," I posed, "you too are a descendant of the bloodline. Which presumably means you're descended from … Jesus?"

To my surprise, Michael took it in his stride. "Yes, I am asked this question a lot, and it's a difficult one to answer because of the elevated status attributed to Jesus today. But I have to be honest with you and say *yes*. In fact it is common knowledge in our family, but you must remember that we don't view Jesus as an incarnation of God, as so many people in the modern world seem to do. We see Jesus as an historical person, a 'king who did not reign', as the Jewish chronicler Josephus wrote about him."

"And do you think Josephus was speaking literally?"

"Yes, of course. Jesus was of royal stock, of the bloodline, descended from King David. It says so clearly in the Gospels. He was the rightful heir to the Throne of Israel and Judah."

"King of the Jews."

"Precisely."

"So why do you think he never reigned, as Josephus says?"

"Oh, that's simple. Because the Romans installed a puppet monarchy on the Jewish Throne in the form of the Herods, in much the same way as the Anglo-Dutch bankers installed a puppet monarchy on the British Throne in the form of the Hanovers, who are now the Windsors. There's no difference."

I pondered this for a moment. Then: "The Doctor told us there's a department within MI6 that holds genealogical documents proving that what you say is right, and that the reason these documents are kept under wraps is to suppress knowledge of the Stewarts and their claim to the Throne."

"To suppress knowledge of the *bloodline* and *its* claim to the Throne. Look, I don't wish to give you a history lesson but let us talk about Diana's Stewart blood for a moment. The reason Diana was brought into the Windsor fold was first and foremost to reintroduce the Stewart strain into the Royal Family, something they have to do every few generations. It is not widely known, in fact it has been well and truly covered up and you certainly won't have been taught this at school, but Queen Victoria was illegitimate. She was not the daughter of Edward, Duke of Kent as is recorded in your history books because Edward was barren, and as Edward was the only one of Victoria's 'parents' to have even the slightest drop of Stewart blood in his veins, the Stewart strain became extinct in the Royal blood at that time. It remained so until today—until Charles married Diana, in fact. I repeat: the reason Diana was brought into the Windsor fold was first and foremost to reintroduce the Stewart strain into the Royal Family and by so doing deflect any legitimate Stewart claim. Do you see? It was a political marriage, I can assure you."

I remembered that the Doctor had spoken about what he'd termed *political and masonic viticulture—the grafting of bloodlines from one vine to another, one family to the next* in order to maintain possession of the bloodline. I'd asked him to be more specific: *How can you possess a bloodline?* I'd put to him. *Marry into it, produce children, get rid of the mother,* he'd replied. He'd added: *Of course, this only creates a bastardized strain of the original bloodline, but it's enough to fulfil the ambitions of those who possess it.*

"A political marriage," I heard myself say, echoing Michael's words. "Diana was purposely selected to marry Charles in order to reintroduce the bloodline gene into the Royal Family. But she became too popular and the combination of her popularity and her Stewart heritage made her a threat. That's what you're saying, right?"

"Exactly. The Stewarts have always been a threat to them. We still are."

"And you think she could have been murdered for this reason?"

"Absolutely, yes, especially when you consider she was planning to marry an Arab-Muslim and have his children. Would they have carried the gene, too? The whole thing just got out of hand."

Just then, JB returned from the bathroom and it was time to wrap things up.

"Subjects leaving the building," the woman in jeans and camel tweed jacket said into her mobile phone as she turned her back on the Duke of Wellington statue and headed off along Leith Street into the anonymity of Edinburgh's suburbs.

"It was good to meet you, Michael," I said. "Thank you for your time."

"My pleasure."

We'd just exited the hotel on Princes Street and were preparing to go our separate ways—Michael back across town to his apartment just off the Royal Circus, about half a mile away, and JB and I to the airport. Sending a furtive glance to the opposite side of the street, to where the Duke of Wellington was still attracting a handful of admirers, I noticed that the woman in jeans and camel tweed jacket I'd seen on our arrival was no longer there. Maybe I'd overreacted, I told myself. Maybe I'd let my paranoia get the better of me again. I gave my attention back to Michael.

"Thanks again. We'll be in touch."

"I look forward to hearing from you." Then he said: "And be careful. They'll be watching you now, even if they weren't before!"

He laughed out loud, then turned and headed off along Princes Street and into St Andrew Street, leaving JB and I even more confused than we'd been before we met him.

44

Over the following weeks and months I actually came to know Prince Michael quite well, and the confusion we'd felt following our Edinburgh lunch was, at least to some extent, allayed as both JB and I were able to hold more relaxed and in-depth conversations with him and gain a better understanding of where he was at and why the Doctor and our mystery kidnapper had wanted us to talk to him. By the time our book finally arrived some twelve months later – and almost two-and-half years late, I might add – Michael had visited my home and stayed overnight on several occasions, and it would even be true to say that he'd become a good family friend. *Stuart Little*, Katie had christened him, after the Hollywood movie of the time—a fitting soubriquet for the diminutive Prince of the Royal House of Stewart, it has to be said. For his part Michael was more than happy to give his time to our project, and even agreed to write a foreword for the book. Which he did. Perhaps it was the best part of fortune, then, that in the end the book *did* arrive late. At least we'd had time to properly prepare Michael's interview and foreword for inclusion in the first edition.

And his involvement didn't stop there, either. Michael also joined JB and I on a number of our book signings and media appearances, both on radio and TV, and was happy, too, to play his part at our speaking events, where he often opened the show with his edifying but entertaining preamble on Diana and her Stewart heritage. And its consequences. Indeed, as per the arrangements we'd made on the telephone barely forty-eight hours earlier, we were fully expecting him to be at this night's conference as well, having once again planned for him to give the opening talk. But for reasons we had yet to discover, this night Michael wouldn't be coming…

"Have you called him?" It was early evening. JB and I had just arrived at the conference centre and were heading across the car park towards the main entrance. The sign above the doors read: PRINCESS DIANA: THE EVIDENCE, A PRESENTATION BY JON KING. We pushed through the double doors and shouldered our way through the milling crowds in the foyer, past the stall where Jackie was selling copies of the book, and finally out through the fire exit on our way backstage to prepare for the talk.

"I've called him several times," JB was saying as we exited the foyer and made our way along the gravel pathway hugging the back of the building. "For some reason he's not picking up. It keeps going through to his voicemail. It's just not like him."

"Well, keep trying."

We entered through the backstage door.

Michael's unexplained absence was bothering me. It seemed to have added a disquieting edge to the evening, made me feel prickly, like an unwanted omen had reared its head and had threatened unpalatable things. I wasn't in the best of moods as it was, it had to be said; I'd learned earlier that day that Katie wouldn't be coming to the talk, either, and the news had flattened me. *I'm at mum's*, the note had said. *I need time to think. The kids are fine. Lunch is in the oven.* It felt like I'd been kicked by a very large, very angry mule. Okay, we hadn't been getting on so well of late; the endless book signings, the media appearances, the public speaking events—they'd been eating up all of my time and more and I hadn't been giving our relationship the attention I should have been giving it. The same old story. I held my hands up to that. But even so the last thing I'd expected was to arrive home from work at lunchtime and find that Katie had packed a suitcase and moved out, lock-stock, kids and all. I felt like giving up. I felt like walking out of the conference centre this minute and jumping in my car and driving over to Katie's mum's and pleading with her to change her mind, to come home, to bring the kids with her. But even if I did, what would I say?

Sorry babe. This'll be the last talk I do. The last book I write. The last time I put my work before our marriage. The last time I make lame promises like this one only to break it the very next day.

No, it would be pointless, I knew. She wouldn't listen. Why should she? It wasn't the first time I'd been found guilty of this particular crime and I felt sure Katie wasn't about to accept that it might be the last, either. And anyway, I was in too deep now. I couldn't just walk away. I couldn't just disappear from the conference centre and leave a packed house to sit and stare at an empty stage. And neither, if I was to be honest, could I allow the bastards who'd followed me and harassed me and monitored my every move for the past four years – the same bastards who'd murdered Diana – I couldn't let them see my weakness and assume they'd got the better of me because of it. My weakness, of course, was my desire to keep my marriage a marriage, keep it a living, breathing thing: a loving thing. I couldn't let them see that I was prepared to put sentiment before conviction. What a stupid, proud fool.

And then, of course, there was Michael. I was worried about him. I had this bad feeling. It wasn't like him to ignore our calls, to duck under the radar without letting us know where he was or why he'd decided not to come. It wasn't like him at all. By the time JB and I had found our way backstage to the dressing room and I'd thrown on my suit jacket and tie and gathered up my folder containing the guide notes for my talk, fair to say my stress levels were stretching the scale.

"Packed house again," Mark said, triumphantly, throwing back the door as he bounded into the dressing room, clearly impressed by the evening's turnout. He was rubbing his hands enthusiastically. "You ready?"

"As I'll ever be," I said.

"Where's Katie?"

"You tell me."

"She's not coming," JB told him. "And neither is Prince Michael." He followed me out of the dressing room.

Enthusiasm well and truly doused, Mark about turned and followed us both along the short passageway to the auditorium entrance. He didn't say another word.

A few moments later JB was on stage, filling the void left by Prince Michael's absence.

"Good evening, ladies and gentlemen. We're here tonight to present evidence that Princes Diana's death was not an accident, but that she was murdered. In just a few moments I'll be introducing you to someone with whom I've spent the past four years investigating this case and writing this book." He held up a copy of our new book, in view of all present. "The book the British Government tried to ban."

A ripple of anticipation, complete with discernible murmurs, came back from the audience. From the side of the stage I caught JB's eye—he knew, like I knew, that they held high expectations of us. An anxious look between us then he turned back to face the front and continued with his introductions.

Meanwhile I stood in the wings and stole a sly glance at the audience.

As Mark had commented, it was a packed house, I could see that clearly enough. There wasn't an empty seat anywhere that I could tell. True, over the past weeks and months we'd signed books and given talks the length and breadth of the country, sometimes to as few as thirty or forty people, other times to a hundred or a hundred-and-fifty. This night, though, there were ten times that many—fifteen-hundred absorbed faces fixed intently on the stage, and JB's introductory speech. It gave the evening a new sense of proportion as I scanned those faces now, feeling their anticipation, their tension, their sense of not knowing quite what to expect. Had these two nobodies, Jon King and John Beveridge, really uncovered evidence that Diana was murdered? Could it really be that the government – the Royal Family – might have ordered her assassination? If not, then who? Their desire to know was almost palpable, and despite having given countless talks just like this one, I felt nervous. More so than usual. I hoped I could give them what they wanted.

"So without further ado can I ask you please to welcome on stage our main speaker for the evening, Jon King."

Anxious applause filled the auditorium as JB turned and handed me the stage, shaking my hand and mouthing *Knock 'em dead* as we passed one another, he heading for the wings, me centre-stage. I placed my folder on the rostrum and opened it.

The audience hushed.

My heart pounded.

"On the thirty-first of August, nineteen-ninety-seven," I began, "Princess Diana, together with Dodi Fayed and Henri Paul, died in a car crash in Paris. The French Inquiry concluded that the crash was a tragic accident, that chauffeur Henri Paul was drunk, that he was driving too fast and that the pursuing pack of paparazzi forced him into making a fatal mistake. Not only was Henri Paul three times over the drink-drive limit, we were told, but his blood also contained twenty-point-seven percent carbon monoxide, an impossibly high level sufficient in any other circumstance to have rendered him unconscious. But of course he *wasn't* unconscious. Quite the opposite. CCTV footage obtained from the Ritz Hotel in Paris shows that in the moments leading up to the fateful journey Henri Paul was fully awake and alert, chatting coherently to hotel guests, escorting Diana and Dodi to the waiting car and, at one point, even bending down and tying his shoe lace and then standing up straight again with ease. The actions of a perfectly sober individual. Indeed, I put it to you, ladies and gentlemen, that Henri Paul was *not* drunk, that the paparazzi did *not* chase Diana's Mercedes into the crash tunnel as claimed but that British intelligence agents were at work that night and it was *they* who chased her into the tunnel and caused her car to crash. Deliberately." I paused, a calculated pause, long enough for the grit in what I was saying to leave its mark. You could hear a pin drop. Then: "Official claims that Diana died in a drink-drive accident," I said, "and the spurious assertions made by the authorities in support of these claims, are untrue—all part of the meticulously planned and executed cover-up by MI6 and certain other departments within the British government. You're being lied to, ladies and gentlemen. And tonight I intend to prove it."

As I put our case to the audience – the jury – I tried not to look at any one face in particular for more than a heartbeat. Problem was my heart was in overdrive, beating like an old-school flick show, frame on frame, as if it too was being chased by unseen pursuers. I tried not to let it show.

Holding up a copy of a report we'd obtained, I said: "In my hand is a report by one of the world's leading forensic scientists, Peter Vanezis, Regius Professor of Forensic Medicine at Glasgow University. In an independent study, Professor Vanezis, together with his team of three other highly eminent forensic pathologists, analyzed the findings of the French autopsy on Henri Paul and the procedures of the French pathologists in reaching those findings. The report concludes that the blood on which the drink-drive verdict was based could not have belonged to Henri Paul. I repeat: *the blood on which the drink-drive verdict was based could not have belonged to Henri Paul*. Either by mistake or design, ladies and gentlemen, as the report concludes, the blood sample was switched. The question is, of course, who switched it? And why?"

As one the audience sucked in a short, sharp breath, and then rustled in their seats, as though unsure they should even entertain such a thought. My task, I knew, was to convince them that they should.

For the next hour or so I delivered our case and presented our evidence with as much passion and clarity as I was able. Some points aroused more concern than others, drawing further gasps from the increasingly involved audience. Other points were accepted more readily. Of course, to prove beyond doubt that Diana had been murdered was an impossible task, I knew that. To even imagine that as a result of our investigation and the arguments we put forward MI6 might be brought to account in a Court of Law was naïve in the extreme. I knew that, too. But then that's not what I was here to do. I was here to encourage people to question the facts as known, and to provide them with the ammunition with which to do just that. If I could convince enough people that the official verdict was not only unsafe, but fundamentally flawed; if I could reinforce the already cynical public mood with sufficient faith in its own suspicions about Diana's death, then we had all the more chance of forcing the government into calling a public inquiry. And that, more than anything else, was my goal.

For the next hour or so, then, I presented them with the still-unanswered questions and unresolved anomalies an inquiry would be forced to address:

Why was the fact that Princess Diana was unable to wear her seatbelt 'because it was jammed' never investigated by the French Inquiry? Had the seatbelt been fixed deliberately?

Why was the fact that the Mercedes' front right tyre had been mysteriously slashed never investigated by the French Inquiry? Did they believe the tyre might have been slashed deliberately?

Who stole the Mercedes at gunpoint prior to the crash and mysteriously returned it, minus its original EMS computer chip, which controls the steering and traction control? Who replaced the EMS chip?

Who was driving the white Fiat Uno known to have collided with the Mercedes as it entered the crash tunnel? Why was the Uno never found? Or its driver? Or its passenger?

Who was riding the high-powered motorbike that overtook the Mercedes as it entered the crash tunnel? Why was this motorbike never found? Or its rider? Or its pillion rider?

Who was sat astride the second motorbike seen parked broadside across the exit slipway, preventing Henri Paul from turning off the riverside highway and heading up to Dodi's apartment? Why was this second motorbike never found? Or its rider?

Who was driving the second Mercedes that tailed Diana's Mercedes into the crash tunnel and was seen speeding away from the scene immediately after the crash? Why was this Mercedes never found? Or its occupants?

Who was driving the 'small dark-coloured hatchback' car that tailed Diana's Mercedes into the crash tunnel and was seen speeding away from the scene immediately after the crash? Why was this vehicle never found? Or its occupants?

Why did the French emergency services take almost two hours to get Diana to a hospital that was only three miles from the crash scene?

Why was the crash tunnel swept clean, disinfected and reopened within hours of the crash, destroying crucial forensic evidence?

Why was Diana's butler, Paul Burrell, ordered to burn Diana's blood-stained clothes immediately after the crash, destroying crucial forensic evidence?

Why were all ten CCTV cameras lining the route from the Ritz Hotel to the crash tunnel, including the traffic camera mounted above the tunnel's entrance, unable to record any of the car chase or the crash itself? Who turned them off? Who disabled them?

Whose blood sample was stored at the morgue in a vial marked 'unknown male'? This was the sample on which the drink-drive verdict was based. It was never DNA-tested or formally identified as belonging to Henri Paul. It contained 20.7% carbon monoxide poisoning, the kind of level one might expect in the blood of someone who had just committed suicide by inhaling exhaust fumes in an enclosed space, not from the body of someone who had died in a car crash, instantly, on impact, and was thus unable to breathe in any of the fumes from the crashed car. Four of the world's leading forensic scientists asked these same questions, and concluded that the sample could not have belonged to Henri Paul. So whose was it?

And more to the point: who switched the original sample for this bogus one?

Why, against all standard procedure and in contravention of French law, did senior British diplomat Keith Moss give the order for Diana to be embalmed only hours after her death? Was it to cover up the possibility that she was pregnant? The formaldehyde used in the embalming process corrupted all toxicological tests and thus made it impossible to tell. Who instructed Keith Moss to make this decision? Was it his bosses back at MI6?

Why did London's two most senior police officers, Metropolitan Police Commissioner Sir Paul Condon and Assistant Commissioner Sir David Vaness, conspire to withhold vital evidence from the French

Inquiry, evidence entrusted in them by Diana's lawyer, Lord Victor Mishcon? Was it to perpetuate the cover-up already in full flow?

Why did the French Inquiry fail to investigate Henri Paul's connections to British and French intelligence? Why did they not investigate Henri Paul's fortune of £170,000 stashed in multiple bank accounts, £43,000 of which he'd deposited in the final eight months of his life and all of which he'd deposited in cash? Henri Paul's annual salary was £20,500—why did they fail to investigate where this money had come from? Was it because they knew the money had been paid to him by his intelligence handlers for 'services rendered', and that to reveal this would have blown his cover as a British and French intelligence agent?

Why did the French Inquiry fail to investigate the evidence given by former MI6 officer, Richard Tomlinson? Why did French intelligence agents try to prevent Tomlinson giving evidence in the first place by threatening him and beating him up? Did they fear what he might reveal?

And what of French paparazzo, James Andanson?

Why did the French police let Andanson off the hook on the strength of such a flimsy alibi?

Why was Andanson not questioned about his presence in the crash tunnel—about the fact that he'd boasted to friends that he was indeed in Paris on the night of the crash, that he was in the crash tunnel and that he witnessed and photographed the immediate aftermath?

Why was James Andanson found dead in his burnt-out car, 400 miles from where he was supposed to be? Was it to silence him? Was James Andanson murdered?

Why, following his death, was Andanson's office at the SIPA press agency in Paris broken into by an armed gang? To recover the compromising photographs he'd taken in the tunnel immediately after the crash?

Did these photographs include evidence of MI6 involvement in Diana's death?

Did James Andanson work for MI6?

Why were none of these points investigated by the French Inquiry?

And there were other points, too, some more significant than others, some more observable than others, more provable even. When pieced together, I proposed to an all-attentive audience, these points formed the matrix of perhaps the biggest and most far-reaching conspiracy of the twentieth century.

"Only a public inquiry can unravel this conspiracy," I put to the swarm of wide-awake eyes fixing me as I wrapped up the first half of my talk. "Please sign our petition and help us force the government's hand. Thank you."

A few minutes later my own hand was wrapped around a polystyrene cup steaming with the hot black coffee I'd just purchased from the backstage vending machine. It was interlude time; I'd just concluded the first half of my talk and I was making my way through the crowded foyer with Mark and JB. I wanted to check in on Jackie, who was still tirelessly manning our book stall, see if she needed any help. No doubt due to the adrenaline still coursing my veins my mood had taken an upward swing since we'd first arrived — the talk was going well, audience reception was good, and to judge by the jostle of interested punters milling around the stall, the book was selling well, too. Jackie was inundated.

"Looks like we need to give Jacks a hand," Mark said, and peeled off, squeezing his way through the mass of shuffling bodies over towards the book stall.

I turned to follow after him, one arm out in front of me to fend off the mass of bodies and prevent my coffee from spilling on them. Or me. Before I'd managed to turn all the way around, however, to take even the first tentative step, I saw something – or *someone* – that stopped me in my tracks. In that instant every light in my head went out, simultaneously.

I froze.

For a beat I simply stood there, rooted, my eyes disbelieving, my mind turning somersaults as manically it strove to keep the panic I was suddenly experiencing on the inside. It seemed like my heart had stopped beating and my chest was caving in. For sure my lungs had stopped pumping breath. Over by the entrance, through what suddenly seemed like a swirling mass of strangely shaped bodies congealing there in the middle of the foyer, I'd just spotted someone I never imagined I would ever see again: someone I'd last seen some four years previously, on a Saturday, at Avebury Stone Circles, a week before Diana's death. On that occasion this someone had given me nightmares, my dizzying mind recalled, and it felt like those same nightmares were resurfacing in me now, spontaneously, bubbling up from some unfathomed depth like cold spectres. I could scarcely believe who I was looking at.

"Jon?" JB said, following my gaze and fixing on the colourless, craggy face staring back at us across the crowded space. "Are you okay? You look like you've seen that ghost again."

"A ghost with a gun this time," I said without looking at JB. I'd already discarded my coffee on the nearest windowsill and had started to slice my way through the crowd over to where the ghost was standing.

JB started after me.

A few moments later we both followed the American out of the door.

•

"Good to see you again, Jon," the American said, and tipped his head at JB. "I take it this is the famous John Beveridge."

"People call me JB."

"Oh, yes, I know. I know pretty much all there is to know about both of you."

We were outside in the car park, standing twenty or so yards from where we'd just exited the conference centre, JB by my side, the American opposite. It was growing dusky, the light falling in thin shadows across the American's gouged features, giving them a pasty, almost sinister edge. His eyes, though, were smiling, and I couldn't quite make out if he'd come as friend or foe.

The latter, I was about to learn.

"I caught some of what you were saying in there," the American said to me in his slow, Southern drawl. He was referring to the first half of my talk. "You've put together a pretty strong case."

"Thanks…"

"I especially liked the piece about intelligence agents being at work in Paris on the night Diana died. Man that really made me smile. I can see them all now, running for cover, disappearing over the hills and ducking underground to avoid being caught. They all must be terrified." He grinned, as though amused by his own mocking humour.

I wasn't quite sure how to take it. So I ignored it. "You'll be staying for the second half, then?"

"Oh, no, I think not. Thing is, I have a prior appointment. I have to leave in just a few minutes." He left a small pause, turned his eye to nothing in particular, then back at me. I couldn't help feeling he was playing with us. "Anyways, I heard that you were giving this talk so I figured I'd drop by and say well done, you know? Congratulations. I've been real impressed with the way you took on what I told you all those years ago, even more so with the way you carried out your investigation and pieced together such a convincing argument. You even managed to get your book distributed over here—against all the odds. Very impressive." He sucked his teeth. "Yep, we couldn't have scripted it any better if we'd tried. Didn't even have to work it. You just played right along, like the conscientious conspiracy theorist I always knew you to be, the consummate sandman, sprinkling false hope on the eyes of the grieving masses, telling everyone exactly what they wanted to hear. You did a real good job—"

Before I could respond he added:

"—Just like we intended."

"Sorry…?"

Just like we intended.

"Fact is, without you we'd still be trying to figure out how to deal with those grieving masses, all those bleeding hearts out there who can't accept what must be done to maintain the status quo. There's a lot of 'em."

I still wasn't sure exactly where this was going, but wherever it was I knew I didn't want to go there. My gut was beginning to wrench. "Look," I said, not sure quite what else to say. "I really don't understand—"

"Then let me spell it out for you, Jon," the American said, his tone suddenly armoured, his eyes hard on mine. "You were set up."

"What…?"

"You were set up, plain and simple, trussed up like a shop-front mannequin. Trouble is the mannequin has broken the rules."

"Rules? What rules? What are you talking about?" I wasn't sure if it was quite the shrewdest move to argue with such a gnarly special forces veteran. But I found myself doing it anyway. "What do you mean by mannequin, anyway? I'm nobody's pawn if that's what you're trying to say."

"Oh but that's *exactly* what you are, a grade-one errand boy. You're what's known in the trade as a cut-out, a courier of carefully managed information: information we wanted in the public domain anyway; information we wanted the public to chew on without them knowing it was us feeding them."

"No…"

"We needed a champion, you see, someone to rouse a little national fervour, give the public a release for their anger at the untimely death of their princess. We figured someone like you would take the bait. We just didn't figure you'd take it this far." He paused, his eyes firming over with ultimatum. "You've served us well, Jon, better than you know. But now it's time to back off—"

"Back off…?"

"—Safely, while you still can."

"That sounds like a threat."

"Take it as you will. I'm telling you as it is. I want you to drop your call for a public inquiry."

"What—?"

Drop your call for a public inquiry.

"—But we've invested years of our lives in this. We're not about to just give up and walk away, not now."

Beside me I could sense JB growing more tense by the second. He tugged at my arm. "Come on, Jon. We don't need to listen to this."

"Oh but you do," the American warned. "You need to listen good."

"Or what?" I fired back. "You'll kill us, too? Should we check our brakes before we drive home tonight? Or is it the straightforward bullet in the head for us?"

A smug grin turned the American's lips. "Oh, we don't kill people like you, Jon," he said. "We use 'em to our advantage."

"You bastard…"

"We told you what we wanted you to say and now we're telling you to stop. If you refuse you'll be on the front page of every tabloid in the country, I can promise you that. I can see the headlines now: the crazy conspiracy theorist who claims the CIA forewarned him of Diana's assassination."

"But that's true and you know it. You're the one who forewarned me."

"The UFO chaser who believes the moon landings were faked, that Roswell was real and that the American government possesses alien technology—"

"What…?"

"—Or how about this one? The man who believes some acid-rock story about Diana's Stuart bloodline being responsible for her death, and that a nine-inch Belgian in a sporran and a kilt is the true King of Scotland. Oh, that reminds me, have you read the news?"

He pulled a folded copy of the *Sunday Mail* from his coat pocket and tossed it my way.

I caught it, unfolded it, and almost immediately fell backwards as the headline screaming back at me caught me full in the face. *Fake King Of Scots Flees To Belgium*, it read, and went on to say how *the self-styled HRH Prince Michael of Albany faces fraud charges over his applications for British citizenship and a passport*. I knew instantly that, fake king or genuine pretender, the American and his buddies had fitted Michael up.

"Where is he?" I demanded to know, realizing now that this was the reason Michael had failed to show up for tonight's talk.

"Like the paper says," the American said with a lopsided sneer. "He's in Belgium, where he belongs. But there's no need to worry yourself. He's safe, if that's what you're wondering."

"All I'm wondering is how you people sleep at night," I said, and stared back down at the headline and its accompanying article.

A nine-inch Belgian in a sporran and a kilt, the American had said. He was of course referring to Prince Michael, whom we'd first met via our extraordinary rendezvous with the Doctor and his anonymous colleague—the Doctor whom we'd met on the London Eye, and his colleague whom we'd met down by the river following our abduction from outside BBC Broadcasting House. If we'd had any doubts up to this point, all had now come perfectly clear. That the American had just mocked me for believing the *acid-rock story about Diana's Stuart bloodline being responsible for her death* meant that he knew about our contact with these two shadowy characters, and that in turn surely meant they'd been part of the plot all along—didn't it? That is unless they too had been set up, but I failed to see quite how. *Marry into it, produce children, get rid of the mother*. The Doctor had convinced us that Diana's death had been due, at least in part, to the royal bloodline from which she'd descended: that some secretive, and powerful, neo-Templar group had wanted to restore that bloodline to the Throne using her as an unwitting figurehead. Crazy? Perhaps. But Michael had also reiterated this claim and, indeed, had told us that he too had been approached by this same secretive group, but that he had rebuffed their approach. Had Michael been in on it as well? I thought about this for a brief moment, and quickly realized: *no*. Michael had been as much the fall guy as John or I, of course, I was certain of that. The Doctor, on the other hand, with his tales of Muslim-Christian conflict, of a Jacobite uprising and a messianic bloodline so powerful it ruled the Western world … oh yes, the Doctor must surely have been the feeder we'd long suspected him of being; our meeting with him must surely have been arranged for one reason and one reason only: so that the Doctor could feed us information so very far off the beaten track that, whether true or not, it would serve by association to corrupt and discredit the evidence we were presenting in our book. *Our God is Jehova*, he'd said. *Theirs is Allah. And never the twain shall meet*. And again: *Interlopers they may be, but their control of the bloodline is supreme. And because it is they occupy the seats of Western power today*. Again still: *You are aware that Diana was a Stuart by blood, that she too was a descendant of the Bonnie Prince and the original bloodline? She was a bigger threat than either of you realize*.

And we'd fallen for it, lock-stock. Indeed, the only good that had come from all this was that we'd actually got to know Michael – the man, the prince – but even he'd now been spin-dried, it seemed: deported, thrown out, sent back to Belgium.

And there, sure enough, was the giveaway.

Michael had been in Scotland since 1976, actively pursuing his claim to the Scottish Throne in the full glare of the Westminster establishment. Why hadn't he been thrown out before now? Sure, he'd faced a few hassles, had had his home wired, his passport revoked, his birth certificate rewritten to support the 'Fake King Of Scots' headline glaring back at me now. But only now, today, after more than a quarter of a century – now that he'd started speaking publicly about the death of Princess Diana, and winning public support for his own cause in the process – only now had he been sought out and crushed. It spoke volumes.

I tossed the paper back to the American. "There was no need to do this to him," I said. "You've ruined him."

"Exactly," the American said, snatching the paper from the air and holding it up so that its headline yelled back at me. "Let this be your warning. This is what happens when you piss off the wrong people. Born in exile, die in exile, end of story. He should have kept his royal mouth shut." He stared me down for a long moment. "Let it go, Jon, or you too will end up like this—a laughing stock. All your hard work will have been for nothing."

"Only if people buy it," I said, defiantly. "Only if the public believe the spin."

"Oh they will. Remember what I told you all those years ago?" He fixed me now with a glare so cold it made me shiver. "We can make anybody believe anything."

I remembered. I shivered again.

"If you know what's good for you you'll let it go now. I can't be responsible for what might happen if you don't, but a very public character assassination will be the least of it, I can promise you that."

He held my gaze for a moment longer – long enough that I knew I'd been formally warned: no *threatened* – and he turned and walked away.

I crumpled, right there on the spot, folded in on myself like an empty glove puppet. I felt so deflated it seemed as though every ounce of energy had been sucked from me, every fighting thought from my head, every last breath from my lungs. In that moment, as I stood and watched the American disappear across the car park, beyond the perimeter wall and out of sight, I realized there was no truth left to fight for, that everything we'd achieved would count for nothing if we dared to ignore the American's threats. We were beaten. We would have to do as he said. And that was the end of it.

45

"You were there, JB. Tell Mark what the man said."

I stormed into the backstage dressing room, throwing the door wide so that it slammed heavily against the bare stone wall, JB close on my heels. Mark scurried in behind us.

"What are you waiting for?" I barked. "Tell him what he said."

JB went to convey the message to Mark. "He said—"

But I cut him dead. "He said we've been set up is what he said. You, me and the dog makes three. We've all been stitched." I threw off my suit jacket and angrily loosened my tie. Then started pacing aimlessly. "Beautiful," I said, as though to myself. "Absolutely beautiful. They wanted us to do it all along."

"Who?"

"MI6. The CIA. Whoever. They wanted us to do it from the very beginning. From the moment I first met the American. Can you believe it? They actually *wanted* us to do it."

"What?" Mark said. "What did they want us to do?"

"Exactly what we've done, what we've *been* doing these past four years. Don't you see?"

Mark spun on JB. "For Christ's sake, JB, will you please tell me what he's going on about?"

"Tell him. JB," I said. "For Christ's sake tell him."

"If you give me half a chance I will," JB fired back at me, plainly exasperated. He turned to Mark. "Jon's saying that they've been one step ahead of us all along. He's saying that we've been led up a blind alley without a guide dog and now we've got to back off, or…" He faltered, his words trailing off.

"Or what?" Mark demanded to know.

"Or we'll be sold to the nation as nutters," JB finally told him.

"Nutters?"

"Conspiracy theorists."

Mark looked incredulous. "Well what did you expect to be sold to the nation as—national heroes?"

"You're missing the point," I said.

"What is the bloody point?"

"We've been stung! That's the bloody point!"

Realizing I was now yelling like a schoolyard behemoth I reigned myself in, breathed, raked my fingers back through my hair and endeavoured to explain things in a less aggressive manner. It wasn't easy.

"Look," I said. "We've just been warned off. If we ignore the warning and carry on with our campaign to force a public inquiry we'll be splashed across the national media as nutters. Or worse. We'll face full-frontal character assassination and national ridicule. If that happens every shred of evidence we've gathered will be ridiculed along with us, and our call for a public inquiry will be laughed at. It's the perfect sting."

Mark chewed on this concept for a brief moment, but came back fighting. "Not everyone will believe what the media tells them," he wanted me to consider. "People do have minds of their own."

"That's what I used to think," I said, and swung my gaze out the window, looking out on the car park where we'd just been bulldozed by the American. Up until that moment I'd firmly believed that I'd been a free-thinking individual who'd thought for himself and acted on his own volition in championing calls for a public inquiry. Now I knew different. Now I knew I'd been manipulated every step of the way—operated, like some unsuspecting puppet on the end of a string. It was pointless going on.

"What's important is what you think right now," Mark said to the back of my head. "You're back on stage in five minutes so you'd better get your head straight and—"

"There's no way I'm going back out there," I spun and said to Mark. "No way. Not out there on that stage. Not now."

"You have to. People have paid good money to come and hear you talk. More importantly, they're relying on you for answers."

"They'll have to find their own answers. I'm done with it. It's cost me my marriage as it is. If I go back out there it could cost me a whole lot more. Just go and give everyone their money back and tell them it was an accident."

Just then a figure appeared at the dressing room's still-open doorway, catching our attention and stopping us all dead in our tracks. It was a woman. I wasn't sure how long she'd been standing there or how much she'd heard of our conversation, but she was fixing me with eyes that demanded answers.

"Katie," Mark turned and said. "Thank God you've come. Maybe you can talk some sense into your husband's head. Someone needs to."

With that, Mark and JB promptly left the room, closing the door behind them.

A few moments later Katie and I were standing in the centre of the dressing room, facing each other, within touching distance, but no closer. My eyes were locked on hers.

"It's good to see you," I heard myself say, still not quite believing Katie was standing here before me, but so glad she was. "I didn't think you were coming."

"I wasn't," she softly said.

"So why did you?"

She shrugged. "Just a hunch. I thought you might need me around. Seems I was right."

"I'll always need you around," I said.

Katie lowered her gaze to the floor, then looked back up at me. Questions once again shone in her eyes. "Jon, what's wrong with you?," she said. "I heard what you were saying. It's just not like you to give up."

"They set me up, Katie. I feel so stupid. For these past four years I truly believed I was *fighting* the bad guys. Turns out I've been working for them all along."

"That's not true, Jon, and you know it. You've been fighting for what you believe. You've been fighting to uncover the truth."

"Yes, but that's exactly what they wanted me to do." I could see by the look in Katie's eyes that I wasn't making much sense. I tried to explain. "The CIA guy, the one I told you about. He was here tonight. He told me I'd been set up."

"And you believed him?"

"Well, I…"

She moved closer, laid her hand on my shoulder and spoke directly to my eyes. "You know what I think?" she wanted me to consider. "I think they're worried. I bet they thought you'd have given up by now, that you'd have written a few articles, a book maybe, given a few interviews and left it at that. But you've done so much more." She paused, holding my gaze as though to make sure I was hearing her, taking in what she was saying. "You've given people hope, Jon. You've given them a voice. Look at how they've responded at your talks, your book signings, the radio phone-in shows. It's as if they've been waiting for someone to come along and champion their cause, because by themselves they're not able to. That's what you've done for them."

She scooped up my folder from off the table next to us and pulled out a thick, multi-page document containing more signatures than I cared to count. It was a copy of our petition for a public inquiry into Diana's death.

She held it up to my face. "When people sign this petition it means something to them," she wanted me to appreciate. "You can't take that away from them, not now."

"But it's all such a lie. Now I know that we were set up it all just seems so futile."

"That's exactly what they want you to think," Katie pressed. "That's why the CIA turned up tonight—to make you feel exactly the way you're feeling now. To try and make you give up."

She was right, of course. I knew she was right. But it didn't alter the fact that I'd been played like a novice for the past four years and that, even now, if I decided to go back out on stage and deliver the second half of my talk I'd be kicking against a machine too big and too powerful to make even the slightest dent in its armour—the slightest difference to the fact that, ultimately, it would win. It didn't change that fact at all. Did it?

"You can't give up now," Katie insisted, cupping my face firmly in her hands and pulling me towards her. "You'd never forgive yourself. *I'd* never forgive you." She paused. She kissed my lips. And then she said: "Do it for me, Jon. Do it for *us*. Don't let them think we're weak."

46

Within minutes of talking to Katie I was waiting in the wings at the side of the stage, watching a much relieved JB introduce the second half of my talk. The reason he was much relieved, of course, was that he was able to re-introduce me to the audience rather than have to explain to them my sudden absence. He had Katie to thank for that.

"Without further ado, ladies and gentlemen, can I ask you to please welcome back on stage your main speaker for the evening, Jon King."

As the auditorium gave up a chorus of expectant applause, JB turned and started back towards me, exiting to the wings as I stepped defiantly out on stage. My face was deadpan. In my mind I was frantically rewriting the second half of my talk. If I was to disregard the American's warning and deliver my talk anyway, I'd told myself, then I may as well go the full monty.

Ordinarily the second half of an evening such as this one would have spotlighted motive. I had, after all, spent the opening hour or so presenting evidence that Diana had been murdered, and it followed that, in support of that evidence, I should explore the question of *why* she might have been murdered and *by whom*. This, on any other night, would have been the trusted format. But of course this night was different. This night the CIA had turned up and warned me, on pain of character assassination – *or worse* – that I should discontinue my investigation forthwith, in particular my attempts to force a public inquiry, and I'd come oh so close to acquiescing to that warning. Giving up. But as Katie had just minutes before pointed out, the very fact that the American had come here and warned me in person, face to simmering face, surely meant that he and his bully boys were more than a tad concerned that my efforts were gaining converts. That they were having an effect. Perhaps because of this, or perhaps because of my unexpected *tête-à-tête* with the American and the adrenaline overload our confrontation had stimulated in me – or perhaps simply because I felt inspired by Katie's timely intervention – this night I'd decided to do things differently.

Which is why I'd decided to rewrite my talk.

Making my way purposefully back out on stage I positioned myself once again behind the rostrum and peered out nervously at the audience. My mind was deafening. Their silence was deadly. Glancing down I saw that JB had laid my folder open on the rostrum in front of me. I cleared my throat, and peered back out at the audience.

"I came here tonight with my speech all prepared," I said, a little shaky, holding my folder up in full view of the audience, then closing it, replacing it on the rostrum and pushing it to one side. "But an unforeseen circumstance has demanded a change of plan. Instead of continuing with my pre-prepared speech, therefore, and examining the possible motives for Diana's death, I intend to take you on a journey, an ill-fated journey: a journey of conspiracy, treachery and murder. Frame by frame, move by duplicitous move, I'm going to tell you exactly what happened on that fateful night in Paris—exactly how events unfolded, and who orchestrated them." I paused, and realized as I did so that my nerves were no longer fighting me. Suddenly I felt strong. "Simply put, ladies and gentlemen, I'm going to show you exactly how Princess Diana was murdered, the smoking gun—exactly how she was murdered and by whom."

In the front row I saw Mark and JB exchange puzzled looks as several heads turned in the audience and murmured inaudibly. *What does he mean?* Beside Mark, Katie smiled, her eyes misting with pride.

"Saturday, August thirty-first, nineteen-ninety-seven. According to the Ritz security cameras it was precisely four-thirty-five pm when the Mercedes carrying Princess Diana and Dodi Fayed arrived at the Ritz Hotel. Immediately mayhem broke loose as the waiting pack of paparazzi jostled for position, cameras levelled, the photographers bustling and barging their way to the front in their efforts to shoot their prey…

"…But it wasn't only the paparazzi who had the couple in their sights. There were other faces in the crowd outside the Ritz that afternoon, monitoring events, orchestrating proceedings, feeding information back to the MI6 command centre secretly located at the British Embassy, Paris. Two of these faces in particular would play key roles in events later that evening: French paparazzo and long-term MI6 agent, James Andanson, and MI6 Head of Special Operations Europe, Richard Mason. Both would play their part in the operation now starting to unfold. Both would be present in the crash tunnel at the operation's conclusion. Only one, however, would have the princess's blood on his hands. And that was Richard Mason."

Scanning the auditorium I could see the crowd was breathing as one. I felt myself breathing with them.

"Shortly after seven pm the couple left the Ritz Hotel and were driven across town to Dodi's apartment. As their vehicle disappeared along Place Vendome, Henri Paul left the Ritz Hotel and made his way to a prearranged rendezvous with his British and French intelligence handlers. The pieces of a carefully laid plan were now starting to fall into place. For that plan to work, however, Diana and Dodi would need to change their own plans for the evening…"

Dodi's Apartment, Rue Arsene Houssaye, Paris – 7.14 PM

The scene was pandemonium. Close on 100 paparazzi on scooters and mopeds were laying siege to Dodi's apartment, swarming like rats outside the uptown apartment block just off the Champs-Élysées. They were waiting for the arrival of a princess and her lover. Word had filtered through that the couple had just left the Ritz Hotel and the rat pack had acted accordingly, cutting across town via Place de la Concorde and scything their way through the Champs-Élysées traffic jam on their two-wheeled vehicles in a way that was impossible for Diana's Mercedes. Among the rats assembled outside Dodi's apartment, King Rat and his minion.

Mason put his mobile phone to his ear and threw a furtive glance over at his minion, Andanson. *Do exactly as I told you.* The paparazzo was seated astride his BMW motorbike smoking a cigar, his camera slung and ready for use. He acknowledged Mason with a furtive glance of his own.

Then: "Henri Paul went off-duty shortly after the couple left, about two minutes ago. He should be with his French contact in twenty minutes. He'll rendezvous with us later."

"Affirmative," Mason said into his mobile.

"How are things your end, sir?"

"I would say everything is perfect," Mason reported, scanning the madness happening before him. Though he'd kept a discreet distance between himself and the madding throng, he could still feel its pulse running through him. "It's absolute mayhem here. There's no chance they'll be able to keep to their plans and eat at Chez Benoit restaurant tonight, not with this lot in their faces." Again he scanned the hysterical mass of cameras and their owners. "No, they won't be dining anywhere but the Ritz tonight."

I scanned the audience. They were with me; I could feel it. They were with me on the streets of Paris and they were with me here, now, in the conference centre—eyes attentive, tongues stilled, a sense of real-life drama gripping them, as though my words were being played out on the screen of their minds as I spoke them. I picked up the story as Diana and Dodi were driven back across town to the Ritz Hotel.

"At nine-fifty-one the couple arrived back at the Ritz for dinner. Their plan to eat at their favourite restaurant, Chez Benoit, where Ritz manager Claude Roulet had earlier booked a table for them, had been thwarted by the increasingly frenzied pack of paparazzi camped outside Dodi's apartment. Indeed, as they left the apartment and began their intended journey along the river to

Chez Benoit, that same frenzied pack went with them, swarming all over their car, yelling and barking like a mob of unruly savages and firing off round on round of flashgun bullets through the vehicle's tinted windows. The couple were terrified. So much so that Dodi instructed his driver – in this instance Dodi's regular chauffeur, Philippe Dourneau – to forget about Chez Benoit and drive them directly back to the Ritz instead. They would eat there in relative safety…

"…But here's the thing. If the Ritz security staff were caught off-guard by the couple's unexpected return, strangely, the paparazzi were not. Around a hundred rats were already there and waiting as the Mercedes pulled up outside the hotel entrance. It was as if someone knew of the couple's movements even before they did." I paused for breath, and to accent what I was about to say next. "I put it to you, ladies and gentlemen, that *someone* was MI6."

As row by row the audience realized the implications of that last statement, a gust of strained whispers scurried around the auditorium, heads turning and posing their questions to the person sitting next to them. The whispers lasted only a short time, true. But the questions they posed echoed in the hall for a good deal longer.

Ritz Hotel Underground Garage / Place Vendome, Paris – 11.38 PM

The Mercedes S280 that would shortly drive Diana to her death looked almost out of place down here in the Vendome underground car park. Parked up on Level Three of the Ritz Hotel's exclusive five-storey parking garage it nestled anonymously among a dazzling array of supercars—Ferraris, Lamborghinis, Bugattis, McLarens. Against these refulgent roadsters the S280 looked decidedly ordinary.

Not that this mattered, of course, not to Richard Mason anyway. How favourably the Mercedes compared to some of the most expensive and fashionable vehicles ever built was the least of his concerns. The MI6 fixer was concerned only that this particular limo was the perfect machine for the task ahead. Quite frankly, so far as Richard Mason was concerned, nothing else bore any significance at all.

Closing the driver-side door Mason ran a gloved hand along the S280's smooth, burnished surface. *Perfect*, he told himself. *Just perfect. Unarmoured. Cumbersome. Too slow to outrun the chasing pack. And fitted with the necessary technology to make it crash.* He flicked open his mobile phone.

Three storeys above Mason, in Place Vendome, outside the front entrance to the Ritz Hotel, MI6 officer David Wilkinson was mingling with the increasingly restless pack of paparazzi as they waited for their quarry to emerge from the hotel. Word had reached them that Diana would appear soon, and tensions were already high, each paparazzo to a man primed and ready to attack at the first sight of the couple emerging from the hotel and stepping down those famous red-carpeted steps. The protocol was set. First come, first served; first to the front, first to get that elusive photograph that would change forever the life of at least one of the hungry rats. And his bank balance. As if to accentuate this rat-eat-rat protocol a sudden rush of excitement exploded at the front of the pack, and then just as suddenly subsided to groans and frustrated shakes of the head as the pack realized the couple just emerging from the hotel and climbing in the back of a waiting limo were mere TV stars. Nothing more. A few random flashes as the celebs drove off and attention was instantly back on the entrance. The real stars were yet to emerge.

Just then, Wilkinson felt a vibration in the inside pocket of his jacket. Separating himself momentarily from the simmering pack he pulled out his mobile phone and put it to his ear. Three storeys beneath him, Mason barked an order.

"Get a message to our man in the hotel," he instructed Wilkinson. "We need to be notified of the exact departure time."

"All in hand, sir," Wilkinson reported. "Our man reports DT at ten minutes after midnight, in half an hour's time. They'll leave by the rear door."

"Is our man in place?"

Wilkinson shot a glance and nodded once at James Andanson, seated astride his BMW motorbike over by the entrance to Cour Vendome. On Wilkinson's signal Andanson kicked his bike to life and headed off along the narrow, one-way road, heading for Rue Gambon at the rear of the building.

"Sir," Wilkinson replied. "Our man's in place. Is everything go with the chauffeur?"

"Henri Paul? He's had his money, if that's what you mean. He thinks he's driving them back to Fayed's apartment, then going home for the night. That's all he needs to know."

"But we're sure he'll take the planned route?"

"Of course. With all those paparazzi on his tail he's hardly likely to negotiate the traffic in the Champs-Élysées, is he?"

"No, sir." Wilkinson cleared his throat.

"What about logistics?" Mason wanted confirmed. "All go?"

"Yes, sir. Delta's in place to block the route off Concorde and Alma. The K Team are with the Uno now. They'll be waiting at the entrance to the tunnel." He paused. "All we need now is for them to take the right car."

"Oh, they will," Mason assured him. "Our man will be here in precisely twenty-four minutes to run it up to the hotel. From there Henri Paul will take over. All comm channels quiet from now on." He cut the call and replaced his mobile in his pocket, then ran his gloved hand over the vehicle's gleaming paintwork one final time, this time almost lovingly. In his eyes, violence. "Shame to destroy such an elegant body," he said aloud to himself. And then he said: "Still, she shouldn't go round shagging oily coons, should she."

Pocketing his hands he then headed off towards the elevator.

Some twenty minutes later, Acting Deputy Head of Security for the Ritz Hotel, Henri Paul, stepped into the Imperial Suite's private elevator and its doors swished closed behind him. Once inside he dipped his hand in his jacket pocket and retrieved a plain, white envelope that bulged slightly with the thickness of its contents. Momentarily he caught a glimpse of himself in the elevator's gold-framed mirror, a fitting symbol to the hotel's extravagant façade, he mused. He grinned wryly at his own gilt-edged reflection, then peered back down at the envelope, his wry grin melting to a contented smile as he slid a chubby finger along the back of its sealed flap and opened it. He didn't bother to count the money; he knew the wad of used bank notes leering back up at him from inside the unmarked envelope would amount to the same 2500 French francs he was always paid for this kind of job—for acquiring information on the hotel's high-end guests and passing it back to his handlers. On this occasion the information had been requested not by the French DST, as was customary, but by MI6, and the high-end guests of interest to Britain's Secret Intelligence Service were of course the princess and her playboy lover, Dodi Fayed. Henri Paul was, this minute, on his way up to collect them. Due to the media attention they'd received earlier that day the couple had elected to dine back at the Ritz Hotel—not in the hotel's l'Espadon restaurant, but in the privacy of its most sumptuous suite of apartments, the Imperial Suite. Having feasted and rested, they were now preparing to head back to Dodi's apartment on Rue Arsene Houssaye, just off the Champs-Élysées, where they planned to spend the night. Even though officially off-duty, Henri Paul had been called back to the hotel specifically to act as their chauffeur, a task he was regularly called on to carry out by his secret paymasters, the DST. After all, following dinner and drinks, tongues were prone to loosen in the back of the limo, making his task of eavesdropping information all the easier.

And significantly more rewarding.

As he resealed the envelope and slipped it back in his jacket's inside pocket, he couldn't help but gloat just a little on the enviable fortune his work as an intelligence asset had brought him over these past few years. In French francs he was already a millionaire, secretly, and that meant early retirement was no longer a pipe dream, but a choice he'd already made. That pleased him. He was now counting down the months, looking forward to the day when his final assignment was behind him and he could put his feet up, for good. He knew that day was close.

As the elevator came to rest its doors slid smoothly open, and Henri Paul stepped jauntily out into the carpeted Imperial Suite foyer, shrugging his jacket square on his beefy shoulders and straightening his tie. He knocked twice on the door marked 102 and waited patiently for a reply. He checked his wristwatch—twelve-thirteen am. He had no idea he was just eleven minutes away from completing his final assignment and putting his feet up, for good.

Precisely nine minutes later, as Henri Paul accompanied Diana and Dodi from the elevator and escorted them across the ornate, marble-pillared lobby en route to the hotel's rear entrance, a black Mercedes 600 gunned its engine out front amid a frenzy of paparazzi activity. For a beat the vehicle's wheels spun uncontrollably, scorching grooves in the tarmac before screeching off from under the eyes of the panicking rat pack at an unforgiving pace, an olive-green Range Rover in hot pursuit.

Hey! She's in the Mercedes!

Immediately the roar of scooter-and-motorbike engines firing up filled the night air, accompanied by the sudden dazzle of headlights coming to life, as the pack of paparazzi, believing Princess Diana was in the black Mercedes that had just screamed off in the direction of Place de la Concorde, jumped on their nippy two-wheelers and gave chase. Several of the paparazzi spun off along Cour Vendome in a bid to head the Mercedes off. The rest remained glued to the tail lights of the Mercedes's rear-guard Range Rover. The chase was on, or so everyone thought. But instead of peeling off along Rue de Castiglione and heading for Place de la Concorde, the Mercedes, still shadowed by the olive-green Range Rover, accelerated past the Castiglione exit and on around Place Vendome—*tyres squealing, engine whining*. For all the world it seemed as though the two vehicles were being driven by let-loose boy racers who'd decided to use Paris's most fashionable square as a midnight race circuit. In fact Dodi's regular chauffeur,

Philippe Dorneau, was at the wheel of the Mercedes. The range Rover was being driven by al Fayed bodyguard, Kes Wingfield.

Having completed one terrifying lap of the track the two experienced drivers finally brought the vehicles skidding to an abrupt halt back in front of the hotel some sixty seconds later. The paparazzi had been sold a dummy.

•

Back in the conference hall I was in mid-flow, narrating events as they happened. Absorbed, the audience was mindful of my every word.

"As the two decoy cars screamed away from in front of the Ritz and completed their circuit of Place Vendome, chased by the pack of paparazzi photographers," I conveyed to the captivated crowd, "Diana and Dodi left by the rear exit and climbed in the back of a waiting Mercedes S280, one that had been driven up from the Vendome underground car park just moments earlier. The company who owned the vehicle, *Etoile Limousine*, would later reveal that it was 'the only vehicle available that night'. There were no other limos at their disposal, they claimed. Fact? Fiction? Coincidence? This was the vehicle, remember, that had been identified and fitted up weeks in advance by the MI6 team responsible for the operation; the vehicle that had been stolen at gunpoint and mysteriously returned by the thieves days later, secretly fitted with parasite EMS and ESC chips—the on-board computer chips responsible for controlling the vehicle's steering and automatic traction. The thieves had also fitted it with a Blockbuster device designed to incapacitate its braking system. The car, ladies and gentlemen, along with its occupants, was fated, even before it set off."

I paused, as much for breath as effect. It felt as though raw electricity was coursing my veins at this point, and I needed a moment to settle my thoughts, assemble them in some kind of disciplined order. The atmosphere in the auditorium was charged.

At length I resumed: "At twelve-twenty am Henri Paul climbed in the driver's seat and closed the door, while bodyguard Trevor Rees-Jones climbed in beside him and fastened his seat belt. He was the only passenger to do so. But he wasn't the only one to try. In the seat directly behind Rees-Jones, Diana tried to fasten *her* seat belt as well, but she couldn't; it was jammed. As Henri Paul let his toe down on the accelerator and moved off along Rue Cambon towards Rue de Rivoli and Place de la Concorde, ladies and gentlemen, both Diana and Dodi must have felt desperate, as though the wave of uncertainty that had swelled progressively throughout the day was finally threatening to engulf them. They were now less than five minutes from the Alma Tunnel."

Place de la Concorde, Paris – 12.21 AM

Traffic lights ahead, red. Henri Paul slowed to halt. Checking his rear-view mirror he could see the headlights of a dozen or more paparazzi motorbikes snarling up behind him. He could see, too, Diana and Dodi becoming more and more restless in the back seat, craning anxiously round and peering out the back window at the growing menace on their tail, then ducking back round to face the front. What should he do? Should he wait for the lights to change and risk being ambushed by the rat pack? Or should he jump the lights and accelerate on? The traffic was unusually thin for a Saturday night, he'd already noted, and he felt certain he could make it across Place de la Concorde and onto Cours la Reine without incident. But he was in two minds. He had Mr Fayed's son, Dodi, in the back, after all. The princess, too.

Should he put their lives in jeopardy by taking such a risk?

Still tossing the dilemma over in his mind Henri Paul again checked his rear-view mirror, and saw that the pack of paparazzi was growing by the second, an ever-expanding bevy of growling motorbike and scooter engines, complete with riders, looming fearsomely behind him and burning to chase him down. He flicked a glance back up at the traffic lights. Still red. In that moment Henri Paul made his decision. Letting the handbrake off he slammed his foot to the floor and squealed off across Place de la Concorde, jumping the red light and then a second red light as he powered on past the junction with Avenue des Champs-Élysées and swerved off right along Cours la Reine, down onto the riverside highway, putting distance between himself and the chasing pack. The image in his mirror told him the ploy had worked; the paparazzi were no longer on his tail. No doubt they were still there, he mused, astride their machines, angry now, and vacillating – *should we wait? or should we jump the red light, too?* – still simmering there at the traffic lights, waiting for them to turn green. Allowing himself a small grin, Henri Paul focused on the road now stretched before him. He knew he was far enough ahead of the paparazzi by now that it was impossible for them to catch him.

Slightly, he could relax.

Take the exit at Pont de l'Alma and head up to Dodi's apartment that way, he'd been instructed. *At least then you won't get swarmed by paparazzi in the Champs-Élysées traffic jams.*

And that's why he was now heading along Cours la Reine instead of the Champs-Élysées. It was a standard route anyway, taken by many of the city's cab and limo drivers to avoid the Saturday night gridlock on Paris's most famous avenue. It made perfect sense to come this way, especially now that he'd managed to lose the chasing pack.

With these thoughts in mind he again flicked a glance in his rear-view mirror, and was surprised – and no less alarmed – to see headlights closing on him at speed. A beat later he found himself having to squint into the mirror and tilt his head to one side so that the glare of these headlights didn't blind him.

Who was that on his tail now? It surely couldn't be the paparazzi because he'd left them snarling and growling back at the traffic lights on Place de la Concorde. So whose headlights were blazing in through the back windscreen now, no more than a car's length back?

Again Henri Paul squinted into the rear-view mirror, but the headlights beaming back at him now were so blindingly bright he was unable to make out the vehicle from which they shone, or indeed, whether they were shining from a solitary vehicle or from multiple vehicles. He blinked his eyes, once, then adjusted his line of sight to see that Princess Diana was again grappling with her seat belt in the back, desperately tugging and pulling in a futile attempt to release it and strap it across her body. They were travelling very fast now. Diana looked terrified. Beside her, Dodi looked equally ill at ease, ducking down in his seat and shielding his eyes from the glare of the mystery headlights blazing in through the rear windscreen. In the passenger seat Trevor Rees-Jones unfastened his seat belt and swivelled round to reassure the couple that all was in hand. But all was not in hand, and they knew it. Desperate now, Diana shot Dodi an anxious glance. *Everything will be okay, won't it?* Meanwhile Henri Paul returned his gaze to the road ahead, expertly manoeuvring the Mercedes down under the Pont Alexander III flyover and emerging on Cours Albert 1er.

They were now less than a mile from Pont de l'Alma, on a collision course with destiny.

"When Henri Paul joined the riverside highway, ladies and gentlemen, it was twelve-twenty-two am. Though under some duress he remained unfazed, expertly in control of the speeding Mercedes, confident at its wheel. He was an experienced driver, after all, having undergone several advanced driving courses with, among others, Mercedes Benz. He knew how to handle an S280, even at this speed. What he didn't know, of course, was that this particular S280 had been tampered with."

I paused, breathed. The audience seemed to breathe with me.

Then: "He had no idea he was screaming headlong into a predetermined death trap," I put to the sea of spellbound faces. "That the vehicle he was driving had been stolen and fitted up with a Blockbuster device designed to take out his brakes, and a parasite transceiver to enable an agent in situ to take over his steering and drive the car remotely." I searched the audience for signs of resistance—a hostile look, the shake of a head, even the cynical squint of an eye. I saw none. "So far as Henri Paul was concerned his day's work was all but done," I continued. "Keeping his MI6 handlers abreast of the couple's movements throughout the day; driving them home, now, along this pre-specified route. This, he believed, was the extent of his involvement. He had no idea he'd been set up as the patsy whose blood tests would later tell the lie that he'd been drunk at the wheel, that he'd been driving too fast, recklessly, and that Princess Diana had died as a result of his actions. No, ladies and gentlemen, he had no idea at all that he was being used as the fall guy in such a premeditated and deadly game. But he was about to find out..."

Approach To Alma Tunnel, Paris – 12.24 AM

Take the slip road at Alma, they'd told him. *Head back up to Dodi's that way.*

Acutely aware of the headlights still blazing in at him through the back windscreen, filling his mirrors and whiting out the inside of the Mercedes, Henri Paul indicated right and prepared to take the slip road off the highway just ahead. It would take him up to Dodi's apartment via Avenue Marceau and Place Charles de Gaulle, a route he knew well—well enough that he knew the headlights clinging to his tail would be unable to follow him so aggressively along it without attracting the attention of the police. It was a thought that gave him some comfort. Until he reached the slip road...

What the...?

...In that instant he realized something was very wrong.

Parked broadside across the entrance to the slip road was a motorbike and rider, the motorbike positioned so that it prevented Henri Paul from exiting the highway. Henri Paul's heart almost stopped beating, there and then. The leather-clad rider was staring back at him from behind a blacked-out visor, looking like some kind of futuristic Robocop seated there astride his motorbike in the centre of the slip road, revving his engine, but not moving. For a beat Henri Paul's mind panicked—*who on earth was that? Who on earth was the mystery rider and why was he deliberately blocking the exit off the highway?* There was no question about it: if he turned off the highway onto the slip road he would collide with the motorbike and almost certainly injure the rider as well. He had no choice but to react reflexively and accelerate on towards the approaching maw of the tunnel, a task he managed with some aplomb.

But now there was a second obstacle to negotiate.

What the ... where did that come from...?

A white Fiat Uno travelling at a snail's pace suddenly loomed ahead in the slow lane, its brake lights glowing red as though its driver was slowing the vehicle to an unexpected and abrupt stop, right there on the highway: *right there in front of him.* Instinctively Henri Paul eased on his brakes and simultaneously heaved the Mercedes tight left in an attempt to avoid colliding with the smaller vehicle. But it was too late. *Thud!* At a speed closing on 80 miles an hour the Mercedes hammered into the Uno's tail wing, sending shards of the Fiat's rear-light casing splintering into the air. It took every ounce of Henri Paul's driving skills to retain control of the speeding Mercedes as the impact propelled him out into the fast lane and on past the Uno, down into the tunnel. Curiously, the headlights that had clung to his tail all the way from Place de la Concorde remained on his tail, even now, shadowing him out into the fast lane and past the Fiat Uno. Down into the tunnel.

Who the hell was that driving so close behind him? What was going on? Who was driving the Uno and why did they deliberately get in his way?

The road was full of mad drivers tonight!

As if to punctuate this last thought, just as Henri Paul entered the tunnel a second motorbike suddenly pulled alongside him, as if from nowhere, its pillion rider positioned almost side-saddle and aiming what appeared to be some kind of strange weapon at him.

What on earth was happening?!

And now his steering wheel seemed to have a mind of its own. And now his brakes had stopped responding.

What the hell was going on?

Flash!

"Argghhh...!" Suddenly Henri Paul was blinded by a ferocious flash of light fired in through the front windscreen; the flash seemed to come from the strange-looking weapon wielded by the motorbike's pillion rider. As the motorbike powered on through the tunnel, leaving the Mercedes in its wake and swerving violently out of control, Henri Paul slammed the heels of his hands tight against his stinging eyes and rubbed, uselessly.

Who were they...? Why were they attacking him...?

These were the last actions Henri Paul ever performed, the last thoughts his terrified mind ever processed. Two beats later he was dead.

"Right, I said I was going to show you exactly how Princess Diana was murdered, the smoking gun," I said, my adrenaline up now and feeling like raw energy enlivening every cell in my body, and mind. "That's precisely what I intend to do now."

Beside me, on a small table next to the rostrum, my laptop was sitting open and primed. Stepping to one side I fingered the touchpad and a three-dimensional animated sequence appeared instantly on the screen set up on the stage behind me. It was the 3-D animation our friend Steve O'Brien had designed specifically for us.

"Okay, look, this is the Mercedes," I said, identifying the vehicles in the animation with my laser pen. As I aimed the pen at the screen a small red dot highlighted each of the vehicles in turn. Every eye in the audience followed that dot. "This is the motorbike blocking the slip road off the highway, and this is the white Fiat Uno. Now watch. As Henri Paul realizes his exit route is blocked and accelerates on past the slip road, *here*, the Uno suddenly comes into play and forces Henri Paul out into the fast lane—exactly where they want him to be. As incredible as it may sound, ladies and gentlemen, every manoeuvre the Mercedes makes from here on in will be choreographed, precisely."

I ran a finger across the touchpad and moved the sequence on.

"Of course, this wasn't the only reason the Uno and its occupants were here. Forcing Henri Paul into the outside lane was just one of a sequence of predetermined manoeuvres designed to make the Mercedes crash. Look…"

Again I moved the sequence on. "…*Here,* as the Mercedes overtakes the Uno, the person sitting in its front passenger seat hits a button on the remote control he's holding and a small device known as a Blockbuster explodes beneath the Mercedes's bonnet, blowing out its brakes. Simultaneous with this its steering is taken over by the same remote control, which is tuned to the parasite transceiver inserted by the operatives who stole the Mercedes prior to the crash. In short, ladies and gentlemen, at this point the car was no longer in Henri Paul's hands. It was being driven remotely from the front seat of the Fiat Uno. Henri Paul stood no chance."

A wave of incredulity swept the audience. Seeing for the first time how the operation was most likely carried out was undoubtedly challenging, and perhaps for many, difficult to digest. Even so, none seemed entirely overwhelmed.

"As Henri Paul dipped down into the tunnel this second motorbike here entered the fray," I said, pinpointing the motorbike on screen with my laser pen. "Two operatives were riding that motorbike. In the hands of its pillion rider was an anti-personnel strobe gun, which fires directional pulses of light so intense they're capable of blinding a person for up to four minutes. As the motorbike roared past the Mercedes, its pillion rider fired the strobe directly into Henri Paul's eyes, through the front windscreen—*there!*" Again I fired my laser pen at the screen behind me, its red dot fixing on the motorbike and the Mercedes, which were now side-by-side at the tunnel entrance. "Do you see, ladies and gentlemen? Henri Paul is blinded by the strobe gun and immediately he begins to lose control of the Mercedes. At this point the special ops technique known as the Boston Brakes kicks in, and the Mercedes is seen to perform a distinct and recognizable set of manoeuvres characteristic of this particular operational method, the Boston Brakes. There, look, the Mercedes swerves first one way, then the other way, then back again into the concrete pillar."

The image on screen illustrated the words as I spoke them.

"First one way, then the other way, then back again into the concrete pillar—a telltale sign of the Boston Brakes. At the moment when the parasite is activated and the steering is transferred to the remote, at that precise instant, what's know as a 'downpoint' occurs, a split second where neither Henri Paul nor the remote is in control. For this split second the vehicle is effectively driverless, and it's this that causes the left-right-left manoeuvre to occur as the person working the remote fights to regain control of the vehicle. If you're looking for the smoking gun, ladies and gentlemen, look no further. This is it."

I ran the sequence again, showing how, following the moment of *downpoint*, the Mercedes swerved left, then right, then left again and into the thirteenth concrete pillar of the tunnel's central reservation. "First one way, then the other way, then back again into the concrete pillar, entirely consistent with every other instance where the Boston Brakes has been deployed. And our research shows there have been many such instances." I highlighted the Fiat Uno with my laser pen. "Whoever it is in that vehicle, ladies and gentlemen, they're holding a remote control in their hand and they have just used it to drive the Mercedes into the concrete pillar. They are not innocent French citizens on their way home from a night out. They are not tourists caught up in a tragic set of events. They are private security operatives hired by MI6, and that's why neither they nor their vehicle have ever been found."

Alma Tunnel, Paris – 12.26 AM

The strained, ghostly sound of a continuous car horn. The hiss of gushing steam. The disconcerting groan of metal on metal, grinding and creaking as it struggled to reshape itself following head-on impact with reinforced concrete. The smell of scorched rubber.

This was the scene inside the Alma Tunnel just seconds after Diana's Mercedes had slammed into the thirteenth concrete pillar lining the tunnel's central reservation. The impact had spun the vehicle a full 180 degrees, plus a little more, so that its mangled frame now faced back towards Place de la Concorde and the Ritz Hotel, where it had begun its fated journey barely five minutes earlier. Shattered glass littered the dual-lane underpass. Rivulets of oil mixed with blood spilled from somewhere beneath the wreckage and drained grimly into the nearside gulley, while bits of destroyed chassis and exhaust box lay uselessly in the road, scattered among the glass shards.

Just a few yards back towards the tunnel entrance the white Fiat Uno sat motionless, engine running, doors flung wide, its two male occupants standing one at each of the open doors, gaping morbidly at the still-steaming wreckage of the Mercedes, barely ten yards ahead of them. Neither seemed sure whether to celebrate their success or mourn it. As though for approval they glanced over at the man who had just emerged from another Mercedes, the one that had entered the tunnel tight on Henri Paul's tail. The man gave a curt nod of his head, then turned his attention back to the crashed Mercedes and the two leather-clad operatives checking it over, sizing up the damage, their motorbike parked up just a few yards ahead of the wreckage. One of the men reached into the driver's seat and heaved the lifeless body of Henri Paul off the steering wheel, and the incessant tone of the car horn immediately ceased. The second operative checked the back seat, then glanced over at Mason and shook his head.

She's still alive.

Mason understood, but the look in his eye told its own story: she won't remain alive for very much longer.

"We'll leave her to the French emergency services," he said with a hint of cold cynicism. "She'll be in good hands."

The two operatives jumped back on their motorbike and roared off.

Just then, as Mason was himself about to turn and climb back in his vehicle, a sudden flash of light startled him. He spun, and immediately caught sight of someone he knew only too well. On the other side of the central reservation, parked up in the contra-flow lane, James Andanson was sat audaciously astride his BMW motorbike, camera in hand and aimed in the direction of Mason: *flash!* The escaping motorbike: *flash!* Then the Uno: *flash!* The wrecked Mercedes: *flash! flash! flash!*

Then back at Mason: *flash!*

Little did Andanson know it there and then, but the set of photographs he'd just taken would cost him his life.

Having mentally signed Andanson's death warrant, Mason finally gave the signal to the two Fiat Uno operatives that it was time to leave.

Two beats later the Uno and Mason's Mercedes screamed off, nose-to-bumper, the Uno taking the lead.

In the auditorium I was drawing the evening to a close.

"It took the emergency services almost two hours to get Diana to a hospital less than four miles away," I was explaining to the now subdued audience. "By which time it was too late. She was pronounced dead at four am."

I left a respectful pause at this point, during which JB joined me on stage. I swallowed and cleared my throat.

"On the morning of Diana's death," I concluded, "Britain's new Prime Minster, Tony Blair, made a statement in which he famously referred to Diana as the People's Princess. As contrived and insincere as that statement undoubtedly was, it nonetheless turned out that Tony Blair was right. Diana was indeed the People's Princess—without question the most popular British royal in modern history. True, she upset the Royal Family by her lifestyle and her public attacks on the Queen and Prince Charles.

She upset the world's arms dealers with her enormously successful campaigns against landmines and other anti-personnel weapons. She certainly upset the British establishment by her relationship with and proposed marriage to Dodi Fayed, who was of course the wrong colour, culture and creed to father half-siblings to the future King of Britain. In short, ladies and gentlemen, there were multiple reasons why the powers-that-be would have wanted her out of the way." I paused. "But to identify the one reason above all others, I come back to her unparalleled popularity. The fact is, Diana was so dangerously popular she was able to sway public opinion against the status quo, and in favour of her own causes, something she had spent the last few years of her life doing to unprecedented effect. This, we believe, is the primary reason she was killed."

Beside me, JB held up the A4 folder containing the list of names who'd already subscribed to our petition for a public inquiry. "Before you go home tonight, can I please ask you to sign our petition and help establish the people's verdict—the People's Verdict for the People's Princess. We must force the government to order an investigation. We have a right to know what really happened, ladies and gentlemen. And so does Diana. Thank you."

For what seemed a very long moment a deathly silence gripped the hall as I concluded my talk and prepared to leave the stage. But then, slowly at first, a ripple of applause started to make its way from the back of the auditorium, steadily growing and billowing into a wave of thunderous noise as row by row the audience stood up from their seats and showed their appreciation. Within a few short seconds the wave had engulfed the entire audience, everyone in the hall on their feet now, clapping, whistling, some even cheering. I tipped my head to them in thanks, but knew their sentiment was in truth more for the memory of Princess Diana than the content of my talk. Even so, their response was heartening.

I cast my eyes to the front row.

And saw that Katie, too, was on her feet, the only princess that truly mattered to me beaming back up at me from the front row, her cheeks damp with tears. Without Katie – her tolerance of my obsession these past four-plus years, her unwavering support, not to mention her pep talk in the dressing room earlier – I would never even have been here. If we were to be successful in our efforts to force an inquiry, or even an investigation, it would be as much down to Katie as JB and me. No doubt about that.

Tipping my head one more time in grateful acknowledgement of our standing ovation, I gathered up my unused folder from the rostrum in front of me and accompanied JB off stage. We'd done everything we could. It was now up to everyone else.

Epilogue

18 Months Later...

To say life had got back to any real semblance of normality over the eighteen months or so since the book's arrival in the UK – indeed, since the American had warned me to drop my campaign for a public inquiry – would be to inflate the truth, it has to be said. But things *had* calmed down to some favourable degree. Although still regularly called on to do interviews for TV and radio, as well as for a number of 'Diana documentaries', both in the UK and elsewhere, I had nonetheless been able to spend more time with Katie and the kids during this time, and I'd been truly grateful for that. Of course, for as long as I continued to petition for a public inquiry I had to assume the threat of character assassination still loomed— that one day, as the American had threatened, I might wake up and find my name plastered over the front pages with an accompanying article demolishing my name and reputation. *Or worse*. But so far it hadn't happened. I hadn't heard from the American since his unexpected appearance at the conference hall eighteen months ago, in fact, and it seemed whatever surveillance Katie and I had been under for the several years leading up to the book's release had now been relaxed. So far as I could tell, we were wiretap-free. What might happen in the future, of course, I couldn't say. But for now it seemed the threat I once posed to MI6 and its clandestine operations had diminished sufficiently that I was no longer on their list of 'wanted conspiracy theorists'. Either that, or they'd finally realized my influence on public opinion was negligible anyway—that no matter how long and how hard I banged on about the need for a public inquiry, no one was actually listening. I was simply not worth the effort.

This, at least, was the way things had been until now. Or more precisely, the day before yesterday, when quite unexpectedly Lacey had called me up and asked to meet. It was the first time I'd heard from him in months.

"Usual place, protocols apply," he'd said, as he always said. But this time he'd added: "I have something I think you might want to hear. I also want to put the record straight."

Curious to know what he'd meant I'd agreed to meet him in the 'usual place'—the Pump House in London's Hyde Park, where we'd met all those years earlier, shortly after the death of Diana.

Where we always met.

This time, however, he was to tell me something I would never have imagined possible.

"A dollar for your thoughts," Lacey said, standing suddenly beside me. To appear without warning had been a habit of his for as long as I could recall. He seemed almost to revel in it. "It's my final offer."

I didn't reply, not straight away. I was gazing out from the Pump House over Hyde Park's famed Italian Gardens, the ornamental water feature said to have been commissioned by the love-struck Prince Albert as a gift for Queen Victoria. There was a certain irony, I'd been thinking to myself as I'd waited for Lacey to show—a certain irony in that an elaborate water feature had been built here in honour of perhaps Britain's most unpopular monarch, and that a similar water feature was being planned in memory of Britain's best-ever-loved princess: Princess Diana. I wasn't sure where exactly in Hyde Park the Diana memorial was to be built, I'd mused, but I was quite sure it would be as far removed from Queen Victoria's *Italian Gardens* as was geographically possible. The thought had caused me to smile.

"They're worth far more than a dollar," I turned and said to Lacey after a long moment. "You'll have to do better."

Lacey noted my smile. "Well I can see they're high in amusement value. I'll double my offer, but not a cent more."

"Two dollars it is, then," I agreed. "And you buy the coffee."

A few minutes later we were following a familiar path through the park towards Serpentine Lake and Dell Café, the Pump House and its famous water garden disappearing some way behind us. It was chilly. Overhead grouchy clouds gathered behind a freshening wind, prompting me to pull my collar up under my chin.

"It's been a hell of a ride," I was saying, as a green 4x4 cruised slowly past us with horse box in tow. Momentarily my mind was transported back to the first time I'd spoken to Lacey about Diana's death here in Hyde Park, how I'd felt certain we'd been watched and listened to by government agents, some concealed in green 4x4s like the one that had just cruised past us and headed off across the park in the direction of the Old Police House. No such fear now, though. I could honestly say that I no longer cared who was behind the wheel or even if they might be listening to our conversation. My book was out there, along with any secrets I might once have held. I had no reason to fret, and it felt good. "I've done what I've done and I'll stand by it," I said. "I'm in a good place now. But that's not to say it hasn't been difficult at times. I still carry the bruises."

"I don't doubt it. And what about Katie? It can't have been easy for her, either."

"No, poor Katie. She bore the brunt of so much. But she's good now, as is our marriage. It's good to have at least some measure of stability back in our lives. The investigation demanded so much of us—*both* of us. But I'd say we've come out of it stronger."

"I'm pleased to hear that, Jon. You both deserve at least that much—"

We started to stroll beside the Serpentine.

"—There aren't many people I can think of who would have done what you've done and come out the other end with their sanity intact."

I shrugged. "I don't feel I had any real choice in the matter. With what the American told me, and then you … I just felt I had to do something. That's why I decided to go ahead with the investigation, and ultimately, to write the book."

"Ah yes, the book," Lacey said. "How is it doing?"

I shot him a disapproving look. "I think you already know the answer to that."

"Well…"

"It's doing as well as can be expected, is the best I can say. No thanks to MI5."

"You did manage to get several shipments into the country though…?"

"Yes, but on a distribution-only basis. All licence deals were blocked, as you well know. It was your people who D-Noticed it."

Lacey looked a little embarrassed. "Yes, well," he said. "National interests. I'm sure you understand."

"Well no, actually, I don't understand." I stopped and faced him up. "I'd have thought national interests would have included wanting to know who murdered the nation's princess."

"Not when the nation's government was complicit in her murder." His gaze locked on mine, for a beat, two … long enough that his words grew roots. Then he started off along the road again.

I followed after him. "You know you can be annoyingly patronizing at times, Lacey. I've been meaning to tell you that for years."

"And you, Jon, can be frustratingly naïve. But let's not get into personals." He motioned to Dell Café, just along the way. "Come on, I'll buy you that coffee."

A few minutes later we were inside the café, seated at a window table overlooking the Serpentine. Despite the chill weather several brave souls were out on the lake in pedal boats, doing their best to dodge the geese and the ducks. Considerably more were inside the café, though, doing their best to stay warm.

"So why did you call?" I put to Lacey, knitting my hands around my coffee cup and sipping its warm contents. "What made you want to meet up? I can't imagine it was to ask me about my book sales."

"No, quite." A wry smile suddenly shaped his lips. "Actually I thought you might be interested to know that a decision has been made."

"Oh...?"

"About the inquest. They've decided to go ahead with it after all."

"No way." The news took me totally by surprise, and I almost dropped my coffee cup. As it was it *clunked* as I set it back down a tad clumsily in its saucer. "So what changed their minds?"

He shrugged. "You did, as much as anybody. Your book, your petition, your influence on public opinion. Although they of course will cite some or other legal obligation, in the end it was public pressure that forced their arm. It's surprising the effect a grass-roots campaign can have. With public opinion so strongly in favour of a British investigation the media had little choice but to take up the cause, so to speak, and eventually that's what tipped the balance." He shrugged his eyebrows. "The Royal Coroner himself was forced to step in and ask Metropolitan Police Commissioner Sir John Stevens to conduct an investigation. It really is quite unprecedented."

"My God..." I was still taking it all in, or trying to. "That's good news, Lacey. That really is good news." And then this other thought struck me that immediately discoloured my mood. "I can't help thinking it'll be a waste of time, though, a whitewash, like so many other inquiries."

"Oh, I wouldn't be so sure. An inquest into Princess Diana's death will attract intense public scrutiny. They'll have to take that into account. They'll need to be very careful how they play it." He paused. "Of course, you won't get a verdict of murder," he ceded. "But it does look like a jury will probably be called and that opens the way to a verdict of unlawful killing. If that happens, well ... I'd say that would be as close to an open admission of guilt as you're ever likely to get."

Unlawful killing...

I thought about this possibility for a moment, and I had to admit that in some small way it did change the way I felt. It gave meaning to the nightmare Katie and I had suffered these past five or six years, for one thing. JB, too. It gave meaning to the sacrifices we'd made and even made more tolerable the fact that we'd been so manipulated. Of course, as Lacey had pointed out, no matter how open and democratic any inquest may ultimately profess to be, a verdict of murder would always be too much to expect. But the fact that an investigation had finally been forced nonetheless represented a small victory, all by itself—a *people's victory*. Perhaps that victory might yet further be affirmed in a verdict of unlawful killing, I allowed myself to hope.

A People's Verdict for the People's Princess.

Realistically, that was all I'd ever set out to achieve.

"There's something else," Lacey said a few moments later, almost falteringly, as though finding difficulty shaping his words. He cleared his throat. "I said I wanted to set the record straight ... there's something I wanted you to know, about the American—"

"He set me up," I heard myself say.

"Yes, I'm sorry. I didn't know."

"What do you mean, you didn't know? Of course you knew. You were part of it. You were at the meeting and you knew I was being set up as a cut-out."

"Yes, yes, I know. But I didn't know the extent of it. You have to realize this was out of my league, beyond anything even I had been involved in." He paused. "The truth is we were all used in one way or another. Even me."

"That doesn't make it okay."

"No."

Lacey fell silent for a long moment, staring into his half-empty coffee cup as though searching for the words his mind struggled to find. *The truth is we were all used in one way or another*, he'd said. *Even me.* And the more I thought about this the more I realized that he was of course telling the truth, at least so far as he knew it. Certainly he would never have been party to the full scope of the conspiracy we'd both found ourselves embroiled in, I had to acknowledge that. I had to acknowledge, too, that the likelihood he'd been used by those higher up the chain, just as I had been, was considerable. Not that I hadn't questioned. Of course I had. I'd questioned his part from the very beginning, wondering whether he too, like the American, had knowingly strung me along, fed me scripted information, groomed me for a role I had no idea I was earmarked to play. But the thought that he might have been playing this Judas role all along just didn't sit right. What would have been his motive? Why would he suddenly have sold his soul to a side of the establishment he'd always kicked so heroically against?

I could find no answer.

And there was something else I needed to acknowledge. I'd known Lacey now for more than twenty-five years; he was a friend—someone, at least, I could relax with over a game of snooker and a pint, something I'd done on numerous occasions in the past, though perhaps not so frequently of late. Even so, despite that he was a career spook he was someone I'd learned to trust: someone, in any case, whose pride as an MI5 officer was in his determination to do things the right way. Whatever else he may or may not have been, Lacey was old-school, I reminded myself. He was a decent man, and this now was his way of apologizing to me for his part in something that not even he, for all his years as an active field and target officer, could have had the slightest influence over. He'd been used, I allowed myself to believe, just as I'd been used. Even though he'd known in advance that I'd been singled out as some kind of unwitting go-between, a *cut-out*, it wasn't Lacey who'd pulled the strings: it wasn't Lacey who'd set me up. On the contrary, he'd done his best to help me. But he had nonetheless played the game knowing I was on the blunt end of a wrong deal, and that had left a scar that still wept.

As I glanced across at him now I wasn't sure if I was mad at him for the scar he'd left me with, or thankful to him for helping to suture it. Perhaps a little of both.

"Well I suppose I'd best be going," Lacey said at some length, draining his coffee and pushing himself up from the table. "I probably won't see you in this capacity again—I'm being pensioned off. You'll have to get your information elsewhere from now on."

I nodded.

He turned to go, but stopped before taking even a pace. He fixed me one last time. "Well done, Jon," he said. "You and JB. You did a remarkable thing, considering who you were up against. A quite remarkable thing."

He held my gaze a beat longer, then turned and headed for the door. This time he never looked back.

•

A few months later I was in Hyde Park again, this time with Katie. It was a warm, muggy Tuesday, August 31st, 2004—the seventh anniversary of Diana's death. The *Princess Diana Memorial Fountain* had recently been completed and opened to the public, and we'd thought that to pay the memorial a visit on this particular day might be a fitting way to bring closure on what had, after all, been a rollercoaster of a ride for both of us. It was also, we'd felt, a way for us to pay our last respects.

We arrived late morning, and despite it being midweek the crowds were already milling by the curiously designed monument—a vast, shallow stream bed precision-cut from Cornish granite, kind of oval in shape, along which water flowed and bubbled as it cascaded from the monument's highest point all the way to the bottom, where it came to rest in a calm, tranquil pool. The symbology was evident.

And so were the politics. I couldn't help but note that this particular water feature had indeed been built on the opposite side of the park to Queen Victoria's *Italian Gardens*, a fact I found quietly amusing.

It was pleasant enough, though—toddlers splashing about in the water, tourists enjoying picnics, grateful pigeons feeding unashamedly on the scraps. As Katie and I stood and watched the activity I couldn't help but acknowledge the profound effect Diana had undoubtedly had on people, and I found myself thinking about my meeting with Lacey, here in Hyde Park, just a few months previously. I remembered him telling me that it had been public pressure that had forced the Royal Coroner to order an investigation into Diana's death, and that its conclusion would determine whether there were grounds for a jury to be appointed at the inquest. Lacey certainly seemed to think it likely.

It looks like a jury will probably be called and that opens the way to a verdict of unlawful killing, he'd said. *That would be as close to an open admission of guilt as you're ever likely to get.*

A People's Verdict for the People's Princess.

"I wonder." I heard myself say out loud.

Katie heard me, too. She was standing next to me, her head nestled into my chest. "What?" she said without looking up at me.

"Oh, I was just thinking about something Lacey said, about the inquest. I was wondering what people were really thinking, you know, about Diana's death—wondering what's really going on in their minds and if we'll ever truly get the people's verdict."

Katie pushed herself upright and stole my gaze. "You'd be surprised," she said. "People aren't stupid. They know what really happened."

"Do you really think so?"

"I really think so."

Just then, a tall rangy guy in his mid-thirties – chinos, bomber jacket, horn-rimmed glasses – suddenly passed behind us, wheeling an old lady in a wheelchair. Physically speaking, the old girl looked frail, it has to be said. But clearly her mind was sharp enough.

"It's Diana's memorial fountain," the rangy care assistant was saying to the old lady as he stooped and pulled her tartan blanket up around her hips before wheeling her on along the path. "She died in that accident, remember?" He said it in such a way that inferred he wasn't necessarily expecting a reply.

But he got one. Chewing on what the care assistant had just told her the old lady suddenly perked up and blurted in a passionate, East End accent: "That weren't no accident. She was murdered!"

And with that, the two of them disappeared along the path into the milling crowds.

For a long moment Katie and I simply stood there, speechless, shocked not only at what the old lady had said and the timing of it, but also that she'd mustered the strength to say it with such fervour.

In that moment neither the result of the ongoing British investigation nor the verdict of the forthcoming Royal Inquest seemed even remotely relevant. So far as I was concerned the old lady had just voiced the verdict of the people—

A People's Verdict for the People's Princess.

—And that was all that mattered.

Addendum

In January 2004, in response to massive public and media pressure, the British Government appointed then Metropolitan Police Commissioner, Sir John Stevens, to investigate Princess Diana's death under the code name 'Operation Paget', and to submit his findings to the Royal Coroner.

On the basis of these findings, in October 2007 a Royal Inquest was convened before a jury at London's Royal Courts of Justice. Former MI6 Chief Sir Richard Dearlove and ten other MI6 agents, including Richard Mason, were brought before the inquest and questioned about their involvement in Diana's death.

No charges were brought against them.

On 2nd April, 2008, the jury retired to consider three verdicts: 'Accidental Death', 'Open Verdict' and 'Unlawful Killing'. The presiding judge, Lord Justice Scott Baker, forbade them from returning a verdict of murder.

"It is not open to you to find that Diana and Dodi were unlawfully killed in a staged accident," he ruled.

Despite this, the jury of six women and five men returned a verdict of 'Unlawful Killing', citing the negligence of Henri Paul and the drivers of the 'following vehicles' as the cause of Diana's death. It is the 'following vehicles' element that is of note.

In his autobiography, *Memoirs Of A Radical Lawyer*, defending QC Michael Mansfield would later write:

"The 'following vehicles' element in the verdict was an aspect that very few commentators picked up on, or bothered with, and mostly its implications were not understood. In so far as anyone took any notice, they thought it was merely a reference to the chasing pack of paparazzi. It wasn't: there were other vehicles clearly present, but never traced, and not driven by members of the paparazzi."

In his review of events surrounding the incident, Mr Mansfield also cited a box of Diana's personal papers that had, at the time of the Inquest, mysteriously 'disappeared'; the still-unidentified driver of the white Fiat Uno; the three hours on the evening of the crash during which Henri Paul's whereabouts were unknown; and the disproportionate sums of money deposited, in cash, in Henri Paul's multiple bank accounts in the weeks and months leading up to the crash.

Mr Mansfield concluded: "I have always believed that whatever caused the crash, it was not an accident. And, as it transpired, that belief was shared by the jury at the inquest."

For the record, the jury further cited Diana's decision not to wear her seat belt as a major contributing factor in her death.

Operation Paget Report—Page 421:
"Examination of the seat belts showed that they were in a good operational condition *with the exception of the rear right seat belt, which was found to be jammed in the retracted position* [my italics]."

Princess Diana occupied the rear right seat. It was Princess Diana's seat belt that was *'found to be jammed in the retracted position'*.

Medical experts worldwide have since agreed that, due to the angle of impact, the rear right seat should have been the "safest seat in the car", and that had she been wearing her seat belt, Princess Diana would almost certainly have survived.

Footnote: In 2009, a year after the Royal Inquest into Diana's death, former MI6 officer Richard Tomlinson was granted an official pardon by MI6. In an unprecedented move the spy agency offered Tomlinson a public apology for its 'unfair treatment' of him, and at the same time unfroze his assets. Despite having once been Britain's 'public enemy number one', despite having been hounded, hunted, intimidated, beaten, convicted of breaching the Official Secrets Act and ultimately imprisoned for treason, Tomlinson was once again free to return to Britain without fear of prosecution. In return for his freedom, the whistleblower agreed never again to speak about MI6 operational secrets, or about MI6 involvement in Princess Diana's death.

It seemed MI6 was in the end forced to do a deal to keep Tomlinson quiet, then, despite Richard Mason's preferred plan to terminate him.

Printed in Great Britain
by Amazon